LONDON COVEN: THREE-BOOK COLLECTION

FAMILIAR MAGIC | NIGHTMARE REALM | DEADLY PORTENT

M.V. STOTT

Copyright © 2017 by Uncanny Kingdom.

All rights reserved.

No part of this book may be reproduced in any form or by any electronic or mechanical means, including information storage and retrieval systems, without written permission from the author, except for the use of brief quotations in a book review.

BECOME AN INSIDER

Sign up and receive **FREE UNCANNY KINGDOM BOOKS**. Also, be the **FIRST** to hear about **NEW RELEASES** and **SPECIAL OFFERS** in the **UNCANNY KINGDOM** universe. Just visit:

WWW.UNCANNYKINGDOM.COM

FAMILIAR MAGIC

1

It was the absence of magic that first got me, hitting me like a punch in the gut.

I shuffled forward along the scuffed cobbles of the alleyway, my legs threatening to unhinge and drop me to the ground.

My name is Stella Familiar. I belong to the London Coven, a trio of urban witches, and I had just arrived home to find the door of our home hanging off its hinges. The entrance was dented and scorched, as though someone had blasted their way inside, which was impossible. I stood there, looking at the remains of the door for a few seconds, dumbfounded. *Impossible*. And yet, there it was.

The London Coven is in Hammersmith, West London, just a few streets away from the Underground station. It's situated down a blind alley, the only building at the end of a short cobbled stretch. It's called a blind alley because only those who know it exists can see it; a simple but effective layer of perception magic that makes the alley invisible to most, even when looking directly at it.

But back to that impossible lack of magic...

The coven and the blind alley that led to its door should

have been noisy with arcane energy. Should have been alive with boiling, agitated power; great churning fractals of the stuff. It was home to my masters, Kala, Trin, and Feal, the three most powerful witches in England, and every inch of the place was infused with their sorcery. On top of that, there were the spells of protection; hundreds of them. Anyone that wasn't meant to be within the coven's walls could find themselves stepping into a patch of superheated air that melted the flesh from their bones, or perhaps they'd blink, and just before their heart gave out, find themselves wearing their insides on the outside. There were any number of ways it could happen. Any number of creative deaths to discover. With so many things of the dark seeking to slither inside and do us harm, the coven had to be locked up tight. It was impossible for anything to cross the threshold that wasn't invited, and yet...

The door—

That lack of magic—

I tucked a stray lock of raven-black hair behind my ear, swallowed hard, and ducked through the gap created by the half-off door, straightening up slowly on the other side. A corridor stretched before me; walls of bare grey brick, floor made of exposed hardwood boards. A few doors stood either side of the corridor. Straight ahead was the coven's common room.

The place was dead.

There wasn't a whisper of magic to be heard anywhere. To be felt. To be tasted.

It was impossible.

I know I keep using that word, but that's because it was true.

Every building, every street, every hill and river and grain of sand contains some residue of magic. It's all around us every day. We swim around in it; an invisible sea of Uncanny energy. Even if this place hadn't been a coven, hadn't housed three of the most powerful magical creatures in the country, the very fact of its existence meant it should emit trace levels of magic.

But there was nothing.

I reached out with all of my senses, desperate for anything. For a ghost of some ancient incantation.

I came up empty.

'Kala? Trin? Someone, please answer me.'

Silence.

I stepped into the first room; Kala's reading room, piled high with trashy paperback romances. It was empty, but there were signs of a struggle. 'Kala?' Chairs lay on their sides, broken glass scattered across wooden floorboards. The coven smelt the same despite the lack of magic; that strange mix of cinnamon, freshly-cut grass, and lavender that seemed to permanently drift about the place, no matter which potion was cooked up, or what meal was prepared. The smell of my masters' witchcraft.

I turned back and stepped into the hallway again. 'Intruder, my name is Stella Familiar and you will show yourself or I... or I will...'

I pressed a palm against the wall to steady myself and swallowed, my throat dry. The emptiness was getting to me, giving me the shakes. All magical beings are connected to the power that radiates from the natural world, but few are more connected than my kind. As a familiar, I feed on the magic that naturally occurs, soaking it in like a sponge, night and day, without even thinking about it. It sustains me, makes me stronger, gives me the energy to cast spells. But now, in this place, this empty coven, I was like a junkie whose supply had been cut off after a lifetime of indulgence, my slim but powerful body trembling. I was going cold turkey, and it really, *really* hurt.

It was disturbing how quickly I was affected. A minute had passed, tops, and I was already a shaking, sweaty wreck, struggling to resist the urge to run from the coven, from the blind alley, so I could get a good, strong hit.

I grunted, straightened up, and tried to get my shit together. This was no time for weakness, no time to fall apart. My home had been attacked.

'Intruder, my name is Stella Familiar, and you will show yourself to me!' The words roared out of my mouth with a strength I didn't feel.

There was no reply.

I placed a hand on the door to the coven's common room and pushed.

I tasted death before I saw it; a metallic tang on the tongue that twisted my stomach and told me what I was going to see before my eyes had been given a chance to catch up. A taste like a gun barrel in my mouth.

The room was mostly as I'd left it: a few comfy chairs, a bookcase, a couch, and a long wooden table with ancient texts spread across it. A small cauldron hung in a fireplace, and beside that sat a television on a TV stand. Always the same. Except on this day, some extra items had been added.

There were three bodies on the floor.

Three bodies, but more than three pieces.

Kala, Trin, Feal—my masters, my creators, my coven's high witches—had been torn to shreds and scattered around the room.

Eyes wide, hand to my mouth, I stepped inside.

'No...'

Blood was sprayed across the grey brick walls and splattered across the floorboards, collecting in congealing red pools. It was a horror story. A world gone mad.

This couldn't be happening.

Nothing was capable of doing this to the witches of the London Coven. Together, when connected, the three of them wielded enough power to crack open mountains, to turn the

Familiar Magic

oceans into sand, to make demons weep, and yet my shoes were soaking in a pool of their collective blood.

I crouched and placed a hand on a hunk of meat that could have belonged to any one of my masters. It, like the coven itself, was empty. Not just of life, but of magic. Of power. Something had broken into a place it was impossible to plunder, bypassed the magical safeguards it was impossible to survive, and torn to...

...and murdered my masters. Murdered three creatures of immeasurable power. And then, to finish things off, they'd drained every last drop of magic from the place.

Impossible on top of impossible on top of impossible.

I stood, angry. Angry that I'd allowed fear to infect me. I hadn't been created to feel fear, I'd been created to *instil* fear, and to bring about justice. I cradled the anger and blew upon it, igniting it like the first spark of a new fire. It didn't matter that this was impossible, it had happened. It didn't matter that the kind of power needed to have achieved any one of the unimaginable things done to this coven would be enough to turn me into a puddle of bubbling goo.

None of it mattered.

All that mattered was that the coven had been breached, and my creators, my mothers, had been murdered as though they were nothing. As though they were less than nothing. They'd been ripped and shredded and tossed aside. My nails dug into my palms and drew blood, but I didn't flinch. It felt *good*.

I was going to find out who was behind this and do something impossible myself.

I was going to get bloody, horrifying revenge.

I was nothing but a lowly familiar, but I swore to every god I knew that I was going to avenge my slaughtered coven.

'Listen to me,' I hissed, 'and listen closely. You have made a grave mistake. My name is Stella Familiar, and what has happened here today will be met with a fury you cannot even imagine. Do you hear me? I know you can. Whoever did this, I *will* find you, and when I do, I will rip your beating heart from your chest.'

A noise—

A movement in the corner of my eye—

I wasn't alone.

And I was in terrible danger.

2

Whatever it was that was inside the coven with me, it was taking its time. It was trying to scare me. And it was working.

Normally in this sort of situation—with an unknown assailant stalking me, ready to leap out and tear my throat from my neck at any moment—I'd draw upon the surrounding magic and cast a spell that would turn the creature into confetti. Sling a spell first, ask questions later, that was my usual way of dealing with threats. But there was no surrounding magic. I extended my senses as far as I could, invisible tendrils firing out in all directions, desperately searching for a hint of the Uncanny to draw upon, but everything out there was cold.

This was a dead place, in more ways than one.

The creature unleashed a low, rumbling growl that shook the floor beneath me. I was in deep trouble. I tried to ignore the blood, the chunks of my dead masters, and I reached out again to try and make sense of what I was up against.

A voice—

A single word, repeated staccato—

Kill Kill Kill—

The words rolled in my head as I came upon the thing stalking me. It was a slippery creature, hard to get a clear grip on, but it was obvious it wasn't the person behind this attack. No, this creature was a booby trap.

Time to take stock.

I had no magic to draw on, only the weak power I already had stored inside of me, and even that was dulled by my surroundings, as though my magic was shrinking back in confusion at the emptiness around me. Did the creature keeping just out of view know that? Did it realise I was running on empty? That I'd brought a slap to a gunfight?

No, I didn't think so. It was just toying with me; that's the only reason it hadn't already pounced. It wanted to make me scared to death before death actually came calling.

'Whatever you are, this is already getting boring. Show yourself, but know that I have enough juice in me to make your head go pop. Understand?'

A bluff, but I sold it as best I could. From what I could sense, it was a simple attack beast, left to take care of anyone who stumbled into the dead coven. To take care of *me*. Whatever this creature was, it was the monkey, not the organ grinder.

'Do you hear me, you dumb beast? Show yourself or get the hell out of my house.'

A growl and the floor shook—

A wall in front of me exploded—

A creature erupted into the room, bursting through brick and plaster as though they were matchstick and spit. The horned monster dog bore down on me, eyes burning with red fire, its slavering maw a jumble of razor-sharp teeth. It raised its great head, drool dripping from its mouth and splashing on the floor, mixing with the spilled blood of my masters.

I had to choose my next words carefully. 'There there,' I said. 'Good dog...?'

No, not ideal.

A thought struck me: this monster was created by magic, which meant it must have magic available for me to feed on. I ignored the fact that I should have already been able to sense any magic in my vicinity, and tried to reach out to it, to draw in some of its power, but whoever had created this thing was no idiot. Some sort of extra spell had been cast upon the beast that made my mental feelers slide off it, like I was trying to push two magnets of the same pole together. So that was why I hadn't been able to sense its presence, or its magic? The thing was shielded from me. Whoever had ripped apart my witches and left this booby trap didn't plan on making things easy.

The demon dog took a step forward, a floorboard cracking beneath one of its heavy, cloven feet.

'Stop. Stay there. Don't take another step or you're done for.' I raised a hand by way of a threat and formed a weak cloud of sparks that swam around. I could only hope the monster took it for the beginnings of something more powerful. 'You will tell me your name, beast, and the name of your master, or I will—'

I didn't get to finish the sentence. The creature snorted and began to charge, drool trailing from its mouth. I flung the weak defence spell I'd conjured in the creature's direction as I turned and bolted from the room. I wasn't sticking around to check for damage. I knew the energy I'd unleashed would present the beast with about as much of an obstacle as a cobweb.

I ran some more, arms pumping. A second more and the thing would be on top of me. I stopped sharply and threw myself through the open door to my left, causing the monster to tumble past me, unable to halt its momentum.

I landed on the floor, shoulder jarring, but I didn't have time to register the pain. I rolled on to my knee and turned to the open doorway. I could hear the thing scrabbling to stop and turn. I looked around for anything in the room I could use, a weapon perhaps, then realised I'd jumped into Trin's gallery, which was swamped with easels and canvases and little else. I didn't have time to run back out of the door and head in the other direction, which left me only one option: the window.

My only hope was to get out of the coven and away from the blind alley. Either the thing wouldn't follow me—conjured to stay within the confines of the coven—or it would give chase. If it followed, then my one shot was to make it out of the blind alley and into the street before it caught up with me. After that, I'd pull whatever magic I could from the surroundings to do... whatever I could. I'd have at best seconds to power up, and I already knew that wouldn't be long enough for me to gain enough energy to destroy the thing, but I was out of options.

The corridor's floorboards crunched as the beast headed back to the doorway, back towards me. Its giant, snarling head came into view, and its burning, hellish eyes looked at me. Looked at me with hunger, desperate to taste my flesh.

Okay.

It was now or never.

This was going to hurt.

'Here, doggy,' I said.

I used the last of my power to hurl a chair at the beast's face, hoping to slow it down for even half a second, then I turned, raised my arms over my head, and threw myself through the coven window.

3

Shards of glass swarmed me like angry bees as I burst from the coven and fell hard on the cobbles outside. I heard the beast, its roar barely muffled behind me.

'Get up!' I yelled, and pushed myself to my feet, hands criss-crossed with livid cuts from the shattered window.

I'd made it outside, now I just had to make it another twenty metres to the end of the blind alley, to the streets beyond with their wash of background magic that I could pull on. I could do it.

Maybe I could do it.

No, no; I *had* to do it.

I had to survive, because no one else was going to get revenge for my coven. No one but me. If I died, this would go unpunished. I couldn't let that happen. Wouldn't.

I took a step and my knee almost buckled beneath me. The adrenalin was pumping so strong that I hadn't realised how hard I'd come down during my escape. I staggered and managed to keep just about upright, even if I did step more sideways than forward.

'Come on, you can do it.'

I gritted my teeth and kept moving. I had to make it to the street before the animal took me down.

'Well, look at you.'

The new voice came at me from all angles. I spun around looking for a source, still moving forward, still heading for the street.

'*Such willpower. Such determination. I find myself admiring you.*'

'Show yourself!' I yelled, though, in truth, I hoped whoever was addressing me didn't deliver on the demand. I was as weak and empty as I'd ever been. A kitten could have knocked me down.

'*Keep going, Stella. Don't make it easy for me. I want you to struggle and hope and strive. It makes the inevitable all the sweeter.*'

The voice seemed to change from word to word, making it impossible to pin down. Impossible to work out who it might be. I knew every sorcerer, every member of the Uncanny that passed through London; if I heard their true voice, I'd know who it was in an instant. Another trick. More powerful magic, used to evade and disorientate.

'Why have you done this to my coven? Answer me!'

'*No,*' said the voice. '*But you should know... they screamed for mercy, Stella.*'

'Shut up.'

'*Oh, they begged me for it. Even as I tore strips of flesh from their bones with my teeth. They tasted... weak.*'

I stopped in my tracks, rage clouding my senses. 'I'll find you! Whoever you are, I will find you and I will kill you!'

Mocking laughter swirled around me, only to be replaced by the crashing of the coven wall as the beast leapt through and into the blind alley.

Bashed-up knee forgotten, I turned and ran. The creature howled and gave chase. I wasn't going to make it. I could feel the ground shaking beneath me as the animal grew closer with each bound, feel its hot breath beating against the back of my neck. Five metres to go until the end of the blind alley, until the street and its magic welcomed me.

It would be about four metres too far.

The beast reared up on me, claws cleaving the air. I screamed and hurled myself to the side, crashing into the wall so hard it's a wonder I didn't dash my brains out. The creature tried to stop, but stumbled and rolled out of the alley, roaring in frustration at having come so close. The beast was vicious and strong, but not gifted with brains.

I pushed myself back up and ran for the street. Grinning madly I stumbled out of the blind alley, and the dead veil—the absence of magic—was pulled away from me. While the shoppers of Hammersmith High Street screamed and ran from the insanity, I inhaled a great gulp of power. My every nerve ending tingled as the magic, weak as it was, washed over me and soothed my jangled nerves. So dizzying was the rush that I closed my eyes, a beatific smile spreading across my face, and almost forgot about the giant devil dog about to feast on my guts. My eyes opened again and I took up an attack pose, legs spread, arms up and outstretched, ready to unleash whatever spell came to me.

I didn't have time to consider my attack.

The animal was already just metres away, teeth bared, the fire in its eye sockets raging hot and red. As it leapt for me, I felt a weakness in my knees. I always thought, when death came for me, that I'd be able to face it boldly, but there I was, shaking like a coward. Unable to form a clear thought as six or seven half-formed invocations formed a knot in my head, and the certainty of death seized my heart.

I'd failed.

I would die, and my witches' murders would go unpunished.

I closed my eyes and braced for the end.

4

After five or six seconds, I began to wonder why death was taking so long.

I opened my eyes to find myself looking not into the furious, twitching face of a monster hell-bent on tearing my skin off, but into the face of a man. He looked to be in his mid-thirties, with short, messy, dark brown hair, and was wearing an expression of utter surprise. In his hand he held a spoonful of cereal, which had suspended its journey to his gaping mouth.

'Hello,' I said.

'How did...' he started. 'I... I mean, where did...?'

Somehow, I'd jumped from standing in the street, about to be chewed on like the favourite squeaky toy of the Godzilla of dogs, to being laid out on my back in a strange man's kitchen. It was odd, but given the circumstances, far preferable to the former option.

I sat up sharply and took in my surroundings. The man jerked back, losing his spoon, which fell into the cereal bowl with a milky plop.

'Have you seen a big monster devil dog thing?' I spluttered.

'Have I *what*?'

I pushed myself to my feet and looked around. The kitchen was cramped, with dirty dishes piled high and a tile floor that clearly hadn't been cleaned in months, if ever. I darted for the kitchen window, trying to see if the thing had managed to tail me.

'There's a monster after me. Have you seen it?'

'Of course I haven't seen a bloody monster!'

'Good. It was about to kill me and is probably very, very angry that it's not crunching my bones between its teeth. A thing like that doesn't like to skip a meal.'

'Doesn't it?'

'Well, of course it doesn't, it's the whole reason they're created. Think it through... um...' I gestured with one hand, 'name?'

'What?'

'Your name, what's your name?'

'David.'

'Oh, I knew a David once.'

'Most people do.'

'He was eaten by a bear. Well, a powerful sorcerer pretending to be a bear. Well, a demon pretending to be a powerful sorcerer, pretending to be a bear.'

'Right. Of course. We all know people like that.'

I was babbling, my brain spinning. I turned from the window, satisfied that the devil dog wasn't about to leap through the wall at me. My heart was still beating a hundred miles an hour, and I realised I'd been saying things to a normal that they weren't meant to know. But then, this wasn't a normal sort of day. Someone had murdered the witches of London.

'So are you going to, I don't know, tell me what you're doing in my house or—'

I raised a finger and pressed it to his lips. 'Shh, David.' Closing my eyes, I extended my senses out as far as they would go, searching for any hint of trouble. Any sign that I'd been followed. There was nothing. All I felt was the normal background magic of the place. I was safe. Well, safe for now. Which meant I hadn't failed. Not yet. And as long as I was alive, I was going to do everything I could to exact revenge.

'I don't know how, but it looks like I shook the thing. Best guess I have is that the half-formed spells that sprang into my head as it leapt at me must have combined, formed some weird cocktail, and snatched me away from danger, dropping me, well, here. Where is *here*, by the way?'

'Can I talk now?' asked David, lips smushed by my finger, still.

I pulled it away. 'Go ahead.'

'Thank you. My name is Detective David Tyler, and you just broke into my kitchen. Not the smartest of moves, what with the whole detective thing I just mentioned.'

My first thought was to raise my hand, conjure up something devastating, and toss it in Detective David Tyler's direction. Then I realised that was a bit rude, especially considering I'd just appeared from nowhere and interrupted the man's breakfast. On top of that, with the danger having passed, it suddenly hit me how weak I was. The fight, the strange lack of magic in the alley and the coven, the death of my witches... my masters... it was all too much. It was crushing me.

'Okay, so I want you to start answering a few questions now, or—'

He cut off as my knees buckled and I collapsed to the floor.

'Whoa, hey, sorry, are you... okay?'

'I'm fine,' I said, attempting to stand, only to find myself curling into a ball on the floor.

'Hey, you can't just—'

'Please. Help me. I'm in danger.'

'From what? And please don't say a monster.'

'I don't know. I heard a voice. Lots of voices.'

'A gang attacked you? Is that what those cuts came from?'

'I need a place to rest, just for a little while.' My limbs were wet noodles. I was ready to pass out.

David pinched the bridge of his nose. 'Oh, this is a stupid, bad decision I'm about to make, I can feel it. I've made enough dumb decisions in my life to know. I once dyed my hair blonde. Did not suit me.'

'I can stay?'

David crouched down beside me. 'Okay. But I'm locking the door to your room.'

He must have carried me, because I found myself in a bedroom I didn't remember walking to. I lifted my head from the wonderful softness of the pillow to see David stood in the doorway.

'Thanks,' I told him. 'You're a good person.'

'Some might say "idiot", but I'll take "good" for now.'

I smiled and he smiled back. It was a nice smile, open and friendly.

'I must be mental,' he said, then lifted a key, waggling it back and forth. 'One night, then you're going to tell me the truth. That or I'm taking you on a guided tour of the police station. Right?'

'Right.'

'Good. Okay. I left you a glass of water on the side, there.'

'Thanks, David.'

My eyes closed before the door did, and sleep had its way with me. I heard the key turn in the lock, and then I was gone.

5

I opened my eyes.

I was in the common room of the London Coven.

Power rolled around the place in great waves. It coiled and it flowed and it sparked; every colour imaginable, strobing endlessly. It was beautiful, intoxicating, and very, very moreish. To most people it was invisible, but not to someone like me: a familiar, a creature of the Uncanny.

I spread my arms wide and washed my hands through it, watching as the magic danced and weaved around my fingers. Few places in the country were as soaked in the stuff as this place.

My coven.

It would be too much for some. An amateur sorcerer or fledgling magician that walked into this building would most likely find themselves drowning in the coven's magic, or at least driven insane by it. But then very few people ever came here. The coven was not open to visitors, and was protected from the outside world by layer upon layer of spells, hexes and wards.

Or, at least, it had been.

I looked down at myself. I was naked.

'This is just a dream,' I told myself. I always knew when I

was dreaming, and I'd had this dream often enough. It was the day I was created.

'Familiar, I name you Stella,' came a voice from behind me. It was Kala's voice.

'Why Stella?' came a second voice; Trin's.

'It was the name of someone who was kind to me once. Many centuries ago.'

I turned and looked upon them. My witches. My creators.

'Well?' said Feal, who had so far remained silent. 'Can you talk, or did we forget to give you a tongue?'

'I can talk,' I replied. I felt tears prickle my eyes and fought to hold them back. In reality, all three of them were dead. But not here. Not in my dreams. Here they'd be able to live forever.

'You are this coven's familiar, from now until your life is taken,' said Kala. 'Do you accept your fate?'

I nodded. 'Yes. I suppose I've nothing better to do.'

Feal snorted, amused. One of the highlights of any day was making her laugh. Now she'd never laugh again. Not really. Not outside of my dreams.

A familiar is created to serve a coven. Most witches don't like to step beyond their home too much, especially when their home is as heavily protected as this one. So they use their familiar—created by them, for them—to step out into the world and do their leg-work.

I fetched. I carried. I delivered warnings, and worse. Much worse. Anything my masters asked of me. Most familiars are not expected to last long. They are sent out into danger, they are not always expected to return. But I had, for sixty years, served them happily. But now... a familiar was not meant to outlast its masters.

I felt the anger rise in me again and clenched my fists. I would get whoever did this to us. Whoever it was that murdered my coven. I would track them down, and I would make them scream in pain.

'She looks angry,' said Trin.

'Can you blame her?' replied Feal. 'After what she let happen?'

That caught my attention, snapping me out of my anger. 'What? What are you talking about?'

'What are you talking about?' repeated Kala, mocking me.

'It's your fault—'

'Your fault—'

'Your fault—-'

They stepped towards me slowly, making me back up until I was pressed against the wall. Without thinking, I drew in additional magic from the air, ready to defend myself. The witches stopped and watched as the wash of power in the room flowed towards me.

'I-I...' I bit my lip, trying to calm myself so the magic would stop lapping towards me.

'You think you can attack us?'

'She means us further harm yet, even in death.'

'No! I'm your familiar! That's who I am, that's all I am. I would never do anything to hurt you! Not any of you, you know that!'

'You know that—'

'You know that—'

Mocking me again, but wait...

'What did you say?' I asked.

'It's your fault we're dead, familiar.'

'Your fault—'

'Your fault—'

Their voices...

It was only now I was noticing, or perhaps only now I was being allowed to notice...

The witches spoke, but not with their own voices. Each word came out as though a different person had spoken it, just like the voice I'd heard in the blind alley outside.

Another trick.

'I'm not a big fan of people attacking me in my dreams,' I

told the stranger, 'especially not when they use the bodies of my masters to do it.'

'Oh—'

'She catches on—'

'Took her long enough.'

I drew the magic toward myself, spoke the words, and threw an orb of energy that turned the three fake witches to ash.

Breathing heavily, trying to ignore the guilt gnawing at me, telling me that I'd just burned up my own coven despite what I knew, I stepped forward. I poked at the ash with my foot.

'Come on, you coward, show yourself.'

Silence.

Would it be as easy as that? Well, it was my dream after all; maybe it was giving me this simple victory. Building my confidence and—

A scream as a hand burst from the ashes and gripped my ankle. I yelled out in shock despite myself, and tried to pull away, but the alabaster white hand dug its ragged yellow fingernails into my skin.

'Get off me!' I cried.

I tried to pry the fingers free. They felt like ice. As I struggled, a second hand burst from the ashes, then a third, pulling me down. I raised my hands to form a spell, but more fists shot from the floor, striking like vipers, gripping me and pulling me into the floor.

It was just a dream.

Just a dream, that's all it was.

I tried to calm myself by repeating that over and over.

This is just a dream. A nightmare. It doesn't matter what happens to me here, I'm going to wake up in Detective David Tyler's spare room at any moment, covered in sweat, breathing heavily, but alive.

'Are you sure of that, Stella Familiar?'

'Are you sure?'

'Sure?'

The words, spat out in a hundred different voices, swirled around me, over and over, like a ribbon made of razor blades, and now all that was left of me above the floor, above the ashes, was my head. I closed my mouth to stop myself from breathing in my masters' remains.

'I'm waiting for you.'

'I'm waiting.'

'Waiting'

Any moment now, I would wake up.

I had to.

Any moment.

Any moment...

...now...

I closed my eyes tight as the ashes swallowed me up.

6

'How did you get out?' asked David.

I looked up from the bowl of cereal I was eating and did my best to offer a cheery smile. 'Morning.'

David was wearing jeans with a snug, dark green shirt, his hair still expertly tousled. He looked good.

'You haven't broken my door, have you?' he asked. 'That's a nice door. I like that door.'

'Had a bit of a bad dream.'

'Were you naked? I'm always naked in my nightmares.'

'Very naked.'

David sat down opposite me. 'Tell me more.'

'My masters tried to attack me, I killed them with magic, then I was dragged into the floor by a dozen arms that burst up out of their ashes.'

David nodded slowly. 'I see. My naked dreams usually involve me having to take an exam I didn't study for, but okay.'

I nodded and leaned back in my chair. 'Sorry I broke your curfew, but I couldn't get back to sleep after that, so I decided to make myself useful. There's coffee in the pot if you're thirsty.'

David narrowed his eyes and went to investigate, pouring himself a cup.

'Careful, I like it strong,' I said.

'Me too,' he replied, taking a sip. He coughed, and when he turned around, his eyes were watering. 'P-perfect.'

'Thanks for letting me stay. Not everyone would allow a woman who'd broken into their home to sleep over.'

'Well, I'm not every man. In fact, if my ex-girlfriend is right, I'm barely a man at all.'

I snorted. He was funny as well as kind. David took his place opposite me again, raising the cup of coffee to his lips, then thinking better of it and placing it on the table.

'Well, thank you anyway, I appreciate it.'

'So... my door?' he replied. 'Did you pick the lock, or...?'

'Oh, I just used a simple trick to open it. Apprentice-level magic. Kleptomancy. It's the kind of thing you learn on day one.'

David did his slow nod again. 'I see.'

'Do you?'

'Almost definitely not.'

'Oh.'

'Magic?' he said.

'Magic,' I clarified.

'And by "magic", you obviously mean...?'

'Magic.'

'Got it.' More slow nodding, this time combined with a look in his eyes that said, *"Careful, crazy ahead".'*

For some reason, it felt right to fill him in on my world. Like I owed it to him. Like sharing my pain with him would make it just a little more bearable

'Look, Officer David Tyler—'

'Just David will do—'

'David, I know you're not of the Uncanny. To you London is just another place, full of people, and buildings, and noise, and fried chicken shops, and everything can be explained. But what if I were to tell you that everything you knew about London, about the entire world in fact, was wrong?'

'I'd say you and my ex would get along like a house on fire.'

I stopped and stared into his eyes, unblinking. 'I'm being serious, David.'

He leaned back in his seat and folded his arms. 'No, you're being a nutcase, and if you're going to continue being a nutcase, I'm going to have to take you down to the station for further questioning. I may be nice, but I'm not that nice.'

I stood sharply, my chair toppling to the floor. David rose, one hand out in a calming gesture, the other reaching to his pocket. I wondered what he had in there. Some sort of spray, or maybe one of those extendable batons?

'I'm not going to hurt you, David.'

'Good, getting hurt is one of my least favourite parts of the job. Though maybe I'd take it over all the paperwork, and the sandwiches they serve in the canteen. Awful.'

'I'm not going to hurt you,' I said, 'I'm going to show you. Show you that I'm telling the truth.'

David's hand retreated from whatever he had stashed in his pocket. Good. He'd given me a place to sleep things off, the last thing I wanted was to put him down on his arse.

'Okay, you're going to show me that magic is real?'

I nodded.

'How? I'm sorry but I don't have a pack of cards on me, and as far as I can tell, you don't have a hat to pull a bunny out of.'

I snorted and shook my head. 'You normals, you see only one, thin slice of reality. You're looking at the world through a crack in a door.'

The background magic of David's house washed around me, but I didn't need to draw on it for this little demonstration. My own natural power would be more than enough to prove my point.

'Ready?' I asked.

'Oh, completely. Let's see this magic then. Unless you're talking out of your bum because you're insane.'

'Detective David Tyler?'

'Yes?'

Ancient words ran through my head as I reached out one hand and pushed them towards him. 'Shhh.'

I watched, amused, as David waited for something to happen, for the fireworks to begin. Perhaps disappointed, perhaps satisfied that I'd been lying all along, he smiled and opened his mouth to say something—

Only no words came out.

'It's no use trying,' I said, as David's eyes opened so wide they were in danger of falling from their sockets.

He gripped his throat, pulled at his tongue, walked around in a little circle of panic, all the time trying and failing to speak. Finally, he stopped and turned to me, mouthing some words, wide and slow.

'*What have I done?*' I repeated. 'I cast a spell on you. Just a little one. It's called the Spell of Silence and it robs anyone it's cast on of their voice. For a short time anyway, or until the spell is reversed.'

I pictured the words in my head again, but this time reversed them, before reaching out to him: 'Speak.'

'—uck is going on? I...! Wait... I can talk! Hello? Hello? This is David.' He looked up at me, immensely relieved. 'I can talk!'

'Yes, congratulations, you're neck and neck with a two-year-old.'

He stopped rubbing at his throat, and the relief began to drain from him as a horrible reality dawned.

'That was... was that...?'

'Magic?'

'Yeah. That was magic, wasn't it? I mean, sort of, magic-magic. David Blaine, but not tricksy bullshit.'

'Your face has gone very pale.'

'I'm just going to sit down and tremble for a moment or two, if that's okay?'

'Okay.'

David sat down at the kitchen table and placed his head in

his hands. 'This is insane. This is all completely insane. It's the job, isn't it? It's all those times I got bashed over the head chasing criminals, finally catching up with me.'

This happened a lot when normals were confronted with magic. With *real* magic. They tried to shrug it off, to make sense of it in a way that didn't shake their world view to rubble. One demonstration would not be enough.

'Would you like to see more?'

David looked to me, eyes wide, and shrugged. 'Can't hurt. Unless it can, in which case... still yes.'

I smiled and got ready to blow his mind.

7

'Is that... that's me!'

David hopped to his feet and backed up, staring with a mixture of confusion and wonder at the replica of him I'd made appear between us. This David—this simulacrum of David—glimmered with colour, with magical sparks that popped and fizzed around it. It wasn't solid, it wouldn't fool anyone into thinking it was the real thing. This conjured David was see-through, like a ghost. It took more power than I knew how to cope with to create a true double; a double that could replace someone and fool even the closest of their friends.

'Officer David Tyler, meet Officer David Tyler.'

The copy smiled and waved to him. 'Hey there.'

'Okay. Okay, that is very disturbing. Also, I am at least an inch taller than that, and my shoulders are a lot broader.'

'Afraid not.'

I passed my hands through the double and he began to break apart, drifting away like smoke.

'Bye, David,' said the simulacrum, 'it was good to meet you.'

David waved to his double as it faded from view. 'You too...'

'Well?' I asked. 'Feeling convinced yet?'

He looked to me. I knew what he was feeling. Bewildered, excited, terrified. I'd seen the emotions pass over more than a few normals in my time working as the London Coven's familiar.

'Stella.'

'Yes?'

'What did you put in that coffee?'

I sighed and dropped my chin to my chest.

'That's all this is, must be. You put something... something illegal in my coffee and now I'm seeing things. Hallucinating. Tripping off my tits. That's all there is to it.'

'Nope.'

'No?'

'Definitely not.'

He put his hands on his hips and huffed for a second, searching for what to say next. 'Well... I'm still getting that coffee tested.'

'Stop. You know it's not true. You know what I showed you was real, admit it.'

David's breathing slowed as he calmed down and took a seat again. 'Okay.'

'Okay?'

'Look, I'm not completely closed-minded,' he said. 'I'm open to the idea of, you know, the supernatural. Aliens. All of that spooky shit. But... look, this is just a lot to wrap my head around this early in the morning, okay?'

I sat opposite him and reached out, placing a hand over his. I thought he might pull away, but his hand remained under mine. 'You've no need to be scared of me, David.'

'Who said I was scared?'

'Your hand is trembling,' I replied.

'Okay. Maybe a touch, you know, terrified, but definitely not scared.'

'Magic is real. I use it to help people. I suppose you could say I'm the magical equivalent of you.'

'So, you're a what? A magic detective? Harry Potter with a badge?'

I smiled. 'Sort of. I'm the familiar to a coven of witches.'

A long pause.

'Okay,' said David. 'Witches. Coven. I'm following.'

'London is a hub of the Uncanny. All kinds of magical sorts run around these streets. If they were left to do whatever they wanted, it would be chaos. It's my coven's job to try and keep things under control.'

'So these witches, are we talking big floppy hats, broomsticks, black cats, giant warty noses?'

I laughed and shook my head. 'No, I'm afraid not. They look more like a group of middle-aged women at a knitting circle. Well... *looked*.'

'Looked? As in, past tense?'

I pulled my hand away and closed my eyes, hoping for dark, but instead seeing that room, empty of magic, covered in the blood and torn flesh of my masters. My creators. My friends.

'They're dead. Murdered.'

'Murdered? Okay, I need to call this in, the police can—'

'No. The police can't do anything, this is way beyond their, you know, *remit*. This wasn't a simple break-in. Nothing can get into my coven that isn't invited. Believe me when I say that place is locked up tight. If you'd tried to wander in and we didn't want you there, your heart would have exploded out of your ribcage before you took a second step.'

'Right. Okay. Gross, but cool. Go on.'

'Whoever did this to my coven is...' I shivered despite myself, 'they're powerful beyond anything I've ever come across before, and they're going to come after me. They already tried, that's how I ended up here. Somehow. Not sure of the specifics, but I'm grateful for the end result.'

'Look, if what you're saying is true—if someone just murdered a bunch of women—I'm not going to look past that. I don't care how high and mighty the killer is, I'm involved now, end of discussion.'

'You already helped me. Kept me safe.'

'That's my job, Stella. I don't take a lot seriously, but the oath I took? That I do.'

I sighed and nodded. 'Okay. So I owe you the truth, and you're probably not going to like it.'

'Well, today's the day for surprises that make me want to poop myself, so go ahead, what is it? You're not best buds with the Loch Ness Monster are you?'

'We've met, but no.'

'Okay, I'm probably going to want to circle back to that another time, but go on.'

'Here's the thing, David, by helping me, you might have placed a big, neon target on your back.'

David did one of his slow nods again. 'So, some almighty magic man is probably going to try and murder me?'

'Yes. Sorry about that.'

David sighed and rubbed at his eyes with the heels of his hands. 'I've only been up twenty minutes...'

8
―――

Murder, magic and mayhem were a lot to take on an empty stomach. I'd finished off the last of David's cereal, and seeing as the only other food in his wreck of a kitchen was a bowl of rotting fruit, we made our way to a nearby cafe. It was the sort of place that stank of the last decade's fat and cigarette smoke, with sticky, plastic table cloths and chipped, stained tea mugs.

'I'll pay,' I said.

'Oh, yeah, you're definitely paying,' was David's reply. Which, given the circumstances, was fair enough.

We sat in silence as David ate, the quiet giving me a chance to think things over. And over and over. The witches were dead, so where did that leave me? What was I without them? I only existed because they decided I should. My entire purpose for being was to do as they commanded, but now nobody was left to command me. I wasn't even a person, was I? Not really. So what did that make me now? Now that I was just me.

David finished his pile of bacon, sausages, beans, and mushrooms, and pushed his empty plate aside, patting his stomach and reaching for a napkin.

Familiar Magic 35

'You didn't have to have the most expensive breakfast on the menu,' I said.

'No, I think I really, really did.' He turned his head to the counter and waved his hand, 'Garcon! Another round of your very whitest toast once you've got a mo.'

The woman behind the counter looked up with hangdog eyes and grunted.

'Well, at least you're talking again. For a moment I thought I'd accidentally unleashed the silence spell again.'

'Not funny, Stella. Not funny at all.'

'A bit funny.'

David eyed me, then broke, smiling and shaking his head. 'You know I should have you in cuffs already and be dragging you down to the station. This is insane.'

'I'm not the one who should be in chains.'

'Okay, let's say I believe what you're saying. Magic is everywhere and there's a freaky underworld that only super woke people like you know about. What makes you above the law? You walk the streets as the rest of us, or at least, I'm assuming you do. Unless you fly. Ooh, can you fly? Can you make *me* fly?'

'We're not above the law. And no, I can't fly.'

'Aw.'

'There's just a different kind of accountability in my world.'

'The London Coven.'

'Exactly. We keep the peace. Or we did.'

A plate piled high with pasty toast and butter pats was dropped between us with a distinct lack of hospitality.

'Thanks, Nora.'

Nora grunted and shuffled away, her body wobbling like a bin bag full of mayonnaise.

'So,' said David, 'it seems to me like someone didn't like being told what to do by your lot, and decided to do something about it.'

And that "something"—ripping apart the people I loved

and turning them into hunks of dead flesh—was going to get them killed.

'Maybe. They could be acting on revenge, I suppose. The reason isn't important, I just need to find out who was behind it.'

David slowed his toast buttering and looked up, serious for a moment. 'And what happens then?'

'And then I'm going to take them down.'

David nodded, took a bite of his toast, and sank into thoughtful chewing for a few seconds. 'You know that's against the law, yes? Like, properly, incredibly, illegally against the law.'

'Well, when I'm done, you can arrest me. Or try to anyway.'

David stopped and eyed me for a second, then broke into a grin. It might have sounded like a joke, but at this point I really didn't care. What had been done to my coven... revenge was all that mattered. Cold, violent revenge. What happened to me after that was beside the point, just so long as whoever committed the murders screamed in agony at my feet first.

'Toast.'

Another plate piled with more white bread was plopped into the centre of the table by Nora.

David looked up at her. 'Nora, I think one extra round is enough... Nora?'

The strange tone in his voice caught my attention. I looked up to Nora expecting to see her sagging face and hangdog eyes, but instead I saw something else.

Something terrible.

Her face was twisted and distorted, like someone had torn it off and glued it back on in the dark. Her mouth was a crowded mess of yellowed fangs, and her eyes were missing, leaving two dark hollows.

'Jesus...' said David, his voice a trembling hush.

'David, run, she's—'

The movement was so swift I didn't see it coming. Instead, I found myself sliding across the floor on my back, my right cheek throbbing from the back of Nora's hand.

'Stella, watch out!'

Shaking the stars away, I lurched to my knees, only to find Nora eating up the distance between us.

Around us, chairs were falling and people were screaming, a mad rush for the only door, and away from this sudden explosion of violence.

I needed to make sure Nora kept her sights on me and not on any of the fleeing bystanders, so I did the stupid thing and ran directly at her.

It felt like a head-on collision with a truck.

I bounced off her into a wall, the back of my head connecting so hard I almost passed out.

The café was empty now apart from me, David, and whatever the thing was that had possessed Nora. Time to get to work.

I staggered up and drew in some extra magic from my surroundings, ready to—

Nora's hand gripped my throat, and my handle on the magic words was lost. The palm of her hand burned my flesh.

Lifting me as though I weighed no more than a bag of sugar, Nora picked me up with one hand, slid me up the wall, and regarded me with a drooling, lopsided grin.

Any second now, she was going to lean forward and sink those teeth into my face. I needed to get my shit together. To stop letting pain and fear cloud my thoughts, and find the right spell to—

The hand around my throat opened and I dropped hard to the floor.

'My name is Detective David Tyler. Step away from her and put your hands behind your head.'

Nora turned from me, revealing a livid gash on the side of her head. David was stood, extendable baton raised, other hand out, warning Nora to keep her distance. He must have struck her with the thing. He'd more than likely saved my life, at least for a moment or two longer.

'I said my name is Detective David Tyler. You will surrender yourself or I will use further force. Now get on your knees, hands behind your head.'

I got back to my feet, throat throbbing, and circled wide towards him.

'David, no, you can't talk a thing like that down. Hit it as many times as you like with your little stick, it'll only keep coming.'

'*Hey, David, thanks for saving me from being choked to death a few seconds ago,*' he said. 'Oh, don't mention it, you're welcome.'

Nora laughed with a sound like metal twisting. 'You will both die now. Die like those stinking whore witches.'

'So I take it good ol' Nora here has been possessed by something magical and evil?'

'You catch on fast, Detective.'

'Well, the fangs, the empty eye holes, the super strength, they teach us to look out for these little clues at police pre-school.'

'Nora is dead. Whatever has claimed her is all that's left now, and we are in a lot of danger.'

The Nora monster shambled towards us. 'I will rip and I will tear and I will grind your bones between my teeth.'

'Oh, Nora, we used to share such sweet pleasantries.' David raised his baton and charged forward.

'David, no—!'

Nora grabbed his arm mid-swing and tossed him across the room like a rag doll. He came to a crashing halt out of sight as he flew over the serving counter.

'David!'

'I will kill you first, familiar. Send you to the dark pit your creators now dwell in.'

Okay. It was time to put a stop to this. 'You know Nora, you're kind of big-headed for a lowly pit demon.'

Nora stopped, head cocked, confused for a moment. That moment was all I needed. The café was old. The building had stood for over two hundred years, and was chock-full of ancient, strong magic.

I pulled it into me and pictured the correct order of words. It took only moments, and then, screaming with fury, I punched a fist toward Nora and unleashed the spell.

It surged from me, a golden lasso, dripping like molten metal, and swamped Nora. Her empty eye sockets widened as the lasso tightened around her midriff, strangling her like a boa constrictor.

'Catching on now, Nora?'

She staggered back, clutching her head as it began to swell, the bones of her skull cracking, skin tearing. Any second now it would be over. Nora knew it too. She lowered her hands from her rapidly inflating cranium and looked at me, smiling, even as death came to claim her.

'That's good, familiar.'

'Who are you? Tell me your name. Tell me!'

'And where would the fun in that be?'

She laughed.

And then her head exploded.

9

When something like that happens in public, it's best not to stick around too long.

I grunted as I propped David against an alley wall ten streets away from the café. Leaning back on the opposite wall, I inhaled slow and deep, trying to catch my breath and rub some life back into my muscles. I was in good shape, but he was heavier than he looked.

So, that was attempt number two on my life. Whatever it was that destroyed my coven, it hadn't forgotten about me. I was a loose end it intended to tie up. But how had it found me? I did a quick check on myself, trying to locate any magical prints left on me that would help it zero in, but came up with nothing. Nothing that I was able to sense, anyway.

'M-my name is... I am a detective police man and you...'

I squatted down on my haunches next to David as he came to, his bleary eyes gradually coming into focus as they locked on mine.

'Hello, David.'

'Hello, magic lady woman.'

'Careful there, you took a bit of a knock.'

He rubbed his head, confused. 'I had the weirdest dream

Familiar Magic

that old Nora at the café became possessed by some sort of monster and tried to kill us.'

'Yes, sorry, that wasn't a dream.'

'Oh, I was afraid you might say that,' said David, using the grimy alley wall to find his feet.

'Careful, you've been out of it for almost six minutes.'

'Don't worry, I get hit on the head a lot. So, what happened to Evil Nora?'

'I cast a spell on her.'

'A nice spell, like the hologram one you showed me?'

'Afraid not.'

'A wild stab in the dark, but is it connected to all the blood you have across your face and dried in your hair?'

I nodded. 'Yes, I sort of made her head explode.'

David's eyes went wide as he made to speak, stopped himself, and then threw up noisily. After breathing in a few times slowly, then wiping his mouth, he looked up at me again. 'That was down to the bash on the head, not the... you know...'

'Me exploding someone's head.'

'Oh, God, I'm making small talk with a murderer.'

'I didn't have a choice. Nora was already dead, I told you, and we would've been next.'

'Right, yes. Okay. This is just, you know, tricky, for me to get to grips with. I went to bed last night and everything was semi-understandable, and now there's magic, and demons or ghosts or whatever, taking over the body of my favourite cafe owner and trying to murder me.'

'The good news is, things aren't going to get any better for a while.'

'Yes, that *is* good news.'

I smiled and helped him back up to his feet.

'Right, if you don't mind, I might just head off to work now and pretend none of this ever happened. Just really lovely to meet you, though. Let's not keep in touch, deal?'

I grabbed David by the sleeve as he tried to walk away, yanking him back. 'You can't go.'

'Oh, yes, I really can.'

He pulled himself free and carried on walking. Seemed like we were going to have to do this the hard way. The words flashed through my mind as I extended my arms towards David and unleashed the command. There was a *whoosh*, followed by a slightly strangled yelp, and David found himself pinned, upside-down, against the alley wall.

'You know this is assault, right?'

'You can't go. Well, you can, but not without me.'

'Are you holding me hostage? Because no one is going to pay a ransom. My family are very, very cheap.'

I smiled and released him, slowly, so he slid into an undignified heap on the ground. 'I told you, there'll be a target on your back now, too.'

'So now whoever it is that murdered, your, you know, witches, is also going to kill me?'

'Very probably.'

David stood. 'You know, I'm starting to not like you very much.'

'The thing that took over the cafe owner, it knows you're with me. It will try to use that. Interrogate you, torture you. Pull your limbs off one by one to try and get to me.'

'Okay, I think I get it. That's enough detail, thank you.'

'The only chance you have of getting out of this alive is to stay by my side until it's all over. Believe me, I'd much rather be on my own, too, but if I let you walk away, that's another death on my conscience.' I pictured my witches, torn to pieces on the floor of the coven, and shivered.

David sighed and kicked at the ground. 'Fine, okay, but you're going to listen to me. I'm not a passenger, I'm a detective. A good one.'

I arched an eyebrow.

'Well, not a terrible one, at any rate. I'm a solid six-and-a-half out of ten. Seven, on a good day. You can use me.'

I went to argue, then stopped and sighed. He was probably right. It wasn't my usual job to find clues and piece together a case. Up until now, I'd been told what to do and where to go by my masters. They'd say *go there and do this to that person,* and off I would go. I was a blunt instrument. A delivery service. Not the brains. And now I was alone, I was going to need all the help I could get.

'Um, Stella?' said David, pointing over my shoulder with a strange look on his face. 'Are you seeing her, too?'

I turned to see a remarkably tall woman, standing seven-feet high at least. Her head was shaved and her dark skin shone as if lit by an inner light.. She was dressed in brown sack-cloth robes. 'Familiar, you are required,' she said, her voice deep and certain, then she turned and walked out of the alley.

'A friend of yours?' asked David.

'I don't have friends,' I replied, then followed after the woman.

'No? I'm making a shocked face here,' said David as he jogged to catch up, 'turn around and look at my shocked face.'

I didn't turn around.

10

The Monk—because that's what she was—sat cross-legged and eyes closed on the floor of the tube train as it hurtled towards Greenwich. No one noticed her, no one pointed, or took pictures of her with their phones. No one even saw her. The Monk radiated a spell that allowed her to remain invisible to any bystander she didn't want looking at her. To step around her without even realising there was anyone to step around. I could see the spell weaving around her in brilliant, coiling ribbons of gold.

'She's a big one, eh?' said David.

'She is tall, yes. Are those the detective skills you were bragging about earlier?'

'Har-de-har. So what does she want?'

'Did you hear her say another word after we left the alleyway?'

'No.'

'Then you know just as much as I do.'

'Yeah, I very much doubt that. So who is she?'

'A Monk, a keeper of the Sorcerer Tree.'

David did one of his slow head nods to indicate that he had absolutely no idea what I was talking about.

'Don't worry, if we're heading to the church in Greenwich, you'll see it for yourself soon enough.'

As the train continued to speed through the dark tunnel, I thought about my witches and hoped this diversion wouldn't keep me too long. As it turned out, it wasn't a diversion at all.

The Church of the Sorcerer Tree is an ordinary-looking three-storey house sat in the centre of a residential street. At least, that's what it looks like to anyone passing by outside, and to any neighbours. They had no idea that it housed a spiritual order who watched over an ancient wonder.

The Monk paused at the door as she opened it, and looked back at me. 'You might want to prepare, the Church may still feel barren.' She turned back and bent low so she wouldn't hit her head on the doorframe.

'This doesn't look a whole lot like a church,' noted David.

'You'll see.' I replied.

I stepped across the threshold, followed by my companion.

'What in the...?' said David, looking around in disbelief. We had not stepped into a corridor, nor a room that you might expect to belong in a house like the one we had been taken to. No, this place was much larger, much different, to what the outside suggested. It was more like we'd stepped into an immense, gothic cathedral.

'Well, that's not normal,' said David, his voice echoing as he gazed around at the space he'd found himself in. At the stone columns that stretched up and up, to a ceiling that was out of view.

The dark stone of the walls were broken up by giant stained glass windows and immense tapestries that colourfully displayed historic depictions of myth from throughout the Uncanny world. Images of a giant beast whose skin was fire, the Magic Eater, striding across the country, setting it ablaze.

Pictures of wizards battling great packs of werewolves. Depictions of a dark angel, trapped within a cage of glass.

But most of all, there were pictures of the tree. The Sorcerer Tree.

The actual tree dominated the building. It burst up from the centre of the church and stretched high above, its upper branches lost from view. The Sorcerer Tree was as wide as six people laid head to toe, and its huge branches jutted from the great trunk at broken arm angles, bare of leaves.

David stepped out of the Church and into the street, bewildered, then stepped back in again. 'How is this possible?' he asked, looking around him in wonder.

'The Church doesn't exist inside the house, the house is just a portal to another place. To this place.'

'So you're saying the door of the house is sort of a magic door?'

'If you like.'

'Okay, right, gotcha. Magic door. Just a bloody magic door, that's all, of course it is.'

As I walked further into the Church, it was clear why the Monk had issued me a warning before stepping inside. It was also clear that this journey had not been a diversion, but part of the same case I was already investigating.

The Church's background magic was muted.

It wasn't like the Coven—where it had been drained entirely—but it was still enough to be a shock to my system. I had been inside the Church just once before, almost thirty years previously, and it had throbbed with magic, fed it by the Sorcerer Tree. But today its magic was weak, and the Sorcerer Tree looked different. There was a giant, ragged split right down its trunk, almost splitting the thing in two. It looked like a giant had struck down at it with an axe.

'It's been here,' I said.

The Monk nodded. 'When I arrived, the Church was entirely empty of magic, the Tree desecrated. The Church should already be full of magic again, but since the attack, the Tree is weak. Look...'

She placed a finger to my temple, and for a few seconds, I saw the tree as she did. On my first visit, when given this insight, I'd barely been able to look directly at the Tree, such was the ferocity of the magic exploding from it, but this time... this time it was muted. A hazy wash lazily rolling out from the Tree, its wound a black, throbbing void.

'Bless the Tree.' The Monk pressed a fist against her forehead and bowed before the tree, then straightened up. 'Follow,' she said, and walked towards one of several arched corridor openings that led off from the giant main antechamber.

'What, exactly, is that super, big, crazy tree?' asked David.

'The Sorcerer Tree,' I explained. 'The Monks believe it gave birth to the very first people capable of seeing and using magic. That it is a God, of sorts. It radiates a kind of pure, old magic that nourishes them. Or it did.'

'So that tree is God? Makes about as much sense as anything else, I suppose.'

The stone corridor opened up into a small chamber. Inside, was a thing from a nightmare. There was a man, stretched out on a simple cot. He was trembling, his eyes closed. He'd been skinned. Completely. His entire body was slick and red raw, all blood and exposed muscle and veins.

'Oh my God,' said David, turning away, a hand over his mouth. I'd like to say it affected me in the same way, but I'd seen the same and worse in my many years.

'How is this person still alive?' I asked.

'Force of will,' replied the Monk, as two others gently dabbed at the skinned man with damp rags.

'Tell me what happened,' I said, not able to look away from the horror movie in front of me.

'Half of us had been out foraging at the back of the supermarket,' the Monk replied. 'When we returned, the Church was empty of magic, the Tree desecrated, and all the monks who had remained behind were dead. All but this one, who was barely clinging to life.'

'Has he been able to tell you anything?' asked David, shielding his eyes, still. 'A description maybe of who did this?'

The Monk shook her head. 'They cling to life as they wish to tell us. To tell us who defiled the Sorcerer Tree. But their damage is too severe and they are locked in this unconscious state, death creeping towards them, unable to give voice as they are desperate to.'

Apparently, the Coven and my witches were not this bastard's only target. It seemed like they were attacking any great seat of the Uncanny in the city. Draining it of magic and murdering all who stood before them. But why? What was their end game?

'What do you want me to do?' I asked the Monk.

'We cannot seek direct retribution, it is against our beliefs. But you can. And must.'

'I plan to. But if he can't speak, he can't help me.'

The Monk nodded. 'That is why I brought you here, and why we have been keeping our brother comfortable enough to cling to life until I did so. I can make him speak, but it will be the end of him. His body and mind are too far gone to withstand consciousness for more than one brief occasion.'

'Do it,' I replied.

'Whoa,' said David, 'didn't you hear what she just said? It'll kill him. Maybe we should get him to a hospital or something.'

'He's already dead,' I replied, 'the only reason he hasn't stopped breathing yet is because he wants to tell me who did this to him. Who did this to my coven. Understand? This is what he wants.'

Bug-eyed, David ran his hands through his short hair, then waved the Monk on. 'Sure, fine, whatever you say.'

The Monk clapped her hands together, and somewhere in the Church a great gong was struck. The stone chamber began to shake, dust falling down from the ceiling like dirt into a grave. The Monk kissed the palm of one hand and placed it against the mortally wounded monk's forehead. His eyes snapped open and he lurched up, a shrill scream escaping his lipless mouth.

'Easy, fellow, easy,' said the Monk, as the man fell back on his blood-soaked bedclothes, his body shaking violently.

'Death, death is here,' said the man, the sentence escaping from his rasping, gurgling throat, a red-raw and fat tongue struggling around each word.

'Who did this?' I asked, stepping towards the dying man as his fingers clawed at the air, chest struggling for breath. 'Tell me while you can. Who did this to you? Who desecrated the Sorcerer Tree?'

The man's gurgled gasps ceased, and his hands stopped their twitching as he turned to me. 'Like nothing. Like... ancient. So old. So... pow... so powerful...'

'Show her what came here,' said the Monk, taking the man's wrist as I knelt down at his side. She pressed the man's hand to my forehead. 'Show her what did this.'

He nodded, blood dribbling out of his mouth. He didn't have long left.

'Show it to me.'

'I can... show you... I can... show...'

Cold rushed over me and the room shook again, then cut to black. I was in the man's mind's eye. In his thoughts, his memories. He was showing me what he could.

I walked into the black. Slowly, light began to weave into the dark, and I could see a man in sackcloth robes stood before me. It was the dying monk as he had looked before the attack.

'What is its name?' I asked.

He shook his head.

'What happened?'

'I do not know how it arrived into the Church,' he said. 'Suddenly, there was only screaming and death.'

Images flashed around us; memories rushing around the dark. Monks running, screaming, dying.

'Show me what did this. I need to see it.'

The memories warped and faded as the monk peered into the dark. 'It is here. It is here with us. Look!'

He pointed into the black, his finger trembling. Something was moving out there. A patch of the dark that was even darker than what surrounded us. Fear was not something I usually entertained, but as the thing crept slowly towards us—indistinct, giggling—I realised my hands were trembling, too.

'It took my skin slowly,' said the dying monk. 'I was unable to move. It nibbled with its teeth, then dug its fingers in, tearing strips away, whistling while it worked.'

The shape in the dark began to whistle, and the monk staggered backwards. I turned to see he was now like he was in reality: skinless, grotesque, dying. He fell to his knees, coughing up a mouthful of blood that splattered on the ground and dripped down his chin.

'It eats... eats all. It hates... so... much hate...'

Time was almost up.

I ran towards the dark, quivering, whistling shape that was creeping towards us, desperate to see it clearly before the connection broke. Before the monk died.

'I'm coming for you!' I said, but no matter how fast I ran, I never seemed to get any closer to the intruder. Just black on black, twitching and whistling.

A scream, and then I was pulled away.

I was back in the church, the monk dead on his cot. I stood slowly, worried my legs might give out beneath me.

'He's dead,' the Monk said, quietly. She lifted her brother's sheet and covered him with it.

'Did you see who did this?' David asked.

I turned to him, eyes wide, jaw moving without speaking.

'Hey,' he said, gently taking me by the arm, 'it's okay, you're okay.'

'Who did this?' asked the Monk, turning from the dead man.

'I don't... I couldn't quite see. Something of the dark. Something terrible. I think... I think the memory itself knew what he was doing and killed him before I could get a clear picture.'

A burble of loud voices from down the corridor caught our attention as a young monk rushed into the chamber. 'The Tree! The Tree!' she screamed, then turned and ran back down the corridor.

We rushed after to find the main church room in chaos.

The Sorcerer Tree was burning.

'No,' was all the Monk could say as she looked up at the flames ravaging the Tree, tears pouring down her cheeks.

The other monks were stood in a circle around the blazing tree, trying to use their magic to douse the flames, but it was clear it was having no effect. They were not ordinary flames, they raged with blues and coppers and purples, and grew more fierce with each spell poured upon it.

'Leave,' said the Monk.

'We should call the Fire Brigade,' said David, reaching for his phone.

'No use,' said the Monk. 'Go. And Stella, find it. Stop it. Kill it.'

I took hold of David's sleeve and pulled him towards the exit as the Monk joined her fellows in their circle of power, singing in exaltation of the Tree as the powerful, magical flames that ravaged it began to spread. Great jagged cracks appeared in the stone floor, the columns trembled, and the stained glass windows melted and ran as liquid from their frames.

'Get out! Everyone get the hell out of here!' said David as the flames crept towards the unwavering monks, but they continued to sing to the Tree as it died, and as death came for them, too.

'They won't. They can't,' I replied. 'But we can. Come on.'

The cool air from the street hit us like a bucket of ice water as we ran from the Church of the Sorcerer Tree, and the door to the simple house that led to it slammed closed behind us. To walk down this street, you would have had no idea of what was going on beyond that door, beyond that portal. There would be no evidence of the destruction, of the death within.

That creature—that patch of twitching darkness—had destroyed my coven, and now it had killed the Sorcerer Tree. Destroyed its church, its followers, and I was still no closer to understanding what it was, or how I was going to stop it.

How many more would suffer while I fumbled in the black like a clueless child?

11

Every city in England has a place like The Beehive: a place for Uncanny types to socialise, to drink, to gossip, to mingle in a neutral setting. Outside there were rivalries, jealousies, even vendettas, but inside, all of that was expected to be left behind. Under The Beehive's roof, we could relax in peace and be ourselves, away from the prying eyes of normals.

At least, that was the idea.

Because someone had murdered the coven of witches that maintained the peace in London, and today, the Sorcerer Tree —which had stood for millennia—was burning. I would tear apart the city looking for the beast behind that, even if it meant upsetting the patrons of The Beehive.

'I already told you, there is no street up here on the left, it's a parade of old shops and then a dead end.'

I strode on ahead, despite David's complaints. 'That's because it's hidden from the likes of you.'

'Um, the likes of me?'

'You know, *normals*.'

'That sounds a lot like racism, Stella.'

I stopped in front of the blind alley. Much like the street the

London Coven was situated on, the alley that led to The Beehive was hidden from all but those who should know of its existence.

David stopped by my side and stared blankly.

'What?'

'We're here.'

He looked ahead, then back to me. 'Oh, God, you're mad, aren't you? Magic and mad. That's quite the cocktail.'

'Look, David.' I pointed down the blind alley.

David followed my finger.

'Oh, I see it!'

'Really?'

'No, of course not.'

The correct phrase entered my head and I released it towards him. 'David, look now...'

He shook his head and looked in the direction I was pointing once again. 'I told you, there's nothing over... wait... wait a second, where did...?'

I smiled as I looked at his handsome features hanging slack, eyes wide. 'Come on, you can buy me a drink.'

I strode into the blind alley, David trailing behind, arms outstretched as though it was all some trick, and he was about to walk into a wall.

At the far end of the alley stood the pub, just as it had done for hundreds of years now, its wooden sign with a faded picture of a beehive, gently creaking in the breeze. Pushing the door open, I stepped into The Beehive and felt the thin skin of a protective spell part around me, like I was stepping inside a giant soap bubble. The Beehive had a few pretty decent protection spells placed on it, one of which dampened the worst kinds of magic its patrons might choose to throw at one another. Like I say, the rules were clear about violence staying outside of the premises. The Beehive was meant to be a safe zone, but the place sold alcohol, and wherever you found alcohol, you were liable to find bloodshed.

So, the spells of protection.

They didn't rob patrons of their abilities entirely, but they deadened magic to the degree that nothing lethal could be chucked about. Fist fights still broke out of course, just like any other pub, but spill a short-tempered wizard's pint, and you weren't going home in a body bag.

'What is this place?' asked David, looking around at the old-fashioned pub, straw scattered on its dark, uneven floor. 'Why don't I know it? I know all of these streets.'

'You only think you do. There are many streets that people like you would swear don't exist, but they do. London is full of them. We call them blind alleys: streets hidden from all but those who know they're there. Now you've been to this place, you'll always be able to see it.'

David stopped suddenly. 'Wait a second... a year back I was chasing a guy, murder suspect, and he legged it into a side street. I took the corner and suddenly he was nowhere to be seen. We checked every house, and there were no streets he could have ducked down, nothing. Could he have...?'

'Probably. Sounds like you were chasing someone with magic. You should be grateful he found a blind alley, if you'd caught him, it probably wouldn't have ended well.'

David shook like a dog throwing off water. 'You know, this is all more than a bit creepy.'

'You get used to it.'

I scanned the early drinkers, recognising many of the faces. Most were friendly, but some had felt the wrath of my masters through me. Upon seeing me, they turned away, looked at the floor, their drinks, the wall. Word travelled fast in the world of the Uncanny, and a tale as juicy as this one would have been around the city a hundred times by now.

The witches of the London Coven were dead.

'So what are we doing here, then?' asked David.

'This is The Beehive. Anyone who is anyone, high or low,

passes through here. If someone knows who or what is behind all this, they're probably sat in this pub right now.'

David scanned the bar. 'How many of these people could make my head pop like you did Evil Nora's?'

'Oh, at least half of them, but not in this place. The worst they can do here is break a stool over your skull.'

'Good to know. Okay, so here's what we're going to do: I'm going to announce that I'm a police officer, and you're, you know, a magic police officer, or whatever, and tell them we want to talk to them all, one by one. Just ask a few questions, nothing heavy. Deal?'

'Okay.' I turned from David, picked up a chair and launched it across the room. The wall on the far side of the bar brought it to a crunching, splintered halt. 'Listen to me,' I bellowed. 'You know who I am and you know why I'm here.'

All eyes were on me, then the nearest exit, but the only way out was behind me. No one was going anywhere.

'Consider this a lock in. Someone in here knows what happened to my witches, and I will beat each and every one of you into a bloody pulp if they don't start talking.'

'Or,' said David, 'you could ignore me completely and do that. Either one, really.'

12

My fist met Razor's face with a satisfying crunch.

'Tell me what you know!' I demanded.

He looked up at me, a red river running down his chin, and spat something solid on the sawdust floor. Rage growled inside of me. It felt good. Good to unleash my pain on someone else's face.

'You shame your dead masters by acting this way,' he hissed.

Now he was really asking for it. I grabbed him by his thick neck and shoved him, making his head snap back and bounce painfully off the wall.

'Stella, stop!' cried David.

'Don't worry, this piece of crap has done far worse to far too many. Isn't that right, Razor?'

Razor was an eaves, and looked like a mole that had grown up into a man. He was squat and thick-limbed, and had a mouth full of small, sharp teeth that could bite through a man's finger as if it were candy floss. An eaves traded in information; all of their kind did. They collected news and hearsay, and would pass it on for a price. The cost? A taste of magic. They were limited in what they could actually use magic for, but it fed them, and allowed them to conceal their homes from anyone bearing a grudge. This was a particularly useful talent for an eaves like Razor, who was about as nasty a piece of work as you might find in London, and had collected a wealth of grudges.

'I've just made my way here from the Church of the Sorcerer Tree,' I said.

'So?'

'Whoever killed my witches just burned the Tree to the ground, and the monks with it. Now, you're going to tell me everything you know about that, or I'm going to beat you inside out.'

'I ain't heard nothing.'

'I know you've heard something, Razor, so tell me now and maybe I'll make your pain brief.'

He smiled, exposing a recently-broken tooth. 'You think now your masters are gone that you can do whatever you want, Familiar?'

I punched him in the gut by way of an answer, causing him to crumple to the floor at my feet.

'Stop this,' rumbled a deep voice.

The owner of The Beehive lumbered into view. Lenny was a mountain of a man, with caterpillar-thick eyebrows and a grizzled beard. Everyone respected Lenny—respected what he could do with his coal shovel-sized hands—but not me. At least, not today.

'Stay out of this, Lenny,' I urged, 'you know what's happened.'

'I do, but this is my gaff, and there's no fighting here.'

'Listen to him, little familiar,' said Razor, a giggle sliding out of his busted mouth that scraped across my skin like a blade.

'I know you, Razor. I know the kind of grim corners you hang out in. I'm going to give you one more chance to tell me something useful, and then I'm going to start breaking bones.'

David put a hand on my arm. 'Stella, come on, this isn't the way you conduct an investigation. Well, maybe in the '70s, but not today.'

I turned to him angrily. 'Don't tell me how to do my job. Someone murdered my masters, my family, do you understand?'

'I understand—'

'No you don't!'

'Normal, you need to get her out of here,' said Lenny.

'Oh, sure, I'm going to drag the head-popper out of here. Good plan, Andre the Giant.'

They argued back and forth, but I tuned them out. Turned them to static. My focus was trained on Razor and that bloodied smile of his. He knew every piece of scum that hid in the shadows of London. Either he started being helpful, or I was going to kill him.

'You wouldn't. That's not how you do things,' said Razor, reading the look in my eyes.

'Maybe. But things have a way of changing.'

I grabbed Razor by the collar and dragged him towards the exit, throwing him out the door and into the blind alley.

'Oh, shit,' said David.

I marched after Razor, cutting off his escape and exiting The Beehive's magic-dampening bubble as I did so. I felt my powers sharpen, felt the surrounding magic rush into me.

'You can't do this!' yelled Razor, cowering against the alley wall, spittle flying. 'You have no right!'

'Yesterday someone pulled the witches of London apart, piece by piece. Plucked bones from sockets, tore flesh, and worse. That means, today, I can do anything I want.'

I formed the words in my head and thrust my hands towards Razor, unleashing a ball of flame. He screamed and hurled himself out of its path, the fire singeing his leather jacket.

'Stella,' said David, emerging from The Beehive. 'Stella, come on, this isn't you. I mean, maybe it is you, I barely know you, and you did make an old woman's head explode, but I like to think I'm a pretty good judge of character. It's one of the few things I know I'm good at, and everything tells me that you're not, well, a violent psycho.'

'Listen to him, Familiar. This isn't the way. This is not how your witches would want you to treat me. I helped them plenty over the years. Fed them all sorts of information.'

'You think you can speak for them, Razor?' I punched out another spell that snapped his head back, cracking it against the bricks behind him and sending him down to his knees. My fist erupted in flames. 'Tell me what I need to know or I swear I'll turn you into a grease spot.'

'Stella, come on, stop,' said David. 'I've seen a lot of bad coppers in my time on the force. Coppers who take bribes, and bully to get what they want. You don't want to be one of them, trust me.'

I turned to David and looked into his eyes, ready to unleash a fresh stream of justification, but something about the way he looked back made the words freeze in my mouth. I suddenly felt small, weak, vulnerable.

'David... David, they're dead. Someone came into our home and murdered them.'

My flaming fist sputtered out, and David took my hand in his. I wanted to pull away. Wanted to turn back to Razor and beat him until my knuckles broke. Make him scream. But I didn't. I stood still, vision blurring as tears prickled my eyes.

'I don't know your witches, but I know the law and I know real justice. You don't get that by turning into one of them,' said David, aiming a finger at Razor. 'You need evidence. You need to know. Need to know for sure. And then...'

'And then?'

'And then you make them pay.'

I turned to Razor, who was crouched on the ground still, cowering. 'Please, no more,' he begged.

'Tell me what I need to know.'

'The Den Club. Go to The Den and ask Anya why she and her kind were heard laughing about the attack. Toasting it. Patting each other on the back like they had a hand in it. Go ask them. Go ask at The Den.'

I stepped back as the news sunk in. If The Den had a hand in this…

I stepped aside as Razor took the opportunity to barge past and go flailing from the blind alley.

'Should we go after him?' asked David. 'No is a response I'd be more than happy with.'

'Let him go. He told us what we need to know.'

David leaned back against the alley wall, clearly relieved that it was all over. 'Well, that was all more than a little intense.'

I frowned as I looked at the scorch marks my magic had left on the alleyway's brick walls. I was getting out of control, I knew it, but I didn't feel like reining myself in. Not yet. Not until whatever had crept towards me in the black of the skinned monk's memories was dead.

'Are you okay?' asked David, cutting into my brooding.

'This is my life, David. Always has been, for longer than you've been alive. I'm fine.'

'If you say so.' He didn't sound convinced, and I couldn't bring myself to meet his eyes. 'So what's next?' he asked.

'Next?' I said. 'You heard Razor. Next we need to walk into The Den and talk to a succubus.'

'Right. You know sometimes how you regret asking a question…?'

13

The Den hunkered at the end of a street in Soho, its neon sign burning like the lure of an angler fish, pulling unwary prey into its hungry belly.

'So when you say we're going to talk to a succubus, I take it that's not a euphemism?' asked David.

'Correct.'

'Great. Remind me why I can't just forget all of this, head back to the office, and investigate a nice, old-fashioned stabbing or something?'

'Anya and her family are succubi,' I explained. 'They feast on pleasure. Pain. Anger. On any heightened emotion.'

'Monks worshipping giant God trees, secret streets, witches... this is insane. You do realise how insane this all is, yes?'

'No.'

'No, I suppose you probably don't, what with you being a big chunk of insane yourself. No offence.'

I stood by and watched as the patrons of The Den furtively filtered inside. Apart from the neon sign announcing its existence, the facade of the club was simple, nondescript, and there were no windows to give a glimpse at what might lurk within. Just a door and the sign, and that was all.

The Den made dreams come true; the sort of dreams you kept to yourself. The club offered all sorts of illicit delights, from gambling, to sex, to bare-knuckle fighting, to bondage, to... much, much worse. It wasn't just a place for a succubus to hang out and indulge their ways, everyone was welcome, be they Uncanny or otherwise. All types of people would hear whispers of the place and find themselves drawn inexorably towards it. None of them would have heard of it, or even noticed it, until that whisper in the dark. Only then would they walk by and see it, and once that had happened, it would be all they could think about. There was some magic to it that neither I nor my witches had ever quite been able to crack. Inside those walls, pleasure waited. No judgment; whatever was desired was supplied. Even the most strong-minded of people could find themselves bewitched by the place. Obsessed with it. And then Anya, the head succubus, had you. Owned you.

I turned to David and saw how he looked at the place. A curiosity, a hunger.

'So anything goes in there?' he said. 'Anything you could want?'

'Clear your perverted mind, Detective.'

'What? I wasn't thinking about anything. Almost anything. And certainly not naked, peach-bottomed women covered in jelly, if that's what you're thinking.'

'I wasn't. At all.'

'Well. Good. Me neither.'

'The Den leads people astray by offering them what they want; which means you're definitely going to need protection.'

'Like what? A shooter?'

I closed my eyes as I placed my hands on his head.

'What is happening now?' he asked. 'I'm not sure a head massage is really appropriate at this point.'

'You know, you really do talk a lot.'

'Yeah, you're not the first person to tell me that. Hey, that sort of tingles.'

I opened my eyes and took my hands off him. 'I've just placed a protection spell on you. It should stop the worst of the place from getting its hooks into you.'

David frowned and massaged his temples. 'Oh, thanks. Come to think of it, that jelly idea doesn't seem half as appealing now. Not that it ever did, of course.'

'Of course.'

'Now, custard on the other hand...'

I resisted—very hard—the urge to slap the grin off his face. 'Come on, follow me and stay close. They can be civilised, but the monster is only a blink away. Don't trust them for a second.'

'Don't trust the succubus monster people, got it.'

I strode towards the entrance to The Den. Two large doormen stuffed into bulging suits eyeballed us as we approached.

'Well, what do we have here?' asked the first. He was seven-foot, twice my width, with a glistening, bald head.

'Just what I was thinking, mate. What do we have here?' His partner in thuggery, almost as tall, equally as bald, with a nose that had been flattened so many times that breathing through it was no longer an option.

Jack and Jake had been the doormen for The Den since before I was created. I'd never found out exactly what type of Uncanny they were, but one thing was for sure: they'd lived a hell of a long time, and they enjoyed nothing more than someone stepping out of line. Then they could punch, head-butt, and kick that unfortunate person way, way, way out of line. So far out of line that being able to walk back into line was extremely unlikely.

'Jack, Jake, always a pleasure,' I said, in a way that I hoped clearly communicated that it wasn't at all.

'You know she don't like you in her place, Familiar.'

'Yeah, you know that.'

'She knows that.'

'Exactly.'

'Hi, I am also here,' said David, raising a hand. 'Detective David Tyler. In the immortal words of Judge Dredd: I am the law.'

'Don't show them your—'

'Here's my badge—' David pulled it out and brandished the badge with a clearly practiced flourish that might, in other circumstances, have received the desired reaction.

I sighed and turned to the doormen, offering them an apologetic look.

'Not looking for trouble, lads,' said David, 'we'd just like to step inside your sex-house and ask your boss a few questions.'

Jake and Jack scanned the badge, looked up at David, then at each other, and burst out laughing. It was the kind of laughter that ran deep, bending the pair double as they grasped at each other for support, tears streaming down their knuckle-scarred cheeks. It's not the sort of thing that fills you with confidence.

'Ooh, a detective, Jack!'

'A detective, Jake!'

'Oh, I'm so scared!'

'Absolutely terrified!'

Fresh hysterics gripped their giant frames as David put away his badge with all the dignity he could muster. Which wasn't much.

'If you two have finished,' I said.

'So you want to talk to Anya, huh?'

'Anya's who you're looking for, is it?'

'Yes, and I'm pretty sure you know why,' I replied.

They nodded as one.

'The witches of the London Coven are dead,' said Jack.

'Witches are dead, that's what I heard,' said Jake.

'That's what I heard, too.'

'Yup.'

'And how do you know that, guys?' asked David. 'Wouldn't be a little inside knowledge, would it?'

The two doormen shot David a look of such cold-blooded doom that he had to take a step back.

'You're gonna want to keep your normal on a short leash, Familiar.'

'A very short leash.'

'Cos there's nothing we like more than playing with a normal, is there, Jake?'

'You got that right, Jack.'

'Hey, don't think you can intimidate me, pal, okay? I'm the one with authority here,' said David. Jack stepped forward and looked down at him, smothering him in his shadow. 'Just so long as that's clear,' David continued, his voice barely audible. 'Over to you, Stella.'

'We're going inside and we're talking to Anya. If either of you two think you can stop us, please, take your best shot.'

The doormen turned to me, their eyes hooded and dark. I drew in the surrounding magic as it looked as though things might explode. I'd had to grapple with the pair before, but they were strong and could take a lot of magic being thrown at them, and still keep coming. Wherever possible, it was wise to avoid taking them head-on.

The pair broke and laughed again, Jack opening the door. 'In you go little familiar, and your pet detective, too.'

'Yeah, in you go. Anya was expecting you anyway.'

'Expecting you, she was.'

'The guilty always do,' said David.

'What was that, normal?'

'Nothing,' David replied, his voice high and sharp. 'Shall we go in then? Stella?'

I shook my head and followed David inside.

14

It was warm inside. Uncomfortably so. The interior of The Den was all shadowy nooks and private booths with red velvet curtains. All around us, naked bodies writhed and squirmed. People were led around on dog leashes, chained women were whipped until their flesh ran red, and men pummelled each other into unconsciousness. We saw other things, too: things you don't even want to think about, because they'd come back to haunt you later.

'How is this place even open?' asked David. 'None of this is legal. Especially what that woman over there is having that horse do.'

'I think that's a donkey.'

'Well, pardon me.'

The place stank. The cloying taste of sweat and blood mixed with other bodily fluids, assaulting my senses, making me dizzy. It may have been the afternoon outside, but it was always three a.m. in The Den, and the echoes of screams and moans never abated.

'Just stay close, will you? I said. 'There are some bad people in here.'

'Really?' David replied. 'That lady over there using a cheese grater on a man's testicles seems just super.'

Stella...

I ignored the voice, I knew it was only in my own head. We walked into the belly of the club, heads turning briefly our way as we passed, before returning to whatever depravity they'd gone to The Den to indulge in. Some of the faces you might have recognised: politicians, athletes, even royalty. Everyone has something they want—something they're ashamed to want—and The Den was the place to get it. A place without shame, that was impossible for most to resist.

'Wait a second, that's... is that..?'

'Yes,' I replied.

'How does none of this end up in the papers?'

'This is the place you go to do whatever's in the dark recesses of your mind, because you know it never leaves these four walls. It never leaves these four walls, because the place belongs to Anya and her succubus family. To spread what you saw—to try and make money out of it, to blackmail—that gets you a home visit. A one-time and very final home visit.'

'Ah...'

I nodded. 'The only people allowed to make use of what goes on in here are Anya and her family.'

Stella, you let us die—

Let us die, Stella—

The voices of my dead masters, needling at me. I knew what it was of course: it was this place trying to find a weakness. A desire that I would give in to and indulge. Do that and I'd be in their hands. I'd been here on several occasions and had grown to manage the power of the place. To cope with it and ignore it. Or at least, that's what I thought. Of course, I'd never walked in there with any real, overwhelming desire before. I wasn't created to desire. But this time I had one.

Revenge.

'We need to go upstairs,' I said, 'to Anya's office, right now. That's where she'll be.'

David was looking at me funny. 'Are you okay there, Magic Lady? Hope you don't mind me saying, but you look a bit like a junkie who's about to pull a knife on me.'

'I'm fine!' I heard how loud my voice was, how fierce. I closed my eyes and tried to breathe. I needed to give myself a little of what I gave David outside.

Don't ignore us, Stella—
Revenge—
Kill for us—
Spill blood for us—
Now!

I'd been stupid, arrogant. I needed to cast a protection spell upon myself before—

'Hey, I heard those bitch witches is dead, huh?' I turned to find a wall of flesh before me, a pair of horns twisting up from his forehead, a sneer upon his flattened face. 'Sounds like the good times are here at last!'

And then my brain seemed to implode.

I drew the magic in the room toward me and thrust my hands out, unleashing an explosive force at the man that smacked him across the room. He collided with the far wall, his head cracking like an egg, his body dropping to the floor unconscious.

'Stella, whoa, calm down—'

Without a second thought, I flicked my wrist and David corkscrewed away from me—

No time to stop—

No time for restraint—

Only for anger and violence and bloody, awful, wonderful revenge on...

On who...?

Everybody!

I drew the magic into me again, wallowing joyfully in the

screams and the panic, cheered on by the voices in my head as I unleashed spell after spell, and bodies were tossed around the place like pieces of discarded laundry.

I wasn't going to stop.

I was going to make everyone in the place cower in fear and pain before I gave them the release of death. Then I'd find the others, the other dark Uncannies revelling in the deaths of my masters. I would make them all cry in terror. I would make them scream and bleed and die—

'Oi, little familiar—'

I swung around in a rage, teeth bared, ready to sink them into flesh. Jake, one of The Den's doormen, waved at me.

'That's right, look at me, Mister Distraction, over here. Go on then Jack.'

'Right you are, Jake.'

Jack's voice came from behind me. I only had time to turn halfway around before something solid struck me on the side of the head, then out went the lights.

15

I came to, my head throbbing from whatever it was that had cracked me over the skull. I didn't open my eyes at first. Instead, I tried to let my senses spread out and tell me where I was without giving myself away. Unfortunately, my play-acting wasn't fooling anyone.

'Awake at last, Stella.'

I recognised the deep, sultry voice that seemed to caress my skin. Anya. Owner of The Den, and the head of London's succubus family. The game was up. I opened my eyes.

'Tell your doormen that if they try to knock me out again, I'll turn their spines to jelly.'

I uncurled from the floor and attempted to hide my unsteadiness as I pushed myself up to my feet.

'Always so feisty. It's why I like you, Stella.'

She tossed a wave of thick raven hair over the shoulder of her emerald green dress and leaned forward to show off a generous décolletage. 'Why I don't just sit astride your chest and suck you dry, I have no idea.' She licked her perfect, bee-stung lips.

Jack and Jake were nowhere to be seen. Someone as strong

as Anya didn't need bodyguards, it was other people who needed to be protected from her.

'Before you ask, I'm having a really wonderful time,' said David, who was chained to the far wall, his eye swollen.

'Who attacked him?' I asked, spitting the words in Anya's direction.

'Yeah, that would be you, remember?' asked David.

I thought back to the moments before I'd been knocked unconscious. To the fury and bloodlust that had raged through me, and to a rather startled looking David Tyler, as I'd smacked him across the room. I was relieved to find that The Den's grip on me was gone, and that I was in control again.

'It seems you misbehaved in my club, Stella. You know I don't take kindly to those who interrupt the serene debauchery of my clientele; it's bad for business. I want everyone to know this is a safe space for them to do very unsafe, nasty, cruel things, and I can't have the likes of you giving the establishment a bad name.'

I snorted at that. A *bad name*. There were few worse places than The Den in the whole of the Uncanny Kingdom. The only reason my masters hadn't closed the place down long ago was because they needed to keep the succubus family happy, busy, and contained. Sometimes diplomacy meant letting awful things slide for the greater good. I'd learned that the hard way.

The office I was in was luxurious and expensively furnished, with a large antique desk at its centre. Anya strode across the parquet floor to a drinks cabinet, her curves rippling beneath the thin satin dress that clung to her like a second skin. She poured something red and thick into a crystal glass and drank it slowly as she moved towards David, running her fingernails down his cheek. Not hard enough to break the skin, but hard enough for him to think she might.

'People will know if I go missing,' said David.

'Shut up,' I said.

'I'm just saying, I'm a detective. The last thing a place like this wants is the police sniffing around. They'll have you down the nick before you know what's hit you.'

Anya laughed. It wasn't a pleasant sound, and it made me tremble despite myself. She gripped David's jaw. 'Such mean words from such a pretty mouth.'

'Okay,' said David, his words coming out slightly garbled. 'Maybe we could stop right now before this all goes too far. What do you say?'

Anya smiled. 'I say that I am curious as to what it is that hides in the dark crannies of your tiny mind. There's something in there, isn't that right? I can see it. Something bad lurking inside, waiting. I can always see the dark, no matter how hard it tries to hide from me. What do you long for, Detective? What makes your blood boil, your loins twitch? Don't be shy....'

'Stella, any time you're ready to lend a hand...'

I stepped forward, fists clenched. 'Anya, stop, now!'

Before I had time to think, she bounded across the room and pinned me to the wall by my neck, her eyes completely black.

'Stella, darling, tell me why I shouldn't break you over my knee and feast upon the emotions of you and your new pet?'

I pulled the magic in the room towards me, ready for a fight—

'You dare?' asked Anya, and with a scream, she threw me across the room. A wall brought a sudden halt to my flight, the thickly-carpeted floor catching me.

'Leave her alone!'

I heard David yelling as I scrambled up off the floor, head swirling. Anya walked towards me slowly. She wasn't scared. What reason did something as powerful as her have to be afraid of a lowly familiar like me?

'Isn't that sweet? The normal tries to stick up for you. The damsel in distress.'

'Yes I... wait, is she the damsel, or me?' asked David. 'Don't answer that. Look, I understand you're very powerful and scary and sexy, but I am an officer of the law. I don't care who or what you are, and you will respect that.'

Anya turned to David, licking her lips.

'I mean... if you want to.'

'Such bravery for something so vulnerable. I almost admire the sorry thing,' said Anya.

'Don't pay him any attention, focus on me, Anya. I'm the one you have to reckon with.'

'I heard about what happened to the witches,' said Anya. She turned her back on me, a sign of power. Of contempt. She knew that nothing I could do could trouble her. That she could take me any time she wanted.

'My masters were always good to you,' I said, trying to hide the quiver in my voice.

'Only because they had to be. You know as well as I do that if they could, they'd have chased every succubus from England, never mind London. But even they had their limits, so we came to an... understanding.'

I took a step towards her, ready to throw a spell if I had to. 'Did you have anything to do with their murder?'

Anya stopped and turned to me, one eyebrow raised. 'Who has been whispering such nasty ideas into your ear, Familiar?'

'So you don't deny it?'

Anya sighed and walked across her office, taking a seat behind her desk. 'Now, what possible good would it do me to kill the witches of the London Coven, hmm?'

'Because no matter what horrible stuff you get up to, you're still living within constraints, and that must burn you up inside.'

She smiled, leaning back in her chair. 'I won't deny that, on occasion, it has vexed me. The knowledge that we could be doing so much more. That we could turn the whole of this city into one big, writhing, pleasure palace. But I respect the witches. Let me rephrase that: I *respected* them.'

The word stung. They were gone. Past tense, now. The fragile peace between all the different stripes of the Uncanny that stalked the streets of London hung in the balance, and I was the only one left holding it all together.

'So you're denying all knowledge?'

Anya shrugged, picking up her glass and taking another sip of the dark liquid it held. 'The first I heard about it was when Jack and Jake passed on the news. Said everyone was talking about it as they came in the club.' She stood and walked over to David again.

'Hey there, Miss Head Succubus Lady; sorry about all that police talk earlier. Please don't do anything horrible to any bits of me. Especially to my main bits.'

Anya turned to me, smiling. 'You know, I like your little poodle. He's funny.'

'Oh, thanks,' said David, giving her two thumbs up.

Anya opened the locks on his chains, and David warily stepped towards the door.

'Okay, well, Stella, perhaps we should, you know, get the hell out of here before our fine hostess changes her mind and decides to make our insides our outsides. What do you say?'

I wasn't ready to go yet, I hadn't got an answer that felt right. 'You look me in the face, Anya, and you promise me you had nothing to do with this.'

Anya walked towards me. I stood my ground, ready to stare her down. 'Hear these words, Familiar. I had nothing to do with the murder of your masters. In all honesty, the idea that something, anything, could enter your coven and do that to the witches of London terrifies me.'

I searched her eyes and saw nothing but the truth. Another dead end.

'Come on, David, let's get out of here.'

'Best news I've heard all day. Though to be honest, that wouldn't be hard, it's been kind of a bad news-heavy sort of a day.'

David opened the door and hopped outside. As I reached the exit, I paused. 'If you hear anything...'

'You would talk to me as though I'm an eaves? I should kill you just for that.'

'I mean it. I need to know.'

'I am not your informer. I make promises to no one but myself and my family. But know this, Familiar... you are in terrible danger. A thing that could do that to the witches... I'm not sure what power could stop it.'

I shivered as I stepped out of Anya's office.

16

We exited The Den, ignoring some snide remarks from the doormen, Jack and Jake, as we passed by them. Part of me wanted to turn around and unleash some frustration on the pair; get into a real knock-down, drag-out fight. Maybe that would have made me feel a little better. Or maybe Anya would have joined in and left me an emotionless smear on the paving stones.

'Well, that was one of the most terrifying places I've ever been,' said David, as I silently brooded at his side. 'But at least we got some good info. If you believe her, anyway.'

I stopped and turned to him, confused. 'Good info? In what way was any of that *good*?'

'We can scratch a suspect off the list. Okay, it's not as good as finding out who did you wrong, but every name we can dismiss narrows things down. That's police work. If things keep on like that, it's only a matter of time before the culprit finds themselves under a spotlight.'

I snorted and carried on walking, but he was right. It didn't make me feel any better, though. I didn't want to go about this on the slow path, I wanted the monster behind this in front of me right now so I could throw my fist in its direction.

'Uh, I think we might have taken a wrong turn,' said David.

'What?' I'd been lost in my thoughts. When I looked up, I saw the streets of Soho no longer stretched before us. In fact, there were no streets of any kind. We were in the middle of a rural landscape, on the side of a steep hill with long grasses being teased in every direction by a swirling wind.

'A really, really wrong turn.'

To the left of us was a set of worn stone steps leading up to the hill's summit.

'I know where we are,' I said, and headed for the steps.

'Great. Care to share?'

'We've been summoned by The First,' I replied.

'Not any clearer, Magic Lady,' said David, as we began to scale the steep set of steps.

'The First Witch. This is her place.'

'Is it Yorkshire? It looks a bit like Yorkshire. Apart from that lake of boiling tar down there.'

'It's not Yorkshire. It's not anywhere you or any other normal will have heard of.'

I'd never been there. There was no reason why The First would want to talk to a familiar. At least, there hadn't been a reason for her to bring me here before. Now there was. The London Coven had fallen.

'So The First Witch, is she a nice, non-scary sort of a woman?'

'I don't know. I've never met her and I've never been here. I only know where I am because of what I am. It's in my genes. My bones. I look around and I just know where and who.'

After more than two hours of scaling the steps, the summit never seeming to come any closer no matter how high we climbed, the ground suddenly evened out to reveal the entrance to a cave.

'Christ,' said David, gasping for breath, 'I hope we don't have to run away screaming any time soon, because my thighs are buggered.'

'It's okay, we're safe here,' I said.

'What now, then? Do we go in for a chat?'

'Yes.'

'Okay.'

David stepped forward, but I pulled him back. 'Just me. She won't want you in there, tainting her dwelling.'

'Tainting? I know my aftershave is a bit on the strong side, but that's just rude.'

I smiled, just slightly, then left David behind.

'Okay. I'll just stay here, then. Pining for you.'

I stepped into the inky mouth of the cave, the sound of the outside world cutting out instantly. I shivered as I edged forward, the dark licking at my skin. A light flickered in the distance, and I moved towards it. A fire was burning, and an old woman sat cross-legged before it, prodding the flames with a metal poker.

'What's the weather out?'

'It's warm,' I replied.

The First nodded and spat into the flames. They shot up as though vodka had been poured on the fire.

'Sit,' she said. I lowered myself to the ground and watched The First as she continued to tend the fire. She looked ancient. She *was* ancient. Her hair long and thin, her face gnarled like old bark, limbs like sticks, but her eyes... her eyes looked young. They seemed to glow with life, with mischief, with knowledge.

'So,' she said at last, 'you let your witches die?'

'I didn't... I wasn't there to—'

'I've no time for excuses, familiar,' she spat on the fire again and a tongue of bright purple flame burst from the logs. I felt my heart quicken as faces seemed to dance within these new purple flames. Three faces: the faces of my dead masters.

'Pity. Good girls, those three,' said The First. 'Always good for a giggle.'

I nodded and felt a tear rolling down my cheek.

'Ach, now, now, enough of that. Unseemly for a familiar to cry, especially when there's revenge still out there, waiting for you.'

'I don't know who did it,' I said.

'No. I've had a poke around, asked the fire to show me, but…' she frowned and shifted. 'It shows me nothing.'

Sighing, The First stood, her joints cracking, and shuffled over to a table that had not been there moments before. On it, stood a large jug and two clay cups. 'Coffee?' she said, lifting the jug.

'No. Thank you.'

'Suit yourself. I like a pick-me-up cup at this time of day, myself.'

She sipped the coffee, smacking her lips in appreciation. 'Yours is not the first coven to fall,' she said.

'This has happened before?'

'Hm? Oh, no, not like this. I'm just telling you it happens. Covens fall. Not anything that can be done about it, sometimes.'

'If I'd been there…'

'You'd be dead too. Think you, a thing of spit and will, could do something that those three witches couldn't?'

'I'm all that's left.'

'You are that.'

'I'm not good enough.'

'Right again.'

'So what should I do?'

The First shuffled back to the fire, standing beside me. I felt her long, bony fingers begin to stroke my hair.

'Do your best, I suppose. There's no replacements coming any time soon. Not the way it works. Oh, they'll come eventually—a new three for London—but not for a few hundred years at least. That's how long it takes for a new witch or three to appear. Not born, not created, one day they just shuffle out of the dark of my cave and join me by the fire. But not yet. Not for a long, long time. So you're it.'

'But I'm just a familiar, created to do their will. Created to wear out, to die, to be replaced. I'm not even supposed to last as long as I have.'

'Oh, you love to bellyache you, don't you? It's not you that's kicked the bucket, remember, so smile a little.'

'Why have you brought me here?'

'To look at you proper. Get the measure of you. To see whose hands London is in now.'

'And what do you see?' I asked, afraid of the answer.

The First wandered back to where she had risen from earlier, and lowered herself back down. She sipped at her coffee and resumed her tending of the fire with the poker.

'I see... potential.'

'Enough?'

The First's warm, glowing eyes darted from the flames, looking into mine for the first time since I'd arrived. 'Perhaps.'

I wanted to ask more questions, to ask what I should do next. Tell her that I was confused and didn't know which move to make. Didn't know if I *had* any moves worth making. That I was lost and angry and afraid. But before I could, The First spat upon the fire again and the flames swelled like a dying star, blinding me.

By the time my eyes had cleared, I was no long sat in her cave.

17

I sat at David's kitchen table as he made himself busy with the kettle.

'Do you take sugar?'

'No,' I said, running my hands through my hair, feeling more tired than I should have. A cup of tea was placed before me and I wrapped my hands around it, warming myself. *Potential*. That's what she'd said. I had potential. But what good was that? Potential wasn't enough, not at this point, not to find and take down a thing capable of doing what this bastard had done. I needed to be an expert, not a novice. Not something that *could* become something useful one day.

'All in all, I'd say it's not going well so far, eh?'

'No.'

David nodded and blew on his tea. 'Still, now I know there are creatures like that Anya woman walking the streets of London, I can live the rest of my life in a state of blind terror. So that's something.'

I smiled. I kind of admired the way David could keep a bright face on things, despite the world-tipping situation he'd found himself in. Before I arrived, he thought he knew what the world was. It was simple. And now there was magic. And hidden streets. And monsters. And here he was, making me a cup of tea and trying to cheer *me* up.

'What now then?' asked David, taking a sip from his mug, then jerking back with a hiss as the too-hot tea burned his lip.

'I don't know,' I replied. And the truth was, I really didn't. I wasn't used to picking up the clues myself. I did what I was told. I carried out instructions. I had no experience of putting a case together, of solving a mystery. I was out of my depth and it made my stomach churn. The knowledge that I was the only one who could find out what had happened to my masters and bring about justice, and yet I didn't have a clue as to how I was going to go about it.

I'd hit a dead end.

I was a failure.

The witches of the London Coven had been murdered and I wasn't up to the job I'd vowed. To take revenge upon whoever had slaughtered them. Rage rushed over me and I screamed, throwing the cup of tea against the wall.

'My mum bought me that mug.'

I glared at him, then broke. 'I'm... sorry.'

'Hey, no biggie,' he replied, smiling softly.

'You know, what you did back at The Den... what you said to Anya... that was very brave of you.'

'*Stupid* might be a better word for it.'

'It's never stupid to be brave,' I replied.

'That's definitely not true, but I'll take it. So what's next?'

I shrank in my chair. 'I don't know.'

'Right, well, okay, let's just have a little think about this. What we're carrying out here is a murder investigation, right?'

I nodded.

'Okay, well it seems to me that we've missed a step.'

'What step?'

'Any good investigation starts at the scene of the crime.'

I felt myself grow cold. I closed my eyes and saw the

common room of the coven again. The blood, the destroyed bodies, the lack of any magic whatsoever.

'Hey, what's wrong? What is it?'

'I don't think... I don't think I can go back there.'

'I understand it's not pleasant, but—'

'No! You don't understand. You don't understand at all!'

'Hey, come on, calm down—'

'That was my family, David. My family. They brought me into this world and I let them down! And now I've got nothing and nobody.'

I kicked the chair away from me and turned from him, ashamed to realise I was crying like a baby.

'You're right. I don't understand. I've never lost anyone I loved. Even my gran is still up and kicking. But you want to do right by them, yes?'

'Yes.'

'Then we have to go back there, no matter how tough it is. No matter how scary. Because if we don't, the bad guys are going to win. And you never let the bad guys win.'

I felt his hand gently touch my arm, and I allowed him to slowly turn me his way. I didn't want him to see me like this. For anyone to see me like this. Tear-streaked and vulnerable. I was strong. I was created to be strong. But in that moment, I felt like I had nothing left. No fight, only empty, bewildered fear.

David smiled and rubbed at my tears with his thumb.

'It's okay, Magic Lady. I may be an idiot, but I know how to carry out an investigation. This is my thing. Trust me.'

I put my hand over his and nodded, breathing long and slow to get a grip on myself again. 'I'm sorry.'

'It's okay. Your family died yesterday, those tears just mean you're not quite the robot I'd started to take you for. Maybe there's even a real person with annoying emotions in there, too. Something besides rage would be nice.'

We stood for a second, just smiling at each other, then I pulled away and dried my face. It was time to get serious.

'It might be dangerous,' I told him. 'In fact, it almost certainly will be. Last time I was at the coven, there was a monster there waiting for me.'

'That's okay. I believe in you, Stella Familiar. You won't let anything bad happen to me, or to you. And together, we're going to find out who or what murdered your family. And then we're going to bring them to justice.'

I nodded, and for the first time I felt glad—really glad—that he was with me. He wasn't a burden, an annoyance standing in my way. He was my friend. Together, we were going to solve this thing.

18

The blind alley opened up in front of us. At its far end, sat the London Coven.

My birthplace.

My home.

'I take it you're not just staring at a brick wall, right?' said David.

'See it,' I said, pushing the spell towards David.

'I'm not ever getting used to that. One moment, it's a wall, then I blink, and suddenly there's a whole other place I can walk into.'

I stepped into the blind alley with David on my heels. I realised with relief that the alley had already begun to refill with background magic. A least I didn't have to deal with the withdrawal symptoms that had left me so weakened last time.

'This alley,' said David. 'The cobbled road, the stone walls, this is older than the last one. How long has your coven been standing here?'

'A long time.'

'Not quite as specific as I was angling for there, Stella.'

'This was my masters' home and seat of power for over three-hundred years. But the London Coven itself has stood for longer, they just took it over from the people who looked after London before them. My witches should have continued here, continued to serve the city, for several hundred more years. Now they're gone, and this place doesn't have a successor to take their place.'

'What about you? You're still here.'

'I'm no witch. A witch has more power in a single thought than I have in my whole being.'

'What does that mean for London?'

'Nothing good, David.'

'You know, you really have a way with an unnerving answer, Stella. It's a gift, I mean that.'

I trailed one hand along the brick of the alley wall as we walked, feeling the history, the residual power that throbbed from stones that had stood for so long. I tried to draw in that power to bolster myself, to make me stronger than I felt. I needed it. Because as the coven grew closer with each step, my lungs would barely pull a breath. A childish fear had overcome me, as though I were cowering under a blanket from the bogeyman. Something terrible—something that I had never come across in my decades of service—had walked into my home and done the unimaginable, and I was scared to face it, no matter how much I knew I had to.

I felt a nauseating sense of unease, a sense that I was way out of my depth, that I hadn't been able to stop it, that I still hadn't been able to do anything about it. A terror at the fact I was about to see those dead, ripped-apart bodies again. The bodies of my family that I had abandoned and left to rot. Would they have started to smell? Would their putrefying odour infiltrate my nose, my very being? Would I taste it on my tongue? I feared I would carry that smell with me for the rest of my life. A phantom stench that would cling to me forever more. A constant reminder of the horrors that had fallen upon our house.

'Are you okay?'

I turned to David, realising I'd stopped walking.

'It's all right,' he said. 'You can do this.'

I nodded, but I couldn't reply. I worried if I tried to that only a childish whimper would come out. I felt David's hands on my arms.

'Hey, hey, listen to me, Stella. Don't let them do this to you. Don't let the bastards who tore your world apart win. You owe it to your witches, and you owe it to yourself.'

'I let them down, David. I let them—'

'Stop. A bomb's gone off in your life, but you're alive, and as long as you're alive, you've got to stay strong and stay determined. You don't get to break down until whoever did this to you is brought to justice, okay?'

I somehow managed to sketch out a smile as I straightened up and shook off the worst of it. 'Okay.'

'There we go. Let's get in there and do our job. Show them they messed with the wrong familiar.'

'Yes, let's do it,' I replied, trying to force all the authority I could into my voice. Somehow I managed to make my feet move again, and the two of us walked towards the coven, boots crunching over the broken glass that littered the cobbles from my desperate escape.

'David?'

'Yes, Stella?'

'Thank you.'

'That's okay. Feel free to return the favour when you get a moment, because I am seriously shitting it right now.'

19

The bodies were gone.

All of the ripped up pieces of my witches had been taken, leaving only dark, dried blood rusting the floor. Part of me was outraged that they had been removed, that they weren't here waiting for me to give them a decent burial. A larger part of me was glad I didn't have to relive the carnage that had become of them. Did that make me a coward?

'What's that smell?' asked David.

I breathed it in and the corners of my mouth twitched up momentarily. 'Cinnamon, freshly cut grass, and lavender. The smell of home.' Not just of home, of life. For me, it was my first real memory. Before I had even opened my eyes for the first time after being created, I'd inhaled once deeply, through my nose, and the smell of this place had become part of me. Now it just reminded me of what I'd lost.

'So whoever was behind this must have come back for the bodies?' said David, walking the room gingerly, studying every square inch for anything even remotely resembling a clue.

'There was a creature here waiting for me when I got back. A clean-up service in the form of a giant, devil dog that was left to mop me up when I walked in. It's what I jumped away from when I found myself in your kitchen.'

'Well, that's something.'

'What is?'

'Whoever is behind this can be sloppy. Or too sure of themselves. Probably both. That means they have weaknesses, and weaknesses can be exploited. Sooner or later, we'll find something that leads us to their door.'

I found a little fresh hope sprouting inside of me. Was David right? Because it was true, leaving a mindless beast behind to finish me off rather than seeing to the job personally, rather than making sure, had been an error. They had left a survivor behind at the Church of the Sorcerer Tree, too; at least for a while. Yes, whoever had done this was strong beyond measure, but far from infallible. They had a weak spot. Everyone and everything had a weak spot, an achilles heel. It was just a case of finding it.

David scratched at his chin. 'You said when you came back that the place was drained of magic, right?'

'Completely. That shouldn't be possible. Especially not here. Every street, every building, every blade of grass emits some trace of background magic, but somehow whoever did this sucked the whole place dry.'

'Tell me more about the coven's security measures.'

'I told you, the witches had layer upon layer upon layer of protective spells. No one but those three and myself were able to walk in or out unscathed. And only us four would be able to remove or even temporarily nullify them.'

'Could those be "sucked dry"? David asked. 'The magic of the protection spells, just like what happened to the background magic of the place?'

'No, that's different. The spells, they were fixed. Removing them would be like trying to suck a bowling ball through a drinking straw. The only way to get rid of them fully is if you know what they are, the name they've been given, and how to mute them. That's the only way it would be possible for them to be stripped away.'

David stood up from where he'd been crouched studying the blood splatter patterns across the hardwood floor. 'You know what that means, then?'

'What?'

'It means someone must have shared the names of those spells.'

I bristled and marched towards him, my head hot. 'I'd be very careful what you say next, normal.'

'Hey, hey, chill your boots, Stella, I'm just following the evidence so I can piece together the most likely scenario. If what you say is true, then whoever stripped away the magical security of this place must have figured out a way to bypass it. Which means either someone told them—an inside job—or they, I don't know, overheard one of you.'

I snarled and turned away, stomping to the other side of the room before I gave in to the impulse to grab David by the neck and squeeze. *An inside job*. There were only four people who could have told them, and three of them were dead. That just left me.

'I didn't say anything to anyone.'

'Hey, did I say that, Miss Hair-Trigger? Look, here's what we know: they found out somehow. If you can think why or how that might be, then we have a thread to pull at. This is police work, Stella. This is how you get things done. You don't ignore the facts because they make you uncomfortable. You look, you gather, you make connections, and you follow those connections all the way down the line until you find out who did it. And then you win.'

I sighed and turned back to him, anger fading. 'So what now?'

'Now you die.'

That voice... no, *voices*. Each of the words like they were spoken by a different person.

'Um, please tell me that throwing your voice is another of your many talents?'

'Where have you taken their bodies?' I demanded, turning in a circle, searching for some sign of the monster.

'Oh, I fed all of the meat and bones to my dogs. My "devil dogs", as you call them. They chewed them up, yum-yum.'

I unleashed a blast of energy in anger, not even realising that I was doing it. David ducked and scrambled to the side as the room shook.

'Face me! If you're so powerful then stop these stupid games and show yourself! Look me in the eyes and see if you can take my life!'

'Not the best idea to encourage a psychotic murderer, Stella.'

'Listen to the normal, Stella Familiar. Maybe you'll live a little longer.'

A movement in the corner of my eye—

I turned in time to see a shadow step from the open doorway—

'Over there!' I ran for the door, my only thought to catch, to confront, to kill.

'Stella, wait!' David screamed, though the words sounded dull beneath the sound of my heart boom-booming in my head.

I searched for the right words, strung them together, and felt a tide of power wash through my arms and into my hands, ready to be unleashed. *Begging* to be.

'I'm coming for you!' I burst out of the coven, ready to go down fighting.

20

I raced into the blind alley, my fists boiling with an energy so intense that it made the air around them ripple. A single word from me and the energy would surge from my hands and blast into the man of many voices who thought he could mock me. Mock my masters. Kill my masters.

'Where are you?'

I heard a million different laughs in a million different voices, jabbing me from every angle. I couldn't think straight, the desire to tear this piece of shit to pieces was too strong, and I began to unleash volley after volley of magic into the alley. Bricks exploded, rubbish caught fire, but all the time that laugh kept going. That biting, sharp laugh, as the stranger watched me throw a useless temper tantrum.

'If you've quite finished, Stella...'

'Come and get me, you bastard, you coward.'

'But we're having so much fun. Why spoil things now?'

'Stella—' David was at my shoulder, breathing quickly, terrified. 'Stella, I think we should get away, now.'

'No! The creature that tore up the witches is here, and I'm going to finish it. I owe it to them.'

'Here? Who's here? It's just a trick. It's probably got, I don't know, speakers set up or something, because look around, there is no one here. No man, no monsters, just us. Just me and you.'

I felt the air swell around me. I recognised the sensation. Something was forcing its way into being. Forcing its way into existence. Something was being conjured.

'Did you feel that?' asked David, stretching his jaw as though his ears were about to pop.

Before I had a chance to reply, a concussive blast of air hit us, throwing us through the air like a piece of newspaper caught in the gust of an oncoming train. The two of us struck the alley wall and crumbled to the cobbles.

'What the...?'

'David, don't move—'

I heard them before I saw them. For a second they were shrouded by the grey smoke that accompanied the blast, but I heard their growls. Light began to pierce the smoke. Twin balls of fire. One set, then two, then three.

'What is that?' asked David.

I knew what it was. As the first paw of the three devil dogs stepped out of the smoke, I stood and flexed my shoulders. The last time I had only faced one of them and it had almost been the death of me. I had been weak, staggering through a world empty of magic, terrified as the impossible reality of my masters' murders gripped my heart in its icy fingers. This time was different. This time I was swollen with power, with magic, with fury. This time I was going to rip them to shreds.

Moving as one, the three devil dogs lifted their heads and roared to the heavens, ready to do what their master had created them for: to kill.

I drew the magic towards me, feeling it eagerly fill me as David tried to pull me back—

'Stella, come on, let's get back inside, we can barricade the door!'

'No. I'm not running.'

'Stella, come on, this is crazy, look at the size of those things!'

I didn't have time to argue. A flick of my head and David—his eyes wide with surprise—was lifted from his feet and thrown through the air and back into the coven. I heard him land with a thump and a grumble as I shut the door on him and willed it to remain so.

'Well,' I asked the air, asked the hidden puppet master, asked the devil dogs, 'are you going to do something, or should I just get on with it and start killing?'

The first dog bolted towards me, claws tearing up the cobbles, jaws trailing long, toxic ropes of slaver. I let fly a scream and a surge of magic erupted from me in a great, gushing stream, ripping into the beast's hide. It screamed like a puppy as the magic tore up its left flank, causing it to careen to the side and into a wall, so hard I could hear the crunch of its bones.

I laughed. 'Did you think this would be easy?' I'm Stella Familiar of the London Coven, you dumb mutt.'

I roared a war cry as I threw out my right arm and a torrent of fire welled forth from my palm and turned the broken devil dog to ash. I didn't wait for the next attack; I turned on my heels, both fists cocked and ready, and sprinted toward the two remaining dogs. They came at me as one, but froze mid-step as I swung out my left hand and sent a lashing orbit of white light spinning their way. I heard a yelp of confusion from one of the dogs, followed by a blink of its eyes before it fell apart in two halves, cleaved down the middle, its organs landing with a wet slap on the cobbles.

'Very impressive, Familiar,' came the many voices.

I ignored them, turning my attention instead to the final, still-frozen dog. As I stopped before it and stared into the twin fires of its eyes, the simple thing suddenly understood what was about to happen. What it was about to lose. I could taste its fear. And it tasted *good*.

I thrust my burning hands into the monster's chest, blasting through bone and tissue to tear out its giant pulsating heart. The dog huffed once then toppled to the ground, and I threw away its heart like the rubbish it was.

'That's it. They're done. If that's all you've got for me, then you're in big fucking trouble.' I felt the devil dog's blood on my hands, warm and sticky, and almost felt like licking my fingers with satisfaction. 'Well? Why won't you speak now? Are you done? Did you run away?'

The devil dog with the missing heart twitched on the ground before me. I stepped back into a boxer's stance, hands up, power pulsing from my fists.

An arm thrust out of the corpse. And another. Something was pulling itself out of the dead dog and into the blind alley. Something with long black hair, coated in gore. Then the same happened with the devil dog I'd split in two. Viscera-painted women crawled towards me, leaving bloody slug trails behind them. I should have dispatched them immediately. Should have already unleashed the power swelling in my hands, but I was frozen to the spot. I recognised the women. They were my masters.

'Your fault.'

'Your fault, Familiar.'

I staggered back as their dead, empty eyes bored into me with raw hatred, all the power I'd built drained from me.

'Please, I didn't know, I couldn't help, I didn't...'

My witches screamed in unison as they crawled jaggedly towards me, their mouths opening wider and wider still until it seemed their entire heads were one huge black hole, ready to swallow me down into the darkness.

I backed into the alley wall and the damp cold of its brickwork soaked into my back and snapped me out of my panic. This was just a trick. A deception. That's all it was. All it could be.

They were almost upon me as I pulled in the magic around

me and—with tears in my eyes—screamed and unleashed all the power I could on the witches. My masters. The blood-coated lies created to break my spirit.

And then the screaming stopped.

The only sound now was the wind and my own heartbeat throbbing in my ears. Nothing was left of the witches—the lies—not even ashes. I drew what magic I could back inside of me as I stepped forward, my knees ready to give way, but I knew that I was alone. Whoever it was that was behind all this had already gone. It had done what it set out to do. It had poked and prodded at me, made me shake and scream with fear, tested my limits, my strength of will. It was playing games, and it was enjoying itself far too much to take me off the board just yet.

'David—' I waved my hand across the coven door, allowing it to be opened again. 'David, come out, it's safe.'

Silence.

'David, come on.'

The door didn't open.

My eyes widened.

No...

I was running before I really even understood why. I threw open the coven door, hoping, dreading, knowing. David wasn't waiting for me. The only thing greeting me was a pool of fresh blood on the floor.

David's blood.

21

The door to The Beehive swung inward, smashing back against the wall under the force of my boot.

'Where is he?'

I stepped inside, feeling the pub's magic-dampening bubble part around me as I entered. It meant I couldn't make anyone's head explode with a few well-chosen words, but that was okay. I wasn't looking for anything that fast. My fists were all I needed.

I'd reached out for David, trying to sense him, trying to find out where the many-mouthed creature had taken him. I'd been with David long enough that I should have been able to recognise his, for want of a better word, "scent": the impression he left in the magic that surrounds everything. He'd been stolen away from me mere seconds before I'd found the pool of his blood, so I should have been able to sniff him out without much difficulty.

And yet, there was nothing. No sign of him. Not a trace.

I'd searched the coven from top to bottom, chased along the blind alley, run wildly around the streets of Hammersmith. I must have looked like a total head case as I sprinted around, goggle-eyed, taking random turn after random turn, hoping to see or sense something. Anything.

But he was gone.

And that's when I realised I'd been played. Whatever was behind all of this, whatever was hiding behind those hundreds of voices, it wasn't trying to kill me. It was distracting me. Prodding at me, throwing obstacles with giant teeth in my path until my anger took over and I pushed David out of the way. Then, with my back turned and fists throwing fury, it had been free to take him. First it murdered my masters, the only people I was close to. Now, the first person that came into my orbit, the first person I had taken under my wing and allowed to get close to me, had been snatched away, leaving nothing but a scarlet reminder on the floor.

But no body.

No corpse.

No shredded pieces of flesh this time, waiting to greet me as I entered my coven.

And that was the only thing that gave me hope. Gave me the sense that maybe, just maybe, David was still alive. That this thing wasn't done playing just yet. That it was going to keep David alive because it wanted me to come and find him. To try and fight and take him back. At least, that's what I had to tell myself, because what else did I have?

I'd dropped into David's life and turned it upside-down. Exposed him to the kind of darkness and danger that no normal should ever have to know about. It was my fault he was who-knows-where with who-knows-what, his life hanging by a thread. So this wasn't just about revenge anymore. I had to find this thing and I had to beat it, otherwise David's death would be on my hands. Annoying, brave, strong, funny David. I couldn't let that happen.

I wouldn't let it happen.

'Razor! Get out here, now!'

I stalked towards him, causing the other patrons of The

Beehive to part before me. They moved back, relief washing over their faces as they heard me call out for someone beside themselves.

'Stella—'

I shot Lenny a look, a look that told him all he needed to know. He nodded and turned away.

'Razor!'

The door to the bathroom squeaked and Razor stepped into the bar. At first, he didn't notice me. Instead, he looked at the nearest few tables of drinkers, saw the way they were hunkered down, shoulders hunched, ignoring everything.

'What's going on?'

He turned and saw me, saw the smile on my face that didn't reach my eyes.

'You've been a bad boy, Razor.'

'Shit—'

The only exit was behind me, so Razor spun on his heels, almost falling over in his hurry, and bolted back through the door towards the bathrooms. I gave chase, shoving the door open so it cracked against the wall as I ran through. I stepped into the men's room, the sharp stench of piss burning my nostrils as I padded towards the closed cubicles.

'Get out here, Razor.'

'What d'you want with me? I didn't do anything.'

I stopped in front of the closed cubicle door Razor was trying to shield himself behind. He may as well have been hiding under a sheet of wet paper for all the good it would do him.

'You lied to me, Razor. You know that's not a good idea.'

'Lied to you? I didn't lie to you. I mean, I have done, of course I have, I've lied to you lots of times, but not recently.'

I grunted as the sole of my boot connected with the cubicle door and turned its lock into shrapnel. I found Razor squatting inside, quivering, his feet on the toilet seat.

'I came to you looking for information, Razor. Information

about what happened to the witches of the London Coven. Information about the piece of shit that murdered them. And you spat up a lie.'

'What?'

'You sent me on a wild goose chase. And now my friend has been taken.'

'What are you talking about? You're crazy. Someone help me! Lenny! Anyone!'

I grabbed Razor by the throat and squeezed until his eyes bulged out on their stalks. He beat at my face with his fists but I barely felt the blows.

'You're going to give me something I can use, or you're going to die in here, Razor. Die in a toilet. Do you hear me?'

With a roar, I twisted and threw him across the bathroom. He crashed into the mirror and fell hard into the sinks. I smiled as he groaned, rolling and falling to the dirty, tiled floor. I was strong. I was born strong. Right now, with the anger and adrenaline coursing through me, I was unstoppable.

'Please… please, I don't know what you're talking abo—'

I landed a boot in his side and heard a rib crack. It made me smile.

'Wait, please, just wait—'

Razor winced and slid back until he was pressed against the wall, one hand to his busted side.

'Give me a name, Razor. Give me something I can use.'

'I swear, I didn't send you wrong.'

I grimaced. Even now he was trying to feed me lies. He saw what was about to happen and lifted his hands to try and placate me—

'Stella, wait. Just… just wait a second. Look, okay, I heard about the witches, and this might surprise you, but I'm not happy about what happened. I'm not. This city without the witches? Chaos is coming! They held all of this together. Stopped the whole of London from falling to bits.'

'I'm not hearing any names, Razor…'

'I didn't lie to you, or whatever you think I did—'

My fist met his jaw and blood spat from between his busted lips.

'Stella, I haven't spoken to you in weeks!'

What was this? A game? Did he think he was being funny? Did he think I was stupid?

'I came in here and I beat a name out of you Razor.'

'What are you talking about? No, you didn't!'

Enough. I grabbed him by the collar and threw him back against the mirror again so that his head left a fresh crack and a spray of red. He screamed as he fell, tried to make for the door. Bad idea. I took hold of him and threw him back until the side of the first toilet cubicle halted his momentum, crumpling like cardboard under the force. I couldn't kill him with magic inside The Beehive, but I could toss him around like a rag doll until he stopped moving.

I stalked towards him as he coughed up a fresh glob of blood.

'Stella... Stella, I'm telling you the truth. It was playing a game with you. That's all.'

I stopped. *A game*. That rang true.

'Go on.'

'I swear, Stella. I swear on everything my clan holds dear, I did not feed you any false intel. I haven't seen you since this whole thing started. It played you. The thing played you. It pretended to be me and sent you running after nothing.'

I crouched by the destroyed cubicle and gripped Razor by the balls. He screamed long and high as I twisted.

'Give me a name!'

'I don't know any—'

A twist, more savage this time.

'You always know something, Razor. Always! You swim in the filth all day; you taste a piece of every dark thing that goes on in this city.'

'Please, I can't, I can't—'

'I'll tear these things off and choke you with them, Razor.'

He screamed again, his animal howls bouncing off hard tile.

'Please-please, it'll kill me if it knows I said anything—'

'And I'll kill you if you don't. Give me a name.'

Razor's chest was rising and falling spasmodically, his eyes pinned open as though they were about to pop out. He was terrified. Beyond terrified. Of me, I could see that, but not just of me. He knew who had killed my witches, knew who had David, and it terrified him.

'Please-! Please don't make me—!'

I grabbed a shard of the broken cubicle wall and jabbed it into the meat of his thigh.

He screamed.

I laughed.

I twisted the shard in his thigh—

'Mr. Trick! Its name is Mr. Trick!'

22

True names hold power.

In the right hands, a true name can be a useful thing. But was Mr. Trick a true name, or just another part of the game? Another sleight of hand. A tripwire to send me sprawling to the ground, to be laughed at once again as I dragged myself up out of the dirt. To be stomped on and made an idiot of, yet again.

I left Razor bloody but alive in a puddle of his own—and various other peoples'—urine. I had work to do; a friend to find and a monster to strike down. But first I needed to find it, and to do that meant crossing a line. I'm only a familiar, and I don't have the knowledge or capability to do the kind of magic that I needed. Black Magic. Bad magic. The kind of spell I needed was forbidden. It latched on to an Uncanny's essence to pinpoint them, to show the user where they were. I might be too lowly to grapple with such spells, but I knew of a man ancient and powerful enough to do whatever he liked.

I pushed open the door to L'Merrier's Antiques, which sat snugly down a side street off Portobello Road. A stale fug wafted over me as I crossed the threshold, and motes of dust danced in the ensuing breeze, illuminated by the few shafts of light that managed to penetrate the shop's dim interior. Every inch of the place was covered in curiosities, large and small. Some were what you might expect from an antiques shop: old lamps, bits of furniture, ceramic ornaments, the usual. But the usual stood side by side with the unusual. Artefacts of bygone eras, antiquities spawned from the country's mysterious underbelly, the Uncanny Kingdom.

I could see, half-hidden in one corner, the partial skeleton of an angel wing, its feathers long since decayed. Sat on a shelf between an original first copy of the *Complete Works of Shakespeare* and a football signed by the 1966 England World Cup team, jutted an actual unicorn horn. All of these wonders and more lived in this place.

'L'Merrier...'

'I have lowered my protections and allowed you to enter my establishment, little one. Be thankful for that.' Giles L'Merrier's voice rolled from the shadows like silk as he moved into view. He wore a floor-length gown over his bulky frame, covered in ancient symbols. Despite his girth, he moved gracefully, seeming to glide rather than walk.

Despite what he'd told me, I hadn't felt the presence of any warding spells when I entered.

'I didn't notice any protections,' I said.

He smiled and interlocked his fingers, resting his hands on the bulge of his large stomach. He stopped in a shaft of light that bounced from his bald head, almost dazzling me. 'A lowly familiar such as you? Of course you did not feel it, creature. I create spells of protection on a much higher plane than a familiar could ever hope to exist in. You are a bug. An ant scurrying underfoot, unaware that at any moment I could bring that self same foot down to crush you.'

'I get it, you're super powerful. Can we move on?'

His smile twitched into a frown, but just for a moment. 'Do not test me, little one. I have not taken the life of an Uncanny in many years, but I will not hesitate to do so if you disrespect me again.'

He was trying to scare me, and I don't mind saying it was working. He may not have killed in years, but everyone in London and far beyond knew of his history. Of the stories. The true stories of Giles L'Merrier: the man who once strode the globe as though it belonged to him. Who had gone to war with the most fearsome black magicians of the age, and had never walked away the loser.

'I came here to ask for you help,' I said.

A smile quirked his lips. 'No doubt you have come to buy a trinket for your coven. A set of silverware, perhaps, or maybe a nice Toby jug? I can do you a very good deal.'

He knew full well that wasn't why I was there. The smugness he radiated made me ball my fists, made me want to give him a hard smack to the jaw. That wouldn't have been my wisest move.

'My masters are dead.'

'Ah, yes. 'Tis a shame, it's true. They served London well for many centuries.'

'The Church of the Sorcerer Tree is gone, too.'

'Pah. Pious ninnies worshiping bark. I am sure we shall all miss them greatly.'

'Someone is attacking great seats of the Uncanny in London, L'Merrier.'

'Perhaps. Though if that were true, would they not have come directly here? Where else radiates power as strongly as my little shop?'

L'Merrier was renowned for his enormous self-regard, but he wasn't exaggerating when it came to the power he possessed.

'I need you to do something for me.'

'Oh, I do not do requests. I'm sorry to say I am not coin-operated.' He turned from me and began to glide back into the shadows. 'You know the way out.'

'You owe my coven a debt!'

He paused, his giant head turning to look back at me. 'Is that so?'

'My witches helped you a decade back and they never called in the debt.'

'And now you are?'

I swallowed and nodded, my heart fluttering.

L'Merrier laughed. 'The London Coven is dead, with no witches in place to take the reins. The debt is gone.'

'No. The London Coven lives on in me.'

L'Merrier turned fully towards me now as he arched an eyebrow. 'You?'

I nodded and tried to make myself look big. And less terrified.

'Oh, little one, that is adorable. But I think not.'

'I will carry on my masters' work. It is my duty. What I was made for.'

'You are a trifle. A marionette moulded from dirt, spittle, and force of will to do the bidding of others. Of great women. You are the monkey, not the organ grinder. My apologies to monkeys everywhere for that dreadful slur on their kind. Now, if you do not wish to make a purchase, you will leave.'

'No, I came here to—' I blinked and found myself outside, looking at the door to L'Merrier's Antiques. Grunting, I pulled some magic towards me and punched forward, allowing the power to unleash and throw the door open, smashing the handle into the wall and leaving a divot in the plaster. I marched back into the shop. L'Merrier was waiting, his face slightly redder than moments before.

'You dare, familiar?'

'The debt stands and will only be paid when you do the thing I want you to do.'

L'Merrier sighed and swatted one hand back lazily. I braced myself as the spell caught me and lifted me from my feet, pinning me to the ceiling, my head cracking back and throwing spots in my vision.

'L'Merrier, please—'

'Begging now? My, my. You come into my shop and make demands. Tut-tut, little one. I should dispatch you at once you for showing such arrogance. Pluck your limbs from their sockets one by one. What say you? Shall we begin with an arm? Left or right, hmm?'

'L'Merrier, the witches of the London Coven are dead! Murdered in their own seat of power, and it is my duty to get revenge. Do you want their deaths to go unpunished?'

He wavered, considering my words. 'They were good women, 'tis true. For witches, that is.'

'My masters did a lot for you, even in the short space of time I was their familiar. Do you not want their killer found? If they could take down the London Coven, who's next? Who's safe? Maybe they'll pay this shop a visit.'

He twitched his hand and I fell to the floor, my head jarring as the wooden floorboards caught me. I groaned and rolled on to my back. L'Merrier glided into view, leaning over me.

'What is the animal's name?'

'His name... his name is Mr. Trick.'

23

We were standing in the basement of L'Merrier's Antiques, or at least that's where I thought we were. In truth, he hadn't allowed me to walk there, he'd simply clapped his hands and there we were. For all I knew, his inner sanctum was located inside a mountaintop in Tibet, or underneath a betting shop in Ealing.

The sanctum was dressed simply. A desk and chair was set against one wall and a rug sat in the room's centre, upon which L'Merrier stood. I could see neither a window or a door. No evidence of a way in or out.

'Stay within the circle,' said L'Merrier. I looked down at the brass ring inlaid into the stone floor in one corner of the room. 'It is unbroken and infused with magic. As long as you do not step out of it, you will be safe.'

'What about you?' I asked.

'This is my sanctum; the sanctum of the mighty Giles L'Merrier. The things of the dark would not dare to touch me within this place.' He puffed out his already considerable chest. 'Familiar, understand this: using a name to locate a member of the Uncanny Kingdom is of the black arts. I am friends with the Nether, but you... you may be upset by some of the things you are about to see.'

'I can take it,' I replied, trying to ignore the prickle of cold sweat on my neck.

'Very well, then we shall begin.' He clapped his hands and it sounded like thunder, shaking the room.

'Ruma-Chk-Ella-Ruma-Chk-Ella—' His voice rolled out, deep and powerful.

The temperature in the room immediately dropped twenty degrees, and I shivered as my breath fogged in front of me.

'Hear me. Know me. Know what I want. What I can do with a single thought. Know what I demand.' On and on he went, around and around, repeating the mantra.

Something skittered across the floor, just out of view. I almost stepped back in surprise, in fear, at which point my foot would have broken the circle of protection. My magical senses began to recoil at the unnaturalness flooding into L'Merrier's sanctum. My first instinct was to pull in the magic surrounding me, ready to defend myself, to attack, but the room was no longer bathed in ordinary magic. It was flooded with black magic. Corrupt magic. If I soaked that up, there was no telling what it might do to me.

'Chk-Ella! Chk-Ella! I, Giles L'Merrier, the wonder of mankind, have a name for you. A true name!'

There was a shape in the room. It looked almost like a person, but wrong. Stretched out. Bent. Its flesh was crisp and blackened. It didn't have a face, just a giant mouth, full of teeth. A snake's tongue slithered out to lick at the air. Two horns curled and wound from its forehead.

'I am here,' it said, its voice a harsh whisper that turned my stomach into a fist.

'I seek the whereabouts of a stranger,' said L'Merrier. 'I will give you a name, foul beast, and you will reveal him to me.'

The creature wasn't listening. It was looking at me. 'I know you, little thing. Yes I do.'

It stepped towards me, its movements twitchy, unnerving, as though I were watching a film with frames clipped out.

'Beast, I command you!' cried the wizard, but the demon wasn't listening.

The whole of my back was slick with sweat, now. I wanted to run, but the moment I did, I would be outside the protective magic of the brass ring, and the thing would chew my bones to dust.

'You don't know me,' I managed to say, my voice a childish stutter.

'Do not speak with the thing, familiar,' roared L'Merrier, setting his jowls wobbling.

'Oh, yes I do know you,' whispered the creature, speaking to me. 'I have. Have yet to. Will. We all will. The dark knows you.'

A sonic boom as L'Merrier clapped his mighty hands together once more. The demon winced and turned from me, its attention recaptured.

'Yes, look to me, thing.'

'The magic man seeks our council once again,' snarled the creature, its mouth oozing black ichor.

'I have a true name in my possession, and I demand you show me the man I seek.'

'Why should we bend to you?'

'Do not play games or speak falsely with me, foul creature. You know me. You know this sanctum, the shapes I have drawn, the words I have spoken. The magic that flows through this place is without question. In here, with me, you are bound to tell me answers.'

The creature raised one ragged nail and drew it down its cheek. Thick, black blood oozed from the wound and the beast giggled. 'Go ahead, ask and ask and ask.'

'The name of the person we wish to find is Mr. Trick,' I said.

'Ah, yes. The one who did slay the witches of London.'

L'Merrier's turned to me, eyes blazing, then back to the

demon. 'Ignore this insect. I am the one who asks, the one who is in control. The one who—with a few well-placed words—could turn you to ash.'

'You would threaten a thing of the dark?' asked the creature, tipping back his horned head and regarding the wizard with hooded eyes.

'And more besides,' L'Merrier replied, coolly. 'You know me. Know what I have done. Do not think that your destruction is beyond my power.'

The creature giggled again, and my knees shook.

'Very well,' said the demon, 'look...'

The beast's hand shot towards L'Merrier, gripping his broad forehead in its filthy hand. The wizard threw open his arms and screamed as the ground threw up a sheet of flames around him.

'L'Merrier!' I screamed, shielding my face from the heat, from the blinding burst of light. Had the thing killed him?

And then the blanket was lifted. The dark magic was gone. The flames were dead. On the floor, sat L'Merrier, head in his hands. He was trembling. That might have been the image that scared me most of all about this whole thing. The mighty Giles L'Merrier, quivering like a child.

'Is it over?' I asked.

He looked up to me, his eyes wide. 'I know where the thing you seek resides. But... it is like nothing I have ever...'

He stopped, stood, and strode across the room, grabbing a pen and paper and scribbling down an address. 'Here.'

I took the piece of paper and read it. I knew where it was. Knew where the monster that had murdered my family was hiding. Knew where David, my friend, was being kept.

'Now get out!' demanded L'Merrier.

'What if we take on Mr. Trick together? I am only a familiar, as you're always keen to remind me. Maybe together we could—'

He rounded on me, eyes full of fire. 'The debt is paid, familiar. More than paid. Do not come to me asking favours again.'

'Wai—'

But before I could even spit out the word, I felt an outdoor chill cool my skin. I was stood outside of L'Merrier's Antiques again, only now the sign on the shop door read CLOSED. I looked at the address on the piece of paper, then stuffed it into the pocket of my leather jacket.

I knew where the thing was.

The thing that had succeeded in frightening even Giles L'Merrier.

And I was going to kill it.

24

I felt my stomach turn over as I lowered myself through the manhole and into the sewer. It's amazing how often my line of work dragged me sloshing through these subterranean, waste-clogged tunnels. The dark Uncanny hid in these disgusting places knowing that the upstairs world wanted nothing to do with them, but that had never stopped me paying them a visit.

I let go of the ladder and my boots splashed down in something horrendous. I grimaced and wafted a hand in front of my nose.

'Fresh.'

In an instant, the smell of piss and shit was masked by the fragrant aroma of a summer meadow. I knew it wasn't the wisest move to close off one of my senses while I was hunting, but I was so full of fear and anger that I was worried—if I didn't —the stench would overpower me and have me chucking my guts up.

I slid my hand into my jacket pocket and felt the crumpled piece of paper that bore Mr. Trick's address. Who knew how long the thing would remain at that location? I wanted to go straight there and confront whatever it was, but knowing what it had been able to do, and having seen the look in L'Merrier's eyes, I knew it would be a mistake to go rushing in head-first. I was a weak Uncanny compared to many, so to even stand a chance, I needed to be as powerful as I could possibly be. To be topped up with enough magical juice that it was practically leaking out of my ears. And that meant paying a visit to the fairies.

I looked back and forth down the sewer tunnel, stretching out my senses as far as they would go. I made a choice, turned to my right, and set off.

One way or another, I knew this thing was almost over. Mr. Trick would be where the piece of paper said he was. I felt it, deep in my gut. And the way things had been going, I was sure he already knew I was on my way. That he would have felt L'Merrier stretching out into the dark to locate him. He wanted me to find him. Wanted a final confrontation. I felt like I understood the thing, its motives. It wanted to play with me, like a cat with a wounded mouse. But not forever. Letting me know its whereabouts meant it was tired of playing. Now it wanted to take me off the board and start a new game elsewhere.

A flicker in the distance, a stuttering pinprick of white light in the stinking dark. *Here we go.* I chased after it, filthy liquid exploding from my footfalls as I ran, soaking into the bottoms of my jeans.

What was I doing underneath London, chasing a fairy through a shit-smeared tunnel? I was there because real fairies aren't the whimsical creatures they're depicted as in kiddie books. Think of them more like flies, feasting on waste, passing on infections. Dumb animals that live only to breed, and the way they do that? By laying their eggs in a host. Generally, a human host. They're not above sneaking into your house after dark and filling you full of eggs while you sleep, but for ease of access, they mostly prefer a passed-out, homeless person. Here's how they operate: they extend what looks like a stinger from their rear ends and sink it deep into the unconscious person's stomach, injecting hundreds, sometimes thousands, of eggs. The infected person will wake up the next morning with a stomach-ache, but they won't suspect anything. Why would they? Fairies aren't real.

In a few short days, the host will find their stomach horribly distended, but they won't look for help. Instead, the infection tricks the victim's brain into seeking out a place to hide. That's when they find their way to the sewer. Down there, out of sight, they will writhe in agony for up to a week, until, finally, their stomach splits and tears apart, ending their misery. Then, from out of the host's cored husk, pours a cloud of new fairies, ready to repeat the process all over again.

We Uncanny people do our best to cull their numbers to stop the human population from plummeting, but the fairies do have their uses. The creatures are chock-full of magic. Magic that can be extracted and devoured. Many use it as a sort of drug. There are dens all over London in which Uncanny people lounge about on beds, drinking down the magic from a freshly-dead fairy, getting drunk on the hit of magic coursing through their system.

So that's why I was here. Stalking through a fairy-infested sewer. I needed to power up for a fight.

The fairy I was following was so fast I was beginning to lose sight of it. As I ran, I reached out a hand—

'Here—'

I placed the magical words together in my mind and felt energy fly from my palm, catching the fairy like the sticky tongue of a lizard, and drawing the thing into my grip.

'Got you, you little monster.'

It wriggled in my hand, squealing in its high-pitched but unintelligible voice.

'Take me to your home.' The creature went still and blinked rapidly in confusion as the spell took hold. 'Well?' I insisted.

The fairy nodded and I unfurled my fist, allowing the creature to hop into the air and take flight on its dirty wings. It flew away from me, slow enough that I could jog and keep up.

One fairy holds a nice amount of magical juice, but not enough for the fight that lay ahead. To win that, I'd need to find a whole nest of the things and take my fill.

Ten minutes later, the fairy pulled to a stop and hovered mid-air, allowing me to catch up. It pointed eagerly into the gloom, and when I squinted, I saw it: a large nest stuck high to the sewer wall, writhing like a blister full of spiders.

'Thanks,' I said, patting the fairy on the head, then I tore it in two and sucked out its innards. I gasped, my eyes opening wide as the magic filled me, warming my innards like I'd downed a triple whiskey.

'More.'

I threw what was left of the fairy to the ground, then reached up and thrust a hand into the nest, snatching out a fistful of fairies.

'Stop wriggling,' I said, then filled myself so full of magic, I thought my body might go supernova.

Okay.

Nothing else to do.

No reason to put it off any longer.

It was time to finish this.

'I'm coming, David.'

I left fifty fairy corpses swilling around in the watery filth before I made my way to the nearest manhole, praying to everything I held dear that David was still alive.

25

It was an ordinary street in Ealing, West London; a nice stretch of three-bedroom houses, tucked safely away from any busy roads. The sort of street that nice families with money lived on. People who went abroad three times a year, and left the kids with a live-in nanny.

Ever since I'd read L'Merrier's scribbled-down address, I'd been confused. I'd expected Mr. Trick to be lurking somewhere sinister, somewhere barren. Somewhere he could hide away from prying eyes. But here I was, in a densely-populated and well-to-do street, tracking down a monster.

I walked forward, down the broken white line of the road, my senses on high alert, searching for any sign of an ambush. Any magical booby traps that might turn me inside out in a heartbeat. I didn't think for a moment that this monster was going to make things easy for me.

I was so full of bubbling, raging energy from the fairy banquet that it took me a minute to notice something familiar: just like the blind alley and the coven when I'd discovered my witch's bodies, this street was completely empty of magic. Not even a remnant, not a wisp of smoke twisting in the breeze. Just like home, just like the Church of the Sorcerer Tree, the impossible had happened, and every ounce of the area's magic had been removed.

Is this how it liked things, this Mr. Trick? Liked to live in the empty? A barren place scorched clean of magic?

I still had no idea how that was even possible. It shouldn't be. Mr. Trick was unlike anything I'd ever taken on before. Maybe unlike anything *anyone* had taken on before. There were plenty of creatures that could feast on magic, suckle on it to feed themselves or to grow in power, but I knew of none that could scrape a place clean of any trace of it.

I figured this was what Mr Trick did to disorient any Uncanny who came his way. A means of putting them on the back foot before a confrontation, making them easy pickings in a fight. I imagined Mr. Trick liked to watch as his victim began to sweat, twitching like junkies, gasping for magic. Good. Because unlike last time, I didn't feel any withdrawal. I was so hopped up on fairy juice that it cancelled out the effect of there being no surrounding magic. I wasn't weak and I wasn't scared. I was ready.

'Who are you?'

The voice came from behind me. I whirled on my heels, hands instantly alive with power, ready to unleash. What I found was a small boy, maybe six years old, looking at me from the door of one of the houses. He was dressed smartly and had neat hair, like he was on his way to church.

'Looks like it might rain,' said the boy, his voice flat, empty of emotion.

'Where is he?' I demanded. 'Where's David?'

'If it rains, we shall get wet.'

Was this Mr. Trick? This skinny boy? Could it really be? Or was this just a puppet of his? A part of the thing's game. A bauble to distract me with, to keep me off-kilter and guessing.

'I said, where is David? You'll tell me or I'll take your head clean off.'

'Dead. Or alive. Here or elsewhere. Up or down, a smile or a frown? It's so hard to keep track in this day and age, don't you find? And lose? And find again?'

I began to walk towards the boy. His eyes stayed fixed on mine, an empty smile on his rosy-cheeked face.

'Don't think talking in riddles is going to stop me. Either you tell me what I need to know or I'll beat it out of you.'

The boy laughed, the sound coming out in a multitude of voices at once. I clenched my right fist, the energy burning, desperate to be unleashed.

'Nice of you to come and visit, familiar.' The speaking voice had changed now, shifting into the style I'd heard before, as though a different person were speaking each word.

'I know your name, Mr. Trick.'

'Mr. Trick, will come to town, and all of the Uncanny shall fall and frown.'

'Is that what you want? To kill us all?'

'So many dead and worse besides. Dead fairies, floating in filth under the streets of old London town; oh, what a dreadful sight to see. You know, when I was last here, the city was nothing but a huddle of wooden buildings. Even then, the stink of magic tainted the place.'

The thing was crazy. Had to be. Some sort of self-hating Uncanny? That was a new one.

'I'm only going to ask you one more time: where is David?' I threw a line of molten power that exploded from my palm like a lava lasso, scorching the brickwork to the boy's right.

'Your temper is a terrible thing, familiar. It'll get you killed, or worse. If you want David, just come along inside and find him. Mother said it's okay, you're expected.'

The boy turned and disappeared into the house. I paused for a second, aware that I was almost certainly walking into a trap, but I didn't see what other option I had.

I paced forward and stepped through the open doorway, my breath now rapid and short.

I stopped in the entrance corridor, the temperature inside a good ten degrees colder than the street outside. The house I found myself in looked perfectly ordinary. A cosy, middle-class place, with plush carpets, a vase of brightly coloured flowers on a table against the corridor wall, and pictures of a smiling family.

I turned and looked back to where I'd come from to see the front door swing shut of its own accord, cutting off the view. Cutting off the exit.

And then the door vanished.

I ran to it and felt around but couldn't find any sign of the exit, just rough brick, solid, like it had been that way for years. Like it had always been that way.

'Stella...'

I raised two glowing fists and whirled around to see the boy skipping out of view at the other end of the corridor.

'I'm coming for you!' I screamed, hurling a ball of energy in front of me to show I meant business, crisping my own hair as I sprinted through it. I rounded the corner to find the corridor ahead empty, a staircase to my right.

'Pssst, familiar—'

The boy was crouched at the top of the stairs, looking down at me through the banister.

'Enough with the messing around, Mr. Trick. Are you going to stand and fight, or are you going to keep hiding behind this boy?'

I felt it before I heard or saw anything; a prickle on the back of my neck that told me I had to get moving. I turned to my right, just in time to see the glint of a large knife, its blade embedded in the banister where my head had been just moments earlier. Still holding the knife's handle was a woman in her late thirties.

'Drat,' she said, 'you weren't supposed to move, you were supposed to get stabbed.'

'Oh, I don't think Mother likes you at all, familiar,' said the boy, as his mother yanked the blade free and swung it in an arc, only just missing my neck as I threw myself backwards, landing with a crash on the floor.

'Mother knows best,' she said, and stamped on my knee. I cried out in pain and reflexively tossed up a ball of flame that engulfed the woman. Her hair caught fire, then her whole head, but the woman didn't flail, or fall, or even yell out as her flesh broiled. Instead, she giggled.

'What are you?' I asked, as the boy appeared at her side, holding her hand.

'We're bad and bad and bad all over,' he said. 'Isn't that right, Mother?'

'Right as rain,' she replied.

They stepped towards me, the flames dying and revealing the woman's blackened face, flesh scorched, eyeballs running down her cheeks like slug trails.

'Where is David?' I kicked back across the floor and tried to scramble to my feet, my knee sharp with pain.

'Already hurt?'

'Already?'

'You're even less sport than your bitch whore witches.'

I snarled. 'You made a mistake coming into my city. Into my coven. If you think you're going to walk away from this alive, you're wrong.'

I didn't stop to think; I found the right words leap into my mind and unleashed a concussive wave of energy, sweeping the pair aside and depositing them in the kitchen. I ran for the stairs, taking them three at a time, any pain in my knee forgotten. I moved from room to room, searching for any sign of David, until there was only one door left. I turned the handle and shook the door, but it refused to open.

'Who is that?' asked a voice from inside: David.

'David, it's me, are you okay?'

'Just great, apart from being kidnapped by a creepy mum and her even creepier son.'

It was so good to hear his voice.

'Step back.'

I placed my hand over the lock, placing the correct phrase together in my mind. The lock clicked as it opened, the door swinging inwards. I found David tied to a chair in the centre of the bedroom.

'David!'

'Well, you took your bloody time.'

'You're welcome. Now come on, I'm getting you out of here and then I'm coming back to finish this thing.'

I pulled a knife from my jacket and sliced through the ropes, letting David shrug them off.

'I knew you'd come,' he said. 'Well, hoped you would. You or Superman. I'm glad it was you though, as Superman isn't real.'

'David, we don't really have time for your babble.'

'Right, imminent danger, consider the babble stopped. But thanks. Thank you for not letting me die. That would have been really shit.'

I smiled and just about resisted the urge to hug him. David followed me as I made my way back to the stairs, trying to ignore that tickle that was telling me this had all been far too easy. This couldn't be the end of it. They weren't going to let me just run out of here with him, were they?

I soon got my answer.

'Stay close to me,' I said edging forward, my right hand ablaze, lighting the way.

'If I was any closer you'd be giving me a piggyback, Magic Lady.'

They were waiting for us downstairs. We were going to have to fight our way out. As I reached the top of the stairs, I took a breath to ready myself. I turned to David. 'Are you ready for this?'

He opened his mouth to reply, but then his eyes widened as he looked past me.

I didn't have time to react.

A flash of something whistled past my head and the knife found its target, entering David's throat up to the hilt.

He looked at me with confusion, unable to understand what had just happened. I think he tried to speak, but all that came out was blood, coughed up in a violent spray.

'No—' I put my hands to my mouth as he stepped back, then stumbled, then fell to his knees. He reached up and took hold of the knife and pulled it from his neck along with a torrent of blood.

'David...'

He looked at me one last time, then fell to his side, blood pouring from his throat and forming a scarlet pillow around his head.

I walked towards him in a daze, unconcerned about any threat to myself. I fell to my knees.

A corpse before me.

I'd failed.

First my masters, now David.

What good was I?

What was I if I couldn't keep those around me safe?

The boy and his mother were holding hands as they stepped from the stairs and into the corridor.

'Mr. Trick has been a bad boy, hasn't he?'

'Hasn't he?'

'Hasn't he?'

I couldn't think straight, couldn't fight.

'No more,' I said. 'No more.'

I felt all the anger, the fear, the despair, and the shame boil up inside of me like a storm. It met the still-untapped reservoir of magic I'd drunk down, and without thinking, without putting any magical form together, I stood and threw back my head, arms outstretched, and screamed. Power exploded from me, rampaging down the corridor, around the house, like I was a volcano erupting, destroying everything in its path. The walls cracked, the windows shattered, everything around me was turned to ash.

I couldn't tell you how long it lasted. Perhaps a second. Perhaps an hour. Then, like a switch had been flicked, it was over and I fell to the blackened floor.

26

I'm not sure how long it took me to get back to the coven, or how I even got there. Maybe I walked, maybe I took the tube. The world was a daze, a dream, an awful lie. I found myself back in my room, curled up on the bed I hadn't slept on since this whole thing had started. I felt weak, drained of energy. Whatever I had unleashed back in that house in Ealing had completely sapped me.

I'd thought that I was walking into the final confrontation. That whatever happened between me and Mr. Trick, that one of us wasn't walking away. One way or another, I was going to save David. It didn't matter what happened to me, I just had to stop Mr. Trick from taking that one life.

And I'd failed.

Mr. Trick had no intention of attending the grand finale. He'd just lured me in to make me suffer once again. To take something that had become dear to me, and not even give me the release of death. No, he had more in store for me yet.

I couldn't remember seeing him, seeing the boy and his mother, or anyone else—not after I'd unleashed all of my pent-up magic. Their bodies had been completely destroyed by my outburst, David's too, but no part of me thought it was over.

Those things weren't Mr. Trick, they were just playing pieces being pushed around the board. Testing me, seeing what I had.

I could picture that look in David's eyes as I tried to close my own. The incomprehension. Had he even known what had happened? That there was a kitchen knife embedded up to the handle in his throat?

I should never have involved him in this thing. He was a just a normal. No, that's wrong, he wasn't *just* anything. He was a brave man, full of light and kindness, and I'd been too wrapped up in my own thirst for revenge to do the right thing. To realise that involving him in a mission against the most powerful Uncanny I had ever known was only going to end in calamity.

My body felt heavy. This was different to what had happened to my masters. They could handle themselves. They didn't need my help to keep them safe. They were always safe. Well, always had been before Mr. Trick came to town.

Mr. Trick will come to town, and all of the Uncanny shall fall and frown.

Uncanny and normal alike. He wasn't fussy.

A noise from the corridor.

A floorboard creaking as though someone had shifted their weight upon it.

I sat up and stared at the gap between the door and the floor.

A shadow passed, something moving quickly away.

I didn't bother asking who it was, I already knew.

Mr. Trick had come to town.

It was time for this Uncanny to fall and frown.

But not without a fight.

I wouldn't fall without throwing everything I had left in me at the thing, no matter how ineffective it might be. I wouldn't give the monster the satisfaction of a meek shuffle towards death's door.

I drew the magic in the room towards me as I padded

toward the exit and opened it quietly, peering out into the gloom of the corridor beyond. No sign of anyone.

I opened the door just wide enough and slipped out of my room, my right hand fierce with magic; a raging lantern, leading the way.

I could hear the murmur of hushed voices drifting from the coven's common room. I moved forward, and as I got closer, a chill crept across my skin.

I shivered and broke out in gooseflesh.

The voices became clearer:

'I told you.'

'Me too.'

'She was not ready.'

'How could she be, a thing such as her?'

'Spit and force of will.'

'Dirt and rags.'

No...

This was...

I knew those voices.

The power in my right hand grew weaker, then sputtered out altogether as I pushed the door open and stepped inside the common room.

In the centre of the space stood three figures. Three women more powerful than any other Uncanny of London, even though to look at them you would assume they were nothing more than three middle-aged women attending their weekly knitting circle.

Kala, Trin, and Feal.

The witches of the London Coven.

My masters.

My creators.

'Look how she gawps,' said Kala.

'This isn't possible...'

'You think anything exists that could take us out? In our own coven? Our own seat of power?'

'This is just... just a dream, a nightmare, that's all. That's all it can be.'

'You really are pathetic,' said Kala. 'This was a test.'

'A test?'

'I told you she'd fail,' said Trin.

'Yes, but I never thought she would fail so completely.'

I fell to my knees as confusion overtook me.

'Well, fail she did,' said Feal, 'and you know what comes next.'

My masters nodded as one: 'We must destroy her.'

27

The world had become a nightmare.

Ever since I'd first walked into the blind alley that housed my coven, I'd felt things spinning further and further out of control. Further into unreality, insanity, and now...

I looked up again through tear-blurred eyes to see my masters stood before me, smiling. Mocking.

'I don't believe you,' I said.

'Why would we care about a thing like that? Like what you think? What is that to us? What is your opinion worth?'

'It is nothing.'

'Nothing at all.'

'You are just a thing.'

'A tool we created to take care of the drudge and the filth.'

'You're not a person.'

'Not a person.'

'Not even nearly.'

I stood and staggered backwards, angrily wiping away tears with the sleeve of my leather jacket. I reached out with my senses, searching for signs of the trick I was seeing, because that's all this could be. No matter how real it seemed, no matter how much my emotions boiled and told me it was true, this was Mr. Trick's doing. It had to be.

'Oh, that is cute.'

'You feel it, too?'

'Of course. Her puny little magical tendrils eagerly snuffling around us like a retarded pup, searching for signs of falsehood.'

My senses recoiled as I failed to find any lies. They were alive, really alive. They didn't seem like some pretence. As far as I could tell, the three women in front of me were the trio of witches that had created me. The ones I had served without question for decades.

'She sees the truth of it.'

'Why? Why did you do this to me?' I looked at their smirking faces, and for the first time in my many years of life, I felt like I wanted to tear them to pieces. Wanted to draw in every scrap of magic and throw it at them. Wanted to knock them down and stamp them out like they were on fire.

'Your face flushes, Familiar.'

'Ooh, Trin, I believe she wishes us harm.'

'Us!' cried Trin. 'Her own creators.'

'You think something as worthless as you could harm a hair upon our heads?' said Kala.

They laughed, but there was no humour in it, only malice.

I sank to my knees. My fists were hot with energy, but I couldn't bring myself to do anything with it. Not just because they were right—me going against them would be like a fly taking on a T-Rex—but because, despite it all, they were my masters. My creators. For want of a better word, they were my gods. And what right did I have to attack a god?

I wasn't a person.

I was a thing.

A thing they owned.

'Just do it,' I said. 'Do it if you're going to.'

My head sank, eyes closed, as I waited for them to put an end to my long life. If this was who they really were, I didn't want to exist anymore. I thought about David again. About how I'd let him down. My own stupidity had got him killed. My failure to pass their stinking "test". Well, fuck it all. Fuck everything. Time to die.

And maybe I would have done. Maybe that would have been the end of my time, of this story. But then I noticed something. Or perhaps I should say I realised for the first time that I *didn't* notice something. I opened my eyes and a smile spread across my face.

'Why are you smiling, Familiar?'

'She has gone mad. Accepting the truth.'

'Accepting the end.'

'The end at our hand. Because we created her—'

'And so we will also end her.'

I began to laugh, loud and crazy. Crazy with relief.

'What is it?'

'What?'

'Answer us!'

I was a step ahead for once. I knew something he didn't.

'This was really good. I mean, *really* good. You almost had me. I was even sure it wasn't true, and yet you were still able to make me question my doubt. To believe this lie. But you made a mistake. Like David said, you're sloppy.'

'Do not talk to your masters like—'

'Oh, shut up. You're a lie. Another trick. You know how I know that?'

The three witches looked at me, dumbfounded, and I savoured the moment for several seconds.

'Tell us!'

I inhaled once, deeply, through the nose, then breathed out. 'You got the smell wrong.'

The witches looked at one other, not understanding what I was saying. It felt good.

'This place always smells the same. It's my first memory,

that smell: cinnamon, cut grass, and lavender. The scent of the London Coven. And you overlooked it. Even I almost did.'

It was time for this trick to end.

I pulled the magic towards me and unleashed it at them in a great, fiery torrent. They stood dumbly as my magic swirled around them in golden arcs of molten fire. Then the screaming began. They wailed and thrashed as the magic penetrated their bodies.

'Well played, Stella,' said Mr. Trick, many voices as one. *'You actually won a round, but I'm afraid the game isn't over yet.'*

I picked up a chair. 'It soon will be,' I snarled, and launched the chair at the squirming, screaming pretend witches. It turned them to ash on impact and carried on, breaking through the far wall. No, *tearing* through. The wall wasn't brick, it was paper. How had I missed that?

The entire room began to sag and collapse. I ran for the tear I'd created and leapt through as the pretend coven fell.

28

I was in the street in Ealing again; Mr. Trick's street. I'd never left. Never stumbled back to the London Coven after unleashing all of the raging magic I'd devoured. After burning everything around me.

It had all just been another trick.

Christ, was I tired of all this childish playing around.

He'd even filled the fake coven with enough magic for me to accept it. Now the illusion had wilted and I'd stepped out of it, I felt the emptiness of his street again. A street impossibly drained of all magic. It gnawed at my stomach like I was starving hungry, but I'd drawn in enough magic from the fake coven to feel some power inside me. To stave off the sweats and the shakes. But it wouldn't be enough. Not to face this creature. I was walking towards who-knows-what without the safety of the fairy magic coursing through my veins.

Who was I kidding? Even with that power inside of me, I didn't stand a chance. There was no difference between then and now. I was still walking naked into a pit of hungry lions. But it didn't matter. All that mattered was seeing this through, finally, to the end. To face the thing responsible for all of this, and not back down. For the witches of the London Coven. For the monks who had peacefully dedicated themselves to the Sorcerer Tree. For David. Most of all for him.

I flinched as all of the doors in the houses that lined either side of the street shot open, and out stepped the same two people to stand and stare at me as I walked past. The same mother and child as I'd encountered last time, over and over, in front of every house, her arm around his shoulder.

'He's waiting for you,' they said in turn as I passed.

'Mr. Trick has come to town, and all the Uncanny, shall fall and frown.'

I waited for one of them to break ranks, checking over my shoulder every other second, eyes darting from door to door, but they stayed where they were, calmly watching as I moved along the centre of the road.

'It's okay,' said that familiar multitude of voices, *'it's almost over. You're almost done.'*

'Show yourself,' I commanded.

'I'm afraid I won't let you go easy. Oh, it's going to hurt. You're going to wriggle and scream and beg, beg, beg for me to stop. And I will look down at you, your blood on my face and my teeth as I smile, and I will say, "No".'

His words itched at me. Invaded me. His words were fear and I was breathing them in.

'You want to see me? Really see me?'

'Get out here!'

As I walked, I began to notice something strange happening. The street was devolving. As I moved forward it was like I was actually moving back. Back in time. The houses, the brickwork, neat gardens, cars, were becoming wild grass, trees, forest. It should have been jarring, but somehow it seemed natural, a seamless flow.

Within a few more steps, the street was gone entirely. I looked back, but all I saw was a dirt road and trees, as though the street of houses had never existed. I didn't know what magic this was, even worse, I couldn't even *feel* the presence of magic. This was sorcery from a whole other plane. The kind a bug like me could never see or feel.

'Mr. Trick, I know your name, and I think I know what you want. To devour all magic. All magical practitioners. To scorch it all from the planet. To stamp it all out until there's only you left. So come on, stop playing games. Stop being a coward. Come out here and take my life from me. See if you can put me down.'

I didn't look into the tree line. I could sense things in there. Impossible, dark things. Maybe if I saw one of them clearly it would burst on to the dirt track and swallow me whole. Where on Earth was I? Was this place real?

'This is London, Stella. A small sliver of old London that refused to die. Isn't it beautiful?'

The voices came from everywhere, it was impossible to get a fix on him. I felt my hands burning hot with power, desperate to leave a mark on the monster before he snuffed me out.

'No people, no cars, no chemicals or magic tainting the air. Free of the stink of the Uncanny. Almost free...'

My heart hammered in my chest like it might burst from my ribcage at any moment and make its escape.

'Why do you hate the Uncanny so much? You're part of it, you're the most powerful Uncanny I've ever—'

I was cut off as the unseen beasts of the forest screamed as one, drowning me out. Finally, silence fell again.

'Sounds like I hit a nerve there, Mr. Trick. Tell me, where did the evil warlocks, wizards, and witches touch you?'

A mighty crack to my right. I turned to see a giant oak tree falling in my direction and leapt out of the way, rolling in the dirt as the tree struck down by my side and shook the earth beneath me.

I pushed myself to my feet and staggered back, looking for a sign of any more trees about to fall, but all seemed calm again. He didn't want to kill me that way. Whatever happened, Mr. Trick wanted me dead by his own two hands.

'Nice try, but your aim was a bit off, there.'

When I looked around I saw a large wooden hut in front of me, directly in the centre of the dirt road. Instead of a door, an animal skin covered its entrance, gently undulating in the breeze.

'Is this it? Is this where you're hiding?'

Silence.

He was in there. *It* was in there. I knew it. My every nerve ending was screaming at me that he was, and that I had to turn and run. I breathed long and slow, then reached out a hand and pushed the heavy animal skin aside, ducking as I stepped indoors.

The hut was dark and smelled like dirt. I blinked several times and my eyes began to adjust to the dark. There was a hunched figure crouched in the far corner of the room, draped in a thin blanket. It rose and fell rapidly as the figure sucked in short, sharp breaths.

My stomach churned, my senses retreated. Refused to interact with the person, knew I was in the presence of something beyond dark. Beyond horror. Beyond death.

Mr. Trick was waiting for me.

'I'm here,' I said, my voice a croak, my throat dry.

No response.

Hand trembling, I reached out to the figure, took hold of the blanket, and whipped it away. The material was damp.

Still the figure didn't stand, didn't move.

I reached out again, took hold of the person's shoulder, tried to turn them.

'Mr. Trick, I'm here. Here to end—'

The figure twisted round, thrusting up to his feet, face rushing towards mine, teeth bared, eyes crazy—

I screamed and fell back to the floor, my mind refusing to believe what my eyes were seeing.

He stepped towards me as I pushed myself away across the floor—

'No-no-no—'

He leapt over me, grabbed me by the collar, laughing and pushing his face towards mine.

It was a leering, mad face, with wild eyes and a rictus grin.

And it was a face I recognised.

It was David.

29

Somehow, I wriggled free and half staggered, half fell, past the animal skin door and back out onto the dirt path that led through the forest of London.

I stood to see the mother and son clones emerging from the surrounding tree line and applauding wildly as David stepped out of the wooden hut. He bowed and threw out kisses.

'David, how are you… I don't—'

This was a lie.

Another lie, that's all. Did he really think he could fool me again?

'Hello, Stella.'

The world tilted.

It couldn't be true.

That voice.

Two words, two different voices.

'My name is Mr. Trick, and I'm here to tear your city down.'

The unseen beasts of the forest stamped their feet. The trees shook and the ground trembled.

'Listen to them, Stella.'

This was just another trick, that's all. Like the witches, my masters; a lie inside of a paper coven. I just had to sniff out the lie again, find the mistake, and then all of this would warp and crumble, and the snake would slither out to be stamped upon.

'You're a lie. You're not Mr. Trick. You're just another puppet. Another playing piece.'

'Oh no, I can see why you would think that, but I'm afraid this really is the final act. Even the best of games has to end eventually, and this is where I take my trophy.'

The mothers and the sons clapped and cheered wildly before being silenced with a gesture from David. From Mr. Trick.

'I saw you die.'

'Even eyes can betray. Sad.'

I felt fire in my hand and threw my arm out, unleashing a blast of magic. It hurtled towards David, who made no attempt to jump out of the way. Instead, he raised an eyebrow, and the ball of furious power stopped. It hung in the air, rippling with energy.

'And I thought we were friends, Stella. To think I let you stay in my home when you were hurt.'

'That was David. You're not him.'

He sighed and the ball of magic reversed and lurched towards me. I did my best to jump out of the way, but it struck my legs, corkscrewing me through the air, making my skin burn. I landed in a painful heap, limbs twisted.

'With you this whole time as you struggled and failed, failed, failed. What a nasty trick of me to play,' said David.

'Why?'

'Why not? Why should I let my devil dogs eat you up right away when there was so much more to be had from you. To watch you yell and run and search for clues like a good little familiar. All the while with me at your side. You can be a brutal thing at times, can't you?'

Could it really be true? I remembered my confusion when I

opened my eyes to find myself in his house. I'd been moments from death as one of Mr. Trick's devil dogs lunged for me, too flustered to string an incantation together, and then all of a sudden I was somewhere else. A nice, safe house, miles from where I had been, with a stranger looking down at me.

With David looking down at me.

Mr. Trick.

'I think she's putting it together. Finding the pieces slot neatly.'

The mothers and sons cheered once, high and sharp.

I realised with certainty that I'd entered another world—a mad world—and the last thing I wanted was to die there. I turned and ran, the people that lined the path laughing and pointing as I passed them by.

'Where are you going, Stella? The end is the end is the end,' called David. 'When Mr. Trick comes to town, all the Uncanny will fall and frown.'

A bend in the path, and David—Mr. Trick—was stood in front of me. I pulled up short and darted into the forest, batting aside tree branches that fought to slow me down. This was a mistake. This whole thing. Trying to face Mr. Trick, and now running off the path. Nothing good would come from running into a forest full of monsters.

'Stella. Stop. It's over. Now lie down in the dirt like the filthy creature you are and wait for the heel of my boot to grind against your eyes.'

There was no time for a pithy reply, all there was time for was running and fear. A real, primal fear. Mr. Trick, this place, this past London, it was like it had found the primitive part of my psyche and was jabbing it with hot pokers. In all my decades of life, I couldn't remember ever feeling such blind fear. The kind of fear I imagined a child might feel as it lay hot under the blanket in bed, trying to ignore the thing lurking inside the wardrobe.

I stopped to catch my breath. Where the hell was I running to? Was there even a way out? Was there a way back to London proper, or was I just sprinting further and further into Mr. Trick's nightmare world?

A scream.

No, *hundreds* of screams.

Human, but not quite; more animalistic, hungry.

I turned to see all of the mothers and sons, their faces masks of fury, mouths wide, teeth bared, running through the trees towards me. No time for magic, for spells, I couldn't even think straight to put the right incantation together. All I could do was run.

I heard them behind me, desperate to feel me in their hands, under their feet, between their teeth. They wanted to rip me apart, I knew it. I looked over my shoulder, they were falling over each other in their desperation to get to me. The looks in their eyes… I'd never seen anything like it. Anything so dark.

I yelled as I ran straight into something and bounced back, landing painfully on the forest floor. No time for pain, for stopping. I hopped up into a crouch, dimly aware of the sharp complaint of my ankle, and prepared for the first wave of mothers and sons to pile on to me—

But they were gone.

I couldn't see them, couldn't hear them. The only sound now was the noise of my own heavy breathing.

I wasn't going to get out of this. I couldn't run from him. Couldn't step out of old London and make it back to my coven and lock the door. What happened to my witches was proof enough that no one and nowhere was safe from this thing. Sooner or later, he was going to track me down.

I didn't want to die.

I especially didn't want to die at this monster's hands.

This twisted bastard.

But I was out of options and tired of running.

And yet, I refused to run another step. Refused to give the beast that satisfaction.

So I sat. I lowered myself to the forest floor and crossed my legs. All around me, always out of view, I could feel great, ancient creatures moving through the forest. The ancient fears made flesh that lived in this place.

'They are beautiful,' said Mr. Trick, stepping out of the shadows and sitting opposite me.

'Give David back.'

Mr. Trick arched one of David's eyebrows.

'I know he isn't you. He can't be.'

He tilted his head as he regarded me, then shrugged. 'Well, okay, you got me.'

'You're just a thing, hijacking his body. You've crawled inside him and used him.'

'But he's so warm and comfortable,' he replied, smiling. 'I think I may stay in here for a while, holding on to his spark. His soul. Squeezing it between my hands so it squirms and screams.'

'You're trying to make me angry. Make me frightened. I think I'm done with that.'

He nodded and reached forward, taking my hand in his. I tried to pull away, but found I couldn't. Without a word, he broke my little finger. The snap rang out like a rifle shot. He let my injured hand go, and I clung to it, trying not to scream.

'You don't make the rules, familiar. I am the dark. The terror. I am the thing that frightens the monsters. I will make you feel any way I wish. And then... then I will devour you. Take your spark and store it inside of me, next to all the others. Next to your poor, poor witches. They're in me now, thrashing around. It tickles.' He licked his lips.

'Talk all you want,' I said through gritted teeth, the pain in my hand sharp.

'Sticks and stones, eh?'

I didn't respond. Part of me was screaming to get up and

run again, but sod that. 'If you're going to kill me, come and have at it. I won't go easy.'

'Isn't she brave?'

The monsters in the forest roared in agreement.

'Well, perhaps I can break you yet, before I swallow you down...'

I shivered despite myself, wondering what he meant. More broken bones? Or would he nibble off my skin, like he had with the monk? I could take it. I'd have to.

'Here,' said Mr. Trick, 'let me show you something to make you scream...' He reached out his hands and grasped me by the temples and...

...I...

...I could see...

...I was a fragment and...

...Don't let...

...I was lost, lost, lost, and...

The fog cleared and I was stood in a familiar place; the blind alley that led to the London Coven.

'What is this?' I asked, but my words were silent.

The door to the coven opened and I saw myself step out.

A dark shape rushed past me, towards my other self.

I tried to shout out to warn her, to warn me, but couldn't.

The shadow became a person of sorts, and it whispered in the other me's ear. And then I realised where I was.

I saw myself turn to the door of the coven and watched as my hands swept over and over again, forming ancient patterns as I spoke secret words under my breath.

No...

Oh, God...

I couldn't have!

The other me stopped and turned away from the coven, walked down the alley, walked past me and turned out of sight. I looked back to the shadow figure and watched it push open the door and step inside.

It was my fault.

All those protection spells. Layers upon layers of magical protection that nothing could ever get through unscathed, and only four people knew how to take them down: my three witches and me.

I'd let the fox into the hen house.

30

Mr. Trick had done something to me, whispered some magic in my ear, and I'd unlocked the coven for him. Allowed him to step into the most protected place in London, and tear my witches into bloody pieces.

'No!' My voice rang loud and high, suddenly audible again as I found myself back in the forest, curled up on my side, a child sobbing in the dirt.

Mr. Trick looked down at me, smiling. 'There's that pain. That scream. That delicious anguish.'

I wanted to believe it was a deception, but I knew that it wasn't. Now I'd seen it, it was like a door had been unlocked in my mind. I could remember it happening now. The strange compulsion to remove the protection. The satisfied feeling I'd had as I walked away. The confusion as I stepped out of the blind alley, and the knowledge of what I had done disappearing. I'd turned on the spot, wondering if I'd forgotten to take something with me. I'd almost gone back to the coven to check for the thing I couldn't remember, but shrugged it off and walked away.

My fault. My fault. My fault.

Just a stupid, weak familiar. A weak spot that had been taken advantage of.

And now all of London was going to pay. Maybe all of the Uncanny Kingdom.

'What say you, Stella? A rum do and no mistake. Oh, I let them know you'd shown me the way in before I had my wicked, gruesome way with them. I think they were a little annoyed. Sorry.'

'You bastard…'

I stood and felt what magic I had surge through me and explode from my outstretched hands at Mr. Trick. It was no use. He swatted my best aside and stepped forward, grabbing me by the neck and hurling me against the nearest tree. My back hit hard and I fell to the ground, the wind punched out of me.

'Would you like to see how I finished them off? The fun I had? Oh, I took my time.'

'Please, don't.'

I felt his cold hands grasp my head again and—

I was in the coven's common room. My witches, my brave masters, were giving everything they had, but the creature I'd let in was too strong. It brushed each spell aside. It was a mouse playing with its scampering food. They were bleeding, exhausted, terrified. I had never seen them scared before. It broke my heart.

'Watch, familiar. Watch me play.'

'That's enough. Please, I don't want to see…'

I tried to close my eyes, tried to turn my head away as the dark figure rampaged through the coven, tearing flesh, opening wounds at will, but I could feel Mr. Trick's hands on me, holding my eyes open, keeping my head still.

'Watch me play, Stella. It's so, so beautiful.'

The attack was not fast. He blocked any chance of escape and took his time to break them down. To give them hope that they could turn the tables, then smack them down again. Near the end, the witches of London struggled to meet each other. Dragged their shattered bodies across the floor, leaving trails of dark blood behind them. I could see it in their eyes now, the certainty that this was it. They'd done what they could and it was all about to be over. I felt the tears rushing from my eyes, soaking my cheeks.

'Aw, it's almost over,' Mr. Trick lamented, 'but don't worry, we can watch it again and again and again...'

'Please. Please don't show me...'

I wanted to die. For him to kill me at last and have it be over.

But then—

Oh!

Then I saw something. Something *wonderful*.

As I watched the dark shape in Mr. Trick's shadow play attack my witches, I saw them hold hands. They did not fight, did not run. Instead, I saw their lips move as one, saying the same words. Words I recognised. Casting a spell only my witches could have created, and only when working together as one.

I began to laugh.

'Stop.'

I was hysterical now, howling. Shaking with great gales of laughter that hurt my stomach.

'Stop it!' said Mr. Trick.

The coven whipped away like a cloth being yanked from a table, and I was back in the forest. Mr. Trick rocked back on his heels, confused.

'Is this madness? Have I broken you so easily?'

'I'm sorry, it's just, you're making a habit out of this.'

'Of what?' He studied my face, my smile. 'Making a habit of what?'

'Well, first you let me live when you really should have taken care of me right away. Then there was the lack of smell in the pretend coven earlier. Not a details person, are you Mr.

Trick? A little too arrogant for that, too sure of yourself. But this one? This one is a big boo-boo.'

'What? Tell me!' His voice roared out, the trees shaking, my hair blowing back, but I didn't shield myself from it. I walked forward, walked towards Mr. Trick. Now I saw fear in *his* eyes. 'Don't you see? They left the door open for me to walk in.'

'Your witches? They are dead. Dead! I killed them, tore them apart, left them as nothing more than meat and rags on the floor! I swallowed them down, ate their spark. I did that! Me, me, me!'

'Yes, but not before they left me a gift; and thank you for letting me see it, because otherwise I'd never have noticed.'

Mr. Trick blinked slowly. 'What did they do? Tell me what they did.'

I smiled. 'It's something my masters created called the Achilles Curse.'

His lips twitched. 'No. No, no, no... that's not.... not possible.'

'A weak spot. A chink in your armour. Know where it is, and even a fledgling sorcerer could take you down.'

Mr. Trick backed away. 'Where is it? Where?'

'Now, those who cast the spell can't take advantage of it,' I went on. 'Magic has rules, it can be a right bitch like that. But me? I can use it. They left it for me. One last job for the familiar.'

Mr. Trick screamed and raised his hands, ready to throw everything he had at me.

'Hush,' I said. He froze, unable to cast the spell that would surely have killed me.

I walked slowly towards him, savouring his terror.

'Now it's you that can feel fear. That can know what it's like to beg for your life. I feel you struggling against me, but it's no good. There's no point. I know where your weak spot is, and I'm focussing my magic on it. You can't stop me.'

'You think you can put an end to me? You think I can just be—'

'Oh, please shut up. I'm going to kill you now. For my witches, and for David. Goodbye and fuck you.'

I placed the right words together and a flaming sword appeared in my hand—

'No!'

'Oh, yes—'

I thrust the sword into Mr. Trick's chest and he screamed, his mouth growing ever larger until I thought his head was going to split in two. Magic erupted from him in great flaming torrents, forcing me to stagger back. He shook violently, like he was having a fit, and shapes began to burst from him, tearing his flesh open to escape and circle around us. These were the sparks he'd taken, the souls he'd eaten. It was clear he'd feasted often and for many years, and I knew my witches must be up there among them somewhere.

'I did it,' I said. I hoped they could hear me.

Mr. Trick's body fell to the ground and something dark and wet began to crawl out of him. Began to crawl out of David. This was Mr. Trick's true form. His true body. Dragging itself out of David's corpse. The form looked drained and withered, and was dripping with foul black goo. I wondered what it had been, how it had become such a horrific creature. It looked up at me, its face smooth and featureless apart from two giant yellow eyes that met mine imploringly.

'Beg all you want,' I said, 'you won't find mercy here.' I reached out my hands, fire shooting from my palms, and reduced the thing to ash.

Mr. Trick was dead and gone.

I'd done it.

Mr. Trick had come to town, and a lowly familiar had put him down.

I'd started this whole episode seeing impossible things, and now I'd done something impossible myself. I'd destroyed the most powerful creature I had ever met.

'Stella...?'

I whirled round to where David's body lay. He wasn't dead! Not quite, but he would be. I ran to him and cradled him in my arms, fussing at the open wounds that covered him, the giant gaping hole that Mr. Trick had crawled out of.

'David. Oh, God, David, you're going... you're going to be...' I couldn't finish the sentence, because he wasn't going to be okay. His wounds were too severe. He was seconds from death. I thought he'd died once, but this time he really would. This time he was really done for...

...unless...

I looked up at the sparks still swirling around in a confusion of magic. It was forbidden, I knew that. It was the dark arts, black magic. It was especially bad for a thing such as me to use it, and maybe it wouldn't work anyway. But...

I stood and lifted my hands to the sky, head thrown back, looking up at all of the sparks rushing around like a tornado. All of those Uncanny souls. So much magic in one place, for this moment only, but would it be enough? Would *I* be enough? Would I be able to harness it and channel it correctly, or would it burn me up and leave me a husk on the ground?

'Sod it,' I said. 'Let's do this...'

The forms shaped in my head. The forbidden forms. I felt the energy of the forest change. I was a lightning rod, a thing of pure focus. I tensed and tried to ready myself, but as the first spark rushed into me, I heard myself scream. All the Uncanny sparks, the souls, entered me one after one. I could feel my bones burning, my flesh twisting. They were tearing me apart.

No-no-no—

'You will... do what I want... I... I control you... I demand it... I... demand...'

I felt the dark energy I was tapping into, and it terrified me. Whether it worked or not, there would be a price. A familiar like me couldn't play with this side of magic, not without paying a toll down the line. It didn't matter. I didn't care. All that mattered was winning, was pulling one life back from Mr. Trick.

Throat raw from screaming, I lowered my arms and looked at David on the ground before me. I knelt beside him, my body on fire, and I gathered him into my arms, his head lolling back.

'Stella... I think... I think I'm going to...'

'Shh now, David. Everything is going to be okay.'

I craned my neck, placed my lips upon his and I blew into him.

The power, the sparks, the dark magic, rushed from inside me and into him. He jolted from my arms and hung in the air in a brilliant ball of light, the trees around us catching flame, David at its centre. The whole world was screams and fire and blinding light, and it was too much, too much, too much—

And then it was over.

David fell with a thump to the ground, the sparks gone, the dark magic gone. All was silent. I slumped back, every part of me in agony, trying to catch my breath. I was alive. I'd managed to harness all that magic, tap into the dark plane, and somehow I'd survived.

But what about...?

'Stella?'

I rolled over and crawled towards David, my head coming to rest on his stomach.

'Yes?'

'That really, really hurt.'

I smiled. 'You're welcome.'

31

A month later, back at the London Coven, back at my home.

My body had just about recovered from everything, though I still walked with a bit of a limp. I'd stopped coughing up blood in the mornings, too, so that was good. For a while, it had felt strange to return to this place. To decide I was going to live there still. But it was my home. I wouldn't let Mr. Trick win by forcing me out. This was where I belonged.

'Hey,' said David as I entered the kitchen. He put a mug of coffee down before me. He'd recovered much quicker than I had. All the dark magic that had saved his life had fixed him up pretty well.

I wrapped my hands around the mug and not for the first time wondered what the price would be for my harnessing such black magic. There was always a price. I looked up at David and knew I'd do it again in a heartbeat.

'Hey, have I thanked you yet for saving my life?' he asked.

'Only about ten times a day for the last month.'

He patted my shoulder and sat opposite me. He'd described what had happened to him as a sort of dream. He was aware at times that something was inside him, willing him to act in certain ways, but he hadn't been able to do anything about it. At other times, he hadn't known anything was wrong at all. Mr. Trick had only used him for brief bits of time, until he'd staged his disappearance. From then on, until Mr. Trick had crawled out of him, he'd been completely cut off and unaware of anything. As if he was in a deep, dreamless sleep.

'So today's the day?'

'Today's the day,' I said, nodding.

'You're sure? I saw you pretending not to limp when you walked in here.'

'London has been without its witches for too long. Without the protection and order of this coven. Well, I might only be a puny familiar, but I'm of here, and until someone better comes along, I'm going to carry on doing what I was created for: keeping the Uncanny of London in line.'

'With me by your side, right? Remember, this is my city, too. Now I know all of the spooky stuff that goes on here, it's my duty to make sure people are safe. And you can use the intelligence I get through official channels. You know it makes sense.'

I smiled and nodded. Truth be told, I could do with the help, and he knew things that I didn't. People, places, ways to go about investigations. What to look for and how to fit clues together. I needed him. Not that I'd say that to him, he had a big enough head as it was.

Also, I didn't *want* him to go away.

I wanted him to stay with me.

'Stella Familiar and Detective David Tyler,' he said, 'taking on anyone who tries to upset our city. This is going to be fun. Me and you, a crime-fighting duo. Ooh, like Batman and Robin! Bagsy I'm Batman.' He whistled and began cracking eggs into a pan.

There was another reason I wanted David close by. Well, another two reasons. He'd played host to the most powerful creature I'd ever come across. Was Mr. Trick gone for good? Would David now become a weak link, the creature's way to crawl back into this plane? There was no way of knowing. And then there was the fact that I'd used black magic on him, and who knew what the long-term effects of that might be? No, I wanted to keep my eye on him. To protect him. Maybe protect others *from* him.

'It's not going to be an easy ride,' I said. 'The Uncanny world is a dangerous one, as I'm sure you're already very aware.'

'Hey, danger is my middle name.'

'I can't believe you just said that with a straight face.'

'I am pretty much shameless,' he replied with a grin.

'Oh, and David?'

'Yeah?'

'You're definitely Robin.'

The witches of the London Coven might be dead.

And I might not be a fraction of what they were.

But it didn't matter. I'd walked into Mr. Trick's world and taken him out, and I'd do whatever it took to see off anything looking to take his place.

That was my job.

My whole reason for existing.

My name is Stella Familiar.

Created by the witches of the London Coven.

And this city will be protected.

NIGHTMARE REALM

1

Blood sprayed across my face, but the creature kept moving.

'Run all you like, you're not getting out of here alive!'

A panting noise at my side let me know that David had caught up to me. He looked at my clenched fists spitting arcs of magical energy from my knuckles, saw the gore covering my face.

'Here,' he said. 'Have a wet wipe.'

'Maybe later,' I replied.

'It's lemon scented...'

In the short time I'd known Detective David Tyler I'd become used to his sense of humour and the way he used it most during bad situations.

This was a bad situation.

We were chasing down a monster that ate and replaced family dogs. If that doesn't sound so bad, just wait until you hear the rest.

This creature—despite looking like an eight-foot-tall skinned orangutan when not disguised—sits in your home being fed and petted like loyal old Rover, panting and wagging its tail, and then, once it's nice and settled, it gets to work. The creature, known to the Uncanny as a "best fiend", for hopefully obvious reasons, secretes a noxious gas. The gas is invisible and gives off no smell, but has a very particular effect on those within its household.

It gets them pissed off.

The family begins to turn on each other. Old grievances sting anew. New grievances are given fire. Even made-up resentments will arise; anything to stoke the toxic feelings and make the formerly happy family scream and shout at one another.

And then worse. Much, much worse.

Someone, at some point, will be pushed over the edge. Maybe it will be the father, it often is. It might even be the youngest daughter, braces still on her teeth. The best fiend will sit, quivering, in the corner of the room, pumping out more and more of its gas, until finally one family member creeps up on another, kitchen knife in hand. A rolling pin. A pillow to force over a sleeping face. A match and something flammable.

The family will be found—what's left of them—and their neighbours would be shocked and tell the papers that they seemed so happy. So content. Such a nice household.

No one will pay any mind to the family pet sat on the pavement, watching as the police arrive, the fire brigade, the TV news. Not even when it wag-wag-wags its tail and takes off down the street.

So why does the best fiend do all of this? Apart from being a complete bastard of a monster? There are a few theories on that, the most popular being that it somehow feeds on unrest. On anger, and pain, and fury. It sits on the edge of things, a raw pink nightmare, soaking up every shout, every narrowed eye, every dark thought that bubbles and brews in its presence. Drinks it all in until the family are dead and its belly is full, and then off it goes to sleep it off for a few years, before waking up and seeking a new family to destroy.

Well, not this time.

This time I'd received a tip-off about one of the best fiend's hibernating spots, and had arrived just as it woke and twitched its way out of the sewers.

I thought it would be an easy job. Thought the creature would be dazed after its years of sleeping, its belly grumbling and defences down. Using the Amulet of Kanta—created to cleanse a house of such a creature—I would focus a spell on it, and hey presto, end of problem.

But no one warned me just how tough and vicious these things were.

So, yeah, it hadn't quite gone to plan, hence David and I running through the streets at night, me slinging spells at the fleeing thing as he puffed and panted by my side.

'Do you see it?' I asked.

'Three o'clock,' he replied.

I turned. 'I don't see it!'

'Other three o'clock, uh, nine o'clock,' he yelled, pointing in the other direction. 'Sorry, I'm more of a digital watch man.'

We ran.

I don't mind admitting I had a huge grin on my face as I readied for the attack, heart beating, body coursing with magic as I soaked in the area's natural reserves. This was what I did. What I was created for. To hunt monsters and keep the normals of London safe from the worst the Uncanny world had to offer.

'Over there,' yelled David.

I followed his hand to see the best fiend pressed against a wall, desperately looking for a way out.

'It's run into a dead end,' said David. 'Not the brightest bulb, is it?'

I thought otherwise. This thing had—at a conservative estimate—six-hundred deaths to its name, spanning more than nine centuries. Whatever it was, it wasn't stupid.

I held out my hand as we approached the best fiend, and

David tossed me the amulet. The metal was cold but fizzed with energy, needling my skin like static.

Best fiends were catalogued centuries back by a warlock who had taken it upon himself to rid England of the vile creatures. Unfortunately, the monsters could withstand a great deal of magic, which allowed them to escape even the most accomplished magicians. It would sometimes take six or seven concentrated assaults to see the things off, so the warlock went to his workshop and created the Amulet of Kanta: a tool fashioned from the remains of one of the creatures and designed specifically to combat the best fiend problem. Instead of focusing his magic on the creature itself, the magician would focus his spell into the amulet, which would redirect the spell towards the monster in a concentrated form, ending it once and for all. Don't ask me how it works exactly, or why it only works on best fiends. All I know is that, according to the warlock's instructions, it does the job.

David and I stood a few metres from the monster, its black eyes flicking every which way, desperate to find a way out. Except there was only one way out this time, and it wasn't going to like it.

I held out the amulet and concentrated. The surrounding magic flowed towards me as I placed the correct word form together and fed the result into the amulet.

It began to glow.

Dimly at first, then brighter, and brighter still, until it hurt to even look at the thing, though it remained cold in my hand.

I think the best fiend screamed. I hope it did. Hope it recognised the tool in my hand, burning fiercely, and knew what was about to happen.

'Goodbye,' I said, and the amulet unleashed the intensified power.

It surged in red and blue molten lines of furious energy that smashed into the creature, pinning it to the brick wall, then coiling round and round, over and over, in ever-tightening circles.

And then the best fiend exploded.

I hurled myself to the side as blood and chunks of bone and flesh shot in my direction, landing with a jarring thump. I stood, smiling and wiping the gore from my face, sliding the empty amulet into the pocket of my leather jacket.

'Eat shit, monster.'

'Wh-wha...?'

I looked down to see David looking up at me, dazed and laid flat.

'What happened?'

'When the monster exploded a chunk of it hit you and knocked you out.'

'Oh. Which bit?'

'A big wedge of torso I think. Mostly stomach.'

David nodded. 'Okay. Well, it's probably about time to get drunk then, right?'

I smiled. 'Oh, yes.'

2

'Fill these up if you would, Lenny,' said David, sliding two empty pint glasses across the bar.

'Don't I get a "please", Detective?' asked the giant barman and owner of The Beehive, the most popular Uncanny drinking hole in London.

'I'll put a little sugar on top if you throw in a bag of cheese and onion.'

Lenny grunted and went about his business.

My name is Stella Familiar and I belong to the London Coven. Once upon a time it was home to Kala, Trin, and Feal, the three most powerful witches in the country. Together we were, for want of a better term, the "police force" of the Uncanny in London. I was their familiar. The blunt tool they created to deliver warnings and—more often than not—beat the hell out of monsters. We were winning the battle until the most powerful creature I've ever come across, Mr. Trick, murdered them and left their bodies in bloody pieces.

'To another monstrous turd, successfully dispatched,' said David, raising his pint glass.

I reciprocated, then glugged a third of my drink in one go.

'Whoa, slow it down, booze hound.'

I answered with a burp.

'How are you still single?' asked David, rolling his eyes and digging into his bag of crisps.

It had been three months since I'd taken out Mr. Trick. Three months since I'd discovered the creature was hiding inside David. Getting rid of it had almost killed him. I'd had to tap into the dark realm to save his life. That was a big no-no. A witch's familiar using black magic? There'd be a price to pay for that, that was for sure, but right then I had other things on my mind. Since my coven had been destroyed I bore the responsibility of protecting all of London on my shoulders. The rightful protectors of the city were dead, and now here I was—their simple, blunt instrument—trying to fill their shoes. Was I up to the job? I wasn't a tenth of the Uncanny they were. I was just a creation, something they'd conjured into life sixty years ago to do their bidding. Was I even really a person? I had no parents, no birth certificate. One day I hadn't existed, and then the next I just had, exactly the same as I looked in the mirror today. No growth, no childhood, no ageing, always this. Always the same.

Then there was David.

The effects of my black magic aside, there was also the matter of him having unwillingly hosted the most powerful creature I'd ever met. I'd dealt with Mr. Trick. Killed him. At least I hoped I had. That's the thing with magic, with the Uncanny – nothing can ever be for sure. Maybe David would turn out to be a weak link. A toehold for Mr. Trick to cling on to and pull himself back into the world. Back into existence. There was no way of knowing for certain.

So many questions and dark thoughts fighting for space inside my mind. I'd never had to cope with such worry and responsibility before. Not like this. The only way I could keep my thoughts from going to dark places was chasing monsters and drinking beer.

'Penny for them,' said David, pouring the remaining crumbs from his crisp packet into his mouth.

'I was just wondering at what point tequila slammers might make an appearance.'

David was just about to answer when I felt the hairs on the back of my neck dance as the air behind me turned suddenly cold.

'Stella Familiar,' said a voice I didn't recognise. 'We meet at last.'

I swivelled on my bar stool to see a man in a black suit and tie. He had a face with a natural resting point set to a smirk.

'You know,' he went on, 'when my friend told me to seek out a familiar, I imagined a cackling imp sat on a witch's shoulder. But you? Well, you're much easier on the eye.'

'And who would you be?' I asked, polishing off my pint.

'Aw. Thought you might have heard of me. I'm Jake Fletcher, the ex-exorcist.'

'Ex-exorcist?' asked David.

'Very ex.'

'You can see him?' I asked David, surprised.

'Of course I can, I'm drunk, not blind drunk.'

'Yeah pal, I think the reason Stella here is surprised is that you're a normal, right?'

'Right.'

'Right,' said Jake. 'So how in the name of sweet Bruce Dickinson are you able to see a ghost?'

3

'David,' I said, 'maybe have another go at blinking.'

He looked at me, then back at Jake, and finally blinked, shaking his head.

'So, when you say a "ghost", what you actually mean is...?'

'A ghost,' replied Jake, 'As in dead as a dodo, pushing up daisies. I am an ex-man, but not the fruity superhero kind. They call me the Spectral Detective.'

'Right. So there's ghosts as well as monsters and witches and all the rest of it?'

'Afraid so,' I replied, then waved Lenny over to refill our pint pots. 'One for you?' I asked Jake, then remembered the whole ghost thing.

'I'd kill my own gran for a pint, but I'm not in my meat suit. Booze would pass right through me in this state, and I wouldn't want to make a mess of this disgusting, sticky floor.'

'Meat suit?' asked David, sipping from his fresh pint, his eyes scanning Jake up and down. 'Also, can you walk through walls?'

'I can, yeah. And by "meat suit", I mean the guy whose body I possess when I need to chat with you breathers.'

'You possess people?' I asked. 'That sounds like the sort of thing the coven would frown upon.'

'Not if they knew the prick I possessed, they wouldn't. Bloke used to bully me something rotten growing up. One time he handcuffed me to a radiator and stood back laughing while it turned red hot and cooked me.'

He rolled up his sleeve and showed me a scar on his wrist.

'Jesus,' said David. 'Sounds like a prize cock.'

'Still is, but now he helps me do my job, whether he likes it or not.'

'And what job is that?' I asked.

'Solving murders and showing dead people the way to the hereafter. So yeah, forgive me if I bend a little rule here or there.'

I stared at him hard, then shrugged. 'What do I care?' I lifted my fresh pint and blew on the head, making the foam splatter through Jake's phantom form.

'Very mature,' he sighed.

'Okay, I need pee-pee,' said David, getting up from his bar stool and weaving towards the Gents.

I turned back to Jake. 'Well? I take it there's a reason you came looking for me.'

'Something's happening, Stella. Something not good.'

'Could you be a bit more vague about it, please?'

Jake snorted. 'Funny. Listen, I just had to deal with a demon running wild around Camden. Not one of your higher plane demons—this was a low-level turd of a thing by comparison—but it waltzed into my manor like it owned the place. As though the barrier between here and there was tissue paper.'

I shrugged. 'Things slip through sometimes. It happens.' I lifted my glass of tequila and dropped it into my pint glass, watching it sink to the bottom as the two liquids began to mix.

'Look, Stella, I'm not a total amateur. Something's happening. Something bad. I can feel it in my bones.'

'You don't have any bones.'

'True, I feel it in my... whatever it is I'm made of.'

'With all due respect—'

'—None taken—'

'—You have no idea what you're talking about. I've been chasing monsters for sixty years. I clean up messes the likes of you would have no idea about. If anything was going on, I'd be the first to know.'

I took a sip of my new concoction and winced. It was good.

'Are you going to hear me out or just get bladdered?'

I smiled and took another swig.

'Something is happening in this city, Stella. It's like the stitches that hold everything together are starting to fray.'

'Oh, relax, will you? You're dead, put your feet up for an age or two, you've earned it.'

'Stella, this is serious—'

'No. It's not. I'm Stella Familiar of the London Coven. Dealing with evil is just a Tuesday for me. If anything comes my way—anything at all that threatens this city—I'll take care of it just fine. So thanks for the tip, *Jake*, but you're interrupting happy hour.'

I took another mouthful of my tequila beer and smiled as I felt the bar begin to sway.

'I've gotta say, I'm disappointed.' said Jake.

'I'm devastated. Don't let the door pass through you on your way out.'

'I heard you were a big deal. London's great protector. But here I am, and all I see is a stuck-up drunk.' He shook his head. 'See you around, Stella.'

'Hey—' I turned, but he'd already gone. Disappeared in the time it takes to blink. I snorted, then giggled, then wondered what I was laughing about, then giggled some more, enjoying the warm glow of booze spreading through my body.

'Ah,' said David, settling back on his stool, 'that may have been a contender for the world's longest piss. Hey, where'd Casper the Smirking Ghost get to?'

I dropped David's tequila glass into his pint pot. 'Less talk, more drink.'

4

The night air was cold as we staggered back to the coven. I pulled my leather jacket tight and leaned my head back, eyes closed, enjoying the sensation of the breeze buffeting against me.

'Whoa, there,' said David, yanking me out of the way of a lamp post I was about to collide with. He corrected my stagger and steered me on in a straight line. 'So, any idea why I can suddenly see ghosts?' he asked.

'Well, the thing is, ooh, look at that moon. Look how *big* it is. Big moon! Big-ishly big moon.'

I was off my face and had already coated one alleyway with the contents of my stomach before insisting we head to the nearest burger van for a refill. I may have been alive for sixty years, and The Beehive was the place I'd been inside more than any other building, my coven aside, but I wasn't what you'd call a drinker. At least not until a few months ago. Until Mr. Trick happened.

There was a clicking noise and my swimming eyes focused on David's snapping fingers.

'Here we go. Focus, Stella.'

'I'm not drunk,' I said, loud enough to turn the heads of some people at the far end of the street.

'Of course not, and neither am I. So, ghosts? How come I can see them?'

'Prolly... probably something to do with, you know, the bastard. Being inside you.'

'Mr. Trick?'

'That's the tosser. Such a tosser. Evil bastard tosser.'

I felt my eyelids begin to droop and shook it off.

'It's cool though, right?' asked David. 'It seems cool, being able to see ghosts.'

'Second shite. Sight. The Second Sight. Spooky vision eyes, woooooh!' I waggled my fingers in front of David's face until he swatted them away and I almost toppled backwards over a bag of rubbish.

'I wonder what else I can do. Maybe I can do magic. Or X-Ray vision. Or the ability to never have another hangover. Christ, I hope it's that last one.'

I laughed and turned to him, throwing my arms around his neck and hanging off him, looking up into his eyes. They were nice eyes. Had I noticed that before?

'You know, I like you. Being around. Around me. In front of me. And stuff.'

'Well, I like you too. Even if you have made me realise the world is a terrifying place and full of things that want to kill me.'

'You're welcome,' I told him.

'You never said.'

'Never said what?'

'Jake, the ghost, was there any reason he came looking for you?'

'Pfft, just, you know, ghost worries. Ghost things. Thought he knew more than me about what was going on. Bit big-headed.'

As I hung from David's neck, he bent closer and closer until

I could feel his breath against my mouth. Our eyes locked and I felt my stomach begin to do a strangle-swirl thing, and wondered if I was going to throw up again.

David pulled me up and I let go of him, staggering back a step.

'Okay, here we are,' said David, and I turned to see the blind alley opening up before me. It led to the coven, my home. The London Coven, like The Beehive, sits at the end of a blind alley, so-called because, generally, only Uncanny people can see them. The rest of London, the normals, they walk past and never see them. Never see the vast array of hidden streets that thread through their world.

'Okay,' I said, 'bed is calling.'

I looked back to David, unsure what it was I was hoping he might say. He looked at me, smiled, then nodded.

'Yup, better, you know... better head off home. I've got a shift tomorrow and something tells me I'm going to feel like death.'

He turned and headed off down the street. I watched him walk away until he turned out of sight, vaguely disappointed in some way I couldn't quite pin down.

I shrugged and stumbled up the blind alley.

5

I rarely have good dreams these days, and that night was no different. My witches were there of course, Kala, Trin and Feal. I would talk to them and pretend it wasn't just a dream for a while, then Mr. Trick would appear, and nothing good would happen after that.

'They screamed, Stella. Screamed.'

I woke up gripping the bed sheets, the room tilting as my hangover made itself known.

'Oh shit....'

I lurched to my side and heard the splatter hit home in the bucket I'd placed there the night previous. I'd done this enough times over the last few months to know I'd need it, even when I got home blind drunk past midnight.

I flopped back and stared at the ceiling as an image of last night's events flashed through my mind. I had my arms around David, looking up into his eyes. His breath against mine, moving closer and—

Oh, Christ, no. No, no, no.

I stood up and paced the room, feeling something I hadn't experienced in my entire sixty years of life. I was mortified.

Had I really made a pass at David? No. No, he wouldn't

think that. Nothing had even happened, not really, I was just a drunk woman hanging off his neck, that's all. So what if our eyes had locked for longer than normal and our lips had been seconds away from touching? Drunk people do stupid things, and he probably, hopefully, didn't notice anything anyway.

I left my room and headed to the kitchen, pouring myself a tall glass of cold water, downing it, then doing the same twice more.

I'm a familiar, I'm not created to have romantic relationships, or even have romantic thoughts, let alone sexual ones. I don't have time for that kind of thing. Making sure people don't get their heads bitten off by monsters takes up a lot of your time. A partner? Love, marriage, kids? That stuff just wasn't on the cards for me.

Even if I tried to ignore all of that and "date" someone, there was the unavoidable fact that I didn't age. I've lived sixty years and looked the same for all of them. Other people grow old and die, but not me. I'll die alone and look just the same as the day I was born.

I stood and cursed at myself, pushing the thoughts aside. It was stupid, it was impossible, it wasn't right. Just a silly drunken moment that wouldn't be repeated.

I turned my mind to Jake instead; the ghost. I'd fobbed him off in The Beehive, ignored his warning, but it was clear he was genuinely worried about something, even if I'd been too drunk to pay him attention at the time.

Before Mr. Trick, if someone had appeared with a warning like that, I would have taken in everything he had to say and reported it back to my witches. But the witches were dead and gone, so there was no one left to report back to. There was only me, and I didn't have a clue what I was doing. Not really. I was making it up as I went along. Waking up every morning to a cold, empty coven and running out the door, looking for danger to punch in the face. Anything to keep me busy, to stop the fear getting on top of me and prove to myself and all of the

Uncanny that I had what it took to replace my masters. To show that I was good enough. That London would be safe in my hands. That I wasn't just some abandoned tool, collecting dust after the craftsmen left the workshop.

A fellow Uncanny had come to me looking for help, with a warning, and I'd brushed him aside like he wasn't worth my time. But what was I supposed to do with Jake's information anyway? *Something is happening. Something.* That's what he'd said, but what use is that? Being told *something* might be happening is about as much use as not being told at all. There were no specifics there to look into. No leads to follow.

I wished my masters were with me, still. They'd know what to do. They'd know what I should be doing next. No need for thinking on my part, just a job given. A task to execute. A wall to run through.

Christ, life had been simple in those days.

My phone began to vibrate on the kitchen table, snapping me out of my dreary thoughts. I looked over to see David's name. I pulled away from it like it might nip me, then shook my head. I was being stupid. It was just the booze, that's all. Nothing had happened between me and David. Nothing *could* happen.

I grabbed the phone and hit answer.

'What is it?'

'And a good morning to you, Stella. How's the head this morning?'

'Fine,' I replied, ignoring the ice pick lodged in one of my frontal lobes.

'Good,' he said, 'because I've got something that's going to be right up your alley.'

Given where my mind had been, I could only hope he was talking about a new case.

6

I strode into Ealing Hospital, the automatic doors sighing behind me as they closed, cutting dead the wind from outside.

'Six kids?'

'Yup, six kids; they all slipped into comas for no good reason on the same night. Sounds like our kind of thing, right?'

I went over our phone conversation again, trying to come up with a working theory as to what might have happened. A curse? Some sort of sleeping spell? Maybe it was just a coincidence. Yeah, six kids slip into a coma on the same night, totally could be a coincidence. Nice one, Stella.

I marched to the front desk where David was stood. He turned from a uniformed officer he was talking to and smiled, waving. I realised I was smiling back, but managed to stop myself from returning the wave.

'Pretty weird stuff, am I right?'

I grunted and nodded.

'Christ, you sound how I feel. Come on, I'll take you upstairs for a nose. They've put them all in the same room.'

As the lift hummed to a stop and the doors slid open I felt the muscles in my neck tense. David stepped into the corridor and out of view, then leaned back with a quizzical look on his face.

'You coming or just gonna hang out in the lift? I mean, it's a nice lift, as far as lifts go, but come on, chop-chop.'

He ducked back out of view and I followed, turning sideways to slip through the closing lift doors.

Something was wrong with the magic in the air.

Magic is everywhere. It's not something that we Uncanny just call upon, or have burning inside of us; the entire planet, every street, every rock, every car, naturally emits a sort of background magic. I and others like me can see it, washing around us in great, colourful waves. We draw upon it, feed upon it. Cast spells using the power we pull into ourselves. And now, as I walked through the wash of this floor's magic, I could sense something was... off. I didn't know what it was, but it put me on edge. A taste in the air that I couldn't place, but knew shouldn't be there.

'What is it?' asked David, looking back at me, his hand on the door to one of the rooms.

'Not sure. Maybe nothing. Maybe something.'

'Maybe something bad?'

I nodded. 'Let's take a look at these kids.'

I followed David into the room.

Inside were six beds, each filled with a child, flat on their backs, eyes closed, machines by their sides beep-beep-beeping along to the rhythm of their heartbeats.

'Bit creepy, right?' said David.

'Just a bit.'

It was worse in here, that sense of something being wrong. It was apparent right away that something Uncanny had happened to these kids.

'They all look the same age,' I said.

'That's because they are. All twelve years old, and all from a local school.'

'The same school?'

'Not just the same school, the same year and the same class. Miss Henshaw's, to be specific.'

'So, six kids, all from the same class, all went to bed last night like nothing was wrong.'

'Uh-huh, and none of them woke up again. Well, not yet.'

I moved to the nearest bed and looked down at the face of the child laid within it. She was still, face calm, red hair splashed across the pillow. You could barely tell she was breathing. If it wasn't for the beep of her heart monitor, you'd think she'd already slipped away.

But there was something else to see.

To almost see.

I went from one bed to the next, from one slumbering child to the next.

'What is it? What're you seeing, Stella?'

'I'm not sure.'

I squinted and turned my head to try catching something in the corner of my eye. Tried reaching out with my senses to see if they'd pick up anything being purposefully hidden from me.

'There's something... wrong with them,' I said.

'Well, yeah, I put that together myself, Columbo.'

'No, I mean... I'm not sure. It's like I can almost see something. A dark fuzz, a slight shadow sitting above each of them. Only I can't actually see it. Like I almost see it in the corner of my eye, but I don't. It's more that I sense it. Taste it in the magic surrounding each bed.'

'Okay, well, what d'you think that means?'

'It means that something dark has taken these children, and if we don't find out what, none of them will ever open their eyes again.'

7

The first child, the one with the red hair, was called Lucy. She lived in a nice three bedroom house on Clitherow Avenue, a two minute walk from the nearest tube station.

Her mother let us in, David smiling a comforting smile and showing her his badge.

'I've just stopped back to have a shower,' she explained, apologetically, as though we might judge her for not being at the hospital. Was that suspicious? Shouldn't she be there, at the hospital, sat in the waiting room with the rest of the terrified parents?

'That's okay, Miss Callow,' said David. 'We just wondered if we could take a look at Lucy's room.'

She nodded, hands worrying at the cloth of her shirt, then led us upstairs. Lucy's bedroom door was decorated with a sticker that pictured her name written in flower petals. Miss Callow's hand dithered on the handle.

'It's okay,' said David, his voice soothing. He was used to situations like this. 'We can take it from here, Miss Callow. You leave us to it and go take that shower.'

Her mouth twitched momentarily into a smile. 'She always

got up early. That's why I... I shouted up. Then knocked on the door. Then stood over her, nudged her, then shook and shouted. She just wouldn't wake up. I thought she was... at first, you know? Thought she must be, because why wouldn't you wake up if someone was stood right over you? Shaking and shouting at you? Why won't she wake up, Detective? Why won't my Lucy wake up?'

Tears were pouring down her cheeks, but as David went to comfort her she turned away and headed off down the corridor towards the bathroom.

'Okay,' he said, 'let's take a look.'

He opened the door to Lucy's room and stepped inside. I lingered and looked down the hallway to where Miss Callow had disappeared. I heard the shower start to blast, loud enough to almost cover her sobs. Almost. That deep-down love that a parent has for a child, was that what my witches had for me? Had they thought of me like that, or was I nothing more than a device to them? Something they fashioned from dirt, spit, and magic to make their job easier.

'Oi,' said David, popping his head back out of the bedroom, 'you coming in, or what?'

I stepped into Lucy's room, leaving her mother's tortured tears behind.

The room was beyond neat; even the items on the dresser were placed just so. Posters of grinning young men covered the walls.

'Which one's your favourite, then?' asked David pointing to a poster featuring four non-threatening males, none of whom looked as though their face had known the feel of a razor.

'What are they?'

'*What are they?*' he parroted, rolling his eyes. 'You know, sometimes you really do sound like a sixty-year-old.'

'That is my age.'

'Well, yeah, but... look, never mind.'

Lucy's room had a heady scent to it. A mixture of clashing

smells. Chemical, flowery smells from a variety of sprays and creams and fat, multi-coloured candles.

'Lucy's mother,' I said. 'Do you think there's anything in that?'

'What?' asked David. 'You think she might be some sort of evil witch? Or a monster pretending to be Lucy's mum?'

'Well, no, I don't think so. I didn't sense anything off about her, at least not like that. But isn't it a bit weird that she's already left her daughter alone at the hospital?'

'Maybe, but I wouldn't read too much into that. This sort of thing hits people in different ways. I've had husbands who were just informed their spouse had been murdered go into work the same day. Like they've gone into autopilot, going through the motions of their day like everything was just fine. I can understand her wanting to get out of that hospital and take a shower. To feel vaguely human for a minute.'

To feel vaguely human. I understood the appeal, if not the sensation.

I nodded and looked around the room, reaching out with my senses as David began looking through Lucy's drawers.

'You know, I'm not exactly sure what you're hoping to find,' he said. 'Unless there's an empty can of magical sleeping gas under the bed.' He laughed, then looked at the bed for a few seconds. He stepped over, knelt down, lifted the dangling duvet and looked under the bed. He let the duvet drop and turned to me. 'No gas can.'

'Nothing in the air either. Not like at the hospital.'

There was no strange signature to the room's magic. No hints of the dark shadows I could almost see back at the room full of sleeping children.

David sighed and sat on the small, single mattress, the springs creaking as it adjusted to his weight. 'Okay, so we've got six kids from the same class falling into comas on the same night. And all of them zonked out after they got into bed. None of them fell face-first into their dinner, or collapsed in front of the TV. They all went to bed like normal, and the first time anyone knew something was up was when they didn't get up for school the next morning.'

'And now they all have something over them. Something I can't quite see.'

'Right. So...?'

'I'm not sure.'

David sighed again and leaned back, one hand resting on the pillow. He stopped and turned towards it.

'What is it?'

'I heard a crinkle.' He lifted the pillow, there was a piece of paper folded underneath. He looked up at me, one eyebrow raised.

'Could be something,' I said.

'Yeah, or it could just be a love note Timmy had Gina pass Lucy during Chemistry.'

There were just three words on the piece of paper, neatly written with red biro in flowing, joined-up handwriting.

'Well?' asked David. 'Don't keep me in suspenders, what does it say?'

I handed him the piece of paper.

It said *Wake No More*.

8

We checked a few of the other kids' bedrooms but didn't find any other notes. I'd wondered if the note under Lucy's pillow held some sort of curse. That whoever rested their head on it slipped into a coma. Written words can be infused with magic and used like booby traps. Yet the lack of notes in any of the other bedrooms quickly derailed that idea.

Still, it was too strange a coincidence to dismiss, so as David left to head back to the hospital, I made my way home, to the coven, the note stored safely in my pocket.

'Wake no more,' I said, as I walked down the blind alley that led to the coven door. I rolled the words around my mouth to see if any residual Uncanny taste or images emerged just from my saying them, but there was nothing.

I entered the coven and made straight for the main room, throwing my leather jacket over the back of a rocking chair and causing it to creak back and forth noisily before settling into silence again. I remembered how much that *creak-creak-creak* would drill into my head when I was having a bad day. Trin, one of my witches, moving back and forth, a tireless piston, the sound of the chair accompanied by the *click-clack* of her knitting needles as she created an endless supply of scarves, sweaters, and gloves.

Some nights, Trin didn't go to bed at all, and I'd lay awake in bed, squashing earplugs in to try and cut out the noise that seemed so enormous in the dead of the night.

Now I missed that noise.

Sometimes I even lay awake, unable to sleep, because I *couldn't* hear it.

I pulled the note from my pocket and opened it to reveal the neatly-penned words.

Wake No More.

Nothing else. Just one piece of paper with those three words written dead in the centre.

I grabbed a piece of chalk and crouched down on one knee, sketching a simple pentagram shape on the one-metre square piece of black slate fixed to the floor in front of the open fireplace (the fireplace was rarely used, the coven has central heating. We're not savages). Great waves of power washed towards me as I raised both hands above my head and acted as a focal point for the magic in the room. I placed the correct words together in my mind, then pushed my open palms towards the chalk pentagram, infusing it with power. The lines glowed red for a heartbeat, then went back to normal.

I placed the note, open with the words visible, at the centre of the pentagram, then kneeled before it, hands on my thighs, head bowed, eyes closed.

The light in the room dimmed, though I hadn't turned them off. It was the magic, responding to my request. My request to explore, to investigate, to interrogate. I was pushing everything I could think of into the piece of paper, sat in its place of focus within the chalk pentagram. Demanding the power within the London Coven reveal something about the note, about the words. To reveal the curse that had been placed upon it.

I came at the problem from every direction I could think of.

Used any spell or magical command that seemed useful, but they all came up with a big fat nothing.

As far as I could tell, the paper wasn't infused with any magic at all.

The words written upon it weren't cursed.

The ink wasn't laced with anything that might seep out and place a child in a coma after they closed their eyes.

It was just an ordinary piece of paper that Lucy had written three words on.

I swore and sat with a thud on the floor, glaring at the note.

It *must* mean something. I could feel it. This wasn't just some random coincidence. The piece of paper meant something. The words meant something. I just didn't see the whole picture yet.

'Is he here?' I asked.

Lenny nodded and gestured to a far corner of The Beehive. Razor was hunched at a table alone, half hidden in shadow.

'Can I get you another of what you had last night, Stella?' he asked.

I remembered how I felt waking that morning, pictured myself a little too close to Detective David Tyler's lips the previous evening, and shook my head.

I made my way over to Razor and sat down on the stool opposite him.

'Familiar,' he spat.

The last time I'd spoken to Razor I'd left him in a bloody heap on the toilet floor, but that was months ago. Now fresh bruises patterned his face. By the looks of things, someone else had dealt him a beating, and recently.

'You've been in the wars, there, friend,' I said. 'Care to talk about it?'

He glared at me. 'What do you want? Did you come here to attack me again?'

I smiled. 'No, not this time,' I replied.

'Oh, it must be my birthday. Hip-hip-hooray.' He sneered, exposing two rows of sharp, yellowed teeth.

Razor was an eaves: a low-level Uncanny that specialised in knowing things. In skulking around and picking up secrets to pass on for a price. In the case of an eaves, the price is a dose of magic they feast upon. Despite being Uncanny, eaves don't have access to magic in the same way as I do, but they crave its nourishment. If you want information about something, there's a good chance the likes of Razor know it.

I slid Lucy's note across the table towards him. He glanced down, then back up. 'And? What's this then?'

'You tell me.'

'It's a piece of paper, Familiar. I'll take my fee now.'

'Funny.'

He picked up the paper with the ragged nails of his cigarette-stained fingers and sniffed it.

'Where'd you get it?'

'From under a kid's pillow. She went to sleep and never woke up.'

'Aw, you're going to make me cry, here.'

I snatched the piece of paper from his dirty digits and stuffed it into my jacket pocket.

'"Wake No More",' I said. 'What does that mean to you? Have you heard the words used before? As a hex, as anything at all?'

'Can't say I have.'

'Well, thanks, Razor, you've been a big help.'

I stood and began to make my way to the exit, frustrated to arrive at another dead end. I still wasn't used to actually *investigating*. I'd been created to fight, not to gather intel.

'Hey, Familiar.'

'What?' I sighed, half-turning back to him.

'Don't think I've just forgiven you for what you did to me. That was over the mark.'

Was Razor really trying to threaten me? I twitched in his direction and he shrank back into the shadows.

'That's what I thought.'

I turned my back on him and walked out of The Beehive, feeling my phone vibrate in my pocket. I pulled it out. It was David.

'Anything new?' I asked.

'You know, you really need to work on your greetings. Most people go with a friendly "hello".'

'Get to it,' I replied.

'That note we found... I think I might have some new info on it.'

9

The flat belonged to Angie Tyler, David's sister. I realised then that I hadn't even known he had a sister. To me he was just David. A detective in the police force and a friend, and that was all... at least until we got drunk the other night and... no, I didn't even want to think about that.

Angie lived in a terraced house in Acton, West London. The Victorian house had been split into two dwellings, with Angie and her daughter taking up the bottom floor.

Angie opened the door. She was in her mid-thirties with a riot of dyed-blonde curls that she'd attempted to tame with various clips and bands. She didn't remind me of David at all.

'You Stella, then?' she asked.

'Yep.'

'Let her through, Ange,' came David's voice from inside.

I followed her through into the front room. The TV was on, halfway through an episode of *Murder, She Wrote*.

'There she is. Hey, Batman,' said David, hopping up off the couch.

'Robin,' I replied, nodding in his direction.

'What?' said Angie.

'Oh, inside joke, sis', never mind.'

'Right. I'll put the kettle on then.'

As she left the room, David turned to me, his eyes widening momentarily. 'Not one for the big chucks and yucks, my sister.'

'I didn't know you had a sister.'

'I didn't know myself until about six years back. Turned out my dad had been a bit of a twat before I was born and got another woman pregnant. Angie turned up on my doorstep one weekend, telling me she was my half-sister.'

That explained the lack of family resemblance. She must take after her mother.

'Okay, so why am I meeting your sister?'

Amy was thirteen years old and had inherited her mother's mess of thick curls, though hers were dyed bright purple.

She looked up from fiddling on her phone as we entered her room, and stood sharply from the edge of her bed, as if we'd just caught her doing something embarrassing. 'Oi, Uncle Dave, heard of knocking, yeah?'

'Why, what were you doing?'

'Nothing,' she said, her face flushing.

'You know I'm a police officer? Family or not I will cuff you and take you to the station, isn't that right, Stella?'

'Um. Yes. That is right.'

Amy rolled her eyes, but then broke into a giggle. She obviously had more of a sense of humour than her mother.

'Stella Familiar, this is my awesome niece, Amy.'

'Familiar? What kind of a second name is Familiar?' she asked, arching a brow.

'Well, it's the kind of second name I have,' I replied.

Amy looked to David, who, judging by the grin plastered across his face, was enjoying this awkward little conversation.

'Okay,' said David, 'tell Stella what you told me.'

'Which bit?'

'The whole bit.'

Amy sighed and sat back on the edge of her bed, looking down at her phone and sweeping her thumb across it to absent-mindedly scan Facebook.

'It was just after what happened to all those kids. On the news. Not waking up and that.'

She shifted uncomfortably.

'Go on,' David prompted.

'Well, there's this rhyme and stuff that we all know at school, a sort of dare thing, and it's scary even though it's stupid. I know it's stupid, I'm thirteen, I'm not a kid.' Her face flushed again with a mix of embarrassment and anger.

'You're very grown up,' said David. 'Go on.'

'Like I say, there's this rhyme that kids at school started sharing. And then I heard on the news about the kids going to bed and not waking up, and Uncle Dave came over for lunch and he's talking to Mum about it all. Mentions this note he found under one of the kid's pillows—'

'"Wake No More",' I said.

Amy nodded and looked at her knees, then back up at me, her eyes saucer-like. 'I said the rhyme. I was trying to show Carly Fisher I wasn't a baby, so I said it. Said it like eight times, because I'm not a kid, and now, what happens if I go to sleep? Will I wake up again? Am I gonna die?'

A tear escaped her eye and ran down her cheek. David sat next to her and put his arm around her shoulder.

'Hey, Ames, it's okay. You did the right thing telling me, because you know what bad things hate? Me and Stella over there. Nothing bad is going to happen to you, you have my word. Okay?'

She looked up to him and sniffed, wiping away the tears with the back of her sleeve, and nodding. 'You promise for real?'

'For real.'

'Amy,' I said, 'What happens if you say the rhyme? What are you all scared of?'

'It's just stupid, dumb kid stuff, that's all. It's just, the word is, if you say the rhyme out loud, it will come for you when you sleep. It'll find you in your dreams and you'll never wake up again.'

Wake No More.

'What's the rhyme, Amy?' I asked.

'I don't wanna say it out loud again. It's just, it gets under your skin. So Uncle David asked me to write it down instead.'

She stood and made her way over to her little dresser table and picked up a piece of paper. She held it away from her, pinched between two fingers as she walked back to me, like she was afraid it would bite her if she held it any closer.

As I took the note, she gave a slight shudder of relief and quickly made her way to the other side of David, hiding behind him.

The first line of the note was familiar, the rest was new...

Wake no more
Said nobody's child
Kicked and beaten
Turned mean and wild

Wake no more
Said the fearful small
For now I am here
To punish you all.

10

David and Amy talked with Angie for a while as I sat on the couch and sipped my tea, re-reading the rhyme over and over as Jessica Fletcher taught the police of Cabot Cove how to solve a murder.

'For now I am here, to punish you all,' I said under my breath.

The words had weight. On paper, they were nothing, just ink. But as I spoke them, I could feel the darkness that existed within them. Feel the magical shapes they cut in the air around me.

A curse activated by being spoken out loud.

The shapes of the words were strange and made no sense to me. But I could feel things in them. Feel dread. And terror. It was like I could hear a small voice, crying out in pain, at the back of my head. Something alone and terrified and angry. No, not angry, *furious*. A white hot, blind fury.

And there was something else too.

A hunger.

A relentless need to go on and on and on. This wasn't some one-time phenomenon. Six kids went to bed the same night and never woke up, but that was just the beginning. The opening act.

I looked down at the piece of paper again and muttered the rhyme under my breath so only I could hear it. I felt the mess of feelings wash around me again...

More, more, more, never enough, never, never, never—

'For now I am here, to punish you all.'

All.

The children of London were in danger. Every single one of them.

Amy had spoken the rhyme out loud, so there was no way we could leave her behind. The only place she could be was with us, even if that meant filling her in more on the nature of what was happening. Filling her in a bit about me and about the Uncanny. The alternative was leaving her behind and vulnerable to whatever it was that was behind this... this bewitchment.

'She's gonna stay with me for a few days,' David explained to Amy's mum. 'A little uncle-niece bonding time, isn't that right, Amy?'

Amy nodded, looking guilty as hell. Angie shrugged and made sure her daughter packed a bag with enough clothes to last a few days.

'She was a bit easy to convince,' I said later, as the Tube train roared and rocked.

'She's okay. She wants us to have a close relationship, so any time I wanna drop in, or take Amy out, she's all for it. I can't say I feel great about lying to her, though.'

'What would you have told her?' I asked. 'That her daughter might be prey to some malevolent sleep curse? She'd have thought we were crazy.'

'I know, but still. Got a little guilt-seed in my belly.'

'The worst thing we could have done was leave her behind, David. Trust me. I've studied the poem. I've *felt* it. There's something going on with the words when they're all together. Something awful living inside of it. And Amy's spoken them out loud.'

I looked over to Amy, stood holding on to a bar, swaying back and forth, earbuds in and listening to music through her phone. She was just a kid. A little girl who wanted to listen to music, scowl at her mum, and talk nonsense with her friends on the internet. And now she was in the sights of something I couldn't quite see.

I scrunched up the note that contained the full poem, hand in my pocket, and hoped we could come up with something before Amy fell to sleep.

11

'You two are proper mad,' said Amy, as we tried to convince her to walk into a brick wall.

'Go ahead,' said David, 'Just walk right ahead and the wall will disappear, honest.' He looked up at me, grinning, obviously happy to be on the other side of this for once.

To someone like Amy—a normal—there was no alleyway, just a brick wall. That's how it had looked to David, too, until I opened his eyes.

'Go on then, Magic Lady, do your thang,' said David, rubbing his hands together.

'You're enjoying this a bit too much,' I said.

'What can I say? Small pleasures for small minds,' he replied, winking.

I smiled, shaking my head, and pushed a spell towards Amy.

'See,' I said.

Amy began to blink in surprise. 'Uh. No. What? Where did that—?' She pointed at the now visible blind alley, her mouth agape.

'Oh, you see the massive opening to the obviously there alleyway now, eh?' said David, and put his arm around her, leading her forwards. 'Come on kiddo, things are only going to get weirder from here.'

Minutes later, we were sat around the kitchen table, each cradling a cup of tea.

'Um. What?' said Amy.

'Stella here is a familiar.'

'A witch's familiar?' she asked.

'You know about that stuff?' I asked.

'Well, yeah. My mate Jenna, she's well into, like, Wicca and the supernatural and all that stuff. Said she saw a ghost once. But she also said she kissed Tom Bellow, and we all know she was chatting shit there.'

'Whoa, young lady, less of the no-no words, thank you,' said David.

'No-no words? How old *are* you?' replied Amy, folding her arms.

David laughed, and Amy joined in. It was obvious they had a pretty good bond together, even if he'd only known her for a few years.

'So, you believe me?' I asked.

Amy turned and looked me up and down. 'Sure, why not. If Uncle Dave says you're a witch's familiar, then that's what you are. And that alleyway definitely wasn't there until, you know, suddenly it was. So that seems like some real straight-up, legit magic to me.'

'Well, you've taken to the idea a lot quicker than your uncle,' I replied. 'He threw up.'

'Oi! I had just been attacked by a demonically possessed cafe owner.'

Amy giggled.

'So, are you magic and that, too, Uncle Dave?'

'No. Well, I don't think so. I can see ghosts, though.'

'Wow! Cool.'

David swagged his head back and forth. 'Yeah, I suppose so. No biggie.'

'So, you two do what? Solve magic crimes stuff, yeah?'

'That's right,' said David.

'Well, that is pretty cool.'

I smiled. 'I suppose so.'

I pulled the note with the rhyme on it out of my jacket pocket and placed it on the table. Amy sat back in her chair as though it was radioactive.

'So, when did you first hear this rhyme?' I asked.

'Not sure,' she replied.

'Can you think back?' asked David. 'Could be important.'

She shook her head. 'No, it's just... it's been going round the playground for a few weeks. Someone had it written down and it was being passed around everywhere. The rumour was if you said it out loud the thing would get you in your sleep. That you'd never wake up. We were all, you know, joking about it. Trying to get each other to say it out loud. Pretend like we weren't scared of some stupid rhyme.'

Amy's hands were holding tight to each other, fingers interlocked, knuckles white.

'Look,' she said, 'I'm not that small anymore, but I still get scared of the dark sometimes. Scared of waking up in the middle of the night and being on my own. I suppose... I suppose I'm not that grown up. Not really. You must remember what that feels like? When you were a kid?'

'I was never a child,' I replied.

'What? That's stupid, everyone was little once.'

'Not me. I was born like this.'

'For real?'

'Yep,' said David. 'She's a bit of a freak, this one.'

'So, like, you never had a childhood?'

'Well, no. No, I didn't.'

'Oh. That's sort of sad.'

I shifted in my chair uncomfortably, then lifted my cup to take a swig.

'Okay, Ames,' said David, 'go on.'

She smiled weakly at him and nodded. 'Okay. Well, I didn't believe in it. In the rhyme and the curse and stuff. Well, I did sort of, but not really. But when I said the words… it's like I felt something, you know? Like a bit of ice was suddenly at the centre of me. And then I heard about all those kids not waking up, and I just sort of knew they'd said the rhyme. I just knew.'

David placed a hand on her arm. 'That's okay. That's enough. You did good, Ames.'

She flashed a pained, tight-lipped smile at him and nodded, her eyes a little too wide.

'Is that gonna happen to me, Uncle Dave? When I go to sleep tonight am I gonna get taken by the thing and never wake up?'

'Hey, come on,' he took her head on his shoulder and stroked her arm as her body racked with sobs. 'Don't worry about anything, okay Trust me. The best thing you could have done is tell me and the magic lady over there. We kick monster butts for a living, all right? Nothing and nobody is gonna lay a hand on my family, you hear me?'

She sat up, snotty and sniffing, wiping the tears away and nodding. 'You definitely promise?'

'Definitely.'

She seemed a little relieved by that and excused herself to go and use the toilet.

'You know, you shouldn't have done that,' I said.

'Shouldn't have done what?' David asked.

'Promised her. We don't know what's going on. Not yet. All I know is it's something very, very bad, and none of them are safe. Not Amy, not any of them.'

'You'll figure it out,' he replied. 'Got faith in you, Magic Lady.'

It was a good thing someone did.

12

'So, any ideas?' asked David.

We were sat in the coven's common room, staring at the slate tile I'd drawn the pentagram on. Amy was upstairs in one of the spare rooms, settling in. The coven has eight different bedrooms, though only four of them had ever been used in the sixty years I'd been living there: three of them by my witches, one by me. I'm still not sure why the other four were needed. Why they hadn't converted them or used a spell to get rid of them.

'Oi, daydream believer,' said David, clicking his fingers. 'I said, any ideas?'

'One or two,' I replied.

'I don't suppose we're going to be able to just, you know, find the thing, punch it in the kisser and toss it into a cell? Because that would be just smashing.'

'Afraid not.'

'You're a real dream-crusher, Stella. So what do we do?'

'Well, it's obviously got it in for kids. Whatever it is, it wants to harm them. It's not interested in adults, it just wants to take their children. Wants to make them scared. A spooky rhyme, an urban legend, a monster who comes for you in your dreams. It's all designed to freak out kids.'

'Not just kids, I have a touch of the willies myself.'

We sat in silence for a minute or two as we contemplated the shit we were in.

'Oh, I didn't bring a toothbrush,' said David.

'What? Why would you need a toothbrush?' I said, face flushing, my thoughts drifting back to the stupid, drunken, almost... what? Kiss?

'Well, Amy is staying over, so I'm staying over. We can have a slumber party, minus the slumber: me and you two gals. What d'you say? Hair-braiding, pillow fights, *Dirty Dancing* on the telly...'

I arched an eyebrow. 'We're doing this to protect your niece, not to have a party.' I smiled. 'Besides, I'd murder you in a pillow fight.'

We took it in turns to sit up with Amy. I'd placed a simple alertness spell on her, to stop her falling asleep, but someone still had to be with her at all times. Just to make sure. Also, just to keep the terrified teen company.

The London Coven is fierce with magic. David and Amy couldn't see it, but to me it's like living inside of a dry ocean. Multi-coloured waves roll around me the whole time, ebbing and flowing, crashing off the walls. It should be a safe place for Amy. *Should be.*

Two things bothered me. One: I didn't know what the hell was going on. That was a big one. I didn't know what sort of magical, dark force was behind that rhyme. Behind the kids falling asleep and slipping into comas. Who knew how strong it was? Was it strong enough to seep into this place? If Amy were to close her eyes and let sleep take her, would she ever wake up again?

Then there was what happened three months earlier. Mr. Trick. My witches, murdered in their own seat of power. Was this place really as safe as I thought it was? I couldn't assume anything anymore.

I was on first watch and asked her if she'd like to see a film to eat up a few night-hours.

'Okay,' she said. 'Do you have *Dirty Dancing*?'

David threw a pillow my way from the corridor. ''Ave it!' he yelled, then scampered away.

'This means war!' I shouted back, launching the pillow back in his direction with a little magical force behind it.

We found the film online—which turned out to have a pretty good soundtrack—and Amy mouthed along to all the lines. I pulled some of the available magic toward me and pushed an extra protection spell in Amy's direction. I infused it with the right words, the correct phrases, and settled into my chair a little easier as the spells of protection drifted over her like a comfort blanket. Would they actually do anything against a creature that could prey on her in her sleep? I had no idea, but at least it felt like I was doing something.

'Stella,' said Amy, as Johnny lifted Baby high above his head.

'Hm?'

'Am I really in danger? Like… properly in danger?'

I suppose I should have found a comforting way to say it, but if I were her, I'd have wanted the truth. 'Yes. You're in danger. A lot of danger.'

'Right. But I'm going to have to sleep at some point, aren't I? No one can just stay awake forever. I mean, I'm already tired now, even with the magic over me. I can feel my eyes wanting to close and I just want to curl up in this chair and drift off. At some point I'm gonna sleep and the monster will get me.'

'Maybe. But I'm going to do whatever I can to find out what's behind this. Me and your uncle both are. And once we've found the thing, we'll kick its teeth in.'

Amy smiled and nodded and went back to the film.

'So are you and Uncle Dave, like...?' She let the sentence trail off and grinned at me.

'Like what?'

'You know? *Doing it.*'

I felt blood rush to my face. 'What? No! Of course not. Gross. Nope.'

She lifted her hands up. 'Hey, you know, okay, God. You just look like a couple and that.'

'Well, we're not. At all. I mean, no way. Anyway, you're only thirteen – aren't you a little young for this sort of conversation?'

'I'm a teenager, Stella, I've had boyfriends you know?' She caught herself. 'Don't tell Mum, though.'

As the night wore on, David and I swapped back and forth, taking turns to keep Amy company for a few hours at a time, until finally, the sun rose and I sighed with relief. We'd made it through one night.

David entered, yawning and scratching at his midriff, his hair pasted to one side of his head.

'Good morning,' I said, standing from my chair and stretching.

'I know, you two don't have to say anything, I look beautiful in the morning.'

Amy giggled, then faux-gagged.

'Hey, don't be a hater just 'cos I woke up this pretty.'

'Okay,' I said, 'who's up for some breakfast?'

David twitched and reached into his pocket, pulling out his vibrating phone.

'Detective Tyler,' he said, answering. 'Crap, how many? Okay, right, thanks.' David hung up and looked to Amy, eyes wide.

'What is it?' I asked.

I already knew.

'Fourteen more kids didn't wake up this morning.'

I looked at Amy, who sat back in her chair and hugged her knees.

13

I left David to take care of his niece. The plan was that he drag her around the city to keep her awake and active until he heard back from me. Amy grumbled, yawning, but headed off with her uncle with promises of, "Enough ice-cream to make you puke".

Fourteen more children now resided within a ward in Ealing Hospital. That made twenty in total. Twenty kids over the last two nights who went to bed like it was any normal day, closed their eyes, and were taken in their dreams by...

...by *something*.

'For now I am here, to punish you all,' I said under my breath as I marched towards my destination, Amy's note still in my pocket.

I was heading towards *L'Merrier's Antiques*, a shop I'd been ordered to stay away from after my last visit. It seemed more like a warning than a request, but I didn't have a choice. I needed help, and Giles L'Merrier was going to give it to me.

'Little Familiar. Insignificant bug. Fluff from my belly button. You seem to have found yourself within my premises once more. I assume this is some terrible accident on your part?'

'L'Merrier, I need your help.'

His bulky frame was draped in a floor-length gown, ancient symbols covering it. They weren't just for decoration, he had magic sewn right into his clothing. Protection. Giles L'Merrier had lived a long and eventful life. Many a dark Uncanny yearned to see his severed head roll down a gutter, though precious few had the ability to take him down, with or without his protection spells. L'Merrier was one of the giants. A man who had lived for centuries and taken out more enemies than any one person could count. These days he preferred to stay within the confines of his shop and leave the rough stuff to others. No one knew why exactly he'd stepped out of the game, why he disliked people coming to him, looking for help. Some said he was waiting, but no one knew what for.

L'Merrier smiled at me, light dancing around his large, shaved head. It wasn't a smile meant to provide comfort. 'Perhaps you mistook my establishment for a newsagents? Or were you merely passing when you tripped over your own clumsy feet and fell inside? Hm? Surely it can't be that you entered on purpose, because I seem to remember a conversation, ooh, only three months ago, in which I stated, quite clearly, that my debt to your coven was paid and that you should not come to me asking favours ever again.'

I shifted, uncomfortable. 'Thank you for your help, L'Merrier. If it wasn't for you, Mr. Trick might still be out there. Might have killed me, too, as well as my witches.'

'Don't tell me you have returned to flatter. I am not a vain man, neither do I require the adulation of insects.'

'I need... there's a problem.'

'This is London, there is always a problem.' He stroked his

bald pate. 'Tell me, Familiar, where is your new pet? The detective? I thought he'd be scampering at your heels, his little tail wagging.'

'I didn't bring him, out of respect for you.'

'Respect for me?' he replied, raising an eyebrow. 'And yet you return, after I made it abundantly clear that you are not welcome.'

'Some things are more important than my own well-being.'

L'Merrier chuckled. 'How very noble of you.'

He began to move among his shop's shelves, hands dancing lightly across the various items on display. Some were what you would expect to find in an antiques shop, others were far more unusual. Ancient objects of the Uncanny, collected during his many centuries of adventure and exploration.

'Do you know what this is?' he asked, pointing to a glass case that contained a large, blackened object. I peered closer at the thing.

'Is that... a heart?'

'Correct. It belonged to a giant named K'lochenfer. The thing had been terrorising the people of a small village in Belgium. He would visit them once a week to grab a fistful of them to feast upon. I happened to be passing and decided to track the giant to its home. It was a cave of course; giants love their caves.' He smiled as if enjoying a fond memory. 'I crept inside whilst the creature was sleeping, reached into its chest and took out its heart.'

I looked at the heart in its glass case. It must have been three times the size of my head.

'The giant lived for another month after that. Some creatures are not so easy to kill, you know. The beast spent its remaining days searching Belgium for me, until finally the poor thing gave up and collapsed. I dragged its body back to the village and the people ate like kings for a month. Can't say I found the giant's flavour to be all that appealing, personally. Tasted like dirt to me. I'd never chewed such tough meat.'

'L'Merrier,' I said, 'as fascinating as this is, I came here for a reason. I came for your help.'

'And why should I help you? Why should I not render you asunder with a flick of my little finger? I no longer step beyond the walls of this place for a reason. I would like to think that you and others could respect my privacy.'

'Something is taking children. Taking them in their sleep so they never wake up.'

L'Merrier raised on eyebrow and nodded. 'I see. Do you have it?'

'Have what?'

'The rhyme of bewitchment?'

'How did you know I'd have one?'

'Because this has happened before. Many times. The troubling thing is, it should not be happening anymore. Not in London. It should be impossible.'

'Well, it is, I've got twenty kids in a hospital ward in Ealing who went to bed one night and refuse to get up.'

'You do not understand. If what you say is true, if indeed this is the creature I think it is, then we can expect worse than a few children having a lie-in. Far worse. The whole of the city is in grave danger.'

14

L'Merrier read the note Amy had written. The rhyme that seemed to be the trigger for each kid who spoke it being unable to wake up again. He sighed as he read the lines, and nodded sagely.

'You recognise the rhyme?' I asked.

'It is as I feared. The creature has found a way back into the thoughts and dreams of the children of London. It will only spread from here. Within a month, perhaps less, every child in the city will be taken; their bodies left to slumber as their souls suffer in eternal torment.'

He passed the note back to me.

'What kind of creature is it? What's its name?'

'Name? Oh, it does not have a name, you stupid thing.'

'Thanks.'

'It does not have a name because the creature is not really alive.'

'So what? It's a ghost?'

L'Merrier stared at me silently for several seconds. It wasn't hard to work out that I'd said the wrong thing again.

'How do you make it through a day without setting yourself on fire?' he asked.

'Well, sometimes I don't.'

Almost a smile, I was sure of it.

'The thing that created this rhyme is rage and fear and blind fury incarnate. Unconscionable deeds and desire for revenge, weaponised. The idea made reality by a concentration of magic and emotion, exploding out of the infinite possibility and creativity of youth. And it should no longer be able to do the things it is doing.'

He was losing me with this, but the fact that he looked so troubled shook me.

'What do you mean it shouldn't be able to do all of this? Was it killed already?'

He looked at me and smiled. 'You cannot kill a thing such as this. It is not what you and I would consider to be alive, remember. No, it cannot be killed, but it can be prevented. It can be locked, chained, banished from this plane. And it was once, many years ago, when it appeared in our city and began taking children. It was before your time, I believe. Poor Lyla was the familiar then, of course. Tragic thing.'

My predecessor, Lyla. For some reason I always felt funny when she was brought up. No one ever told me what happened to her, but I had enough of the pieces to know that it was nothing good. I think, when they were alive, my witches were surprised that I had lived as long as I had. Sixty years of age. I don't think anyone expected a familiar of the London Coven to make it to such an age.

'I still don't understand exactly what it is you're saying I'm up against.'

L'Merrier bowed his head and sighed, as though dealing with a very stupid child. To him, that was pretty close to the truth.

'Shall I make my words smaller for you, familiar? Would pictures help?'

I felt my fists clench. Yeah, that would be a great idea, Stella. I unclenched.

'Emotions are never more volcanic than when we are young,' he explained. 'Never more frightening and strange and acutely felt. Reason is never more blinded by those very emotions that attack our minds and bodies as though we are a castle under siege.'

L'Merrier began to glide around his shop, hands drifting over his many strange display items. A helmet from some ancient army that I couldn't put my finger on. A shrunken head whose mouth opened as though it was going to scream when his fingers made contact with it. A portrait of himself and three young women, its paint ancient and cracking. I squinted; were those…? My witches? My witches and Giles L'Merrier?

'Oh, I'm sorry, am I boring you?' said L'Merrier, somehow within inches of me, even though, a heartbeat earlier, he'd been at the far end of his shop.

'No, I'm listening,' I said, acting unfazed. 'Go on.'

He snorted and turned his back on me. 'Imagine a bullied child. Bullied by other children. A tale as old as time, wouldn't you say? Now imagine that raw emotion. The raw, explosive emotion of a child. The abject terror. The shame. The unfocused terror and rage. Imagine that happening over and over and over again. A never-ending cycle, picking up a head of steam as all over the city, child after child is made to feel this way. Made to feel this way by other children.'

'You're saying bullying caused this?'

'Simply put, so even your pea-brain can grasp it, the emotions stirred up across this city have come to a boil. The raw emotions met the Uncanny power that is so heavy in London, and an idea was born. An idea of blind retribution. A lashing out against not one child, but all children. And so this thing was created, this thing that exists not in our plane of reality, but that can take a child at their most vulnerable. In their dreams.'

I was finally getting the picture.

'So why the rhyme?'

'Fear. Oh, it wants fear, and that is the first step. A whisper in the playground about a rhyme that can conjure the devil to take you as you slumber. A child will believe it. Oh, they would deny it, but there it will tickle, round and fat in their minds, as they walk up the stairs to bed. And then it has them.'

So, if I was grasping this correctly, what I was up against was not exactly a monster as much as the idea of a monster brought into "reality" by the raw, unchecked emotion of children. Why couldn't it just be a flesh and blood thing so I could punch it in the face?

'It doesn't sound exactly fair. They just created an even worse bully.'

'A creature born of centuries of bullying and made stronger every time a child bullies another. It has life and it has purpose: to unleash hell on children everywhere. To lash out at them for what they have done. To become wrath. It is not a rational being. It exists purely to vent that unthinking anger that every child feels towards their bully.'

'And now I have come, to punish you all.'

'Well, indeed.'

'How did you stop it the first time?'

'Oh, it wasn't me. It was your coven.'

I smiled and felt my heart swell a little, but the momentary feeling was soon laid to waste when the pictures of their dead, shredded bodies popped into my mind's eye.

'What did they do?' I asked.

'They put certain... magical locks in place. Safeguards. As I say, the creature exists in another plane. They blocked that plane from being able to interact with ours. No child should be able to speak those words in the correct order; your masters made sure of that. And that makes me worry.'

'Has someone helped the thing?'

'I think not. London is a focal point of the Uncanny Kingdom, which also makes it a weak point. A point of attack. A crack in the window. The witches of London did not just exist to police this place, they took it upon themselves to hold it together. To stop it sliding off the end of the cliff. Now, it would appear, that since their deaths, some of these locks have begun to, shall we say, spring open. Terrible things are slipping through, and more shall follow.'

'Can you put the protections back in place? Reseal the locks?'

He looked at me in what I thought was a pretty shifty manner.

'Perhaps. Perhaps not. I may be one of the most powerful beings to ever stride across this planet. A colossus. A true master of the light and dark arts. A man who has met the Devil and made him call me Sir. But that does not mean I have mastery over all things.' L'Merrier fussed at his gown, agitated, before turning to me with a scowl. 'To put it bluntly, I have no idea how the witches did what they did.'

Well, this was a day to remember. The mighty Giles L'Merrier, admitting he didn't know everything. A flaw in the diamond at last. I almost danced a jig, but just about managed to keep my body under control.

He went on: 'I only know that the three of them combined were able to set up a web of protective spells that criss-crossed this city and prevented it from falling into chaos. They blocked the worst of the other realms from slipping into our reality. Neutralised certain threats. The power it would need to generate such a web, and to keep the magic fed so it would sustain, so it would not collapse and blow away upon the breeze... it is almost inconceivable.'

Something is happening in this city, Stella. It's like the stitches that hold the place together are starting to fray.

Jake the ghost. He'd tried to tell me that things were falling apart and I'd brushed him off. Had he been right? Had he felt what L'Merrier was describing? The erosion of these magical safeguards my witches had set up?

'So what should I do?' I asked L'Merrier.

'There is always a tipping point that gives "life" to a thing such as this. A single incident that lights the blue touch paper. You must locate that inciting moment: the terrified child, cowering from their bully. Do that and you will find the creature. In other words, you do your job—the one you were created to do—you insignificant glob of sputum.'

15

I left L'Merrier's shop with no invitation to return, and headed back to the coven. As I pushed through the ticket barrier and walked towards the tube platform, my head swirled with all the new information L'Merrier had dropped on me.

There was of course the wider concern. The idea that my witches had somehow kept bad things from slipping into London, and now they were gone those barriers were crumbling. That what Jake had told me was true. But I couldn't get too side-tracked by that. All I knew for sure was that twenty kids in a hospital were being terrorised and might never wake up. That more and more would join them unless I could pin this creature down. This weird amalgam of emotions brought to life to lash out at kids, whether they were guilty or innocent. It didn't matter. All that mattered was that feeling of shame, of helplessness, of fear, of rage, all squashed up together and firing out of a child made to live in terror by other children. Kids it should be playing with, laughing with, not running from.

I felt Amy's note scrunched in my hand, in the pocket of my jacket. I needed to find a way to locate the tipping point. The final inciting incident that had pushed things over the edge and made this creature powerful enough to drag itself into existence. And then, well, we'd get to the "then" once we got there.

The train rocked me back and forth as it charged through the black.

I didn't call David, I wanted him and Amy away from the coven while I worked. I didn't know for certain that what I was about to do wouldn't put Amy in danger if she was there to see it, so I left them to their day-trip and got to work.

I sketched a chalk pentagram on the slate square again and placed the note with the full rhyme at its centre. The magic of the coven washed around me. I closed my eyes, tilted my head back, and drew the energy towards me. Felt it lap against me in great waves, soaking into me, becoming part of me. I trembled with the power, the buzz, heard myself giggle in delight.

For this to work, I'd need to hold and direct a lot of power. More than I would usually take on. Drawing in even a small amount of surrounding magic was pleasurable, allowing this amount to drench me was intoxicating. I licked my lips and opened my eyes, my pupils huge, my cheeks aching from smiling. The magic of my coven had a special effect on me. An illicit thrill. A weaker Uncanny could become lost in it, let its mighty waves break over them again and again until they were buried beneath them.

But I was stronger than that. I was created in this room. This magic was my magic.

I took a step towards the pentagram, tendrils of multicoloured, molten magic trailing behind me. I knelt and held out my open hands to the note, to the words written upon it. I grunted and pushed the power into the words.

'Show me,' I said. My voice eight times my own, a mighty, booming, command.

The last time I'd only had a partial rhyme and no idea what it was exactly I was hoping to discover. This time I had the full rhyme and knew exactly what I wanted it to show me. I wanted it to reveal its history. Its birth. To drag the past into the present. That sort of magic was difficult, almost beyond me. It's only in that room in my coven that I could ever hope to tackle such a thing. And even then it hurt.

A breeze. Wind whipped back my hair. I wasn't alone.

The light in the room had dimmed, the walls seemed distant. Transparent. Were there things beyond the walls, in the shadows?

Wake no more, no more, no more, no more...

The words repeated on the wind as it pulled at me.

I pushed more magic into the note, into the words. They glowed silver and rose off the page, growing larger and larger as they spread to cover the ceiling. Only it wasn't the ceiling anymore, it was the sky. Hadn't I been in the coven? Hadn't I been in my home?

'Show me,' I screamed. I didn't realise at first that I was screaming as the magic surged through me, fed the spell, fed the rhyme, but I was. I could tell because my throat had begun to hurt. Maybe I'd been screaming for minutes, hours, days, forcing the rhyme to give up its secret. To show me its birthplace. To show me where fear turned to revenge. Endless, constant, ravenous, unfocused revenge.

'Show me!'

Damp fingers traced a line across my neck, my cheek, pulled at my hair.

Revenge not against the bully who finally created this thing. Or against any bully. Just against everyone. Every child. All were guilty in the eyes of the cowering, isolated child with the bloody nose and trembling hands.

A figure in the corner of my eye, its movements unnatural, sharp, jerking its way towards me. Trying to distract me? Was whatever owned this rhyme trying to break my concentration?

My link to its spell? Maybe it felt what I was doing, realised what I was attempting.

Was I in danger?

'Show me!'

Wake no more, Wake no more, Wake no more...

I looked down to see a moving carpet of large, black rats flowing past me, their greasy fur buffeting against my ankles, my knees, my thighs.

I spoke the words of the rhyme over and over again, not allowing myself to disconnect from my focus.

A child was crying. A mournful sob at the edge of my hearing.

I was in a school corridor, pressed up against the lockers, a fist coming to meet me, my head snapping back.

More tears now, more voices. So many, one after the other, a chorus of fear.

I was in a field with my sister—

My sister?

I don't have—

I look up to see three boys climb over the fence and point at us, cruel smiles on their faces. I stand in front of my sister, I'm terrified. The biggest one runs towards me and—

'Show me!'

So many screams, so many voices, I can see them all around me, crowding in. They look like ghosts, or afterimages, shuffling, alone yet packed in so tightly I'm worried they might crush me and—

I'm in my bedroom—

I'm in the school toilets—

I'm in an alleyway out of view of adults—

And I'm punched, I'm kicked, I'm spat on and laughed at—

Children's faces, twisted with hatred leering down at me, the soles of their shoes coming to meet my knees as they stamp down and down and down and—

I'm getting lost.

It's too much—
So many—
So many broken children—
So much pain—
Maybe they deserve it—
Maybe the creature is right—
Punish them all, them all, them all—
'You will show me!'
Silence.

The book of the past stopped jumping from page to page and the chorus of crying children ceased. I was alone again. I lowered my shaking hands and pushed myself to my feet, staggering slightly, having to lean against the brick wall to steady myself.

I was in a wide back alley of some sort. There were bins, overflowing. Large bins. I was behind a row of shops where unwanted goods were thrown and rats scuttled. I turned to find a pair of small legs poking out from behind one of the large, metal bins. They were laid out flat. Unmoving.

'Hello,' I said, stepping towards—

The picture warped like film, bubbling as if lit by a match. It was trying to burn the image down. To hide it from me.

'I see it,' I said. 'I know where you come from now. You're too late.'

There was a sound like a thousand children screaming in fury, then I was at the centre of the ghostly afterimages again as furious faces lunged towards me, fists pummelling me, passing right through, freezing me, I had to break the spell, had to get—

I was on the ground. When did I fall? I wasn't behind the shops anymore, wasn't in my coven, I had to get back, I had to follow the breadcrumbs or I might be lost forever, and—

Wake no more.
No more.
No more.

16

I woke up to find David and Amy crouched over me.

'See, she's not dead,' said Amy. 'You owe me a Mars bar.'

I sat up, my head groggy.

'What have I told you about day drinking?' said David as he helped me to my feet.

'Hilarious,' I replied. 'What time is it?'

'Almost ten,' said Amy.

'What? Ten?' I'd been blacked out for hours.

'Yeah, you were supposed to call us to tell us we could come back, remember?' said David. 'Only you didn't call, it was late, our feet hurt like bastards, so here we are and there you were, spark out on the coven floor. What happened? Are you okay?'

'I'm fine, I was just handling some, you know, heavy magic stuff. Must have fed back and knocked me out.'

'Can you play Quidditch?' asked Amy.

'Nerd,' said David, giving her a playful shove.

'Shut up,' replied Amy, scowling.

'What's Quidditch?' I asked.

Amy looked at me in astonishment.

'Our Stella has lived a long but sheltered life,' said David. 'Right, kettle on, two sugars for me. Go on, shoo,' he told Amy, pushing her in the direction of the kitchen to leave the two of us alone.

'So, wanna tell me what actually happened? How'd things go with your antiques wizard?'

I thought back to what had happened before I'd fallen into the black. The hundreds of voices. Thousands, even. Pure fear and anger swirling around me, attacking me, trying to infect me. Whatever it was we were after, it had felt me there, searching. Knew someone was trespassing on its land.

I hoped it was worried.

Hoped it had the capacity for that.

I filled David in on what L'Merrier had told me, skipping the part about the faltering network of spells and safeguards. That was just for me to worry about. For now at least.

'So, a creature—a kind of creature at least—created by kids being bullied by other kids?'

'Yep,' I replied.

'A creature that now targets kids? Seems like it's kind of missing the point there, don't you think?'

'He said it's not a rational, thinking being. All it has is the feelings that fed it, and the desire to lash out at other children that might make it feel that way.'

David shook his head and sighed. 'Well, I suppose that makes some sort of sense. At least as much as anything else has in the last few months. By the way, are we gonna circle back to the whole *me seeing ghosts* thing at some point?'

'Let's deal with one thing at a time. As soon as we've stopped this turd and saved every child in London, maybe then we can take a look at your messed-up brain.'

'You're all heart, Stella Familiar,' he replied, grinning. 'I take it we have a way of helping Amy, right?'

I thought about the place the spell had shown me. The

small legs poking out from behind the bins. 'I think so. I hope so.'

Amy walked in, carefully holding three cups of tea. 'Here you go, I make the best tea, you'd better believe it.'

'Biscuits?' replied David.

Amy grunted, turned on her heels, and stomped back out.

17

David insisted on coming with me.

'She's my niece, I want to help her.'

I agreed to his demand. The truth is, I liked it when he was by my side. For decades I'd handled the dangers of the job on my own, and it was nice to have some backup for a change. To have a partner.

'We're only going to be gone an hour or so,' he told Amy, 'we're just checking out a back alley. You know how it is, the glamour of a police investigation.'

'Why can't I come?'

'Because this is official business. No place for a muggle.'

'Oi!' She chased David around the kitchen, whipping him with a tea towel.

Even though we'd only be gone a short while, and Amy had insisted she felt tip-top and wide awake, I placed my hands on her forehead and put the correct words together.

'Awake. Alert,' I commanded, strengthening the spell I'd placed on her earlier.

'Oh, that tingles like mad,' said Amy. 'Hey, can you give me superpowers? Make me fly like a witch?'

'Of course she can't,' said David. 'Witches can't fly.'

'That's right,' I said. 'Not without their broomsticks.'

I gave Amy a sly wink, causing her to break into giggles. It was a nice feeling. I hadn't had much experience interacting with teens. Or children. Or people, really.

'That should keep you awake while we're out,' I told her, 'but if you find yourself nodding off, call David and we'll head right back, okay?'

'God, all right, *Mum*,' she snorted.

The place I'd been shown by the rhyme wasn't too far. A small, backstreet square behind a row of shops in Acton, just a short hop on the Underground.

As the train shot us towards our destination, I noticed David wasn't his usual self. Now that Amy wasn't around he'd let his cheery face drop, and instead stared at his feet, his expression set. It was odd. He didn't seem like himself at all.

'Hey,' I said, but a combination of the roar of the train and the noise of his own worried mind deafened him to me. I reached out and touched his arm. 'David.'

He turned to look at me, 'I can't let anything happen to her, Stella. She's family. I just... I can't.'

'I won't let it have her,' I assured him. 'I won't. We'll stop this thing, I promise.'

He smiled and nodded uncertainly, then fell into silence again.

There were no legs poking out from behind bins when we reached the place I'd been shown; a squalid area, out of the way of any passers-by. The only people who came back there were shopkeepers throwing out boxes of expired goods, tramps hoping for a safe place to sleep, and people looking to do things away from prying eyes.

'Nice smell back here,' said David. 'It's like a fart farted.'

I took a look down the alleyway and saw the backs of the shops to our left and a high brick wall to our right, both leading to another wall at the far end. A dead end. The only way in or out was behind us.

'You're sure this is it?' asked David.

I nodded. This was the place. As soon as we'd stepped into the alley I could feel it. A fug of old despair that hung in the air, infused with the sharp smell of urine. Actions can leave traces of themselves in the magic that washes around a place. They can scratch a signature in the bricks, even. Dramatic events, events of high emotion, even more so.

Something bad had happened here.

'Hey, you okay?' asked David.

I realised I was hugging myself. 'Yeah, it's just... this is definitely the place. I don't know what happened here, not yet, but it wasn't good. It wasn't good at all.'

'So the monster was created here?'

'L'Merrier told me there would have been a flash point. That years of bullying had built up until one final incident gave the creature the spark to exist. Whatever happened here gave it that spark. This is where it started. This is where a monster was born.'

'And how long ago was this?'

'Not sure. But before my time, so at least sixty years ago.'

A sound.

What was that? Footsteps running? A name being yelled? It was distant, right on the edge of my senses, but it was there.

'The thing that happened here, it's still happening,' I said.

David looked at me, then looked around, turning in a little circle. 'I don't see anything, not even with my new super-awesome ghost vision. I'm calling it ghost vision by the way, because it sounds cool. Better than *brain damage caused by an evil bastard monster,* anyway.'

'I can sense it. Almost sense it. Like it's just out of my reach. But the incident wore a deep groove here, and it's happening over and over again, on an endless repeat. A child running, its name being called, a dead end. Over and over it goes, and it'll never stop.'

'So what do we...' David stopped mid-sentence, furrowed his brow, and shook his head sharply.

'What is it? David, what's wrong?'

'Nothing, I... No... don't let them... Stella—'

He started to back up, away from me, towards the dead end.

'David? What is it? What are you seeing?'

'No!' His eyes were wild now, pure terror, he wasn't seeing me, wasn't hearing me. He was somewhere else, somewhere that scared him to the bone. 'Don't let them touch me!'

He turned and ran, but there was nowhere to go. He hit the dead end, turned, arms up, sliding down the brickwork screaming, arms over his head, tears rolling down his cheeks.

'Don't let them touch me. Don't let them touch me!'

18

I had to get David out of that back alley before he dropped dead from a heart attack.

I grunted as I struggled to lift him.

'David, it's me, Stella. You're okay. Stop fighting.'

'Don't let them, please, don't let them touch me. Get my dad, my dad will stop them, please.'

After that he stopped resisting and went catatonic, paralysed with fear. I cradled him in my arms and headed out of the back alley and into the street, getting a few curious glances from the Acton locals as I turned the corner, lifting a full-grown man like he was a baby.

I managed to get him to a bench and placed him down, dropping into the space beside him and catching my breath. David sat slumped next to me, still frozen, lost in whatever it was the place had made him see. I wondered why the alley hadn't affected me the same way. I'd sensed the dreadful things that had happened there, tasted the terror, the anger and desperation on my tongue, but it hadn't seeped into me like it had David. Hadn't made me mad with fear.

'David, can you hear me? David?' I tapped gently at his face.

'Hey, hear my voice, David. It's me, it's Stella, you're okay, you're safe.'

Nothing.

I looked around, making sure no one was paying attention, then I belted him across the cheek hard enough to make my palm sting.

'Ow! Hey! What d'you do that for?' shrieked David, putting a hand to his reddened face.

'Are you okay?'

'Am I okay? No, you just smashed me in the... wait, how did we get out here? When did we decide to sit on this bench?'

'What do you remember?'

David lowered his hand from his cheek and looked away, distant. 'I was... we were in the back alley, which stank. I mean, just stank. And then... and then I was somewhere else. I didn't feel it happening and it didn't seem strange, I was just suddenly somewhere else. Like the sort of thing that happens in a dream, you know? One minute you're one place, and the next you're somewhere else, or even someone else, and you don't question it. Dream logic. Your brain just tells you this is normal and on you go.'

'Where did it take you?'

David smiled briefly. 'I was in my garden. From when I was born until I hit ten, we lived in a place with a nice back garden. It looked out on some fields. We didn't live in London, then, it was Hitchin, a little place just north of London. More rural. So I'd sit in this back garden and I'd play, right? Drive my little toy cars around, make my He-Men fight each other, kick a ball about, whatever. And then... I stopped wanting to sit in that garden. My mum would ask me why I didn't go out there to play anymore, but I wouldn't tell her. Didn't even like helping to hang out the washing on the line back there. The thing is, I couldn't remember why I didn't want to go out there. I'd blocked it out somehow, and then... well, then we went in that back alley it's like a locked door opened up and I was pushed inside.'

'So it let you see some sort of, what? A traumatic incident from when you were a kid?'

David swallowed and nodded, his hands fussing at his jacket. 'I mean, I didn't remember this at all. The things a brain will do to protect you, eh?'

'What was it?'

He looked away from me, looked into the distance like he was seeing it play out again. 'I was maybe five and I was on my knees in the back garden. I was playing, happy. Mum was inside, Dad was out somewhere. I didn't notice them at first.'

'Didn't notice who?'

He turned to me, fear dancing in his eyes. 'I didn't see the boys. There were three of them. In my memory, they're giants, but they must have only been about eleven. Just three stupid kids who saw a chance to mess with someone smaller than them. To feel strong and powerful. I didn't notice them, but they'd cut through the field and seen me. It wasn't until the first one had climbed over the fence and the other two were following that I noticed.'

He was trembling, that same childhood fear fraying at his nerves again.

I reached over and placed a hand on his arm. 'It's okay, David. You're fine.'

He smiled and nodded, laughed even. 'Yeah, stupid. It was so bloody long ago.' But his eyes turned dark again. 'One of them had a knife. Just a little flick knife. The kind of thing a kid might carry to show off to his mates when no grown-up was looking. To show how tough he was. It was the size of machete to me, though. I couldn't move. It's like I was frozen. I wanted to run—every part of me was telling me to run inside, to scream, to shout—but I just stayed there, on my knees, as the boys sniggered and nudged each other. They ran the knife across my cheeks. My chin. My neck. Not hard enough to break the skin, but hard enough for me to think they were going to.'

'Did they hurt you?'

'No. They weren't interested in that. They just wanted to frighten a little kid. Make them so scared that they'd wet their pants. Yeah, I wet my pants. They laughed, but they weren't done yet. The one with the knife grabbed a chunk of my hair and pulled it so hard it almost came out at the root. The other two held me down as he sawed through it with the knife and came away with a handful. After that they put the blade away and climbed back over the fence with their trophy, laughing some more. I remember just staying out there, on my knees, watching them disappear across the field, then standing and going inside. My mum saw my piss-covered jeans and bald patch and went mental. Demanded to know what had happened. I knew better than to squeal, so I told her I'd tried to give myself a haircut and wet myself when it went wrong. She wasn't impressed, I'll tell you that.' He sighed and leaned back, shaking off the recollection. 'Well, that was a shitty little trip down memory lane.'

'The incident, whatever happened in that back alley, the place is heavy with it. It must have pulled out your childhood trauma.'

'Well, that back alley can fuck right off,' he replied, laughing, before raising a middle-finger in the alley's direction. The laugh was a hollow one, and as he lowered his hand he turned to me, his face grim.

'Stella, we have to stop this thing. We can't let it make any more children feel that way. We have to find it, and we have to kill it.'

19

David was quiet on the tube ride back to Hammersmith. I could tell he hadn't quite shaken off the fear that the trigger location had dragged out of him. I wondered whether that fear was generated by the place, or if it was an effect of the creature it had created. Whatever the case, it was obvious from our visit that it could force adults to experience the worst of their past emotions.

But what about me?

I didn't have a childhood. I was born exactly as I am, exactly as I always will be until something kills me. I had no childhood trauma to attack, but I knew how deep down and painful those kinds of fears could be in other people. People who were actually born and then grew up. Effects of bad events when you're a little kid can scar you like nothing else. That alley, that creature, whatever it was that had affected David, it hadn't done anything to me. There was no childhood and no trauma that it could latch on to.

Lucky me.

As we got off the train and stepped out into Hammersmith, David looked at his phone and swore.

'What's wrong?'

'Amy didn't reply to the message I sent before we got on the tube.'

'Maybe she just hasn't seen it yet?'

'Yeah. Yeah, maybe.'

But somehow I already knew that wasn't true.

We began to walk fast, almost breaking into a run as David dialled again and again, swearing as it went to voicemail, hanging up, and trying, hanging up and trying.

He ran ahead as we turned into the blind alley, the coven door at the other end.

'Amy,' he shouted.

She should be okay.

She should be safe.

I left a spell on her to keep her awake.

Into the coven, David already heading for the common room, to the couch where the previous night I'd sat and watched *Dirty Dancing* with his niece.

And there she was. Curled up and fast asleep.

'Amy, wake up. Come on, Amy,' David patted her, shoved her, pulled her up into a sitting position. She wouldn't wake up.

'Do something,' he said, staring at me, desperate.

I reached out and placed my hands on her temples.

'Wake.'

Nothing.

I tried again, putting more force behind the word, pushing more of the magic of the coven into myself and out through my command for Amy to wake. To open her eyes. To be safe.

After fifteen minutes I staggered back, David staring at me in disbelief.

'What? Is that it?'

'I can't reach her. She's gone.'

His eyes blinked slowly then he turned back to Amy, fast asleep beside him. 'You cast a spell on her. You said she'd be okay.'

I felt the knot of guilt twist in my stomach. I'd had good reason to think she'd be okay. A spell that keeps you awake, keeps you alert, was child's play. I'd thought it would be too dangerous for her to go to the alleyway with us. As it turned out, there was no safe place for Amy. Sooner or later, it was going to get her.

She'd said the lines.

Repeated them out loud.

And that meant she was the creature's to take.

She belonged in the creature's realm now and there was nothing we could do to stop it.

Nothing at all.

'I... sorry.' It was the best I could do. I didn't have anything else to offer.

David closed his eyes, teeth bared like he might yell, then I saw it just melt away. He looked at me. 'What am I going to say to my sister? I'm a detective, Stella. I protect people. How can I tell her I couldn't even protect my own niece?'

'It's not your fault. There's nothing we could have done.'

'So what? What do we do now? We just let it have them? We just let it have Amy? I go to my sister's house and tell her that her daughter is dead? Worse than dead?'

'No. Not yet. Just because we can't protect them, doesn't mean we can't stop this. Doesn't mean we can't stop it taking any more. And she's alive! Look at her. Amy is alive. She's breathing, warm, her heart beating. When I touch her head I can still feel her brain working in there. She's not dead. None of them are. It doesn't want them dead. It wants them alive to feel whatever it is it wants them to feel.'

'So we can get Amy back? This isn't it, she's not going to stay like this?'

'Do you think I'd let it keep her? Let it keep any of them?'

I looked at Amy and I pictured the room full of children slumbering at Ealing Hospital, and I felt my fists tighten, knuckles throbbing, magic swirling around them.

'We're going to show this bastard what we do to things that mess with kids.'

20

It's stupid to make promises you don't know you can keep, but as I looked at David and saw the pain on his face, all I wanted was to make him feel better. Make him feel hope. Make him believe in me.

I wanted that face to go back to its normal, smiling self. To see the sparkle in his eyes again. The idea of that fear eating away at him made my stomach drop.

But it was stupid.

I had no idea if I had it in me to stop this. My witches had done it once, but so what? What was I compared to them? I was a witch's helper, that's all. I didn't have a tenth of their knowledge or a fraction of their mastery over the Uncanny.

But he'd stood there in front of me looking so small, so broken, that the words had just come spilling out. What if I wasn't able to keep my promise, though? What would David think of me then? Would he walk out of this dusty old coven and never look back? Would he leave me behind, a failed familiar, alone in the city?

It didn't matter that I'd made the promise when I shouldn't have. I'd made it, which meant I had to keep it.

David got a call from work and I managed to convince him

to go. It was no good him sitting at the coven with Amy. He should carry on as normal and I'd do whatever I could to wake her up. The truth was, I just didn't want to be in the same room as him until I had some sort of a plan figured out. Some course of action that made me feel as though I was doing my best to keep my promise.

All night I sat with Amy. I'd carried her through into one of the empty bedrooms and laid her out on the bed. I wondered how long she'd stay there. How long until she opened her eyes. Maybe she'd stay in there for good, until her body finally gave out on her. If that happened, would the part of her the creature had taken to its realm die, too? Or would it get to keep that part forever? To torture it for eternity.

I looked through the books of magic my masters had collected over their long lives, searched for anything that might be useful, but nothing came up. If only they'd kept records of some sort, then maybe I'd have an idea how to tackle this situation. But my witches weren't the type to keep records. There wasn't a scrap of evidence anywhere of their centuries of fighting monsters. No records, no reports, no computer files I could use to CTRL-F "*Monster who steals sleeping kids.*"

I walked the coven, going from room to room, lost in my thoughts. The creature didn't live in this reality. Back in the alley where the monster had been born, I felt as though I'd seen a glimpse of its hiding place. Felt its realm rubbing up against our own.

Maybe...?

Was there a way to tempt it out? What if I could manipulate reality at the monster's creation point and pull it into our world? If I could do that—lure it from its safe space and into this realm—maybe then I could kill the thing. Destroy it for good.

Still, just going to the alley and demanding it appear wasn't going to be enough. I needed more. I would need some sort of physical link to the incident. To give me a direct connection to what happened there. Something real. Something related to the creature's birth. I needed to find one of the people involved in whatever crime had gone down there decades ago.

My phone rang. It was David.

'Hi.' I realised my voice sounded small, embarrassed. I coughed and straightened myself out.

'How's Amy?'

'Good.' That was stupid. She was far from good. I didn't want to even imagine what terrors she must have been facing. 'Sorry. She's... there's no change. She's in one of the beds.'

There was a pause on the other end.

'David?'

'Sorry, still here. I think I have something.'

'What? What is it?'

'I did a bit of digging through the files, went way back, checking anything in the past hundred years that mentioned that back alley.'

'And? What did you get?'

'I think I found the incident. I think I found what started all of this.'

David told me what he'd found.

And I realised just why that monster had been born.

21

I met David at the gates to Acton Cemetery. It was dawn, the sun just pulling itself clear of the horizon. Forty-eight more kids hadn't woken that morning. Forty-eight more families, confused and terrified, demanding to know why their child lay dead to the world.

'Are you sure Amy will be okay on her own?' asked David.

I wanted to reassure him, but I also didn't want to lie.

'I don't know.'

'Well, now I feel loads better.'

'She's as safe as anyone can be at this point. No one will be able to get to her at the coven, but if all we do is sit by her side playing nurse, we'll just be watching her die. So let's get on with this.'

I strode through the cemetery gates with David at my side.

It had happened eighty years ago. Twenty years before my witches created me. David had read about it on an old police blotter – a matter-of-fact rendition of something terrible. Something beyond terrible.

Alice Travers had been nine years old, sent by her mum to buy some bread early one morning. She never made it to the shop. Two kids from her year at school had been out early, too.

A boy and a girl who had made it their daily routine to terrorise Alice. Eventually, it led to their expulsion from the school they shared, and Alice had thought it was over.

It almost was.

The two kids knew Alice would be out alone, bright and early. Being sent to the shop for bread was a daily chore. The boy had been the first to see her. It seemed like he was on his own. Alice had run, straight ahead, towards the shops, and the boy had given chase. Alice met the girl soon after, blocking the path ahead. The bullies has purposefully cut off two paths of escape, forcing Alice to blindly run down the back alley. The back alley out of view of any passers-by. The back alley with the dead end.

Alice must have realised right away that she'd made a mistake. Did she know what was about to happen? She must have been terrified but thought, at worst, they'd punch and kick her. Taunt her. Spit on her. Did she have any idea at all about what the two bullies really had in store for her that morning?

I wondered how they'd gone about it. Had they padded towards her, slowly and deliberately, enjoying the fear? Dragging it out until Alice's heart felt like it was going to give out? Or had they run into the alley, sprinted towards her, hungry to get started?

The kids, when the police picked them up, claimed they hadn't meant to kill Alice Travers. That they'd just wanted to teach her a lesson for getting them into trouble. For getting them expelled from school and in terrible strife with their parents. Had they been telling the truth? Was it a case of bullying gone too far? Or maybe a mania had overtaken them, a blood lust as they egged each other on, past the point of no return. Maybe the creature had been there—almost a real thing but not quite—pushing them on and on to keep hitting, keep stamping, one more time, one more time, go on, enjoy the music of screams and broken bones. Dance to the pain.

Give me life.

They'd left Alice's body behind the bins, legs sticking out. One of the shopkeepers found it a few hours later as he went to dump some old stock. Little Alice Travers, just nine years old and dead already. Her body a twisted mess. Who'd think two eleven-year-olds could be capable of such a bleak and vicious act?

The creature knew. And now it had come to punish them all. For Alice. For everyone like her.

'Oi, over here,' called David, waving me to him as he stood over a gravestone. 'This must be it, look.'

Alice Travers, read the inscription, *Beloved Daughter, 1928-1937.*

Such a short life. Nine years and dumped behind some bins.

'So, what now?' asked David. 'I didn't bring a shovel. Are we just gonna knock on the gravestone and invite her out?'

I needed something from the incident itself. Something with a physical connection, and what would give me a stronger connection than Alice herself?

'I'm not sure I feel entirely amazing about this,' said David. 'Fighting monsters is one thing, but robbing the graves of little girls is a bit, you know... much. I'll be leaving this one out of my memoirs, anyway.'

'We need Alice,' I replied. 'If it makes you feel any better, it's just her bones down there, sitting in a box.'

'Right, just a box of kid bones. That does make me feel lots better. Cheers, Stella.'

'I mean, it's not *her* anymore, it's just stuff she left behind. She isn't her body. She isn't her bones. But those bones will give us the best connection possible to what happened in that alley eighty years back. Something to pry open the window between worlds and drag the creature out.'

'So we can kick the shit out of it.'

'Oh, yes.'

'Right. So, are we just digging with our paws like a couple of dogs, or...?'

I raised an eyebrow and gestured for him to stand back. I stood at the foot of the small grave and breathed in slowly. The magic of the cemetery began to wash towards me in great, lapping waves as I made myself a focal point for the Uncanny. The background magic here was strong. This was an old place full of ancient things.

I felt the magic filling me up and reached out with my hands. 'Alice,' I said. 'Alice, come here.'

I fixated on the command, rolling it over and over in my mind. I felt my hands become irresistible, an undeniable force, demanding and insisting.

The ground below trembled a little, then the dirt on the grave plot shook and split.

'Alice. Alice, come here now. Come here.'

Something began to force its way out of the ground. A patch of dirty white that spread and then pushed itself out and into the morning light.

A skull.

Alice's skull.

I lowered my hands, allowing the magic to drain away from me. I felt David step in beside me and we both looked at the small skull that had wriggled free of the earth, its eyes wide black holes.

'Well,' said David, 'nothing about that was a poop-inducing nightmare.'

'Come on,' I said. 'Grab the skull and let's get to work.'

As we left Acton Cemetery, David holding the skull under his jacket, nodding meekly at an old man giving his dog a morning walk, I felt hopeful. We had something to fight with now. Something we could use to pull this creature into the light.

Something to save Amy.

22

Back at the coven I used a pestle and mortar to grind a piece of the skull into a fine powder.

'She's still... she's okay,' said David, entering the coven's main room to join me.

'Good. I've finished,' I said, indicating to Alice's powdered skull before carefully tipping it into a leather pouch, which I placed in my pocket.

'You know, there's something very wrong about all of this. It just feels, odd. I mean, we just ground up a child's head.'

'Believe me, I've done worse.'

David nodded, then shook his head and laughed. 'Jesus, my life was a lot more simple before you showed up in my house, yapping about monsters. I had a life and a job I was good at. Well, pretty good at. Sometimes. And now...'

I almost didn't respond in case the reply was something I didn't want to hear. I swallowed. 'And now what?'

'Well, it's never boring, is it?' he said, and winked.

'No. No, it's not.'

'I just want to say, Stella, I wouldn't change it. I wouldn't want to go back. No matter how bad it gets, I couldn't just turn my back on all this and pretend the Uncanny didn't exist. I couldn't, you know, turn my back on you.'

A heavy silence. I thought back to the drunken walk home from a few nights previous, about what almost happened, then patted the bag of ground skull in my pocket.

'We need to get back to the alley. To the place Alice was murdered.'

David sighed and nodded. 'Yeah.'

'You don't have to come,' I told him. 'I can't ask you to risk going through what happened last time. Not again.'

'Hey, that's my niece in there. My family. And even if it wasn't, kids across the city are in danger. Helping them is my job. It doesn't matter if that's frightening, I took an oath. So let's get on with it, yeah?'

We stood and left the coven, David checking on Amy one last time before we left her behind again. I wondered what it was she was experiencing as she lay still in that bed. What place the creature had taken her to, and what it was making her go through. I almost felt like I could hear her screaming. Screaming in pain, in fear. Screaming for help.

Well, help was on its way.

At least I hoped it was.

23

David had started to talk a lot, even more than usual, and his usual level was like a six-year-old on a sugar high.

'Easily the best Carpenter film, that. *The Thing*. How can you not have seen *The Thing*?'

'My witches weren't really big on movie nights.'

'Well, we're getting that watched. And then we can get on to the others. You'll love *They Live*. It's about this bloke who gets to see the world as it really is, all covered in monsters and that. Remind you of anyone you know?' he said, jabbing a thumb at himself.

I nodded. I knew what this was. David was trying to distract himself. To dampen his nerves as we got off the tube and drew closer to that cursed place.

He stopped as we stood before the mouth of the alley.

'You can stay out here while I do my thing if you want,' I told him.

'No, I'm going in there. You never know, you might need me to help you if, well, if shit goes down and stuff.'

'And stuff?'

'Yeah.'

'Okay.' I walked forward, David following a pace or two behind. On my third or fourth step into the space I felt the atmosphere around me darken, just like the last time. The shadow of the incident, of what had happened to Alice as she ran in there eighty years ago, the devil at her heels.

'You feel that?' asked David, breathing in short, shallow breaths.

'Yeah. It still lives here. Stamped into our reality. Alice's murder at the hands of her school bullies.'

'You realise none of those sentences make me feel even the tiniest bit better, right?'

The first time we came here, David hadn't noticed the way the past had tainted this alley, not until it infected him. This time, it was like he was more tuned into the alley's darkness. It had taken him once and left its mark on him.

'Come on,' I said, and made my way deeper into the alley, taking the leather pouch out of my pocket.

'So what are you going to do, exactly?'

'I'm going to try and summon the past. The incident is still happening, even as we stand here. It's happening again and again, a never-ending repeat. We can use Alice to try and bring it fully into our realm so we can see it.'

'And if you can do that?'

'If I can do that, maybe the big bad will show up too.'

'Well, there's nothing I like more than terrifying hell beasts, so get cracking, magic lady.'

I poured the ground remains of Alice's skull into the palm of my right hand. Felt its coarseness between my fingers.

'*Wake no more*,' I said, then threw the skull dust into the air.

Rather than fall to the ground or get caught by the wind and whisked away, the remains hung in front of us, like someone had pressed pause on the passing of time.

'Is that you doing that?' whispered David.

'Shh.'

'Sorry.'

The remains were caught in the heavy, bleak magic that washed up and down the alley. The skull was part of this alley's story. It wanted it. Wanted to claim it. I closed my eyes and became a focal point for the magic, willing it to flow towards me, to enter me.

'Wake no more, said nobody's child, kicked and beaten, turned mean and wild.'

The alley darkened. It knew the words. Recognised the power they held.

The skull cloud began to swirl and dance in front of me.

'Do you hear that?' asked David, looking around. 'I think I heard a kid.'

I ignored him. Couldn't let him break my concentration. Couldn't let anything break my connection to the magic in the alley, to Alice's remains, to the rhyme.

'Wake no more, said the fearful small, for now I am here, to punish you all.'

I threw my arms out and inhaled, my mouth a vortex, inescapable, the cloud of ground skull entering me, filling my lungs.

'Stella? Stella, are you okay? Talk to me.'

For a moment I was Alice. I saw everything she ever saw, felt everything she'd ever felt. Her whole life opened up to me, every smell, every pain, every half-asleep dawn. It rushed through me, intoxicating. If I wasn't careful I could get lost in it. Could become submerged and lose myself in the confusion. I couldn't let it. If I did I might never escape.

'Wake no more!'

I bent double, screaming, and the cloud of Alice's skull was expelled, exploding out of me, tearing through what we saw of the alley like shrapnel through flesh. The alley as we knew it, in our time, was peeling away and being replaced by something that looked similar, but not quite. An older version. The version of eighty years ago.

I realised I was on my knees, coughing, with David patting my back.

'You know smoking is bad for you, right? Especially smoking the ground up skull of a long-dead child. Seriously, ask any doctor.'

I grunted and stood. 'It worked.'

'Yeah? So, did we travel back in time? Is that's what's happened here?'

'No. Well, not exactly. We're still in the same alley, we haven't gone anywhere, or any-when. I just used the magic in the alley, the memory of what happened here with Alice as the connection. Used it to pull the past version forward so we could see it.'

'Okay, tell me you heard it this time,' said David, looking around.

I did. It was a child. A girl. She was screaming.

'Look,' I said, David following the dart of my eyes.

There was something behind the bins. Two small legs poking out and into view.

'Is it her?' asked David.

We stepped forward and there she was. Alice Travers, her chest rising spasmodically to drag in a desperate last breath or two. Her face a mess, her teeth in her hair like macabre jewels, blood the pillow her head rested upon.

She looked up to us through the one eye she could still open, and then she died.

24

I blinked and Alice was gone, melted away in a heartbeat.

'Jesus Christ,' said David, quietly. 'The report said... well, it didn't go into detail about Alice's injuries. Kids did that?'

I nodded. 'Two little kids. Cruel and savage and bloodthirsty.'

'Where's she going, Jack?'

'Nowhere after this, Tilly.'

Voices at the entrance to the alley. We turned to see Alice, wild-eyed, racing towards us, her two attackers slowing as they entered, knowing their quarry had nowhere to go.

A dead end.

'Hey, it's okay,' said David, trying to get Alice's attention. But of course she wasn't really there. This was a repeat. I shivered as the cold memory of her brushed past us, prickling my skin.

'Is she a ghost? Are they all ghosts?' asked David.

'No. Not exactly. Ghosts still have their own mind, their own personality. Most of them anyway.'

'Like Jake, from The Beehive?'

'Right. This is different. This is a snapshot that the magic in this alley has claimed as its own.'

Alice was backed up against the wall now as the two kids, Jack and Tilly, walked past us.

'They look so normal,' said David.

It was true. They didn't look like murderers. But then what would that look like, anyway?

'Don't come near me, I'll tell. I'll tell a copper.' Alice's voice was small and thin. She knew it didn't matter what she said, Jack and Tilly were going to hurt her, anyway.

Tilly's knuckles connected with Alice's jaw and she fell to the ground.

'Can't you do anything?' blurted David.

'Please,' said Alice. It turned out that "please" was the last coherent word Alice Travers ever said.

Things moved fast then as a sort of mania overtook her attackers. Maybe it was the creature, or the idea of the creature, urging them on. Overwhelming them. Pushing them to go further than they'd intended.

Do it, go on, do it.

I realised with horror that the two attackers were grinning as they went about their work. David tried to intervene but it was pointless, this wasn't really happening. Not now. It was in the past, an imprint of history.

Then came a blast of wind that almost blew the two kids off their feet, halting their savage attack. They turned, shielding their eyes as a bright light illuminated the alley. The brick walls and cobbled ground seemed to warp. A ripple, like a throat swallowing, flowing down towards us.

'What's going on?' asked David.

'Something has just been born,' I replied.

'Wake no more, wake no more, no more, no more.'

The words fluttered around us like feathers, tickling at our ears.

'For now I am here, to punish you all.'

Jack and Tilly were the ones that looked scared now. They

raced for a way out, sprinting from the broken body they'd left in a bloodied, undignified heap behind the bins.

This was it.

This was the moment.

I raised my hands above my head and willed the magic towards me. Alice's skull was still in the surrounding air, and I inhaled some of it back into my lungs.

'Please, Please, Please—'

A foot stamping down and down and I know suddenly I'm going to die and I worry about my mum crying when she finds out and—

'Wake no more,' I said, placing demands in my mind as I said the opening line again. I placed together ancient words that insisted the hidden Uncanny show itself.

'Please, Please—'

The magic around me crackled and popped. Screeched like twisting metal. Something was coming.

'Wake no more, wake no more, wake no more—'

'Stella, look,' said David, tugging at my jacket and pointing all around us.

Shapes were beginning to emerge into this realm. Small shadows, one by one, fading up into view.

'It's... are they children?' asked David.

They were. More and more appeared, crowding around us. All the children laid up in comas in Ealing Hospital. In hospitals all over London. In my coven.

'Amy!'

David ran to one of the shadows. Somehow we both knew it was her.

'Amy, can you hear me? Come on Ames, it's Uncle David, I've come to get you.'

The spell had only partially worked. I hadn't been strong enough to completely pull the creature's realm into our own, only to give us a glimpse of it. An afterimage.

'Stella, come on, do something. She's right here. Save her.'

I closed my eyes and willed the magic into me.

It filled me, made my skin itch, my heart dance, my breath quicken. More and more I soaked in.

'*Show me, show me, show me—*'

For now I have come, for now I have come, for now I have come to punish you all.

Screams.

The children, the shadows of all the children it had taken, were terrified. They scattered, running in and out of view, like they were blinking in and out of reality.

'Amy? Stop, come back Amy!'

She was lost, it was impossible to know which of the shadows was hers now as they merged, ran, panicked, a mass of screaming horror.

'What are they running from?' asked David. 'What can they see?'

A shiver ran up my spine. 'Him,' I replied. There was a man stood before the brick wall, before the alley's dead end. 'They're running from him.'

'*Wake no more, said the fearful small, for now I am here, to punish you all.*'

25

The man, the creature, stood quite still.

He was tall, taller than any normal man, and thin besides. The suit he wore clung to him like a second skin. Perhaps it *was* his skin. His skin forming the idea of clothes. He had hair, brown, a simple short, neat cut, but below the hair there were no features. No face at all, just blank, white skin.

'Is that it? Is that him?' asked David, backing up a step.

'That's the monster,' I said.

'Children? Why do you run from me?' asked the man, somehow speaking even though he didn't have a mouth. His voice was level, calm, soothing, and yet terrifying.

'Children, I am here. There is nowhere for you to go now. Only I exist. Me and my desires. And I desire to punish you all. All the wicked and the small.'

The man stepped forward. Well, I assume he did. I didn't actually see him move, didn't see him place one foot in front of the other and actually step anywhere. It's just that he was suddenly one step forward.

'Why do you hide from me, children? I only want what's worst for you.'

'Stella, I don't... I don't feel good, I...' David was backing up against the wall, his hair sticking to the sweat on his forehead. He began to slide down the wall, lifting up his hands to protect himself. 'Don't let them touch me. Please, don't let them touch me!'

The creature had moved again, another two unseen steps forward.

'Cruel, cruel, cruel. So small yet so full of hate. I would cry and weep, and sob a river of tears, believe me; if only I had eyes of my own. Poor me. Poor, poor me.'

I ran to David, trying to keep the creature in my field of vision.

'David, you're okay, they aren't here. Those kids are just in your mind.'

'They climbed over the fence. He's got a knife. I saw it. He's going to cut me!'

'Interesting,' said the creature, now crouched at my side, staring with the eyes it didn't have at the cowering David.

Its sudden appearance made me jerk away in surprise, falling to my side.

'Please, they're pushing the blade too hard, it's going to cut me. Going to cut me open!'

'Let me see.'

'Get away from him,' I yelled, scrambling to get up and onto my feet as the faceless man reached forward and sank his hand into David's chest, as though his arm and hand were made of smoke.

David's eyes opened wide. I wondered what he was seeing. Did he feel the creature's hand on his heart?

'Oh, yes,' said the creature. 'Such pain. Sad, sad, sad. What is it you would wish to do to those boys?'

'Hurt them. Hurt them badly,' replied David through gritted teeth.

'Now I have come, to punish you all.'

'Oi, monster, over here,' I shouted, waved my hands and

stamped my feet, but the faceless man didn't pay me any attention. It's like I wasn't even there. I wanted to attack the thing. To throw balls of fire at its featureless head, but I couldn't risk doing anything while it had its hand inside David's chest.

'Monstrous children. That is what they are, you know. All and all and all. The victim. The guilty. Interchangeable. One and the same. Anger and violence. Pain and shame.'

David whimpered, curled up on the dirty cobbles, the creature looming over him, its hand still inside his chest. 'I didn't do anything to them. Why did they do that?' he asked, his voice smaller than I'd ever heard it. 'They took my hair.'

That wasn't David the grown man speaking, it was David the young boy. Scared and powerless. The creature was attuned to children, and to childhood trauma in particular. David may not have been a child, but the creature could sniff out his past. His pain. I didn't have a childhood. Nothing for it to pay attention to. So it didn't. I wondered if it even knew I was there.

'I knew a child who killed dogs for kicks,' said the creature. 'She would tempt them with a tasty treat, then lead them out to a field and stove their heads in with a brick, safely out of sight, for she knew what she was up to was wicked and rotten and worse besides. She would collect the bloody mess and throw it into the river, the water rushing the corpse away to bye-bye. Then she started taking schoolmates who ticked her off most thoroughly. In went their heads, the cracking of skulls, and hey-ho, into the river they go. I took her in the end. She said the rhyme and so she was mine.'

Finally, it removed its hand from David's chest and stood.

'David? David, are you okay? Can you hear me?'

He looked up at me, eyes red, mouth quivering and silent.

The creature looked about. 'Children? Where did you go? Do you know, I don't think we're altogether where we should be. Whatever can the matter be?'

It wasn't going to work, I knew that before I tried. I pulled the magic of the alley towards me and, with a scream of effort, punched my hands towards the creature, one after the other, again and again, molten cords of energy arcing from my glowing knuckles to whiplash against the creature.

It didn't even flinch.

It looked solid, more solid than the shadow children, but really it was barely any more substantial. Just a piece of the other realm made visible to us by the spell I'd cast.

David was crying on the ground. The creature turned to him again.

'Ah, the music of tears. I know this tune well. This is my song.'

I ran at the faceless man as he moved towards David again. Screaming, I tried to tackle him, willed myself to make contact, but I passed through him and tumbled painfully to the ground.

'Perhaps we could sing a duet?' suggested the creature, and lifted David to his feet, before plunging both phantom hands into his chest. David gasped, his head snapping back, eyes wide.

'David!'

The sound of children screaming began to swirl around us, growing in volume, almost physically assaulting me, beating me down. I pulled the magic into me in a panic, unleashed it in an unfocused rage, trying to kill the spell. Send this version of the alley, the creature and the children, back to their own realm.

'So sad,' said the creature, 'I feel your pain. I am your pain. I am your urge and retribution.'

David stopped crying and started screaming.

My hands burned hot. I didn't have a choice. It was either pointless or dangerous, but this thing was harming David. Perhaps even killing him. I had to throw whatever I had at the thing and hope for—

The ground shook.

I staggered back, the wall stopping me, the fire in my hands sputtering out as confusion took the spell's place in my mind.

'Oh, don't fight,' the creature told David. 'We're friends, you and I. Best of friends. Best of enemies.'

David's head slowly righted itself to look directly at the creature.

There was something wrong with his eyes.

They were filled with fire.

A white hot glow that seeped from the sockets. Was this the creature's doing? What was happening to him?

'David! David, are you okay?'

He lifted his hands and took hold of the creature's forearms, slowly pulling them from his chest. I'd passed right through the thing like I was a ghost, and yet here was David gripping the thing by the arms.

'Don't want to be friends? Oh, dear. Oh, my.'

David pushed the creature out of him, the power in his eyes had now escaped from his eye sockets and was spreading out, his whole head blazing with white fire.

'David, stop,' I said, weakly. I found myself sliding away across the wall, my arm raised to shield myself from the heat he was generating. This couldn't just be the creature's effect. What the hell was going on?

David spoke, his voice a deep, unnatural rumble: 'Finished.'

He threw out his arms and the raging fire erupted from him, burning down this vision of the creature's realm as the power he unleashed tore my spell apart. Pure, unbridled power flew from him and raged around the alley. I found myself on the ground, covering my head and fully expecting the flames to burn me to ash.

It didn't happen.

Breathing heavily, I peeked out from behind my arms to see the spell I'd cast was over. Whatever David had done had wiped it away. Broken the connection. The other realm was hidden again, and we were back in the here and now.

'Stella?'

I turned to see David curled up on the ground. Whatever

the energy was that had burned around him and killed my spell was gone.

I stood and moved warily towards him. 'David, are you... okay?'

He looked up at me as he unfurled from his foetal position, then slowly pushed himself up, using the wall for support. 'This is definitely my least favourite dingy alley in London,' he said. 'And I include the one where a junkie stabbed me in the guts with a four inch blade. So, you know, stiff competition.'

He rubbed at his eyes, the eyes that had burned with magical power moments earlier.

'It was here, David. The creature was here,' I said, dumbfounded by what had happened. By what David had been able to do.

He placed his palms on his chest, to where the faceless man's hands had entered. 'Amy was here,' he said. 'She was here. Almost here.'

'I couldn't save her. Not like she was. The spell wasn't strong enough.'

David sighed and shuffled forwards as we made our way out of the alley and back into the light of the street. 'So now what?' he asked.

'I'll think of something, don't worry. We'll get Amy back, I promise.'

What had I said about making promises?

26

We found a nearby pub and collapsed into a booth, David's hand noticeably trembling as he lifted his pint glass to his lips. His shakes upset the beer, which rolled down the side of the glass and dribbled over his fingers onto the table.

'Shit,' he said as he placed his glass down, half annoyed at the spillage, half embarrassed that he was still so shook up.

We should have gone straight back to the coven to check on Amy, but who were we kidding? We knew what we'd find: Amy laid out in bed, still as a corpse, no closer to being saved. So, instead we found a dingy corner to numb a bit of the doubt and frustration. I took two big gulps and rested the already half empty pint glass back on the table, holding it tight in my hand.

'It could see me. The creature, I mean,' said David. 'Why could it see me and not you?'

More to the point, what the hell did you just do back there, David?

'I don't know,' I replied. 'Well, not for certain. But I think it must be something to do with what happened to you as a kid. It seemed like you were experiencing that memory again. That childhood trauma. It must have put you on its radar. With me, it acted like I wasn't even there.'

'Well, don't take it personally, but maybe you're not his type.'

I smiled and sipped at my drink. 'Funny, but I think that is exactly it. I was born an adult, so I don't have any childhood pain for it to take notice of. I might as well not exist as far as it's concerned. Maybe it literally can't see me because of that.'

David sighed and shook his head, lifting his drink to his mouth again.

He looked normal.

There was no trace of the power, the magic that had exploded out of him. No evidence of the white-hot flames that had burned out of his eyes, his mouth, his entire head.

'You know, my nut is banging here. I must have hit it on the ground or something.'

"Or something", was right.

Was this connected to his new ability to see ghosts? What the hell had Mr. Trick done to him?

'What are you looking at me like that for?' asked David.

'Like what? I'm not looking at you like anything.'

'You're looking at me like a big-eyed puppy that you're about to put down. What's up?'

'Nothing, just... I didn't like to see you like that. In the alley, I mean. That's all.'

Well, that was sort of true. Just not in the way he would take it.

'Yeah, well, it wasn't exactly a picnic for me, either. You know, I'd happily locked that memory up in the dark recesses of my noggin, and now here it is again. Any time I want to I can picture those three turds stood over me, knife in hand. I can even remember how I smelled after I pissed my pants. Of piss, if you were wondering.' He snorted and shook his head.

I should have told him, I know that. It's like finding out someone has an illness and deciding it's better for them if they don't know. It's never better for them, but I didn't know exactly what it was that had happened to David. It may have had nothing to do with the effect of Mr. Trick living inside of him. Maybe what had happened in the alley was just some, I don't know, natural backlash to the creature messing with him. Maybe, because he was an adult, his body had just reacted like an antibody, fighting off an infection.

It was possible.

No, I didn't believe me either.

'Stella,' said David, indicating past me with his head. 'Oi, mate, turn that up will you?'

I looked over to see the barman pick up the remote control and turn up the sound on the pub's television. It was a news report. A woman with a serious face and serious hair was informing London about the strange spate of children slipping into comas that was happening across the city. Since we'd last checked in, the number had grown.

Eighty-seven.

Eighty-seven kids had closed their eyes and failed to open them again.

'It's spreading,' I noted.

'And the number's increasing each day.'

The woman put forward one viewer's tweeted theory that the children had drunk a contaminated soft drink; a chemical attack by terrorists. The Daily Mail was running with that one for the next day's front page. One crackpot pundit said it was down to the soup of Wi-Fi waves we live in, affecting the brainwaves of developing minds.

The newsreader moved on to discussing the opening of London's fourth cereal cafe, and the barman switched over to the football.

'It's only getting worse,' David lamented. 'What's our next move, Stella? How do we batter this thing?'

27

My witches would have known what to do.

Kala, Trin, and Feal; they would have taken this thing down as easy as you like. The creature wasn't even real, not in the dictionary sense of the word. It was just a magical creation, pulled into existence by the emotions of children. Kala and the rest had already taken it down once, before my time. They'd tackled the thing and beaten it. Protected the children of this city from saying the rhyme. From falling asleep and never waking up again.

But my witches were dead, and whatever safeguards they had put in place to stop this thing, to stop things like it, were growing weak. Now there was only me left to try and stop it. Well, there was Giles L'Merrier, but nowadays he seemed disinterested in the plight of man. Kala used to speak about him a lot. Of the brave and mighty L'Merrier, of the people he would save and the evil he would brush aside and stomp under his foot. She spoke about him with a sort of reverence in her voice, like he was one step above even them. Like she almost worshipped him. But that wasn't the man holed up in his dusty antiques shop. Now it seemed like the world bored him. Irritated him. I wondered what it would take for L'Merrier to step out of that shop and lend a hand.

I sent David to the coven to check on Amy. I didn't want to go back. Didn't want to see her, not yet. Not since the promises I'd made were no closer to being kept. So I walked the streets of West London, pulling my leather jacket tight around me, lost in my thoughts. Or at least that's what I was doing at first. After that I was just pretending to be distracted. Pretending like I didn't know someone was following me.

When you work in my line of business you develop a sort of sixth sense. A little twinge that lets you know when someone is stalking you. I felt the hairs on the back of my neck stand up. A prickle that worked itself up and down my spine.

I knew the routine by now. Knew how to snatch a look at who it was surveilling me without letting on that I knew they were there. I'd stop in front of a shop window, pretending to scan the goods inside, but actually catching a glimpse of the person lingering behind me. Then I'd make a sudden change of direction, turning back on myself. The surprise would cause whoever was following me to stop, to waver, caught off guard. In the split-second it took them to right themselves, I'd learn who was on my tail and what they looked like.

It only took rolling those two strategies out a couple of times to figure out two things: first, it wasn't one person following me, it was several. One was stalking me for a while, for five or ten minutes, then someone else would take their place, like they were part of a tag team. Second: I knew what it was. It was a breed of low-level Uncannies, all from the same clan. I knew that because they always kept to their own, and besides, I knew this one by name.

'Razor,' I said, nodding my head by way of a greeting as I sat on some stone steps, waiting for him to catch up.

'Familiar,' he said, spitting the words past his small, sharp teeth.

'Is there something I can do for you? Your whole clan seems very interested in my movements.'

'Yeah, because I asked them to find you. We eaves know things, hear things. If someone needs to be found, we can track them down.'

'I'm still waiting for an explanation. And believe me, I'm not in the best of moods right now, so if you're just here to piss me off, or try to feed me some more dog shit, I'll be more than willing to take a little frustration out on that ugly mug of yours.'

'So disrespectful. The High-born always are.' He slapped his forehead. 'Oh, I'm sorry, you weren't "born", were you? You were puked out by some witches to do their bitch work.'

I stood, hands throbbing with power, and Razor snarled, baring his teeth.

'A little frustration therapy it is then.'

I raised a fist, magic swirling around it in molten threads, expecting Razor to either attack or run. Instead, he sagged his shoulders and bowed his head.

'What is this? You talk big and then give in at the first sign of trouble? That is very disappointing, Razor. But don't think it'll stop me knocking those yellow teeth out of your skull. I don't like being followed.'

I raised my fist and stepped forward, ready to teach Razor his—by my count—seventy-fifth harsh lesson. But something stopped me. He looked up, and for the first time I saw something in Razor I'd never seen before.

Vulnerability.

'What is it? What's wrong?'

'I... I need your help, Familiar.'

'You need what now?'

'Your help. We all do.' He broke eye contact, like he was ashamed. 'It's our children. We need you to help our children.'

28

Razor and I had never exactly spent quality time together. The extent of our relationship to date had amounted to me tapping him for information at The Beehive, or leaving a cracked tooth in his jaw when he did something to piss me off. Needless to say, strolling down the street by his side felt more than a little strange.

Obviously, I didn't trust him, never could and never would, so I was on high alert the whole time, waiting for the other shoe to drop. Was he leading me into a trap? That seemed the most likely end result, but then what for, and for whom?

We didn't make small talk as we walked, which was fine by me. He led me through the streets of Hammersmith, up back alleys, down blind alleys hidden from the normals of London, through doors that led to places they shouldn't have. He was taking me to his den. To his home.

The eaves hide their nests where no one can find them, even if you've been taken there before and think you've memorised the location, you'll soon find yourself lost and trying to figure out which wrong turn you took. It was one of the things they did with the magic they received in exchange for knowledge. Because when your stock in trade is tattling and telling tales, the last thing you want is to be traceable, otherwise who knows what will come knocking on your door?

Razor and I walked across rooftops then through a door into the sewers, swatting away the curious fairies that lived there. Well, I swatted them away. Razor grabbed a few and snapped them open, drinking down the magical juice within. For some reason fairy magic doesn't have the same effect on the eaves as the magic I gave them. For Razor and those like him, the fairy juice was like chewing nicotine gum. It scratched an itch, but wasn't the same.

Finally, we found ourselves before a large, wooden door that had seen better days. It had been painted bright red once, but now the only paint left on it was huddled in small, peeling patches.

'We're here,' he said. 'Wipe your feet on the way in.'

As he opened the door I looked up at the large, three-storey Victorian house and wondered which street we were on exactly. I looked around me, squinted, but any time I looked away from the house it was like I was wearing goggles that someone had smeared gloop all over. Giving up, I stepped into Razor's house, wiping my feet on the mat inside, and closing the door behind me.

'D'you want a cup of tea?' asked Razor.

'Tea?' I replied, surprised. 'I never imagined you'd be much of a host, Razor.'

'Yeah. Well, I do have some fucking manners.'

He turned and trudged up the staircase. I could hear the noise of a TV seeping down from above. I looked back at the closed door and wondered what the hell I was doing. How was this helping the job at hand? How was this helping me keep my promise to David about saving Amy?

'You coming or what?' asked Razor.

I followed up the stairs. 'You get five minutes,' I told him. 'Some of us have got work to do.'

'Yeah, yeah.'

Eyes peered at me from darkened rooms as I walked, and I heard a few unpleasant words muttered as I passed. I could hardly blame them for that. I'd never exactly been pleasant to the eaves.

The house itself looked like a crack den: an abandoned, dilapidated building that the eaves has found and moved into. Squatted in, made it their own. From the look of the place, not to mention the smell, eaves weren't too house proud.

'In there,' said Razor, pointing to a room at the end of the corridor.

'And what am I going to find in there?' I asked. 'Because if this is some sort of trap, I'll be leaving you with more than a few bruised ribs this time, understand?'

Razor snarled then spat on the threadbare carpet. 'Just get in there you piece of... just, in you go.'

He went inside and I followed. I wasn't expecting what I found. The room was quite large, larger than you would expect for an upstairs room in a house like this. More evidence of magic. They obviously used it for more than getting off their heads and making their dens tricky to locate. The walls were lined with single beds. Next to each sat an eaves, who looked up to me with barely concealed contempt as I entered.

'What is this?' I asked, my voice a whisper.

'You know exactly what it is, Familiar,' replied Razor, and went over to one of the beds, joining a female eaves who was sat next to it.

I moved around the room, from bed to bed. Each contained a small figure. A child. The young of this eaves clan. All had their eyes closed and were sound asleep. The reality of the situation was obvious.

'They spoke the rhyme?' I said.

'Of course they did,' replied Razor.

'How did they get hold of it?'

'We're eaves, Familiar. We listen. That's what we do. Something like that rhyme wasn't going to be passed around our streets without us getting wind of it eventually.'

There were nine beds in all. Nine beds containing nine young eaves.

'How long?'

'First few went down two nights back, the rest since,' replied Razor, one hand resting on the arm of the young eaves in the bed he sat next to. Was that Razor's own child? In my wildest dreams, I'd never imagined he was a father. To be honest, I'd barely given him much thought at all besides what I could get out of him, or what I would do to him if he sold me up the river.

'Why am I here, Razor?'

'Why are you here?' He stood, a snarl baring his sharp, yellow teeth. 'You've got the nerve to stand in this room, to look at these beds, and ask why you're here?'

I tensed and took a step backwards, looking at all the eyes now on me. They weren't happy eyes. They were angry, eager, ready to attack.

'This isn't my doing Razor, I'm trying to stop this.'

'You're *"trying"*? Trying doesn't make our young open their eyes, does it? They're alive right now—just about—but how long is that going to last? Huh? Will they die today? Tomorrow? Is there any way back for them?'

I'd never let Razor talk to me like that. Usually my fist would have connected with his jaw a few sentences in, but I felt weak. Powerless. Because he was right.

'I know what the creature is. I found it.'

'Then why aren't my young awake?'

'I just need to figure out a way to stop it. To destroy it if I can.'

'*"If"*? I bring you to my den, show you this, and all you've got is an *"if"*?'

'I can't promise anything.'

I thought about what I'd said to David. The promise

tumbled out easily then, more than once, because I wanted him to believe in me. I wanted him to believe I was going to take that pain away.

'You know how long it took your witches to deal with this the last time? One day. One morning kids in Hanwell didn't wake up, and by the evening they'd taken care of the whole thing. The creature never affected another child. How many nights have passed this time?'

'I'm not my masters,' I replied.

'No, you're not. You're a weak little familiar that they made out of dirt and spit. A mindless thug without an ounce of their knowledge. You think you're what London needs? That you can just take up the mantle of the London Coven all on your own and keep everyone safe?'

I realised I was backed up against a wall, my heart beating like a jackhammer. He was right. I wasn't as good as my masters, nowhere near. Maybe I didn't have what it took to replace them. Maybe I doing more damage than good.

'I'm trying, Razor. I'll beat this thing, I prom... I'll beat it.'

Razor snorted and his eyes narrowed. 'You'd better. Because it's not just the young of normals being taken. It's everyone's. And we all know whose job it's supposed to be to fix it, so if you don't, we'll be coming for you. All of us.' He pointed to the door. 'Now get the fuck out of my house.'

29

David was slumped on the couch in the coven's main room when I got back, his mobile phone discarded on the floor several feet away.

'Good walk?' he asked.

'Yeah. No. Not really. Razor took me home to see the family.'

David looked at me with a not unreasonable amount of confusion. 'Say what?'

'Oh, he was just showing me what a shit job I'm doing, that's all.'

'Fair enough.'

I gestured at the phone on the floor, 'What's happened now?'

He sat up and sighed. 'I called my sister. Had a nice chat. Lied to her about her daughter, the one in the coma that she might never come out of. You remember Amy, right?'

'I remember.'

'I told her Amy was going to stay a few more nights because we were having so much fun, and that the reason she wasn't replying to calls or texts was because she dropped her phone in the toilet and we were trying to dry it out in a bag of rice. So, I feel really amazing right now and not at all like a subhuman piece of shit.'

I flopped on a chair and pictured the room of slumbering eaves, all being terrorised by the creature in its nightmare realm. They'd have been up and about had my witches been alive. Had Mr. Trick not dropped into our world and murdered them.

'You know, Magic Lady, the whole defeated body language you're rocking there isn't filling this detective with a lot of confidence.'

I waved a middle finger in his general direction.

'Ever the lady. Okay,' said David, 'enough with the sitting around feeling sorry for ourselves stuff, let's actually try and get this sorted out, shall we?'

'Don't you think that's what I want? I don't know what to do, David. Everyone is relying on me to stop this thing and I don't know how.'

'Do I ever seem like I know what I'm doing?'

I raised an eyebrow.

'Exactly, but I still solve cases. Because you don't need to know everything, or even anything. I just have to know the things the case shows me as I stumble around in the dark like an idiot. So let's act like detectives and put everything we know on the table. We do that, we have all the pieces out there, and we'll find what we need to do next. Standard procedure. Come on, what do we know about this thing?'

I smiled. David knew how to give me a metaphorical slap around the face to get me moving.

'Well, we know it takes kids. It's only interested in kids.'

'Okay, that's thing one. We also know it only takes them when they go to sleep.'

'And after they've already said the rhyme,' I said, standing and pacing.

'We know it zeroes in on childhood trauma. That it's drawn to it like a wasp to a sticky bun.'

'Yes, it was even distracted by yours, even though you're a grown-up.'

'Yes, I am a sort of a grown-up, whatever my ex says.'

'It seemed like it couldn't even see me because I don't have any childhood trauma. Or childhood.'

'Okay, another thing we know is that it doesn't really, sort of, exist here. Not where we are, right?'

'Right, yes. In the alley, when I managed to pull its realm into ours a little, I passed right through it. It doesn't exist properly here.'

'So what does that mean? We can't do anything to it?'

I stopped my pacing as a few thoughts started to coalesce. 'Yes. Yes, that's exactly what it means,' I said, grinning.

'Well, I'm glad that tickles you, Magic Lady, but it seems like a teensy bit of a problem from where I'm sitting.'

'I know what we have to do. I think I know.'

'That's definitely a positive. Run with it, Stella.'

'We have to go to the thing's realm and kick its teeth in over there.'

David nodded slowly, 'Okay. Following. Makes sense.'

'If I can get there I can finish this, I'm certain of it. Well, pretty certain.'

'Pretty certain?'

'Sixty percent. Sixty-five, maybe.'

'You're losing me a little. Let's bring this home strong. How do we actually, you know, get over there? To Scary Town?'

'The thing only pulls children into its world, yes?'

'Correct.'

'Then I just have to convince it I'm a child.'

Another slow nod. 'As simple as that, eh?'

'Yes. Actually, no. There's more...'

30

We found him supping a pint in the corner of the Camden Tavern.

'Well, well, look what the cat dragged in,' said Jake Fletcher, ghost and ex-exorcist, as we entered the pub. 'I take it this isn't a happy coincidence?'

'Um, who's this?' asked David, pointing at the man in the booth.

'That's Jake Fletcher, the Spectral Detective.'

David turned to him again, understandably confused. 'What are you talking about? This guy's much better looking.'

Jake scowled. 'You're a real charmer, you know that?'

We were off to a bad start, so I poured on some honey. 'Nice suit,' I remarked.

'You like? Cost a bomb I reckon,' he replied, stroking the lapels of his pinstripe jacket.

'I was talking about the meat suit,' I said, gesturing to the living body Jake was currently possessing.

'Oh, this old thing? Yeah, I sometimes need to avail myself of a living person every now and again. You know, when I've got something important needs seeing to, or when I fancy a drink and a packet of dry roasted. Cheers,' he said, raising the beer, taking a big gulp, and smacking his lips. 'You've no idea what a bugger it is not being able to have a drink whenever you want. Probably the worst thing about being dead.'

'I'm sorry,' said David, 'Are you saying you're currently possessing a living person?'

'Bang on, son. He's quick, isn't he, for a copper, I mean.'

I smiled and sat on a stool opposite Jake. Well, opposite Jake and the man he was currently riding around inside of.

David took the stool next to mine. 'Wait, is this not, well, not illegal, as such, but morally a bit... iffy?'

'I wouldn't get your knickers in a twist about it, mate. Grade-A turd, this one,' he said, prodding the chest of his meat suit. 'Like I said last time, he used to make my life a living hell growing up, so now, whenever I need a living body, I take his. Least he owes me, the twat. Besides, I make sure he never remembers any of it later. No harm, no foul.'

'All right then, I think I might get a drink. Stella?'

I nodded and David went to order.

'So, how did you know I'd be here?' Jake asked.

'A little birdie told me.'

'Oh, yeah?'

'Well, a little eaves anyway.'

'Those little bald guys with the piranha teeth? I had a ruckus with one of them a little while back. Razor he was called.'

I smiled. 'So, that was you who gave him the fresh bruises?'

'Seemed rude not to.'

He certainly had a sense of humour for a dead guy.

'So, is there a reason you two have rocked up in my local?' Jake asked. 'Don't get me wrong, it's always a pleasure to chew the fat with some other weirdos, but I was under the impression me and you weren't too friendly.'

'Have you seen the news?'

He nodded. 'The kids.'

'That's right.'

'I thought that was a bit naughty, yeah. I was going to have a gander at it myself at some point.'

'Right after you'd possessed a former bully so you could get drunk?'

'Priorities, Stella,' he said with a wink.

'This thing attacks children. It's attracted to childhood trauma, and I plan to use myself as bait. I want it to latch on to me and pull me into its realm so I can kick its teeth down its throat.'

'So, you're going to waft your childhood boo-hoos under its nose and hope it takes a bite?'

'Exactly.'

'And how are you meant to pull that one off? I've read about familiars, you're created exactly like you are now, all grown-up. You don't have a childhood.'

'No,' I replied, 'but you do.'

Jake sat back and grinned. 'Oh, I see how it is. You've come begging a favour, have you? Well isn't this a turn up.'

David returned, placing a pint before me and sitting down to take a mouthful out of his own. He wiped the foam from his mouth and looked at the pair of us, silently staring at each other. 'What did I miss?'

'Jake being a prick.'

'Right,' he replied, and took another swig.

'It's funny,' said Jake, 'because I seem to remember, not so very long ago, coming to you with a little heads-up about a potential giant, terrible problem and being told to do one, in no uncertain terms. That stung my cold, dead heart, I'm not gonna lie.'

'You can't blame her for that,' replied David. 'That's just her personality.'

I glared at David, then started on my drink.

'So, what's the deal with you two? Knocking boots?'

'What does that mean?' I asked.

'I'm picturing P.C. Plod here in something frilly, tied to a bed, while you stroll around in thigh-high boots, cracking a whip. Am I close? How close? Seventy percent of the way there?'

'Hey,' said David. 'Why am I the one tied up?'

'We're not a couple,' I said, my voice a little higher than I'd have liked.

'So, what you're saying is, you're available?'

I felt the blood rush to my face and had to swallow the urge to clobber the man Jake was possessing.

'Okay, okay,' said Jake. 'I'm rising above here. So what exactly is it you want from me that's important enough to interrupt pint and peanuts night?'

'Well,' I said, already regretting the words before I spoke them, 'Jake Fletcher, I want you inside of me.'

David coughed and spluttered as his drink went down the wrong way. 'What did you just say?' he gasped.

The way he said it, I sensed something more than just surprise. What was it? Was it jealousy? Did David care for me as something other than a friend?

This wasn't the place. I turned to Jake. 'So?' I said.

'So what?' he replied.

'Are you going to help me or not?'

'Give us a second,' he said, then lifted his pint, draining the last of its contents, before slapping the glass down and unleashing a deep burp. 'All right, Stella Familiar, it looks like we have ourselves a crossover episode.'

31

Jake knocked back eight shots of tequila, then went to the toilets and left the body he'd been possessing unconscious in one of the cubicles.

'Let's rock and roll,' he said, as he walked through the door, back in his ghost form, and headed for the street.

The fact that Jake could possess the living, and that he'd chosen to possess that body in particular, had been the two things that made my plan come together.

I needed to convince this nightmare creature that I was a child. The magic to make myself look like one was simple, but I needed more than that. I needed childhood trauma. Real trauma. And I needed it embedded deep in my brain.

That's where Jake came in.

First, he'd be able to jump inside me and share my body, share my mind. Well, share the bits I allowed him to. Then, when the creature came for me, my magic would convince it that I was a child, and Jake's childhood trauma would seal the deal. The trauma he'd told me about when we first met at The Beehive. The trauma the man he liked to possess had been responsible for.

It was a good plan. It would work. It had to, because if it didn't, I wasn't sure what else I could do.

'So, this is the London Coven, huh?' said Jake, looking around. 'I thought it would be a bit swankier. This place has all the soul of a motorway service station.'

We moved through to the bedroom where Amy was still laid out in her coma.

'Who's this then?'

'My niece,' said David.

'Right. Sorry about that. She still...?'

'She's alive,' I said. 'The thing has her, but she's alive. And I'm going to get her back.'

We moved Amy over so there was enough room for me to lay next to her. I took her hand and rested my head on the pillow. Amy was part one of the plan. My physical connection to her would get the trick rolling. Would fool the creature into thinking I was a child.

'Jake, when you're inside me, don't try to control anything. Don't try to move me. Just sit still and think about the things you used to suffer.'

'Well, this is going to be a barrel of laughs. I'm being sarcastic, by the way.'

'I got that,' said David.

'That's why you're the detective, Detective.'

David pulled up a chair and sat by my side. I held out my other hand and he took it in his. 'You're going to be my anchor, David. My way back in case I need to get out of that thing's realm fast. By holding your hand I've given myself a living, conscious tether back into this world, so whatever you do, don't let go. My life is literally in your hands.'

'If I need to pee really quick, is that okay?'

I shot David a dirty look then turned to Jake. 'Go on then, in you go.'

'Don't worry, darling, I'll be gentle.'

Jake warped and fuzzed, then lowered himself down to

move inside of me. It felt like being dropped into a cold bath as the two of us became one.

'Are you okay?' David's voice, but distant.

'Yes. It's just... it's uncomfortable.'

I shook my head as Jake's memories began to mix with my own. He wasn't possessing me, not completely. If he did, my conscious mind would drop out, and he'd take over completely. No, for this to work we had to exist as a duo. Like we were one and the same.

All right darling, whenever you're ready to stick your head in the lion's mouth.

Jake's voice inside my head. That was weird.

Yeah, it takes some getting used to.

I looked up to David, trying not to look worried.

'Go and kick this thing's arse,' he said. 'Go and show it who it's messing with, then bring Amy back. Bring them all back. And make sure you come back, too, okay?'

He squeezed my hand.

I turned my head and looked up at the ceiling. The magic of the coven washed around me and I pulled it into myself, the colours strobing as they drew towards me.

I was a child. I was a child like Amy. I wasn't a grown-up, I was young, small, still to fully develop.

I felt the spell connecting, felt the spark, the static, between my hand and Amy's.

Time for part two.

I put the correct words together in my mind, then closed my eyes and spoke a single word.

'Sleep.'

32

At first I was nowhere.

A black nothing without sound, without feeling, without time or space.

I tried to look at my hands to stop feeling so dislocated, but I wasn't even sure I had hands anymore. So I sat in the nothing for a while. Or stood in it. I wasn't really sure what I was doing.

Then I was in a room I half remembered from over twenty years ago. It was a bar, somewhere in Soho. Not sure where now, but I remembered being there a few times. I was singing karaoke with a person I'd never met before. At least I didn't remember meeting them. Then I was the person I didn't remember and I was annoyed that this other person, the me I was now stood opposite, didn't seem to know who I was.

'How can you not remember me?' I said to myself, but myself just shrugged, so we started to sing a duet to *American Pie* instead.

You're dreaming, Stella.

'I know that,' I said to Jake's voice.

I was myself again, and left the bar to get some fresh air, only when I stepped out into the street I somehow ended up in a train carriage. I sat and looked at the people at the other end, who seemed to be having a bit of a disagreement. I could see myself down there. It was my first mission for the London Coven. Not just my first mission, but my first day alive. I'd only been created hours earlier, and now there I was, chasing after a monster that could change its shape at will. I often thought about those people. The other passengers whose lives I'd dropped into. I'd made sure to remember each of their faces.

You haven't changed much in sixty years.

'I don't age. I am what I am.'

Like a sexy Popeye.

I just about resisted the urge to punch myself in the head.

I needed to get off this train, to stop thinking about my first day of life, because if I thought about that it would break the illusion that I was a child. That I'd had a childhood at all. Instead, I thought about Amy.

I was sat in bed and my mum, no, Amy's mum, was at the door, smiling at me. Angie, David's sister.

'What you still doing awake, Miss?' she asked.

'Having trouble sleeping, Mum,' I replied.

'Why's that then? You not tired?'

'I am. But that's when the bad thing comes.'

'No use fussing now, love. You've said the rhyme out loud, haven't you?'

I nodded.

'Well, then, damage is done as far I can see. Better off just accepting your fate and getting a good eight hours in. Night, night, love. Don't let the bed bugs bite.'

She closed the door and all was black. I felt the covers on my skin, the cool pillow against my cheek.

You know how dangerous this is? To put yourself up as bait for a monster? To waggle your bare arse in its direction, hoping it'll sink its teeth into your seat meat and drag you into its realm?

'Doesn't matter. This is what I was created for. To put my life on the line for others.'

What if it doesn't come for you?

'It will.'

It came for children as they slept. The children that had spoken its rhyme out loud. It had marked them in some way. Shot up a flare that the creature could home in on. Well, I'd spoken the rhyme over and over again since Amy first handed me the note with all the lines written down.

'Wake no more, said nobody's child, kicked and beaten, turned mean and wild. Wake no more, said the fearful small, for now I am here, to punish you all.'

I'd probably said it out loud more than any of the children it had taken. I was noisy with flares. The sky above me was a riot of bright explosions. It was just a matter of time.

'Jake. Think about the things that man did to you as a child. Think about them and how they made you feel.'

I closed my eyes. I was in a classroom. I tried to stand but found my arm tethered, my shoulder jarring as I strained to get free. Laughter, faces leering in, kids sneering down at me. I was handcuffed. Handcuffed to a radiator. It was hot and the heat was conducting through the metal of the cuffs. My wrist was getting hotter and hotter.

'Let me go!' I screamed, but Mark, young Mark, Jake's bully, just laughed and waggled the key in front of me, letting me snatch at it but keeping it just out of reach.

'It hurts! It's burning me.'

'What a fucking pussy,' he said to the other kids.

We weren't in the classroom anymore.

I was still cuffed to the radiator, my skin burning, Mark leering down at me—at Jake—but now all there was around us was black. There was no noise. Mark still laughed and jeered, spittle flying, but he didn't make a sound.

'Mark? Mark, can you hear me?'

A pressure. Something was coming. I was alone. I grabbed the wrist that had been cuffed but was now free and rubbed at it. There was no burn mark.

I stood.

'Jake? Jake, can you hear me?'

I couldn't hear him in my head anymore.

'Jake?'

The black rippled.

'Night, night, love. Don't let the bed bugs bite.'

'Night, Mum.'

Night air on my skin. Goosebumps.

I looked around. I wasn't in the dark anymore, and I wasn't in my own dreams.

I was in the back alley in Acton. I could see two small legs poking out from behind some bins.

Alice Travers, the young girl beaten to death by her two bullies, eighty years ago.

I was in the creature's realm.

It had me.

33

'David? David, where are you?'

I closed my eyes and tried to feel my hand in his. I wasn't in my own dreams anymore, I was in a different realm of existence, a realm created by this creature when the murder of Alice Travers gave it life. I could easily be trapped here if I didn't make myself an exit point, which is why I had David holding my hand. As long as he kept hold of me, I had a living, conscious link back to my own realm, to what we think of as the "real world", and I could escape from here.

'David.'

There.

There it was.

I could feel his hand squeezing mine. The warmth of his skin against my own.

'I'm here.' His voice was a whisper, indistinct, like a suggestion of a voice carried on the wind.

'David?'

'I'm here, I have you. I won't let go, Magic Lady.'

Without opening my eyes I imagined a door that would lead me back to him. That if I were to turn the handle, open it, and step on through I'd find myself back with him. Back in my coven.

I imagined it was real, then demanded it be real, pushing the command out of myself.

I opened my eyes. There was a door in the brick wall to my right. A neon sign above it read EXIT.

Now my way out was set I could get back to it any time I needed to. But I wouldn't step through it until I had done what I'd come here for.

First, I was going to find the kids. Find them and get them to this exit point. After that, I was going to put an end to this creature. Not block its entrance into our world, not put a lock on its door. Locks weaken, and if this saga had taught me anything, it's that half a solution wasn't a solution at all.

No, this time, my time, I was going to make sure returning to haunt the dreams of children would never be an option, or I was going to die trying.

'Jake, can you hear me now?'

Silence. No smart-arse reply. I couldn't feel him anymore, but I knew he was still there. I could still hear the sound of Mark taunting him. His fear was still in me, and that meant Jake must still be there, too.

I turned to where Alice Travers lay, her face a battered mess, and knelt beside her.

'Hello, Alice.'

Alice's broken lips twitched and her eyes flickered open, the whites bloodshot, one bulging from its socket.

'My name is Stella.'

'Stella?' Her voice had no power behind it. No breath. No life.

'Have you seen any other children here? Maybe a girl called Amy?'

'I think I'm in a terrible way, Miss Stella. Could you call me a doctor? I don't want to die.'

I took her cold, damp hand in mine. 'I'm sorry, Alice, but

you're already a long time dead. What happened to you was eighty years ago.'

'Eighty years? No, it just happened. It's always just happening. I get back up and clean off the blood and then they come running after me again.' She sat up, her clothes tearing away from the dried blood, and pushed herself back to her feet, joints cracking like logs on a fire. 'Look,' she said, pointing to the other end of the alley, 'Here they come again, and again, and again.'

I turned to see her attackers, her school bullies, running into the alley, their faces a mixture of joy and savagery, sprinting towards her. I instinctively pulled the surrounding magic into myself and unleashed a molten arc of power, trying to stop the kids in their tracks, but they ran straight through the spell, not even flinching.

I looked away as they punched and kicked and stamped at Alice. They weren't really alive. There was nothing I could do to stop this. Alice Travers was long dead, and beyond anything I could do. I could only help the kids that were here but still alive, laid up in hospitals across London, in a hidden eaves den, in a room, laying beside me, in the London Coven.

Eventually, the bullies blinked out of existence and it was just me and Alice left in the alley.

'Alice? Alice, have you seen Amy?'

'Yes. She was here once. I remember her. She tried to help me, too, but you can't help the dead, can you? Too late then. Too, too late.'

'Can you tell me where she might be?'

Alice nodded. 'She's where her fear is. Find her fear. Oh, look, here they come again.'

Alice got back to her feat.

'Thanks. I'm sorry I can't help you,' I said, and turned from her, passing the two bullies as I made my way out of the alley.

Alice's scream cut off abruptly as I stepped out of the alley and into what lay beyond. I didn't walk out onto a street in

Acton, as I would have done in the real world. Instead, I stepped into something that looked like a nightmare drawn by Escher. Random pieces of reality were jammed together: rooms, streets, forests, lakes, schools, back gardens, caves, bedrooms, all slapped together by a madman in a dizzying array that made my head swim. There seemed no reason to it. It felt like I might fall into nothing with the next step. There was no way to orientate myself as the different places didn't sit next to each other, but jutted out at every angle.

'Amy!'

Cackling laughter. I whirled around to see a boy in the distance. A black shape, a shadow. Was that the monster?

He stepped forwards. It was Mark. Jake's meat suit. His bully.

'Where are you going, Jake, you fucking queer?'

This realm was reading the fear inside of me, but it wasn't mine, it was Jake's. I wondered what effect this would have on him if he was really here? Would it pull out a primal sense of terror? Would it reduce him to a terrified wreck?

'Oi, bender, I'm talking to you.'

Mark stomped towards me, pulling a pair of handcuffs out of his pocket.

'Sorry,' I said, 'but you've got the wrong person.' I pulled the magic around me into myself and shot the palm of my hand forwards, fire arcing from it and burning the pretend Mark to nothing.

Mark was here for Jake. Somewhere in this jumble of places there was a room or two from Jake's fears, and Mark was there to take him to it. To torment him forever. Well, bad luck, it wouldn't work on me.

'Amy, where are you?'

I reached out with my senses, trying to find something I recognised.

'Listen,' I said, placing the correct words in my mind.

'Please, just stop. Please!'

Amy.

That was Amy's voice.

I closed my eyes and held on to the connection, stepping forward, trusting it to take me to her. I felt tree branches scrape against my skin, felt the cold chill me, then heat make me sweat. I felt the ground beneath my feet change from one step to the next as I moved through the crazy array of places and times that the creature had squashed together in its realm.

I stopped. I could hear girls jeering, the sound bouncing off something hard, like we were inside a tiled room. I opened my eyes, I was in a communal toilet, four cubicles on one side, a line of sinks and mirrors on the other. Four girls were stood in a little semicircle at the far end, a fifth girl in front of them, her back pressed against the wall as the other girls leaned in at her.

Amy.

'God, you're fat.'

'So fat and gross.'

'Why'd you think Josh would even look at you, never mind fancy you, you dirty skank.'

'Bitch.'

'What's wrong with your clothes?'

'Mum can't afford anything decent?'

'Shut up!' Amy cried.

'Or what?'

'What you gonna do, bitch?'

One reached forward and yanked on Amy's hair.

I outstretched a hand and flames leapt from it, burning the mean girls like they were made of old newspaper, until all that was left were the echoes of their nasty little slurs.

'Skank.'

'Bitch.'

'Lesbo-dyke.'

'Amy, it's me, it's Stella. I've come for you.'

Amy shook her head. 'No, you're lying. You're just this place. You're the monster!'

I didn't have time to negotiate, so I grabbed her and pulled her forward, past the mean girls that were beginning to form again, to give themselves bodies and not just voices.

'Where you going, bitch?'

'I'll fucking kill you if you talk to Josh again, you hear me?'

I pushed the door and stepped out, pulling a struggling Amy after me. We arrived on an abandoned train platform.

Amy blinked in surprise then looked at me. 'Stella? Oh, my God, it's you, isn't it? It's really you!'

This platform wasn't part of her fears, this was the location of some other kid's worst memory. Pulling her here had snapped Amy out of her own terror.

'Yes, it's really me. Me and your Uncle David, we came up with a plan, and this, well, this is the plan.'

'How did you get here? You're not a kid.'

'Magic. And a ghost.'

'A ghost!'

'Yeah.

'Oh, cool.'

I gave her a shrug. 'You haven't met him.'

'Oi, bender!'

I turned to see Mark walking towards us.

'Who's that?' asked Amy.

'That's one of the ghost's issues, don't worry about it. Come on.' I threw a ball of fire at the pretend Mark as we headed for the platform exit.

34

We did our best to ignore what was happening to Alice Travers as we arrived in the back alley and approached the exit I'd created.

'So, I'll just wake up, as soon as I step through that door?'

'Yes.' I decided to leave out the "hopefully".

She looked at the door with its flickering exit sign.

'Are you coming?'

'No, not yet. There are too many other kids here, still. I came here to save all of them, not just you.'

'But what if... what if the creature notices what you're doing?'

That was the big question. Sooner or later it would realise something was up and come looking for me.

'If it comes, I'll smack it in its stupid, blank face,' I replied, and smiled.

'You're such a bad-arse.'

'Yes, I am. Now get through the door, your uncle is waiting for you.'

She smiled and opened the portal to a white light beyond. 'Thanks, Stella. Thanks for saving me.'

She turned and stepped through the door, the light engulfing her before the door slammed shut again.

Okay, one down, a shit-load more to go.

I have no idea how long it took me. No idea if time even existed the same way in the nightmare realm. For all I know I could have been there for seconds in real time.

Or decades.

Every new place was boiling with fear and anger. With pain and hatred. It chipped away at me, little by little, even as I found the children, one by one, and led them to the exit.

'Are you okay?' asked one of the kids as I leaned against the wall, trying not to hear the sounds of feet stomping on Alice Travers.

'Yes, just tired, that's all. Go through the door. It's time you woke up.'

And on it went: the image of Mark appearing again and again to torment me, or at least try to. After all, it was Jake's trauma it was reacting to, not my own. The only effect it had on me was to make me increasingly annoyed as I struggled on.

I found all the eaves kids huddled together. They were the only ones not suspicious of me as I tried to help.

'We know who you are.'

'Of course we do.'

'We're eaves, we hear lots of things about you, Familiar.'

Finally, the last one, a small human boy named Tom. I found him locked in an abandoned hut in the woods. In this place the birds didn't tweet, they screamed with the voices of terrified infants. Spiders crawled over every inch of Tom's body as boys ran circles outside, hitting the walls of the hut with sticks and laughing and hooting. I burned them to cinders then carried the boy into the woods. Into the abandoned train station. The classroom. The caravan. The public toilets. Onwards and onwards through the sites of a thousand tortures.

At last we arrived in the back alley in Acton, a dying Alice Travers behind the bins. I pointed to the exit.

'Go on. Wake up. Get out of here.'

'Are you not coming?'

God knows I wanted to. I was exhausted, physically and mentally. This place had pounded against me relentlessly. Trying to find a way in.

'I can't. Not yet. I have one more thing to do.'

Tom nodded. He knew what I was staying to finish. 'He's coming.'

'Who?'

'The monster. The monster man without a face. Can't you feel him?'

'He's coming,' said Alice, agreeing, her voice a death rattle.

'This is nothing but a bad dream, Tom. Go and wake up now.'

Tom shook his head. 'No. This is very, really, real, I'd say. And you can die if it's real. Don't die, Miss.'

And with that, he stepped through the door into the bright white, and the realm was empty apart from myself and poor Alice Travers. Only one of us was real, though. Alice's cries and battered body were nothing but shadows cast by something that was over a long time ago.

The alley rippled and writhed, reality warping around me, making me stumble in my beaten down state. Making me feel like I might throw up. Like the world surrounding me was a boat on a wild ocean.

'Children? Where are you, children?'

Alice Travers was by my side, fear on her corpse face. 'He will be very mad with you. I think he'll want to do terrible, awful things to you.'

My stomach was telling me to go. To run away and hide. To escape the bad man. But that was just this place. I knew that. Infecting me with fear.

I stood my ground even as the cobbles beneath my feet tried to throw me down.

A split in reality at the far end of the alleyway.

It was coming.

He was coming.

Alice ran to hide behind the bins where she'd died.

I clenched my fists as a pretend man without a face stepped out of the tear and into the alley.

'I've looked all over and I can't find them,' it said. 'In every bad place, in every haunted terror. What have you done with my children, Stella Jake?'

35

The creature stood still, arms by its sides, as the two bullies ran into the alley towards Alice Travers to punch and spit and stomp, stomp, stomp.

'Is the music of my realm not beautiful, Stella Jake?'

'You're done, you hear me? You're a monster, and you've just met the woman who finishes monsters.'

I pulled the strange magic of the alley into myself and thrust out a fist, punching an arc of lethal power in the thing's direction. I never saw it duck, or jump, or run – in the blink of an eye it just wasn't where it had been. The magic sailed past and died.

'My children liked to dance to the music of my home. Or hated it. Or clapped in joy. Or ran in screaming terror. So hard to know or understand for sure. Whatever have you done with them?'

'I've sent them home, you piece of shit.'

I grunted with effort as I unleashed another arc of power, only to see the same thing happen. A blink and the creature wasn't where it had been, and the magic guttered and died.

It tilted its head to one side. 'I don't understand. Is that not a home for them? I made it just for them. It only exists to hold them. To haunt them. To torture them. For now I am here, to punish them all.'

'Stay still!' I unleashed arc after arc of power, dragging the magic around me into my body and unleashing it over and over, but it didn't matter what I threw at it, I missed my target every time.

'Stella Jake, why do you fight so? This is right. Your punishment. All children will come here forever and ever, and I will make sure only the very worst happens to them.'

'Run,' said Alice Travers from her pillow of blood on the alley floor.

'I won't run.'

'You made yourself a way out? How did you do that, Stella Jake?'

He passed a hand in front of himself. I turned to my exit, but all that was there now was a solid brick wall.

'David? David!'

I tried to concentrate on him, tried to feel his hand in mine, but I couldn't feel anything. Was I trapped there now? Doomed to suffer in this nightmare realm for all eternity?

'Children? Where are my children?'

I screamed and threw everything I had in the creature's direction. The bricks exploded behind where it had been stood a heartbeat before, shards shooting every which way.

I ran from the alley. The world rushed past me in a jumble as I tried to formulate some sort of plan.

'David? David, where are you?'

I couldn't feel him at all, couldn't hear even the faintest whisper of his voice. I was stuck here, maybe for good.

I skidded to a halt on the abandoned train platform and tried to catch my breath.

'Where are you running to, Stella Jake?' The creature was stood at the far end of the platform. It began to move towards me, closer and closer with each second that passed, never once seeming to actually take a step. 'Are you taking me to my children? Where have you put them? They have not been punished enough for their wicked ways.'

'They haven't done anything wrong. They're just kids.'

The ground where the creature had been a second before exploded as another volley of magic flew from my knuckles and missed the thing.

'They haven't done anything wrong? Oh, that's not true. They hurt. They shame. They kick and they punch. They make lives a misery, and now I am here to punish them all.'

I tried to run as the creature almost reached me, but jerked back, my shoulder jarring. I turned to see Mark grinning at me, my wrist chained to a radiator. And then I was back in the classroom, with Mark and his gang of savages laughing at me as the heat torched my wrist.

'Nothing wrong?' said the creature, stood at the head of the class, its head tilted to one side. 'This is not me, I did not create this. This all happened. And it happens and it happens again.'

'But this is just one bad child, why do you have to hurt all of them?'

'One bad child? None are innocent. All must be punished for the way they made me feel.' As he spoke, his voice began to morph into that of Alice Travers. 'They kicked and they punched, Stella Jake. Punish them.'

'No, Alice. That was just those two children. Punish them, not all of them.'

'No,' said the creature, now using another child's voice. 'Not just them. All. Every day at school I was mocked, spat on, had my money stolen, my face pushed in the toilet, and all saw. No one helped me, Stella Jake.'

'I was taken out to the woods behind school,' said another child, a boy. 'Four kids from my class. They told me for weeks they were going to get me, so I bunked off, pretended I was sick, but eventually I had to go back. The other kids knew what was coming. They knew what the bullies were going to do and none of them stayed. None of them came to help as the bullies crowded around and ran me to the trees. They made me take my clothes off, Stella Jake. And then... and then...'

'Punish them all.'

'All.'

'They're all guilty.'

'Guilty.'

'Guilty.'

'No!' I stood, the handcuffs falling away from my wrist.

'Oi, bender, where'd you think—'

I turned and swiped a hand across Mark, across his gang. They froze, then blew away like burning paper in the wind.

The creature tilted its head to one side. 'How did you do that? You should not be able to do that.'

'My name is Stella Familiar of the London Coven, and I tricked you to get here. This place only has power if you have a real childhood trauma to attack. Every kid has something. Some memory, big or small, that you could hurt them with. Well, guess what? Not me. I never had a childhood.'

'We shall see,' said the creature, and suddenly it was in front of me, plunging its hands into my chest.

I screamed, throwing my head back as its fingers wrapped around my heart.

'There must be something. Something. Something.'

I snarled, gritting my teeth, trying not to pass out from the shock. 'Afraid not. No childhood fears. I was born this way.'

'Nothing. Nothing. Empty and empty and empty.'

'That's right, bitch.' I grunted and shoved the creature away, shivering as its hands left my body.

The faceless man hopped back, and back again, lowering its featureless head into its hands. 'What are you?' it asked in Alice Travers' voice. 'You are not a real person. Where is your childhood? Just nothing, and nothing, and terrifying nothing.'

The classroom shook, throwing me to the floor. I looked up to see Mark stood over me.

'Who are you? You're not him. You're not Jake. Where's my Jake?'

I pushed myself backwards then clambered to my feet as the room began to deform and break apart. Mark began twitching and writhing as the arms and faces and legs of a hundred different kids, a hundred different bullies, burst out of him, their faces twisted with anger, with confusion.

'So empty. Just nothing, and nothing, I am drowning,' said the creature.

I fell through the door as the room bucked and found myself in the bathroom where Amy had been terrorised. The semicircle of girls were now one gestalt beast, their flesh fused together, writhing in confused agony.

'Bitch!'

'Skank!'

'Josh mine.'

'Ours.'

'Ours.'

The tiles beneath the thing opened up, and they fell through. As the floor continued to tear apart I ran from the room and found myself on the abandoned train platform. The creature was waiting for me.

'What is happening?' it begged.

The truth was, I didn't know for sure. My best guess was that as it tried to latch on to my fear, to hold it, to taste it, my absence of a childhood had somehow infected it. I was the common cold, and this alien's tripod was bucking and tumbling.

It stepped forward. For the first time, I actually saw its feet move. Slowly, it walked towards me.

'Stella? Stella. What are you? What have you done? Where are my children?'

'I saved them. Saved them all. And now it looks like you're dying.'

'Dying? I do not die.'

I pointed behind the thing. The platform was crumbling away like sand, leaving nothing behind but emptiness.

'Tell that to this place. Tell that to your body.'

The thing lifted a hand to see that it too was starting to crumble. It lowered its hand, what was left of it, and turned its blank face back to me.

'I am afraid.'

I grimaced. 'Good.'

'You cannot leave. Your way home is gone. I took it from you and I will not return it. We will die together.'

'It doesn't matter. This is what I was created for. To fight things like you. To give up my life in the name of others. So yeah, I'm gonna die, but you know what? This is a fucking good way to go.'

'Stella...'

The creature collapsed as its legs disintegrated, then its arms, its head, until there was nothing left at all. Almost nothing left of its realm, either. Just a few metres of platform and me, watching my time run out.

I thought about David, back at the coven, hugging his niece. Hugging Amy. Taking her back to her mum. Leaving me and this life behind.

I'd done well. I'd kept my promise.

I thought about David.

'Stella?'

I realised I'd closed my eyes, waiting for things to be over.

'Stella, where are you?'

Someone was holding my hand.

'David?'

I opened my eyes. The platform was gone. Everything was gone.

I should have been dead.

David was stood by my side, his hand in mine, holding me tight.

'I found you, Stella.'

His eyes burned with white hot fire. He was like he had been in the alleyway again, when the creature had attacked the first time.

'David, how are you doing this?'

'I heard you. I found you.'

He turned and reached out a hand, pointing. A door with an exit sign above it appeared in the void.

'Come on. Let's go home.'

He walked towards the exit, his hand still in mine, and I followed.

36

All the kids that had fallen into comas survived.

One by one, far and wide across the city, they began to open their eyes. When asked what they remembered, all they said was they'd had a nightmare. A nightmare that a woman in a leather jacket saved them from.

David never told his sister what had actually happened. That Amy had been in a coma, like the kids in the news. He and Amy both thought it better to keep it a secret, and I agreed with them.

'So what's up with your detective?' asked Jake, nestled inside his meat suit again as we sat in The Beehive, getting steadily drunk.

'Nothing. He's just... he's fine.'

'He doesn't remember what he did?'

I shook my head.

When I woke up I found him on the floor unconscious with Amy trying to wake him up. When he finally came to he said he'd been having a dream about fishing on a big lake. Like the last time, he didn't remember changing. Didn't remember his eyes filling with fire.

What he'd done was impossible. Stepping into the creature's realm. Creating an exit and saving me.

'You know, I've gotta say, that was all bloody impressive stuff, Stella. I'd written you off as some stuck-up, snooty cow, but what you did? That took a serious set of ovaries.'

'Well, Jake, it was a pleasure having you inside of me.'

We tapped glasses and got drunk.

Someone was knocking at the door.

I opened my eyes, bleary, the thud of that night's alcohol making my head heavy. It was the middle of the night, who would be knocking on the door in the middle of the night?

Then another thought: who would be knocking on the door to the London Coven at all? No one came knocking here. Not even David, he always called first. He said it was just manners, but I think it had more to do with all the magical protections I'd told him covered the place. He was just worried he'd come knocking, trigger one, and find his head rolling off down the blind alley, which, to be fair, was a distinct possibility.

Another knock.

Every time, three knocks, a beat between each set. They echoed around the coven.

I threw my blanket aside and sat up, bare feet chilled by the cold of the floor.

Three more knocks.

I put on some clothes, my boots, and padded towards the front door.

Three more knocks.

A few metres from the door, I stopped and reached out with my senses, trying to judge what was waiting for me outside. Was it a friend? An enemy? A monster?

'Who is it?'

Three more knocks.

'My right hand is cocked and ready to turn you into a puddle of goo. Got me? So stop playing around and tell me who you are.'

'You know who it is. You were expecting me.'

I blinked with surprise, because suddenly, upon hearing his voice, I did know, even though I'd never met them before in my long life. It was like I suddenly remembered I'd been expecting him to visit. Which was very strange indeed. Was this some sort of spell? Magical suggestion designed to lower defences? No, I didn't think so. I could sniff that out if I knew I was looking for it. This was something else.

I passed my left hand in front of the door's lock. There was a noise of invisible bolts sliding aside, then I reached forward and pulled the door open.

On the other side stood a tall man in a wide-brimmed hat. Well, he was sort of a man. A man that looked like he'd been whittled out of a tree, his face an immobile circle of wood with rudimentary features carved into it.

'Stella Familiar, I am the Knot Man, and I have come to deliver the warning. May I come inside?'

We sat at the kitchen table on opposite sides, facing each other.

'Why are you here?' I asked.

'I am the Knot Man. I walk through many worlds. Many possible realities. Every parallel potential. My job is always the same. To deliver warnings. I've given warnings to kings and I've given them to ordinary men. Men about to become all that stands between the light and the spew of Hell itself.'

'Well, it sounds like you meet a lot of interesting people.'

The Knot Man smiled, only his mouth didn't move, couldn't move, so I don't know how I knew that.

'So, you have something to warn me about?' I asked.

The Knot Man nodded.

'Are you ready to hear the warning?'
I shrugged. 'Okay, go ahead.'
'It is about Detective David Tyler.'
My heart fluttered and I sat up. 'What about him?'
And then the Knot Man told me.

DEADLY PORTENT

1

The screaming came first.

Not just one scream, but a multitude, jabbing sharply into the street and causing the passing foot traffic to put an extra spring in their step as they propelled themselves away from the sound as quickly as possible.

'Well, Stella, that does not sound good,' said Detective David Tyler, a master of understatement if ever there was one. 'Not good at all.'

'Let's do this,' I replied.

As I clenched my fists and made to move forwards, a large, shrieking man shot by me. He'd been ejected at speed from the blind alley that hid The Fenric club, and landed in a bloody mess at our feet. To any of the passing drinkers and characters that patrolled Mayfair at this hour, it would have looked like the man with the windmilling arms was spat from a solid brick wall. A few people gave a double take, but most just kept on moving; you don't get involved unless you have to in a place like London.

David took a knee by the man as he looked up at us, wiping blood from his nose with the back of one hand.

'Have a tissue,' said David, holding out a crisp, white one.

'Where the hell have you been?' the man yelled, grabbing the Kleenex and squeezing his nostrils closed with it. 'We called you an hour ago, what took you so long?'

I helped the man—who was at least twice my size—up to his feet, his knees threatening to drop him again before he propped himself against the wall and tipped back his head to stem the bleeding.

'We came as fast as we could,' I told him. 'Hammersmith and Mayfair are not exactly side-by-side.'

'Yeah, yeah,' he said, or more accurately, grunted. The man (not that he was one, not exactly) was Lodo, the doorman of The Fenric, a five story private members club in the belly of Mayfair. It was a place for the Uncanny to hang out and socialise, a little like The Beehive, but for a more elite set of clientele. There were no sticky floors in this establishment, and the smell from the toilets stayed strictly where it belonged.

No, the Fenric was for a different class of Uncanny. A different breed even. You had to be invited and vouched for by three different members just to be given the address of the place, let alone be let in there. I'd never actually been inside myself of course. I might belong to the London Coven, but I was only a lowly familiar.

'What exactly is going on in there?' I asked.

'Didn't he tell you?'

'Your manager was pretty keen to get off the phone so he could run for cover,' I replied. 'What can you actually tell me about—'

'She's a monster! She's tearing the place apart! Just stop your shitting yapping, get in there, and do your bloody job, you stupid woman!'

I looked at Lobo's wide, popping eyes. At the veins on his neck sticking out like ropes and the spittle on his lips. And I punched him square on the jaw.

As his eyes rolled shut and he slid to the ground with a

solid *thump,* I turned to David. He was looking at me like a teacher would a naughty child.

I shrugged.

David smiled and nodded to the blind alley that housed The Fenric. Both of us could see it as clear as day, even as it remained hidden from the ordinary folk of Mayfair. 'So what d'you think's waiting for us in there?' he asked.

'Nothing good,' I replied.

'We never go anywhere nice,' he sighed.

I strode into the blind alley with David on my tail. 'What do you mean?' I asked, 'I took you on that yacht party on the Thames last week.'

'One of the guests turned into a werewolf and ate the other guests.'

'Yes, but there was free champagne.'

'That's true. And sausage rolls. I like sausage rolls. Well, I like any meat wrapped in pastry, to be honest.'

We stopped and looked up at the Fenric's facade, all dark, weathered bricks and criss-crossed wooden beams.

'There doesn't seem to be as much screaming now,' David noted. 'In my experience on the force, that's never a good thing.'

A window three stories up smashed, causing us to duck for cover as a swarm of shards buzzed down, followed by a chair. The cobbles broke its fall, and also just broke it.

'Come on,' I said, and walked into The Fenric.

Unlike The Beehive, there were no magic-dampening spells protecting this place. As The Fenric prided itself on its higher class of clientele, its lack of dampening was a way of saying, *"We don't have the same sort of mindless riff-raff in here, thank you very much. Our patrons can control themselves without the necessity of some magical flim-flam."* The snooty could be dumb, that was for certain.

As we entered the first main room I half expected to be met by a footman in a powdered wig, but the place was empty, save for a collection of comfy chairs and a discreet bar in the corner. Not one of the chairs remained intact though, and the bar looked like a giant had reached into the room and crushed it in its fist.

A muffled cry came from somewhere above, so we moved on.

'What do you think it is? A goblin? Another werewolf? An eaves?'

'Shh,' I replied.

'A "Shh," huh? Not heard of one of those.'

I ignored David's shit-eating grin and we made our way up the stairs, glass crunching under our feet.

The next floor was much the same as the first: broken furniture, a smashed up bar, and scorch marks on the walls that told me angry magic had been tossed around up there.

To the third floor we crept.

I reached out with my senses, trying to get an impression of what it was we were about to go up against, but whatever it was was powerful and knew how to block me from getting a clear fix.

Fourth floor next, the same story as the others. David stood at my side, panting slightly. 'You're sure there isn't a lift in this place?'

'Okay, last floor, get ready,' I said.

The fifth and final floor is where we found the creature causing all the chaos.

She stood with her back to us as we edged into the room, and was swaying back and forth like the room was rocking. Her hair was a long, dark riot of waves, her clothes black and raggedy. In one hand she clutched a bottle of whiskey, in the other, a ball of red and yellow crackling energy.

'Please, stop her!' said the man with the pinched face who was cowering behind what was left of this floor's bar.

The woman swigged from the bottle as she casually tossed the ball of magic in the man's direction. He shrieked and ducked as the magic sailed over his head and smashed into an expensive-looking art deco sculpture, turning it into slag metal.

'Well,' said David. 'Better do your thing, magic lady. Put her down.'

'I don't think that's a good idea,' I replied.

'Smart move, sister,' said the woman with a slur, turning towards us and performing an awkward curtsy. 'Workers unite!'

She was a familiar.

'David, meet Eva Familiar.'

Eva waved, causing David to yelp and jump out of the way as she accidentally sent a ball of fire in his direction.

'Sorry about that,' said Eva. 'Had the safety off.'

2

It turned out the pinched-face man was the manager of The Fenric. He said his name was Pierre Moreau, though his accent didn't betray even a ghost of French. As we stood in the street and I tried to keep the outstandingly drunk Eva from wandering off, David did his best to placate him.

'The damage!' he roared. 'My god, it'll cost thousands! Tens of thousands!'

'Can't you just do a little, you know, Mary Poppins style clean up?' asked David. 'A click of the fingers and the chairs fix themselves?'

'Stuck up bitch, that Poppins,' slurred Eva. 'You heard me. No time for her. Nope.'

'She's fictional,' I replied.

'Right, right, right, yeah, I know. Course. Who is? Has anyone seen Rambo? Now that's a film!'

Lodo was stood by his manager's side, glaring daggers at Eva. I was hoping he wouldn't do anything stupid, like to try to attack her as she had her back turned, as I could guarantee that would end very badly for him.

'And then there's our reputation,' said Frenchie Le Fake. 'This is not The Beehive!' He almost gagged on the other bar's name. 'We pride ourselves on our relaxed, non-violent atmosphere. But then this... this *thing* turns up, demanding entrance, and refusing to go away!'

Eva twirled, bottle of whisky still in her hand, and pointed at the manager, who hopped behind Lodo with a shriek. 'He was rude about my general demeanor and, you know, potty mouth, and such. The ignorant fucker.' She went for a swig from the bottle, found it empty, and tossed it over her shoulder.

'You see,' replied Pierre. 'You see!'

He flinched and ducked again as Eva raised her fighting hand, then lowered it, barking out a laugh.

We took our leave soon after that. We'd dealt with the problem, it wasn't our job to compensate or clean up. I fought monsters, I didn't sweep up, too.

'So, are you going to tell me who she is exactly?' asked David as the tube train shot us home.

I looked over to Eva, who was stretched out across several seats, sound asleep.

'Eva Familiar. She's like me. Well, not quite, she's much older.'

'How much older?'

'If the stories are true, she's been alive for almost five-hundred years.'

'Well, shit.'

'Yep.'

Eva snorted and rolled over, turning her back on us.

'What is she doing here? I sort of assumed you lot stayed with your own coven.'

'We do. At least we're supposed to. But Eva doesn't have a coven anymore.'

We managed to wake a disgruntled Eva in time to skip off the train, then steered her out of the station and back to my home.

'This it then?' she asked, swaying before the front door.

'Yes, this is the London Coven.'

My place of creation. The sanctuary of the protectors of London since long before the place even used that name. My coven.

'Right. I really need a bit of a piss,' she replied, and let herself in.

'Hey,' said David, 'how did she...? What about all the protection spells?'

'She's a familiar, David. This place knows its own.'

We followed her in.

If it seems like I know Eva, I'm giving the wrong impression. I know *of* her, and I feel a connection to her as we're both familiars, but this was first time I'd actually met her face-to-face.

I'd heard the stories, though. Of the wandering familiar. The very idea of it made me feel funny. A familiar is not supposed to wander from their coven, doing what they please when they please. We're created for one purpose and one purpose alone: to protect the people safeguarded by our covens. But we did have something in common, Eva and I, apart from both being familiars: something terrible had happened to our witches.

'What's a fully grown woman got to do to get a drink in this place?' said Eva, draped over a chair in the coven's main room.

'How long have you been drinking?' I asked.

'What time is it?'

'Ten thirty P.M.'

'October fifth, 1917.'

'David, coffee, strong,' I said.

'Oh, I'm a waiter now?'

'Yes,' said Eva, 'Now don't make us wait-er any longer.' She burst out into tear-rolling hysterics.

'That is the worst joke I've ever... was that even a joke?' said David.

'Wait... er...!'

'Two sugars, please,' I said, and David left the room, still grumbling.

'He's a fine young boy, Stella Familiar. Where'd you find that side-piece?'

I ignored her. 'What are you doing in London, Eva? And why didn't you come here first if you were passing through?'

'You know, this is a much nicer coven than mine. The Cumbrian Coven is all cold and medieval looking. Depressing. I used to go on at my witches all the time about redecorating. Updating the place a little, but would they listen? Pfft.'

The inside of the London Coven looked a lot like an old village pub in many ways, the kind you rarely saw anymore. Dark wood, a large open fireplace, beams low overhead. You could imagine the air thick with pipe smoke and the taste of ale.

Eva pulled a small bottle of something strong from an inside pocket, took a swig, then offered it my way.

'No thanks,' I said.

'Suit yourself,' she replied, and necked a large mouthful.

'Well? Why are you here?'

'Hey, everybody's got to be somewhere. And I'm here,' she said, tapping the arm of her chair.

'So that's it, you were just wandering through?'

'It's what I do these days. Just because you continue to let yourself be tied to a desk, doesn't mean I have to. I'm free!'

She snorted and took another swig before pocketing the bottle. So that's all it was, another stop on her endless wander. Okay. Looks like I was expected to play host, which is not something I was created for.

'So, are you going to fill me in?' said Eva, interrupting my train of thought.

'About what?'

'Oh, you're a secretive one, are you? Your non-normal normal, what's the story?'

I felt my heart skip a beat. 'I don't know what you're talking about.'

'Don't kid a kidder, young one.'

'Milk?' called David from the kitchen.

'Black!' said Eva. 'Like my heart.' She snorted, then began waving her hands around in front of her face. 'Ooh! Look at it go.'

I watched as she washed the colours in the air around herself. The heavy concentration of magic in the coven could be hypnotic; great, multi-coloured waves that swam around the place constantly.

'He's not normal, is he?' she said, getting back to her point.

'He is. He's just my friend. Just Detective David Tyler, that's all.'

'Nah. He's... odd. I'm not entirely—' she burped, then continued '—sure what he is. Lots of, you know, magic bouncing around in him for someone who isn't actually magic. It's fizzing around in that body like a fireworks display. I'm surprised he's able to keep it under wraps.'

I daren't tell her the truth. The truth about David's recent explosive demonstrations of magic. About how, when I'd been cut off in the nightmare realm as it collapsed—the home of a creature brought into existence to torment children everywhere—that David had somehow, impossibly, appeared, eyes burning with white hot flames, and saved my life.

David didn't remember a thing about it. I'd gently prodded at the issue, trying to see if anything would spark, but he was completely oblivious. As far as he was concerned I'd just woken up from the dream state I'd put myself in. He hadn't done anything to help.

A month had passed since then, and David hadn't shown any other signs of that sort of power. In truth, I was hoping whatever it was that lurked inside him had burned itself out. That whatever changes had been brought about by being possessed by Mr. Trick, and by the black magic I'd tapped into to save his life, had guttered out already. Eva's questions had put that idea to bed though.

'Whatever it is,' said Eva, 'It's interesting. I was planning to head off in a day or two, pop up to Manchester to see a man about a God, but maybe I'll stick around longer. I've got this feeling in the bottom of my bottom that something interesting is on the horizon, and my rear end never lies. Not like these tits of mine.'

'Here we go then,' said David, entering with a tray of coffees.

Eva had already crashed out by then, so the two of us shovelled her up and tossed her into one of the coven's spare rooms.

As I lay in bed later, I thought about what Eva had said. Yes, she was drunk, but she'd seen the truth. Her eyes were older than mine, and more attuned to the Uncanny. You can't hide what you are from a familiar that old.

She saw what was inside of David.

She saw what the Knot Man had come to the coven four weeks back to warn me about.

That whatever had happened to David had changed him, and that the change could spell disaster for the whole of London.

3

The next morning there was no sign of Eva, just an empty bottle at the foot of the bed and the covers in a corkscrew on the floor.

I found the note on the kitchen table.

At first I thought it must be from Eva, a thank you for letting her stay, or a message to tell me she'd see me later. What I didn't expect was that it would be from Giles L'Merrier.

The note was business card sized and written in large, flowing letters. It simply read: *To me, now. L'Merrier.*

A summons from the mighty L'Merrier? What on Earth was going on? L'Merrier wasn't one to entertain visitors, least of all from a lowly witch's familiar. Something told me he wasn't inviting me over for tea and biscuits and a gossipy chat.

I rolled the card over in my hands, tracing the crisp edges with my fingertips, wondering what in the hell L'Merrier could want from me. He'd made it quite clear during my last few unwanted visits that my presence in his shop was far from desired. In fact, I got the distinct impression that he rather disliked me. A lot. Then again, that just put me in the same boat as everyone else walking the streets of London. Giles L'Merrier had long ago retreated from the world, a virtual hermit, content to stay hidden away in his shop, his past a thing of whispered, awed myth.

Perhaps this invitation was proof that he'd finally decided to step out into the world again.

I slid the card into the pocket of my leather jacket, fully intending to head straight to L'Merrier's Antiques. You don't keep a man like that waiting. As I reached the front door though, I felt my phone vibrating. It was David.

'Morning, sunshine,' he said, brightly.

'What is it?' I grunted.

'Ah, there's that friendly disposition I've come to love.'

'David...'

'I've got something. A body. I think we've got a new job on.'

David was waiting for me at Ealing Hospital.

I strode in, detectives and medical staff nodding and smiling at me as I passed. Technically, I shouldn't be anywhere near an official police investigation. I wasn't on the force, I had nothing to do with the case, and I didn't even technically qualify as a human being. But I did know magic, and I knew how to use it to cloud the thoughts of normals and make myself welcome in places I didn't belong. I never pushed it too far. All I did was put out a suggestion that I was meant to be there. Just a gentle nudge. People would never be sure quite who I was, but they also wouldn't question it.

Oh look, it's what's-her-name. She's expected. She's down. She's on the list. You know who I'm talking about... what's-her-face.

...And they'd nod politely and let me by, no questions asked. Don't get me wrong, the spell has its limits. The effect crumbles if I stick around too long, but for a quick visit, it does the job nicely.

I followed the signs to the hospital morgue, where I found David stood next to a ceramic slab bearing a covered body.

Opposite was a wall full of small, metal doors, I wondered how many of them hid bodies of their own.

'Hey,' he said. 'How's the booze hound this morning?'

'Eva? Gone.'

'Oh, I thought she might end up taking up in one of the coven's spare rooms.'

'Yeah, well, she hasn't.' I realised that I'd been vaguely hoping that, too. My witches were dead; it was just me and David trying to keep the Uncanny peace in London's sprawling streets now. An extra-experienced familiar like Eva mucking in wouldn't have hurt. I mean, it's not like she really had a coven of her own to go to. She'd been wandering the country, a free agent, for years now. It was time she got back to work.

'So, what have we got?' I asked, changing the subject.

'This is a weird one,' replied David, 'so hang on to your breakfast...'

He reached down to the slab and peeled back the white plastic sheet to reveal the naked body of a man.

He'd been found that morning by his teenage daughter. She'd called up to his room to let him know his morning coffee was ready, and he hadn't answered. Hadn't arrived downstairs, bleary-eyed, hair a mess, desperate for his morning rocket fuel. So, she'd called again, and again, getting louder and more annoyed each time. Finally, she'd stomped her way up the stairs, thrown his bedroom door open, and yelled, *'Are you coming down or what?'*

The final word had caught in her throat as she'd flicked on the light and saw her dad, laid out on his back in bed, quite dead, his body completely drained of moisture. It looked like he'd been left out in the desert to mummify. The man was a withered husk.

'Jesus,' I said.

'Yeah,' replied David. 'This is one for us.'

'This is *definitely* one for us.'

'Oh, it's you again,' came a woman's voice from behind me.

It was Detective Layland, David's partner. She was a hard-faced young woman who, on the few times I'd met her, had made it very clear she didn't like me. Just like the others, she put up with me because of the suggestion magic I pushed at her whenever she got near. She thought I was a specialist of some sort. A gopher from some strange department or other that dealt with the weird stuff, an associate of David's who he'd call in from time to time. If she ever tried to examine the thought too closely—to really subject it to scrutiny—the thought would be pushed out of her mind, like she was trying force two magnets of the same pole together.

Despite the magic, or perhaps, subconsciously, because of it, Layland didn't care for my presence one bit.

'Hello, Detective,' I said, without turning to look at her.

'Another freak show.'

'The body, or Stella here?' asked David.

I raised an eyebrow.

'Please don't hurt me.'

'Any ideas?' asked Layland, even though her voice made it very clear that it pained her to even ask.

'One or two,' I replied.

'Care to enlighten me?'

'Not sure of anything, not yet.'

'Right, right. You see, solving this sort of shit, murders and so on, is kind of my job. We like to find killers, and arrest them. One way of doing that is to share facts, opinions, thoughts, hunches.'

'She has a very good point,' said David.

'As soon as I have something worth saying, I'll say it.'

'So, never then?' said Layland.

David snorted, then took a half step back as I narrowed my eyes at him. 'Hey, come on, that was a solid return of serve.'

Layland sniffed derisively, then headed off. 'Fill me in on whatever shit she spouts, I'm gonna go and bang on the neighbour's doors. You know: police work.'

David grinned at me. 'You know, I think she has a crush on you.'

'How about a little respect, David? We are stood over a murder victim.'

'All right, all right.'

I ran my eyes over the corpse again; at the leathery skin that looked as though it had been left to dry out in the sun for decades. The wide open eyes, their colour drained away. The mouth cracked apart, stretched in a silent scream. The withered tongue that hung from it, burnt to a crisp like a rasher of overcooked bacon.

I didn't like the way my thoughts were turning.

Because I recognised the signs.

Yes, there were a few different ways a body *might* end up in a state like this—and I'd have preferred if one of those ways had turned out to be the actual way—but as I reached out with my senses and probed the corpse for answers, they only came back with bad news.

'I know what creature did this,' I said.

'Why do I get the feeling I'm not going to be over the moon with the answer?' replied David.

'Come on. We have to go pay a visit to Anya.'

'There it is. Bollocks.'

David covered the dessicated corpse and we headed from the morgue and out of the hospital, quickly, before my suggestion spell broke apart.

4

Anya and the rest of her family spent most of their time holed up in The Den, the Soho club they owned.

And fed in.

'You're sure there's a connection?' asked David, warily looking towards the entrance of The Den, its door flanked by Jack and Jake, the two giant, shovel-faced doormen.

'Only one creature I know leaves a body like that,' I told David. 'A succubus did this.'

'I thought you said they were under control these days?'

That was true, or had been when my witches were alive. Since then, who knew? Maybe Anya and her family had decided all bets were off and were starting to step outside of their club to feast.

The deal between the succubi and the London Coven had been struck to put an end to a no-win war. The witches agreed to leave Anya and her family unchallenged, and in exchange, the succubi had acquiesced to limiting their feeding to the confines of their club. They also promised not to drain any of their clientele to death. They got to take a nice, big gulp, and then their victims walked out, alive and healthy.

The Den was a no-holds-barred fetish, sex, violence, and whatever else got your engine running club. Your wildest fantasies could come true within the walls of the place, and the succubus family would then feed on all the wild explosions of emotion unleashed. The building lay hidden in plain sight. A place that you didn't know was there, no matter how many times you walked past it. Not until, that is, you heard a whisper about its existence. About the things you could experience if you went there. And then it sunk its hooks deep and you found yourself walking through its doors, ready to indulge in your most depraved fantasies.

The succubi family had you then, because there was no way you weren't going to return again, not after a taste. And even if you were strong minded enough to resist, enough to want to try to get it closed down, it was too bad, they already had you. They knew your darkest recesses, had them recorded for posterity, or blackmail. And if that wasn't an option? Well, a family member would just pay you a visit as you lay in bed one black night.

The Den had existed, unchallenged, since before I was created.

'Perhaps,' I said, 'Anya and her family have grown tired of restrictions. Perhaps they think they can kill again, now that it's just me in charge.'

'So what's the plan?' asked David.

'The plan is, we talk to Anya. And, if we have to, we stop the succubi from hurting anybody else.'

'And how exactly do we do that?'

'We'll think of something.'

'Phew, that's my worries eased,' said David. I believe he was being sarcastic.

'Come on.'

'I was being sarcastic by the way.'

Told you.

I headed towards The Den, David nipping at my heels. As

we approached, a furtive looking man stepped out of the place and pulled his collar high, his hair stuck to his forehead with sweat, his eyes wide and bloodshot.

'See you again,' Jack said to him.

'See you again,' said Jake.

'No,' replied the man, 'I won't be back.'

'That's what they all say, 'int that right, Jake?'

'That's what they all say, right enough, Jack.'

The man scurried away. That was the thing about The Den. It wormed its way into your mind. Became an addiction. Once you'd had a taste of it, once you'd experienced the kind of things it offered, it was difficult not to make a return visit.

'Well, well, well; look who it is,' said Jake.

'Well, I never, look who it is,' replied Jack.

'I'm not looking for trouble, boys,' I said, making sure to draw in some of the surrounding magic, just in case.

'We never look for trouble,' said Jack.

'Never look for it, do we?'

'Never.'

'It always finds us, though.'

'Always knows exactly where we are, does trouble.'

'Exactly where we are.'

'We're here to talk to Anya,' squeaked David, then coughed to get his voice back into a more masculine register. 'Anya. We're here to ask her a few questions. If that's okay. Please.'

'It's the detective, Jake.'

'Look, Jack, the detective.'

'Are you going to show us your badge again?'

The two slapped at each other, laughing it up.

'No. Not if... you don't want me to.'

'Okay,' I said, as the two doormen regained control of themselves, 'Are you going to let us in or do we have to do it the hard way?'

'Ooh!'

'So tough, I'm scared, really, aren't you, Jake?'

'I am. Very scared indeed.'

Jake turned and opened the door, 'In you go, missy. Maybe Anya will tear off one of your arms or something.'

'Or a leg.'

'Could be a leg, could be.'

We stepped into the club, leaving the two doormen behind, grateful that our little confrontation hadn't turned into something worse. Those two were a pain to fight head-on.

'Remember,' I said to David, 'The spell I placed on you should protect you from the suggestion magic that rolls around this place, but stay close to me anyway.'

'Oh please,' he replied. 'I have amazing self-control.'

'Then stop staring at that woman rubbing oil into her four giant breasts.'

'I was just... checking. Surveillance. That's a police thing.'

I smiled and made my way towards the second floor of the club, towards Anya's private office. The seating in The Den was vinyl, wipe clean, the tables and bar metal, and the walls were covered in dark, red velvet. As we walked I tried not to take in too much of what was going on around me in the sweaty, darkened corners.

'There's no way that's going to fit in ther—' David started saying, before a scream and the sound of a big, wet insertion cut him off. 'Oh, no, in it goes,' he added, correcting himself. 'I feel a bit queasy.'

'Good. Better than the alternative.'

I can't say I relish the times I have to meet Anya, or any of her family, come to that. She's strong, all succubi are, but Anya is stronger than most. Her kind might seem friendly, seductive, even lovable, but they can turn in an instant and tear your guts out with one hand. They like to keep you off-balance, wary, as they prowl in front of you, prodding and poking.

You can never be sure they're going to let you walk away without a fight, or worse.

'Oh my god,' said David.

'What now?'

'I think I just saw Todd over there. He's a desk sergeant I know!'

'Don't stare,' I replied. 'Get your focus back, David, we've got work to do.'

'Right, yes, sorry. But I'm never shaking Todd's hand again. Not after what I've just seen him doing with that gibbon.'

5

Anya was stretched out on a couch in her office, propped up against the arm as she slowly drank something red and thick from a crystal glass.

'Anya,' I said, nodding my head in greeting.

'I see you brought your little friend with you again,' she replied, her voice smooth and playful.

'Hello. Yes. I'm just going to stay behind Stella if that's okay.'

'Aw, I don't think he likes me,' replied Anya, pouting.

'No, no, you're very nice. Not at all terrifying.'

Anya placed her glass down and stood, her red, silk dress that hugged her like a second skin sliding down to cover her bare feet.

'Tell me, detective, how can I convince you to visit my jolly little club without the chaperone?'

'Anya,' I said. 'Someone's died.'

'Careless of them,' she replied, never taking her eyes off David as she seemed to almost glide towards us.

'Do you find me attractive, Detective? I know that you do, I can taste it.'

I took a step to the side so that David was now hidden fully behind me. 'I came here to ask questions, not to watch you flirt with my partner.'

Anya looked at me unblinkingly for several seconds, during which the world seemed to hold its breath. Finally, she smiled and turned from me, heading towards her desk.

'What could you possibly need to ask me about, familiar? And why should I answer? You are not your witches, why should I feel beholden to anything you say?'

'You're right. I'm not my witches. Not even close. But I am of the London Coven, and that still means something. So please, answer my questions, and I'll be out of your hair. I promise.'

Anya settled into her chair like a cat and offered me a dead-eyed smile.

'You know, your masters used to be a lot more fun than you. Such a pity they were torn to pieces.'

I felt my stomach twist and I took an involuntary step forward, fists clenched. I felt a hand lightly touch my arm.

'We have a job to do, Stella,' David whispered.

I controlled my breathing and unclenched my fists, feeling my palms sting from where my nails had dug in.

'That's a good girl,' said Anya.

The truth was, an attack on Anya might have been the last thing I ever did. A familiar going toe-to-toe with a succubus? She could have beaten me into a bag of loose bone shards.

'Okay, if you're not going to stamp your feet and throw your little fists, could you ask the question you came here to ask? I'm growing tired of your company already.'

'A body was found,' said David. 'A dead body, just to be clear. A corpse.'

'And?'

'And this,' I replied, holding up my phone, which displayed a picture of the mummified man's body.

'Strike you as familiar?' I asked.

'I don't believe we had ever met, no.'

I pocketed my phone. 'Notice the way his corpse looked?

He was alive the night previous, then was found like that in the morning. Completely dried out, not a drop of moisture left in his body.'

'Perhaps he had the heating turned up too high.'

David laughed, the sound catching in his throat as I glared at him.

'Sorry, but, you know, that was kind of funny.'

'Anya, you know what I'm asking.'

'You think that he may have met his end at the hands of a succubus.'

I nodded.

'You are treading on thin ice, familiar. If I were you I'd choose my next words very carefully.'

'We're not accusing anyone here,' said David. 'Just a few friendly questions. Standard, you know, police stuff.'

'Oh, I think your partner here is very much accusing my family of something, is that not so, Stella? Do you believe myself and my sisters to be guilty of the poor man's untimely demise?

'You've seen the picture. And I've seen the body up close.'

Anya stood and glided towards me. 'I am the head of the succubus family of London, and whether your witches are dead or alive, a pact was made. I do not break my promises. My sisters do not break their promises. We agreed to feed within these walls and within these walls alone, and never to the point of a subject's death. All who enter, all who we feed upon, walk out of this place alive.'

I studied her face, looking for a tell, but came up with nothing. She seemed to be telling the truth.

'Could another succubus be out there?' asked David. 'One who isn't in your family?'

'No. We would know. I would know.'

'You're sure?'

'We always know.'

As Anya spoke her eyes never left me. A blink and her eyes

were black. She raised a hand, now more like a claw, and ran one rough, long, sharp finger across my cheek.

'Maybe' I replied, 'someone in your family has a got a little tired of living by the rules and wanted to fully embrace their nature. To really sate their appetite.'

Anya's nail stopped tracing my jaw. Instead, the point began to press against my flesh. The pressure began to increase, ever so slightly, with each passing heartbeat; sooner or later she was going to break the skin. Finally, I blinked and jerked my head away.

Anya sneered and turned from me.

'When was the last time you had a, well, a *full feed*?' asked David.

'Too long,' she replied, almost wistfully it seemed. 'We were at war with the London Coven, and they fought with all they had to deny us our feeding rights. The last time I drained someone to death was one evening almost ninety years ago. She was a young thing, perhaps twenty, with lily white skin that had never known the touch of a man. I sat astride her and drank her down. Every last emotion, every desire and fury. All of it, until her perfect skin puckered. The truce was called the next day, after both sides had finally realised we'd fought to a standstill. I am a monster of my word, and neither I nor my sisters have fed fully since, no matter how much our stomachs beg us to.'

'It must be, you know, difficult,' said David. 'I mean, I used to love a nice ciggy, puffed those things all day every day since the age of fifteen, only gave up a year ago. Went on the patches, the gum, but it wasn't the same. It didn't scratch that itch in the same way. I still find myself buying a pack every couple of months, just so I can smoke a single cig before chucking the rest out.'

Anya smiled, 'He's smarter than he looks, isn't he?'

'Oh, thanks. I think?'

'It is difficult, but we are not human. We are not so weak.

We can and do restrain ourselves. No occasional cigarette just to appease the itch.'

I held up my phone again, the picture of the man's corpse still on display. 'You're sure of that?'

Anya's eyes snapped black again for a second before she caught herself and her composure returned.

'You come to my home with accusations, questioning my control over my own family? That shows either surprising bravery, or extreme stupidity. Which is it?'

'I'd say a little from column A, a little from column B,' said David.

'Can you explain the picture, Anya?' I said. 'If it wasn't caused by a succubus, what else could it be?'

'There are any number of things that might have done that, as well you know. I'm sure you yourself could manipulate a spell to do something similar.'

Perhaps I could, but I'd been close to the corpse, and no magic spell had caused it. I would be able to see evidence of that, be able to taste it. The specific Uncanny residue of witchcraft.

'Well, thanks a lot for your time,' said David, in his best police man voice.

'Oh, it's always a pleasure to see *you*, detective. Do come back any time.'

'Yep,' said David, his voice a squeak, before looking to me and pointing to the exit.

'Stella?' said Anya.

I stopped and turned.

'If you come in here and accuse my family on such flimsy evidence again, I will mount and feed upon you until that old body of yours finally gives out. It will be... delicious. Do I make myself clear?'

I nodded and left.

6

We made our way back through The Den, again doing our best to ignore the various acts of depravity going on around us.

'Do you believe her?' asked David.

'Not sure. Maybe. Anya's a very good liar, but then again, why lie? If it really was one of her own, it would make more sense for her family to have jumped us en masse back there and torn us to pieces.'

'Right. Well. That's reassuring.'

Then again, maybe Anya wasn't in quite such close control of her sisters as she liked to think. That's not something she'd admit to easily, or at all to someone like me. No, as far as I was concerned, Anya and her family were still very much in the frame for this, at least until a more likely culprit raised their head.

'Hey,' said David, 'isn't that your new bestest bud in the whole world over there?'

I turned in the direction he was pointing and saw a pile of rags piled upon a couch in a darkened corner of the club. It was Eva, curled up in a ball and snoring as a fat woman wearing leather lederhosen whipped a hairy-backed man in a gimp-mask chained to the wall beside her. As the whip cracked and the man screamed, Eva remained fast asleep, oblivious.

'Shit,' said David, looking at his watch. 'The guv is going to think I've gone missing again.'

'Go. Let me know if Layland has anything new for us.'

'Will do, magic lady. Stay safe.'

I watched him leave. He looked and sounded fine. You'd never know he'd turned into something so... Uncanny, just a few weeks earlier. Maybe the Knot Man was wrong. Maybe Eva was wrong. Maybe it would all be okay.

Yeah, wishful thinking.

I made my way over to Eva and sat beside her.

'Hey.'

'I'm asleep,' she replied.

I shook her and she sat up, groaning, the whites of her eyes as red as strawberries.

'Christ on a bike, I think someone crawled inside my head and knocked some walls down.'

I picked up a glass half-full of something and passed it over to her; she downed it in one and shuddered.

'That's the stuff,' she said, then glanced about to collect her bearings. 'So, where are we, exactly?' She jumped as the fat woman's whip cracked against the gimp's back and he let rip a sharp cry.

'The Den.'

'The what? Oh, yes, yep, I've got you. A whole lot of filthy buggers in here. I mean, I'd heard stories of course, but blimey. This right here is some next level filth.'

Another cry as the whip left a fresh, livid mark.

"Scuse me, love, do you mind,' asked Eva, trying to get the woman to let up her assault for a moment.

'What are you doing here?' I asked.

'I'm a tourist, just taking in the sights.'

'You do know who runs this place?'

'Mr The Den?'

'Anya, a succubus.'

'Oh, one of those sorts. I thought I caught a whiff of something, but then I've stuck so much up my nose recently it can be easy to make mistakes. Know what I mean?'

'Not really.'

Another whip crack, another scream.

'Oi, tons of fun, I won't tell you again,' said Eva.

The woman grunted, her flesh quivering in annoyance.

'So, what are you into then, my girl?' she asked me.

'What?'

'What's your poison? You must've come here for a reason. A little light bondage? Fight club? Daddy play?'

'No! No, no, no. None of that. I came here to ask the succubus who runs the place some questions, about a murder.'

'Ooh, I do love a good murder.'

I pulled out my phone and showed Eva the dried-out corpse.

'Now that, is one ugly fucker.'

'Look like a succubus attack to you?'

Another cry from the gimp.

'One moment, love,' said Eva. She flashed out her hand and caught the whip just as the fat woman was about to give the gimp another bloody streak across his arching back.

The woman turned to Eva. 'Oi,' she said, 'what's your game?'

'Me and my friend here are trying to have a civil conversation, you sack of mayonnaise, and it's awfully tricky with all the screaming.'

The woman shrieked and lunged at Eva, who uttered an incantation under her breath and sent the woman flying through the air, pudgy legs whirling like she was on a bicycle, before a wall broke her fall and she crashed down to the floor, unconscious.

'You know,' said Eva, 'in my experience, women in lederhosen are always very unreasonable.'

'Ladies.'

'Ladies.'

Jack and Jake, the Den's bouncers.

'What is it now?' I asked.

'Familiar's Anonymous meeting is it?'

'Sorry,' I said, standing slowly, trying not to give them any more reason to get agitated. 'The lady in the leather trousers started it when she charged my friend here.'

'Is that so?' asked Jake.

'Oh, is that so, is it?' said Jack.

'Yes,' replied Eva, 'So why don't you two numbskulls toddle off before I rearrange those flat faces of yours, hm? Come on Stella, are we going to chat with Giles L'Merrier or what?"

Eva stood and shoved past the pair, staggering towards The Den's exit. Jack and Jake looked at each other, slowly blinking in surprise, then turned to me.

'Sorry guys, bit of a mouth on her, that one.'

I jogged past to catch up with Eva, leaving the befuddled pair behind before their surprised confusion turned to anger.

7

'Do you mind telling me how you knew I was going to pay Giles L'Merrier a visit?' I asked as the tube shot Eva and I towards *L'Merrier's Antiques*.

'Oh, I saw the summons on the card you keep teasing at without realising you're doing it.'

I pulled my hand away from the card that I was holding on to in my pocket.

'Did you see who delivered it?'

'Nope. But then I don't suppose the big man utilises delivery boys and such, do you? More of a flim-flam and away we magically go sort of message transference, I'd say.'

Well, if anyone had the power to bypass the coven's security so they could deliver a note, it would be Giles L'Merrier. Better that than actually leave his shop, or pick up the phone. If anything, I was surprised he hadn't transported me there against my will.

Eva placed her hands behind her head as she propped her boots up on the frayed seat opposite. 'Lyna, one of my witches, she told stories of L'Merrier over the centuries. Truth be told, I think she had a bit of a crush on the big man. I asked if they'd ever knocked boots and she turned me into a frog for six months.' She threw her head back and laughed uproariously, which drew more than a few concerned glances from the other passengers in the carriage.

'Yeah,' I replied. 'My witches used to talk about the sort of things he'd get up to.'

Eva nodded, using a sleeve to wipe tears from the corners of her eyes as her giggles finally died down.

'Lyna once told me about how a gaggle of witch hunters had the coven surrounded. Before my time this, you understand.'

Before Eva's time was a hell of a long time ago, by the way. If what I'd been told was true, she was probably the oldest living familiar in existence, though to look at her you'd swear she was in her late thirties at most.

'So, they'd tried everything against these Godless fuckers and nothing had worked. What's more, the turds had already dispatched my predecessor. Chopped her up and fed the bits to their horses. Bit grim....' Eva's eyes dropped and her head began to nod.

'Eva!'

'What? Yes?'

'L'Merrier! L'Merrier and the witch hunters.'

'Right! Are we on a train?'

Focus was not one of Eva's gifts.

'So, Lyna and the rest are completely surrounded, their familiar dead, powers drained, thinking they're goners. Would've been too, but then up out of nowhere appears L'Merrier, large as life and twice as fierce. Is that a saying? I think I ballsed that up. Anyway, he had an enchanted tree branch in his big hands, and he whack-whack-whacked each of the witch hunters' heads off, then threw their bodies into Derwent Water, one of the great lakes. Threw their horses in too, for good measure. Trapped 'em for good in The Nether. That's just the sort of shit he did, before he went soft, figuratively and literally, judging by the blubber he carts around on him these days.'

Every story anyone told about L'Merrier in the old days made him sound like some sort of a god. To meet the grumpy sod who never strayed from the insides of his shop, it was difficult to match the two pictures up.

'Do you know why he stopped?' I asked. 'Why he just stays in his shop these days?'

Eva shrugged. 'Buggered if I know, but then even the best of fun gets boring, given time.'

Eva seemed to sag, her eyes becoming hooded, distant, looking at something I couldn't see. I knew what it must be, because I know I often have that expression when I'm thinking about a certain something. David had told me often enough.

'You're thinking about them aren't you? Your witches?' he'd say, and I'd nod, hoping a tear wouldn't escape if I blinked.

Eva's witches were dead, just like mine.

We sat in silence for the rest of the journey, listening to the clack clack clack of the wheels on the track.

8

Like I said, L'Merrier isn't the type of person who encourages visits. As a matter of fact, he's warned me on more than one occasion to never darken his doorstep again. Needless to say, this mysterious summons of his had me more than a little curious.

And wary.

'This the place is it?' asked Eva.

'Yes, the shop with the sign that reads "L'Merriers Antiques" is the shop we're meeting L'Merrier in,' I replied.

'Smart arse.'

I pushed the door open, the little bell jangling to announce our entrance.

'L'Merrier, it's me, Stella Familiar.'

I peered around the shop, packed full of a jumble of strange objects, some everyday, others of the more Uncanny variety.

'Is that a giant's heart over there?' asked Eva.

'Yup.'

'Now that's not the sort of souvenir you pick up in your average gift shop. That's something else, that is.' She stopped and sniffed the air. 'It stinks of magic in here. I mean, I thought your coven was heavy with it, but this place...' She wafted a hand in front of her nose.

'Familiar.' A deep, smooth voice rolling out from the shadows.

'Christ,' said Eva, 'You nearly gave me a heart attack.'

L'Merrier, in his floor-length robe with its sewn on symbols of protection, glided out of the dark, his fingers interlaced and resting on top of his bulging stomach.

'I came,' I said, 'as asked.'

'Congratulations for indicating the obvious, familiar,' he replied. 'I do not recall adding a "plus one" to the invitation.'

'You're bald,' noted Eva. 'Lyna never mentioned anything about you being bald.'

L'Merrier turned to Eva, 'Ah, it is you, the errant leftovers from the Cumbrian Coven. Always running, running, running from her responsibilities. From her true place and purpose. As though she has any future that does not include her return to the dark lakes.'

'Yup, that's me,' she chirped.

Was that almost a smile on L'Merrier's face?

'A pair of tragic orphans in my humble shop; it seems witches are becoming an endangered species, does it not?'

'That's enough,' I said, feeling a little seed of anger sprout. He could say what he liked about me, but I wouldn't stand for him mocking my dead.

'A little fire in the belly, familiar?' asked L'Merrier, one eyebrow raising with amusement.

Eva inhaled noisily, 'You know, Giles, it really bloody reeks in here. It smells like you've been farting out your own brand of magic in a sealed room for twenty years. Crack a window, mate.'

L'Merrier swept one hand in front of himself and Eva found herself pinned to the ceiling.

'Let her down!' I yelled, stepping automatically into a boxer's stance, my hands raised, boiling with magic.

'Short temper on you, chubs,' said Eva, 'you should speak to someone about that.'

There was a heavy, silent pause, then L'Merrier burst out laughing, which was more disturbing than it sounds. With a twitch of his head he killed the spell and sent Eva tumbling back down to the floor.

'L'Merrier,' I said, slowly relaxing and allowing the magic to putter out from my fists, 'Are you going to tell me why you asked me here or not?'

L'Merrier bowed his head, then looked up, fixing me with his eyes. They shone like golden coins in the dark.

'You know why I have asked you here.'

'No, I don't.'

'But you must suspect.'

David.

'There,' said L'Merrier.

'What about David?'

'I believe you had a very particular visitor to your coven recently.'

I shuffled, uncomfortable. 'I'm not sure I—'

'Do not play dumber than you are, familiar, you know exactly of whom I speak.'

Eva raised a hand. 'Not sure I do. Unless it's me. Is it me?'

'The Knot Man,' I said.

'Exactly so.'

'The Knot Man?' replied Eva. 'Have I heard of him? I think I've heard of him. Far as I can tell, having him show up on your doorstep is never a good thing. Though, when is anyone turning up on your doorstep unannounced ever a good thing, am I right? Give me a "praise Jesus" if you know what I'm talking about. Okay, I'm bored now, I'm going for a ciggy outside.'

The doorbell jangled as Eva left the shop, pulling a tobacco tin out of her inside pocket.

'First your pet detective, and now that stray,' sighed L'Merrier. 'Such delightful company you keep.'

'What do you want to say about David?'

L'Merrier moved over to a glass display case, inside of which was what looked like a large hunk of rock.

'Do you know what this is?' he asked.

'No,' I replied.

'This is a piece of Apoc Hill.'

'Is that supposed to mean something to me?'

'No, it is not of this reality, it is of another, parallel earth, but it is relevant to this conversation. The Apoc Hill came to rest in the north, heralding a game. A battle between the light and the dark that almost resulted in that reality's version of Hell rising and taking control of the Earth. Well, of *that* Earth. The Knot Man was there, as he walks between realities. Any time he pays someone a visit, it is just before a point of calamity. So forgive me for being curious when my web jangles and twitches and I look up to see him knock, knock, knocking upon your door.'

The idea that L'Merrier kept watch on things—kept watch on my coven—shouldn't have creeped me out. Knowing his power, I should have expected it. But the idea of him watching me, peeping into my home, still made me squirm.

'What do you think is going to happen?' I asked.

'David is no longer what he was,' L'Merrier replied. 'He's been altered in some way by you introducing him into our world. I wonder what you made him face that changed him so. That is still changing him.'

I thought about the black magic I'd used to bring David back to life after Mr. Trick left him for dead, but I kept it to myself. Despite his own fondness for it, L'Merrier was known for turning others who used the dark arts to dust.

'What is he changing into?' I asked.

'You already know. The Knot Man told you.'

A walking apocalypse.

'He has no control over it, the poor thing,' L'Merrier continued, 'he's just walking around blind in his little life, oblivious to the fact that his body is drawing in more and more power, more of the Uncanny, more potential, and, sooner or later, there will be a tipping point. He's like a black hole, only instead of dragging light into his belly, he's pulling in magic. At a steadily increasing pace, I might add. And then...'

'And then what?'

L'Merrier spread his hands out, his face grave: 'Boom.'

He wants to destroy him. To destroy David. That's what L'Merrier wants, it's what the Knot Man suggested too. No chances, no help, just cold-blooded murder.

'He can control it,' I said. 'I can teach him.'

'Oh no, not even I could do that, and compared to me you are but an ant, crawling across the toe of an elephant. The die is already cast. The power is filling him up. It will turn him monstrous, and then goodbye, London. His end must come, for the good of all.'

I stepped forward, not caring who it was I was talking to, how he could knock me into another plane of reality, David was my friend. 'No one is going near him. I'll help him. I'll stop this and I'll save David Tyler's life. You hear me?

L'Merrier chuckled. 'Headstrong. Always have been. But stomp and pout all you wish, if you do not take care of David, others will. Do you think a visit from a being such as the Knot Man to our fair city will have been seen only by me? No, no. Word is spreading even now among the Uncanny of London. They will come for him. It would be a kindness if you brought David here, to me, I could put him out of his misery. What do you say?'

I felt my head getting hotter and hotter, my nails digging into my palms as I clenched my fists so hard I thought my knuckles might burst.

'Don't you dare threaten him.'

L'Merrier smiled thinly. 'I do not threaten, familiar. I say, and I do.'

'No one is touching him. No one but me. Do you hear me, Giles?'

L'Merrier raised an eyebrow as I tossed his summons card on the floor and turned to head toward the exit.

'Have no doubt, familiar: David must be destroyed.'

I turned from the door as the bell rang above my head: 'Over my dead body.' I left Eva in my wake as I stormed out of L'Merrier's Antiques, the door crashing shut behind me.

'Oi, wait a minute,' she said from around the cigarette clasped between her lips. 'What's up? What did old Giles L'Chubbier have to say for himself?'

'He wants me to kill David.'

'Right. Bit harsh. I mean that aftershave he's wearing isn't for everyone, but still.'

'You have to help me with him, Eva.'

'Whoa now, what gave you the impression I was the helping sort? I'm the drinking, the lounging sort, but very much not the helping sort.'

'Then why are you even here?'

'I'm passing through. Always passing through. On my way from there, to here, to somewhere else.'

'We're familiars, it's our duty.'

'Ha! I washed these dainty, rough knuckled hands of any idea about getting involved in things like this a long time ago.'

'So you're happy for my friend to just die?'

'Well, I wouldn't say happy, but what's your alternative? Let the poor sod massacre millions? Bit out of order, that, love. You just do your best, but be ready to do your worst if you need to.'

My heart was thumping in my ears, my breath short. No one was going to hurt David. It didn't matter what was happening to him, I would find a way to stop it, and nobody, not even the mighty Giles L'Merrier was going to take David away from me.

Whatever it cost me, he would survive.

9

Another alleyway, another dead body. It seems like I've spent half of my life looking at corpses in narrow, damp, dingy passages. The dead stowed away, behind bins, in piss stained gutters. Something for the rats to gnaw at.

David waved and began to weave his way towards us, leaving his partner, Layland, behind.

'Here he comes,' said Eva, 'the old walking apocalypse.'

I watched David as he approached and felt my heart ache. My witches had died; no, been murdered. I should be alone, but I'm not, because at the same time as the worst thing to ever happen to me came about, I met David. I had a friend, a partner, someone who liked and trusted me, and I wasn't going to let anyone or anything harm a hair on his head.

'Hello ladies, beautiful day to look at a dead body in a piss-scented alley, hey?'

As David lead us toward the corpse I thought again about what Eva had said as we made our way over: *'Why are you still doing all of this? Your coven is dead. Walk away, live a life free of a duty that no bastard ever thanks you for doing anyway.'*

I supposed it was a fair enough question. If a coven has, for all intents and purposes, "fallen," why pretend? I was a genie who had been set free, I didn't have to stay in the bottle anymore, didn't have to grant wishes to anyone who picked up my lamp. I could just walk away. Walk away from London, and the constant churn of death and evil and horror.

I could live a normal life.

But what even was a normal life? Normal for me was smashing my fist into a monster's mouth. Running around after unspeakable danger, my heart thumping like it might explode out of my chest. Going to sleep knowing I'd made the city safe for one more night.

I'm a familiar. This is what I was created for. How could I just walk away and pretend like every part of me didn't want to carry on?

I don't know how Eva finds it in herself to stay away from her coven, from her whole county, without going mad from shame. She didn't belong anywhere. Anywhere but watching out over Cumbria, over the lakes, whether her witches were at her side or not.

'There she is,' said David, as we stood over the body of a woman. She wore dirty clothes and a pair of boots years past their best. Just like the last body we saw, hers was drained and mummified.

Eva crouched and sniffed at the body, leaning in so close the tip of her nose practically scuffed it.

'If she licks the corpse I'm never going to hear the end of it from Forensics,' said David, nervously glancing around at the other officers on the scene, some of whom were giving the still crouched Eva some odd looks.

'What is it?' I asked, as Eva stood and pulled out her cigarette case.

'Nothing. Just, you know, the stink of death.'

'Oh,' said David, 'who doesn't enjoy a lungful of that?'

It was a succubus attack, I was sure of it. The face was the same, eyes and mouth wide, a reflex action in the last moments of being drained.

'No I.D. on her, but judging by the location and the way she's dressed, we're pretty sure this one was a rough sleeper,' said David.

'Poor fucker,' said Eva. 'A shit life and a shittier death. Ain't life grand?'

Layland approached, cup of coffee in hand. 'Oh, you invited two weirdos for the price of one; my lucky day,' she said, her narrowed eyes practically piercing my skin.

'Whoa,' said Eva. 'Now that is a face you have nightmares about.'

'Stella, is there a reason my numbskull partner invites you to these things, because I see a second dead body now and not a single helpful word from you.'

'I'm working on it.'

I didn't like the way Layland looked at me. Sometimes it felt like the suggestion magic I pushed out to make the officers accept my presence didn't quite work as well as it should have on her. I probed at her a little with my senses, wondering if there wasn't a distant bit of Uncanny about her, but came up with nothing. Maybe she was just strong-minded enough to notice that something was playing her.

'I think God did it,' said Eva, blowing out a cloud of smoke.

'Oh, God, okay,' replied Layland, and never had a sentence been spoken with so much sarcasm.

'Oh yeah. I mean, if you think about it, God's to blame for everything. Every death. That is, if you believe in a God, of course.'

'And you do?'

'I try not to think too much about it, love, that way leads to madness, know what I mean?'

Layland gave Eva a long hard look: the wild mess of black hair, the ragged clothing that made her look a bit like a goth Stevie Nicks. 'Oh yes,' she said. 'I know what you mean.'

Eva saluted and turned on her heel, wandering away from us.

'You have the best taste in friends, Tyler,' said Layland.

'What can I say,' David replied. 'I attract damaged women.'

Layland sighed. 'You know my previous partner wasn't much for talking, or jokes. We worked together for three years and barely exchanged a dozen words a day. God, I miss Terry.'

David grinned and put his arm around her, 'Come off it, you know you love me, you big grump.'

She looked at him, eyes half shut, and sighed.

'Stella, if you can't give us anything useful, I don't expect to see you on my crime scene, got it?'

'Got it.'

Layland gave me a last contemptuous look, then walked away.

I turned my attention back to the body.

'So, are we still thinking the same thing?' asked David. 'One of Anya's nearest and dearest out on the prowl?'

I stared into the poor woman's wide, dead eyes, all colour drained from them. As far as I was concerned, there was no doubt.

'Yeah.'

'Well that's not good, is it? I mean, that's very, very bad. Three "verys" even.'

He was right. It didn't get much worse.

10

I was surprised to find Eva waiting across the street from the alleyway as I stepped out, still puffing away on a cigarette. I'd expected her to have done a bunk again.

'Hey girlfriend,' she yelled, raising a fist as I approached.

'You know those are bad for you, right?' I said.

'Ah, fuck it. What isn't bad for you these days?'

'Not smoking.'

Eva snorted at that.

'How long have you actually been alive now? It's running into the hundreds of years, correct?'

'Yeah, and it fucking feels like it, believe me. I may have the appearance of a youthful, sexy-as-all-damn-hell female, but my joints ache to buggery and I wake up to take a piss about five times every night.'

'Information I wasn't desperate to hear.'

'So, a succubus gone feral, eh?' Eva continued. 'Nasty shit.'

I nodded, nasty shit was an understatement of epic proportions. Going toe-to-toe with a succubus was practically suicide as it was. There was also the matter of whether or not this was a fresh succubus, new to the city, or whether it was one of Anya's family gone rogue. Neither option was appealing, but the second one meant facing off against Anya and her entire family, and that sounded like a one way trip to the cemetery.

I felt myself shudder a little and reached out a hand towards Eva, who looked at me in surprise before handing over the ciggy. I inhaled and held it for several seconds before letting it fog out of me with a sigh.

'That's it, lady,' said Eva, 'just give in. Life kills you in the end, why try so hard? That's my motto. Not that I have a motto, because that would make me a prize pillock, but if I did. Which I never would. Scratch this whole thing and give me that.'

She grabbed the cigarette back and slumped on a bench, pulling a half-full bottle of gin from her pocket and unscrewing the cap.

'I'm not sure I can do everything that's expected of me,' I said. 'Whatever magical safeguards my witches put in place on the city have decayed and the bad is just getting badder. I've never had so much work, and it's just me and David now, who I'm lying to, and it seems like I'm supposed to kill him or someone else will and it's all a bit, you know, much. What if I'm not good enough?'

'You're not. Accept failure, it's easier in the long run.'

'Thanks.'

She grinned and toasted me with the gin bottle before suckling at it like a hungry newborn. I sat next to her and stared towards the alley's opening as the body of the homeless woman was placed into the back of an ambulance and driven away.

'My masters are dead and I'm here trying to keep some sort of order in London. One coven for a whole city, what were they thinking?'

'That they were witches and therefore unkillable and above questioning. Arrogant sods, the lot of them. Well, death sure showed our respective creators, hey?'

Is Eva what I'd become if I took her advice and just walked away? If I said goodbye to the coven and washed my hands of my duties? How could she have done that? A familiar is built for one purpose and one place. How could shirking her duties not eat her insides away?

I looked to Eva, her eyes half closed, trying to drink from her gin bottle and inhale her cigarette at the same time, her hands trembling slightly. She'd been hiding from her responsibilities for years, and look what it had done to her.

I couldn't become that.

I wouldn't.

'Hey,' said David, making me jump. I'd been so caught up in my own dreary thoughts that I hadn't noticed him approaching.

'Hey,' I said back.

'Thirsty?' asked Eva, holding out the gin bottle and giving it a wiggle.

'Thanks, but I think I'll pass for now.'

'Suit yourself, more for Mama.'

David widened his eyes at me briefly, smiling. I looked past him to see the bulk of the officers leaving, the alley now taped off with a couple of coppers sat slumped in the front seat of their patrol car out front.

'So,' I said, 'What are they making of all this? Layland and your bosses?'

'They haven't got a clue, which for some weird reason really pisses them off.'

I smiled. 'What are they expecting from you?'

'The same as always, results out of thin air, and fast. Only, no matter what happens here, I'm not going to be able to give them any actual results, because the killer is a monster that doesn't exist. Or doesn't exist as far as anyone else knows. All I can do is help you stop it, then it's just another unsolved crime on my ledger. I've gotta say, joining up with you is not bringing any extra sparkle to my career prospects.'

David dropped into the final seat on the bench, his leg pressing against mine and making my stomach do a strange whirly thing. Nothing else had happened since the strange almost-kiss from a few weeks back. The strange almost-kiss that I'm pretty sure he didn't actually notice anyway, and I'd blown up in my head out of all proportion. I'd been drunk. Worse than drunk, hanging off his neck with our faces too close for too long.

'Is no one else going to notice that then?' asked Eva, derailing my train of thought.

'Notice what?' I asked.

'You seriously haven't noticed?'

'What is she talking about now?' asked David.

'Who's "she", the cat's, you know... what is it? Cousin? Or...? What were we talking about again?'

'We haven't noticed something,' I replied impatiently.

'Oh right, yeah. So no one has noticed? I'm the only one, and I wasn't even paying attention.'

'Noticed what?' I cried.

'Lady muck over there! In the doorway of the boarded-up chip shop. She's only been stood watching crime alley for the last fifteen minutes. Keen eyes, you two, this city is in really safe hands.'

I leaned past Eva to see what it was she was looking at. There was a person slouched in the doorway about fifty-metres away. She was wearing a floor-length, purple cloak with the hood up, which was a strange thing to have on, but not for this person.

I could only see a little of her face, but that was enough. I recognised her. It was one of Anya's family.

It was a succubus.

11

The succubus was fast, moving swiftly and with little effort as I sprinted after her, David panting at my heels. What we were going to do if we actually caught her I didn't know. My best current plan was: try not to die horribly. I already saw a lot of holes in that plan.

Just David and I against a succubus was bad, having Eva help out would've been a safer bet, but as we made to chase she'd just shrugged and said, *'I make it a rule not to run unless I'm being chased.'*

I didn't have time to argue with her, or tell her she was shaming familiars everywhere with her cowardice, instead I just ran, pulling in the street's magic as I went, readying for attack.

'She's ducking out!' said David, pointing towards the succubus as she slipped past a group of passers-by and disappeared down an alley. I knew the succubus we were chasing – I'd spoken to her a few times over the years. Her name was Lorna, one of the younger sisters of the family. She'd always seemed one of the more restrained and approachable of Anya's kin; at least you didn't worry quite so much that she'd turn suddenly and try to drain the life out of you. As we turned sharply into the alley to continue the chase, I had to wonder what she had been doing near the crime scene. Had she broken ranks from the family and turned feral, murdering normals for her own satisfaction? Or was she just keeping an eye on the investigation on Anya's behalf? Trying to find out who was really behind the murders.

Well, it looked as though I was going to get the opportunity to ask.

As we reached the end of the alley it opened up into a little courtyard area with no exit. The succubus was down on her haunches at the far end of the courtyard, her back to us, dark purple cape pooling out around her.

'Lorna! It is Lorna, isn't it?'

The hood covering her head twitched a little, but she didn't turn or answer.

'Lorna,' said David, 'we'd just like to ask you a friendly, non-violent or in any way threatening question or two.'

'Lorna, we have two people dead. Two people drained dry. And now here you are. What are you doing here Lorna? Are you just keeping an eye on things? Looking for clues just like us?'

'Or maybe you got a little tired of being on Anya's short leash,' said David. 'Of Stella's pain in the arse rules about what a succubus can and can't do. Hey, I can relate, my mum never let me go further than the end of the street when I first got a bike, but I did anyway. So. This is kind of the same.'

I gave him a look.

'Well, it is kind of. Minus all the murder.'

I indicated for David to hang back as I took a step or two towards the still motionless Lorna. I dragged the surrounding magic into myself, cords of multi-coloured energy whirling around my clenched fists.

'Lorna, the more you don't answer me, the more nervous I get. The more I think you're not here doing detective work. The more I think maybe it's you doing the killing. Persuade me that I'm wrong.'

Things moved fast then. Too fast for me to do much of anything besides tense for impact.

There was a flash of purple as Lorna turned and stood, her cloak whirling past my eyes and its hood falling down to give me my first clear glimpse of her.

It wasn't pretty.

She was in full beast mode.

Her eyes were unbroken pools of black, her face a stretched, razor-tooth-filled gargoyle scream. Before I knew what was happening, she'd swept the back of one elongated, clawed hand across my face and I was airborne, a wall breaking my flight painfully.

There was no time to check for broken bones or open wounds. I hopped up on my feet instantly, my fists boiling with magic, and found Lorna stalking towards David, who happened to still be blocking the only exit.

'Halt in.... the name of the law?' said David.

He wasn't going to just get out of the way, the stubborn, brave idiot, which meant unless I did something fast he was going to end up face down in a puddle of his own brains.

So I did something fast.

I clapped my hands together then pulled, creating a long, magical whip of crackling, bright orange energy, which I swung, striking Lorna across the back.

CRACK.

She hissed and twisted back to me, fury in her ink-black eyes.

'Where do you think you're going, succubus? I haven't even started with you yet.'

All thoughts of escaping by way of a dead David had now clearly deserted Lorna. All she wanted now was to do some very bad and potentially very fatal things to me.

I struck out with the whip again, hitting her across the face, opening a livid cut across one cheek. She screeched and sprang towards me, claws out, ready to sink them into my chest. I dove left, rolled once, then hopped back to my feet, lashing out with the whip again, only this time she was wise to it and caught it before it struck home.

'Oh shit,' I said, and really, really meant it.

Lorna yanked on the whip, sending me flying towards her. I landed in a pile at her feet, the whip no longer in my hand, the world tilting as my brain jarred on impact. I looked up to see Lorna above me with murder in her eyes. As she loomed over me, face twisted with fury, claw raised and ready to strike, I pictured my dead witches and wondered if I'd be seeing them again sooner than planned.

That's when the metal bin bounced off her head and sent Lorna sprawling to the ground.

'Well,' said David. 'Get the up and twat the cow!'

He didn't have to tell me twice.

I leapt to my feet, soaking up the magic in the air like I was breathing in smoke, my fists throbbing with energy.

'My turn,' I said, and punched my fist forward with a scream, unleashing a wave of energy that caught the still-downed Lorna flush and smashed her back against the wall.

I didn't wait for her to gather her senses.

I punched forward again, and again, one fist after the other, the magic surging into me and then exploding out, crashing into Lorna like breaking waves. Taking on a junior member of the family had been a lucky break – she still had enough strength to rip me to shreds given the chance, but if this had been Anya, the chances of me walking out of this alley would have been next to zero.

'Lorna,' I said, unleashing another wave of energy, trying to keep her from gaining her footing and fighting back. 'You know why I'm doing this. You've stepped outside of the pact.'

I looked at her as she squirmed, still in full beast mode, and wondered what could have—

—I blinked, the world swimming back into sharpness, to find myself on my back and looking up at the sky. What the hell?

'Hello, Stella.'

'Hello there, Stella.'

I sat up to find Jack and Jake, The Den's doormen, stood before me with David in their clutches. We were in the courtyard still, but there was no sign of Lorna.

'Hey, Stella,' said David, 'Jack here told me to tell you that if you try anything funny he'll... what was it?'

'Snap your neck like a twig.'

'That's it. That thing he just said. About my neck.'

'And stomp your skull into a bloody paste,' said Jake.

'Oh, yeah,' said David, 'that too. Forgot about that.'

I stood, my fists clenched, ready to fight.

'Which one of you fuckers knocked me out?'

Jack raised a hand. 'It was this fist here.'

'That one there,' agreed Jake.

'One punch.'

'Back of the head.'

'And down she went.'

I looked around, but she'd definitely gone. Lorna had escaped.

'If you're looking for Lorna, we couldn't let you carry on with that nonsense.'

'Not with that nonsense, I mean, you were being very rude.'

'Rude is the word for it.'

I'd had enough.

'David?'

'Yup?'

'Sorry.'

'About?'

I swept my hand across him and he lurched out of Jake's grip, sprawling on the ground a few feet away.

'Like that is it?' said Jake.

'Oh, like that, then?' said Jack. 'Oh goodie.'

I threw a fist forward, then another, striking both in the chest with a ball of crackling power. The bouncers flinched and slid back, like rhinos nudged by a couple of shopping carts. They didn't go down.

They looked at each other and smiled, then back to me.

Christ, I hated fighting this pair.

They charged towards me as one.

I punched out more and more magic, but they were quick on their feet for their size, ducking and weaving as they approached, causing me to leap and roll to avoid their massive bodies crushing me against the wall.

'David, away,' I ordered.

'I'm not leaving you to these lumps,' he replied. 'Christ, why am I so noble?'

'Stella, stay still so we can hurt you,' said Jake.

'Yeah, stay still, Stella, we only want to hurt you,' agreed Jack.

I soaked the magic into me, willing as much of it inside of me as I could. So much that I could see a dim aura glowing from me.

'Come on then,' I said, and began to charge.

Jack and Jake smiled and came to meet me. At speed.

There was a collision. There was a release of magic. There was a lot of pain. And then I was on the ground again, struggling to right myself as Jack and Jake, breathing heavily, helped each other to their feet.

One hand against the brick wall for support, I wrenched my complaining body back up, my head throbbing from the impact, vision swimming.

'Had enough yet?' I asked, my voice wavering.

'Enough?' said Jack.

'We can do this all day,' said Jake.

'Ha, all bloody day!'

They hunched their shoulders and turned to face me, ready to charge again.

I pulled the magic into me, my legs still threatening to drop me back to the ground.

'Enough,' said a voice I recognised. Smooth, commanding, and above all, seductive.

Jack and Jake relaxed and stepped aside as Anya, head of the succubus family of London, slinked into view.

12

Anya's hands caressed the chests of her two doormen, tracing the scorch marks on their starched white shirts.

'Has she been playing rough?' she asked.

'Very rough,' replied Jake.

'But we don't mind that, boss,' said Jack.

'Oh no, don't mind that.'

'We like it rough.'

Anya smiled and licked her lips as she turned and looked at me. 'Go and wait for me by the car, would you, boys?'

Jack and Jake nodded, gave me a cheery wave, then lumbered away.

'Well, isn't this an awful mess?' she purred.

'You lied to us,' I said.

Anya pulled a mock-hurt face and shook her head. 'No. I did not.'

'She's the killer, isn't she, Anya? Lorna, your sister, she's gone feral, broken ranks, and you're here to try and pull her back. Am I wrong?'

She turned towards David, who had his back pressed

against the wall, trying to be invisible. 'Detective Tyler, what a delight to see you again so soon.'

'Oh, hey there.'

'When will you come back to my club, alone?' she asked. 'I see such... fun in you.'

'Pfft, I have such a busy slate at the moment. Otherwise... well, I still wouldn't come as you and that place terrify me. A lot. A lot of terrified.'

'Anya, I represent the London Coven, and you will answer my questions now. Truthfully.'

She turned to me, her mouth twitching momentarily into a grimace. 'Oh, will I now? Are you really the coven, or just all that's left? A remnant clinging on to something that's already dead?'

I can't pretend that didn't sting. That it didn't ring a little bell in my head. Eva popped into my mind's eye briefly. Eva, who was just like me, but had given up her purpose after her coven's destruction. Did she have the right idea after all? Maybe I was holding on to something that was over. I wasn't a witch. What right did I have to try to act as though I were?

'As things stand, I am the coven, Anya. And that means I can't just stand aside. I can't let people in this city die at the hands of the Uncanny, no matter which family that Uncanny might belong to. You know that.'

Anya stared at me a little too long, and I felt a chill caress my skin. I wondered what would happen next. If she'd turn feral and leap at me, sink her teeth into me, gouge my heart open with one claw.

But instead she smiled.

'Yes. I know that. And again, I did not lie.'

'The murderer, it's Lorna.'

Anya bowed her head once.

'So you're telling me you didn't know?'

'That is what I am telling you.'

'The powerful Anya of The Den, head of the succubus

family of London, didn't know when one of her own was breaking the agreement and indulging in a murder spree?'

'I won't tell you again, Stella,' she replied.

I shifted, hands clenched, I didn't like the way Anya spoke to me. L'Merrier was one thing, but Anya got under my skin.

'Where is she then? Where's Lorna?'

'We will find her,' said Anya.

'Sorry,' said David. 'Does that mean you let her escape? You let the murderer get away?'

Anya turned her head in his direction, her eyes suddenly black, causing David to hop back in not the most manly of fashions.

'No offence, just trying to get the facts down. It's the copper in me.'

'Why did you have your pair of idiot doormen stop me if you were just going to let her run away?'

Anya turned her attention back to me, the black in her eyes fading. 'Because she is my sister. My family. She is mine to deal with. She is not yours to bat around or judge, familiar. Is that clear?'

'No,' I said, trying to sound braver than I felt.

'No?' she replied, arching an eyebrow. 'One of these days your bravery is going to be your undoing.'

'Anya, I can't just allow Lorna to carry on killing and wait for you to clean up the mess.'

'Is that so?'

'Yes, and you know it is. I couldn't just step aside even if I wanted to. It's my job to take out whatever's threatening this city.'

'You know, Stella, I really must question that fiercely stated manifesto, considering your current company.'

She turned to face David again.

'Tell me, Detective, how are you feeling?'

David looked past her to me, a little confused, 'I'm good.

Well, pretty good. Good with a side of fear, which is pretty much my default setting these days.'

'You're different than you were the first time we met.'

'Anya—'

'I am? I parted my hair differently this morning, but—'

Anya turned back to me, a humourless smile on her face. 'A little hypocritical, familiar.'

She turned and strode towards the street. 'Lorna is my family, I will deal with her.'

'Not if I find her first, Anya.'

She paused briefly. 'Get in my way, and it will not end well, regardless of your affiliation.'

As she left, David crouched to catch his breath. 'You know, she is really very stressful to be around.'

Anya knew about David. About what was happening to him. L'Merrier was right, the news was spreading. How long before someone decided to try and do something about it?

13

I placed a pint on the table in front of David and dropped onto a stool opposite. We'd retreated to The Beehive to lick our wounds and consider our next move.

'Cheers,' said David, raising his glass and gulping down a few mouthfuls.

I now knew two things for sure. Firstly, the killer was indeed a succubus from Anya's family gone rogue, and secondly, people were starting to find out about whatever it was that was happening to David.

'I'm not going to lie, Stella,' said David, 'I really hope Anya finds that black sheep of hers before we do, because those succubi are not my favourite Uncanny peeps.'

I smiled and took a drink. I can't say I disagreed with him. If Anya managed to get to Lorna first and pull her back into the fold before she committed any more murders, that would be fine with me. You could argue she should have to face some sort of justice for the murders she'd committed, but unless the family agreed, it would mean going to war. Justice couldn't always mean punishment, not in this Uncanny world. It would be up to them how she was reprimanded. Stopping her would more than likely have to be enough. I touched the side of my head and winced a little; a painful reminder of my rumble with Jack and Jake.

'So, what she was saying back there—Anya I mean—about me changing; what was all that about?'

'How should I know?' I replied, feeling like shit as I avoided his eyes, instead suddenly finding the foam on top of my beer super interesting.

'Seemed like she was circling around something,' he said, pushing.

'She says a lot of things. It's what she does. Trying to prick at you, trying to get inside your head. I learned a long time ago to block that crap out.'

David looked at me curiously, then shrugged. 'Yeah, she's a crazy one,' he said, taking another swig of his beer.

I didn't like lying to David, especially when it was about something that might actually hurt him later, but I didn't see what choice I had at that point. I needed some sort of plan of action before I said, *"Hey, so you seem to have turned into some sort of magic black hole, slurping up the juice around you, and at some point there's a chance you might explode and wipe out the city."* As soon as I could cap it with, *"But don't worry, because this is how I save you,"* I was staying quiet. Anything I told him before then was only going to make him worry, and that's the last thing I wanted.

I drained my glass and stood, my stool scraping back like nails on a chalk board. 'Another?'

David looked up at me, then at his own still three-quarters full glass. 'I'm good. Thirsty?'

'Thirsty.'

I made my way over to Lenny, The Beehive's landlord, and ordered myself a second glass full.

'So,' began Lenny, then stopped.

He was never much for small talk.

'So what?'

'Your friend. The not-so-normal normal. People are talking.'

'Let them. He's under my protection. I'll deal with it.'

He slid the full glass across the bar. 'Sure. But maybe you should stay out of view for a while.'

'What are you saying? You want me to leave?'

'People are getting antsy. I see it. I see them coming in and out of here all day. I hear the chatter. Your detective has been coming up a lot lately.'

'Let them talk. If they have anything more to say they can come and see me.'

'All I'm saying is, be prepared.'

I looked over my shoulder, scanning the room. I saw little groups of people, huddled around tables, speaking in hushed voices, stealing glances at an oblivious David, who smiled and waved at me.

'Put it on my tab,' I said, and made my way back over to our table.

'You okay there, magic lady? I mean, you scowl a lot, but even for you, that is one full-on, scowly scowl. That is a scowl squared. That is the mommy and daddy of all—'

I raised a hand to stop him. 'I've got it.'

I took a sip, and took another quick glance around the room.

Now that Lenny had pointed it out, I could practically taste the unease in the room. Before, my attention had been so taken with the Lorna problem, and the fact I was lying to David, that I hadn't noticed. But now I did.

Surely none of them would dare do anything though? Not with me there? I was Stella Familiar of the London Coven. David was safe with me.

'So, what did old Giles L'Merrier want with you, you never said?'

'Hm? Oh, nothing. Just, you know, to call me a few bad names, tell me what a terrible job I was doing. The usual.'

Certainly nothing to do with how you need to be put down before you go nuclear and blow up the entire city. Nope.

'If ever there was a guy with a stick up his arse,' said David, 'it's that man. I mean, don't get me wrong, he rocks that robe like a boss, but he needs to get out once in a while. Mix with us little people.'

I smiled, and then the world seemed to hold its breath around me, time slowing to a crawl. I tried to search my memory to find something that told me I was wrong, that I'd just forgotten, but I couldn't find anything. Because I wasn't wrong.

'David.'

'Hm?'

'How did you know I went to see Giles L'Merrier?'

'You told me.'

'No, I don't remember telling you anything about that.'

David looked at me, incredulous. 'Well you must have done, because I know about it, and I'm pretty sure Giles didn't fill me in. We're not exactly best buds.'

'David, I didn't tell you a thing about that. About his summons, about going, about any of it.'

Was this part of his new, growing power? Somehow he was reading my thoughts without even knowing he was doing it. That was bad, but things were about to get a whole lot worse.

'Oi, why don't you actually do something about him?'

I turned to see a group of men I vaguely recognised glaring our way.

'What did you say?' I replied.

'You're the London Coven. It's your job, Familiar!'

Grunts of agreement from around the pub. I could read the signals. They were scared and readying themselves to do something stupid. Waiting for the bravest of them to work up the courage to attack, then piling on after him.

'Hey,' said David. 'What's going on? What did I do?'

'It's okay, David,' I said. 'They're just drunk. Isn't that right, lads?'

They weren't playing ball though. 'If you won't do anything, maybe it's time someone else did!'

Chairs scraped back as one by one they began to stand.

'Oi,' said Lenny, 'everyone just calm down!'

But there was no calming this now, and no way of getting David out and through the door without getting past a good ten people brimming with murderous intent.

'You really want to do this?' I asked.

'Do what?' said David. 'What are they doing? What is happening here?'

The men nodded. 'What choice do we have?'

'Right,' I replied. 'Come on then.'

And that's when it all kicked off.

14

For a while I assumed I was dead.

There had been a fight. All of the drinkers in The Beehive dogpiling onto us, throwing fists and kicks and more besides. Normally I would have swept them aside without breaking a sweat, but The Beehive has an energy field around it, and our aggressors were determined to keep us inside of it.

So they could kill David.

The energy field is a type of protective bubble that affects the magical abilities of any Uncanny that steps inside it. It doesn't take them away completely, it just dampens things, because drunk people and magical powers are a recipe for death and mass destruction. The field leaves you with enough power to make any fight within its walls extra interesting, though. Extra bits of force behind punches, energy enough to unleash the magical equivalent of a supernatural fist to the nose.

All this is to say that we were taking on about twelve scared, angry people with two fists each and a little bit of magic to give their punches extra meat. David did his best to help out. With the bubble, things were a little more on the equal side, so he dove in and threw his fair share of punches. Still, we were more than a little outnumbered.

This had gone on for a few minutes when I found myself pushing my aching body up off the floor for the fourth time, spitting blood on the ancient, stained carpet, ready to do some damage of my own.

That's when I felt it.

Something was building. It made my skin prickle, my head itch. I began to hear a faint whine, like an engine building speed.

It was David.

Four of them had backed him into a corner, but were now heading in reverse.

'His eyes!'

'Stop him!'

'Get out, we've got to—'

A chaos of noise, of voices, of furniture crashing aside as a vortex began to whirl around David, his eyes turning white as a pure flame began to seep from them. I'd seen this before. Seen it a couple of times in fact, when the magic being sucked into David like a sponge overtook him and he became... something else.

'David,' I said, shielding my eyes, 'David, can you hear me? You've got to stop! You've got to stop or you're going to kill us all!'

I didn't know if he could hear me, he didn't turn to look at me, he just threw his head back, his mouth wide, screaming, and then—

...

...

...

—I remembered a blinding light, a release of energy, a feeling as though the flesh was being melted from my bones—

—and then nothing.

...

...

...

Well, not quite nothing.

If you're aware of the nothing then how can there be nothing? At the very least there was my consciousness, but I couldn't see myself, or anything else, and I couldn't move. It was like I'd forgotten how I did that. How I made my limbs move. How I blinked. How I breathed. Maybe I had nothing to move and nothing to breathe with.

No limbs, no mouth, no ligaments or lungs. Maybe this was what death actually was. Just an awareness, fixed in nothing.

A dislocated consciousness.

I stayed there for a while. It was difficult to know how long, because time didn't exist. Maybe it was seconds, or maybe it was decades.

Then I felt something pull on the nothing that was me.

Something was gaining purchase on me, it felt like it was dragging me backwards. And if something could touch me, could move me, could pull me backwards, that meant I couldn't just be a consciousness, I had to have a physical element.

Just as that thought entered my mind I blinked. I had eyelids. I had eyes for them to cover. Piece by piece I discovered my physical self again as I hurtled back and back, wind screaming in my ears, mixed with an indecipherable babble of layer upon layer of voices creating one painful roar.

And then it was over.

I lay still for a while, body trembling, the fresh wounds I'd received during the bar fight beginning to throb now I'd returned to reality.

But where was I? I wasn't in The Beehive, that was for sure. I sat up and looked around. I was home. I was in the coven.

And I wasn't alone.

I stood, quietly, padding towards the door to the main coven room. Someone was talking inside. No, not someone, three someones.

Deadly Portent

Three someones I recognised.

I pushed open the door to reveal my witches. My three masters and creators, Kala, Trin, and Feal.

'This is a trick,' I said, as I stepped into the room and the three of them turned to look. 'This is just a trick.'

I pictured the last time something like this had happened; that had been down to Mr. Trick. A trap. A magical pretence meant to crush me. A shiver ran down my spine as I looked around, fearful that the creature I'd killed would step out to reveal himself.

'What is she talking about?' asked Trin.

'A trick, just some sort of a trick. Or maybe I am dead after all, and this is the next stage. First nothing, then you start seeing things like... things like you three.'

'Things like us three?' replied Kala.

'I thought you'd gone out,' said Feal. 'Did you forget something?'

I walked slowly around the edge of the room, not taking my eyes off the three of them in case they turned into something else. Something dangerous. Or just in case they disappeared and I lost them again.

'Stella,' said Trin. 'Have you gone quite mad?'

'Why isn't she speaking?'

'I don't know, why would I know? I know as much as you do,' said Feal.

'You're real,' I said.

'Well done,' replied Kala.

'I mean, you're really real, this isn't a trick. This isn't in my head.'

My three witches looked at me, confused. But it was true, I could tell. I could feel it in my bones. This wasn't an illusion. They weren't ghosts. They weren't tricks. This was really them. My three dead masters, resurrected. But how?

'Wait a second,' said Trin, licking her lips. 'Something's happening.'

'What?' asked Feal. 'What is it?'

'Can't you taste it?' asked Kala.

Feal began to lick her lips too. 'Oh! Oh. Time travel.'

'Time travel,' said Trin.

They looked to me again as I took in what they'd just said. They weren't resurrected. They were alive because they hadn't died yet. Mr. Trick had yet to crash into our lives and take them from me.

Which meant...

'Why are you here, Stella?' asked Trin. 'And how? Do you know how much energy, how much power, it takes to skip back into your own timeline?'

'Even the three of us combined couldn't pull that off.'

I stepped towards them, my heart beating ten to the dozen. I had a chance here. Whatever David had done, the magic he had released, it had sent me tumbling into the past, back to before my masters were murdered, and that meant I could save them.

'Listen to me,' I said. 'I need to tell you about something. No, I need to warn you. I need to warn you about what's going to happen.'

Kala stepped forward, waving her arms around. 'Whoa now, hush.'

'Stop right there,' said Trin.

'But, I've got to warn you about—'

'We don't want to know,' said Feal.

'Whatever has knocked you back here will pass. Time travel is only ever temporary. But while you're here, you can't tell us anything.'

'But you don't understand!'

'Stella, we understand.'

I felt myself getting angry, frustrated. Why couldn't they just let me save them?

'Something bad is going to—'

'Silence,' said Trin, and I felt my words catch in my throat. I tried to speak, but I couldn't. She'd cast a silent spell on me. I felt my eyes prickle with tears as I felt the chance slipping away.

'We understand, Stella,' said Trin. 'Something bad has happened, but it hasn't happened yet. You can't do this.'

'Whatever it is, it's already done,' said Feal. 'You can't change it. If you tell us, and we stop it, do you realise the damage that would happen?'

'You cannot change history,' said Kala. 'Not one line. No matter how awful those lines are, they've already been written.'

'Those are the rules, no matter what.'

I wanted to say *Damn the rules*. Wanted to tear them up and stomp them into the floor. Who gave a crap about what damage it might do if I could save them all from Mr. Trick?

'Stella, whatever made it possible for you to be here, it's dangerous,' said Trin.

Kala nodded. 'I can feel it. The power that sent you to us. It's almost too much to bear.'

'Whatever it is,' said Feal, 'it must be stopped. No doubt we've already said this to you, but we're saying it again. Stop it. Do whatever it takes, or else everyone will be in danger.'

The room began to fade as I searched for paper, for a pen. Something to scrawl *"Run. Just run. Mr. Trick is coming!"* but everything around me was turning to smoke. Or maybe it was me.

'Stop them, Stella,' said Trin.

'Whatever it is, you have to destroy it.'

I tried to shout. Tried to scream. Felt my throat grow raw with a hundred silent cries.

And then they were gone.

15

I opened my eyes to find Eva looking down at me.

'It looks like you had one hell of a party in here, love.'

I sat up sharply, my chest heaving. I was back in The Beehive. What was left of it anyway. Every stick of furniture had been reduced to splinters, and glass covered the floor.

'Eva, where's David?'

She looked around and shrugged. 'Maybe he's taking a piss.'

I stood and scanned the four corners of the room, but there was no sign of David, and no sign of anyone else. Of Lenny, of the other drinkers who'd attacked us, just the smashed aftermath.

'There was a fight. A fight between us and, well, a lot of people. They were trying to kill David.'

'Makes sense. Scared people do scared things.'

'And then, David, he... well I don't know what he did, not exactly, but this energy burst out of him, did this to the room, and sent me back in time. For a bit.'

Eva regarded me, surprised. 'You went back in time? Actually, you know, hopped back? In time? Time travelled? In time?'

I nodded.

'Huh. Well that's cool.'

'I saw my witches. They were alive and I spoke to them.'

Eva began to prod at glass shards with the toe of her boot. 'Must be nice. I wonder what I'd say to mine if I had the chance.'

'They wouldn't let me warn them about what was going to happen. All they cared about was me killing David. Everyone wants me to kill David!'

'I don't. Though we should probably shove him on a boat and drop him off on a remote, uninhabited island and let him explode in peace.'

I yanked out my phone, surprised to see it was still working, and hit David's name. It went straight to voicemail. 'Shit.'

'Aha!' cried Eva, as she found the last unbroken bottle of alcohol in the pub. She yanked out the cork with her teeth, spat it against the wall, and took a nice, big swig. 'Every cloud, Stella.'

'Eva, I need your help.'

Eva drank some more, squinting at me. 'I'm not much of a fan of helping, these days. FYI. I'm more of a sitter-outer. And a drinker. And a lounger. I am the Queen of lounging.'

'Just... just help me. Please.'

Eva sighed, drained the bottle, tossed it over her shoulder, then waved her hand at me as she headed towards the door, which was hanging off its hinges. 'Come on then, let's find your super-dangerous-we-should-definitely-probably-save-London-from-him friend.'

I looked around at the destruction and wondered what had happened to everyone else. As if on cue, there was a ripple in the air, a dark blur, the sound of twisting metal, and then Lenny appeared on the ground, back from wherever David had sent him, his eyes springing open.

'I did not enjoy that,' he said, in his low rumble of a voice.

'Lenny, you're okay, thank God.'

Lenny looked around at his pub, then over to me. 'I think you and your mate are barred for a bit.'

'Yeah. I think we are.'

I headed after Eva, my boots crunching glass, as the others began to appear, one by one, back from their own short trips through time. I grabbed Eva and we hung back, out of sight, until they all left, staggering off to lick their wounds. I'd hoped David would appear at some point too, but he didn't.

As we turned down David's street I tried his phone for the twentieth time, but like the previous nineteen, it went to voicemail. Didn't even ring, just straight through to the increasingly annoying recorded greeting.

'Give it a rest,' said Eva, 'he's not answering.'

I glared at her and pocketed my phone.

'Look on the bright side, maybe he disintegrated. Maybe that was it. His big bang, and L'Merrier just overestimated what sort of damage he was going to do. Instead of leaving London a smoking crater, he just broke a few chairs, popped the lot of you back in time for a bit, and then turned himself into a fine powder of some description.'

'So, your brightside is David is dead?'

Eva shrugged. 'Well, better he dies and hurts no one else than, you know, he hurts millions of people, or even maybe you have to kill the poor sod.'

I didn't have a response for that. It was true. If David was okay, all that that meant was that L'Merrier was right, my witches were right. Everyone was right. David was a danger and the danger was only ramping up. What just happened in The Beehive was evidence enough of that. A tremor before the big one. I needed to solve this, I only hoped to God it wouldn't mean my killing him.

Whatever happened, I'd find a way.

I had to.

I knocked on David's front door a couple of times, then let myself in with the spare key he'd given me. A few letters were piled on the welcome mat, which was about all the evidence you need that someone hasn't been home. We went in anyway though, just in case. His outburst had sent me—at least briefly, and in another time—back home. Back to my coven. Maybe it had done the same for him.

'Eva?'

'Hm?' she answered distractedly as she rummaged through a kitchen cupboard and retrieved a box of cereal, which she began to eat dry from the box.

'If David had sent himself home, sent himself here, but to an earlier time, would you be able to sense that?'

Yeah, we're both familiars, but Eva is more skilled than I am. She may have been dulling herself with bad living, but of the two of us she still had more experience, power, and ability.

'Yeah. Probably. Kind of an effort though. To do the sensing bit. Like trying to squeeze out a difficult poo, if you know what I mean.'

'Great.'

'I mean a giant, bone-dry hog of a turd.'

'Thanks, I get it. Can you just do it, please?'

She shoved another handful of cereal into her mouth, then sighed, sending a cloud of crumbs firing out. 'Fine. You know you're a needy bitch.'

Eva sat at the kitchen table and laid her hands down flat, closing her eyes. I felt the magic in the air begin to ripple around me, then surge towards Eva as she willed the Uncanny into her and searched for any signs of time disturbance.

There was a rattle to my left. I turned to see dishes on the drying rack trembling, then cupboard doors vibrating, the light fitting juddering. Eva reached out with her senses, not just into the here and now, but probing fissures to the past. Sweat beads began to form on her forehead, then roll down, her face twitching as her body shook with the effort.

Finally, she opened her eyes and the kitchen fell silent again, apart from Eva taking ragged gasps of air.

'Well?'

'No, I'm not. I'm severely shagged out.'

'Did you find anything? Did David send himself back here but to an earlier point in time?'

'Oh, no. I got nothing besides a damp bra,' she said, scratching her underboobs.

'Fuck.'

David was alive, I knew it. I was sure that if he'd obliterated himself I'd feel it. I had to find him before someone else did and decided to finish the job the patrons at The Beehive had started.

Or before he took out the entire city.

'Come on,' I said, 'let's get to the coven and think of something else.'

'Okay. Also, can I borrow a new bra when we get there? I'm telling you, this one has soaked in a good cup full. It is not comfortable.'

I tried my best to ignore that image as we headed for the front door, opening it to reveal a familiar face.

'Well, well,' said Layland, David's partner. 'Would you look who it is.'

16

I blinked a few times, trying to take in what Detective Lauren Layland had just told me.

'Can you say that again?'

'What's wrong? Hard of hearing now, as well as full of more shit than a backed up turd machine?'

I'd like to say I hated Layland, but the truth was I sort of respected her take-no-crap attitude. Still, I can't say I hadn't occasionally thought about the sound my fist would make connecting with her nose.

'Please, just repeat what you said.'

'I said, have you been in contact with Detective David Tyler since he dropped off the face of the fucking Earth three days ago?'

Yeah. The fight in The Beehive was, it turns out, three days ago.

'Three days?' I repeated, turning to look at Eva.

'Hm?' replied Eva, still more interested in the now almost empty box of bran cereal she was clutching.

'It's been three days since... well, you know.'

Eva frowned, then began to count on her fingers. 'Oh, right, yeah. I suppose it was three days.'

Layland narrowed her eyes at us as I tried to dance around the subject.

'You might have mentioned that,' I told Eva.

'Hey, in my defence, I forgot.'

'That isn't a defence.'

'It had the word defence right there in the sentence,' she said, turning to Layland for support. 'Hey resting bitch-face, am I wrong?'

Layland bristled and took a step forward. 'What did you just say to me?'

'Just ignore her,' I said on Eva's behalf. 'She was dropped on her head as a baby.'

Eva laughed. 'That's actually true. A small section of my skull is made of wood.'

'You're both fucking loonies. And I must be a loony, too, for putting up with you.'

'Detective Layland,' I said, trying to get things back on track, 'we haven't seen David. That's actually why we came here, because he hasn't been picking up his phone and we wanted to check on him.'

'How long have you had a key to his home?'

'Does it matter?'

'Maybe.'

'A while.'

'Want to be a little more specific?'

'About six months.'

Layland nodded, then wrote it down in her notebook.

Eva nudged me with her elbow. 'I do not think that this pig likes you.'

'Nope, and I also don't like you,' replied Layland without looking up.

'I respect that. I'm an acquired taste.'

'I'm ignoring her now,' replied Layland, focussing on me. I didn't like the way her eyes bored into mine. Those eyes that radiated suspicion. An unfocused suspicion, but one that assumed—rightly too—that I was at fault somewhere in all of this.

'The last sighting we have of Detective Tyler was on the street with you, heading through Ealing Broadway on foot. Care to tell me where you were going?'

A hidden pub for magic people that he then wrecked with his ever-increasing and terrifying Uncanny powers.

'We had a drink at a pub to talk over the case. The strange murders.'

'Which pub?'

'I don't remember exactly. They all look the same, don't they?'

Layland snorted and scribbled more notes.

'And then?'

And then I travelled back in time for a while.

'And then I left him to finish his drink, and that was the last I saw of him.'

Layland fixed me with her eyes again, searching my face for any sign of a lie, for any giveaway tics. A standard technique, put the suspect under pressure, make them sweat, and they're more likely to say more than they ought to.

'Okay,' said Layland, flipping her pad shut and pocketing it. 'You'll tell me if he gets in touch, right?'

It was an order, not a question.

'Of course.'

'Detective David Tyler might be soft in the head, but he's my partner. My friend. And if anything has happened to him, and you're in any way connected, then I'll have you.'

I couldn't blame Layland for the way she reacted to me. She knew something was off, and didn't like her partner dragging crackpot outsiders into her cases. The very fact she allowed it, when I knew full well she could block me from getting anywhere near her crime scenes, told me how much she actually respected David. It might piss her off, but she let him have his weirdo friend pop in every now and again. Part of me wondered if it wouldn't be easier just to go to her with David and let her in on everything. On me, on the uncanny, on the world of monsters that shared her streets. But no, too many normals who find out the truth end up dead.

'I believe it,' I replied.

'You'd better believe it,' said Layland, as she turned and got in her car.

'Now that,' said Eva, 'is one hell of a woman.'

17

We made our way back to the coven, at which point Eva staggered off to bed.

I paced the main room and tried not to think about the fact I'd recently been speaking to my dead masters in this very room, if not this time period.

I tried not to think about the fact that I'd had a chance, probably my only chance, to save them. To change history and overturn what Mr. Trick had done. If only they'd listened, if only the three of them hadn't been so caught up in the rules of right and wrong. Maybe if they'd known their lives depended on it they wouldn't have been so quick to tie my tongue and—

'Stella.'

I heard it, but it was faint. A distant whisper on the edge of my hearing.

'Stella.'

It wasn't Eva, she was sound asleep, her door closed. This was a disembodied voice. Something not quite of this realm.

'David?'

'Stella, I... where... am I...?'

David was here, somewhere. Sort of here. I needed something of his to try and focus the pair of us on. I scrambled around the coven, trying to keep him talking, trying to keep in contact, as I searched for something of his.

'David, tell me where you are.'

'I don't... dark... can't seem to...'

His voice was so weak. So far away. A ghost of a thing.

'David, tell me about something real. Tell me about the last thing you remember eating.'

Silence.

My heart leapt in my chest.

'David? David! David, can you hear me?'

Had I lost him? Had I been too slow?

'David!'

'Chips. Bad chips. Greasy, from a van.'

'Okay, good, keep thinking about those chips.'

A pen, one end chewed; David's. I grabbed it and ran back to the main room.

'David, you're lost, but that's okay because I'm here and I'm holding a lifebelt.'

'I think.... drifting apart...'

I grabbed some chalk and drew a pentagram on the large square of dark slate set into the wooden floor, then I placed David's pen at its centre. Dropping to my knees, I willed the magic in the room to flow into me. To assault me. To drown me. Then, with a grunt of effort, I thrust my hands towards the pentagram, feeding it with the magic I'd absorbed.

'David? David, are you still there? Stay with me!'

'Here. I'm still...'

'Okay, okay good.'

I began to focus on David's pen, sat in the centre of the now glowing pentagram. The pen began to float, to glow as ribbons of energy coiled around it.

'I'm going to bring you home, David. Just try to focus. Try to see something that wasn't there before. Can you see it?'

'Not... what are you...?'

I fed more magic through myself into the pentagram, into the spell, the pen glowing brighter and brighter still.

'David, look for it, a faint spot of light, do you see it?'

Silence.

'David!'

I see it.

'Okay; move towards it! Move towards that point of light! You need to grab hold of it, and—'

I fell back in surprise as a hand thrust out of nowhere and grabbed the floating pen.

'David!'

I lunged forwards and grabbed the wrist, wrenching back, pulling David back into this realm, back into the coven. I collapsed back with him crashing on top of me, knocking the wind from my lungs.

I looked up to find David's face so close to my own that the tips of our noses were touching.

'Hey, magic lady.'

I laughed and threw my arms around him.

I placed a cup of tea on the kitchen table in front of David and took my place opposite.

'So, what do you remember?'

'Not a lot. There was a fight, I was getting my arse kicked, and then, well, nothing until you started talking to me about chips.'

It seemed like whatever had overtaken David hadn't knocked him through time, or obliterated him entirely. Instead, it had, for want of a better way of putting it, phased him out of this visible realm and hidden him in another. Like an unconscious move to yank him out of harm's way.

'How am I going to explain going M.I.A. for three days at work? To Layland?'

'We can tweak the spell I use to make your colleagues

accept me at crime scenes. Feed it with a ton of extra magic and make them forget they've even been looking for you. That you've been missing at all.'

David blew on his tea, then looked up at me, making my heart skip. I could see fear in his eyes. The eyes that, the last time I had seen them, had been engulfed with white hot flames. 'Stella, tell me what's wrong with me.'

'I'm not... I don't know. Not exactly.'

'You know enough though, right? L'Merrier warned you about something. I know you didn't tell me, but somehow I know he did anyway. I'm scared, Stella. Make me less scared.'

I wished I could.

'Something happened to you. Mr. Trick, the most powerful Uncanny creature I've ever met, took over your body for an extended period. Couple that with the black magic I used to bring you back to life, and, well, it's altered you.'

David nodded slowly as he took in the information. 'Am I dangerous?'

I paused, then nodded once.

'How dangerous?'

'Dangerous enough that Giles L'Merrier told me I needed to murder you.'

David's eyes widened as he went to speak, stopped, then tried again. 'Okay. Well, shit.'

'"Well, shit," indeed. You're pulling in a massive amount of magic. You're not doing it consciously, it's just happening, and you keep... turning. Having 'episodes', I suppose you'd call them.'

'Did I kill anyone? At The Beehive?'

'No, you just trashed the place and sent us all back in time for a bit.'

'Oh. Cool.'

I thought about my lost opportunity to save my masters. Nothing about that was *cool*.

'What do Giles and the others think I'm going to do, exactly?'

'They think... they think you're like a bomb. Of sorts.'

'Okay.'

'That you're soaking up more and more magic, and, at some point, the end result will be more than a few trashed rooms and time travel trips. The end result will be London becoming a smoking crater and millions of people being... less than alive.'

David shrank back in his chair, trying to take it all in. It's not every day you're told that your future is probably going to amount to you murdering millions of people. All things considered, he took it pretty well.

'Okay, could Mr. Trick be behind this? Could any part of him be hanging on through me, making this happen? One last nasty trick?'

'No, I killed him.' I don't know why I said that with such authority. Why I felt like I had to lie. The truth was, I had no clue, and it wasn't as though I hadn't wondered before if David being alive gave Mr. Trick some sort of weak grip on existence still. Who knew what something so powerful, so other, could be capable of?

'So what do we do?'

'We stop you.'

'Right. 'I take it you're not...?' David mimed dragging a knife across his throat.

'What? No! Of course not!'

'Good. That's good. I appreciate that.'

I hoped to Christ it was true, that it wouldn't come to that. That I'd never find myself having to make that choice.

'But what if it's the only way? I don't want to kill anyone, Stella. I'm not worth all those lives.'

I went to say, "*You are to me*," but bit my tongue.

'You're not going to hurt anyone, and nobody is going to hurt you. We just need to find a way to stop you going boom.'

'You're sure there's a way?'

'Of course,' I lied, 'there's always a way. Trust me.'

David looked at me hard for a few seconds, then smiled and nodded. 'Okay, magic lady. I trust you. But if it comes to it, promise me you'll do the right thing.'

'Don't—'

'Stella, I'm serious. I won't hurt all those people. If you have to, if it's the only way, you do your job and you stop me. Do you hear me? You stop me.'

18

I looked down at the pile of dried-up, withered bodies stacked on top of each other in the centre of the living room. A family of five, a mother, a father, three kids, in a three-bedroom house in Hammersmith.

Lorna had indulged in a sick feast to celebrate our return.

'Why do you keep inviting her,' said Layland, eyeing me evilly, cup of coffee in hand.

It hadn't been easy covering David's absence, Layland especially had needed three or four doses of the spell before she forgot he'd been missing. Even after all that I got the impression she was aware she was pissed off for some reason she couldn't quite put her finger on.

'You force this woman on our crime scenes because you think she can help in some way. Well, this is crime scene number three of this case, and I've yet to hear one useful word drop out of her mouth.'

This really was the problem with our set up. If I was involved, it was because something Uncanny was going on. Something Uncanny that we were never going to just capture, put on trial, and lock up like your normal criminal. As far as Layland was concerned, I was about as useful in an investigation as a house brick. Worse than a house brick. At least with a brick she could pick it up and throw it away. I kept coming back.

'Layland,' replied David. 'Trust me, she helps.'

Layland grimaced at him. 'I can't help but think there's something I'm forgetting to shout at you about.'

As she turned and left us, I dropped onto my haunches to look closer at the bodies. I wanted to really see, close up, the result of my ineptitude. Five more people dead, including children, because I'd failed to uphold my duty to keep the people of London safe. I reached out and touched the arm of the smallest body, a girl named Sally. She'd only recently celebrated her fifth birthday, and now that would be her last, because of me.

Had I murdered her myself? No, of course not, but it was my job to stop things like Lorna, and now she had seven bodies on her slate, and more to come if I didn't get it together and take her down. It didn't matter what Anya had said; that she thought it her mess to clear up and that I should stay out of it. Three days had passed since that confrontation, and still Lorna was on the streets, murdering innocents.

This had to be the last of them. No more. This bitch was going down.

I leaned in to the girl's body. 'I'm sorry,' I said. 'I'm sorry I wasn't good enough, but I'll get her. I'll get your killer.'

The girl's corpse opened her eyes. 'He must be destroyed.'

I jerked back in shock.

'David, tell me you can see that.'

'I see it. And hear it. And I really don't like it.'

The girl's eyes had no colour to them. Two dried out, white prunes sat in their puckered sockets. How was this possible?

'Kill him. Stop him. He is death,' said the girl, her voice dry and whispery, empty of life, of emotion.

Someone was using the bodies to get a point across. Some sick bastard playing with the dead.

And then, one by one, the other bodies began to open their eyes and join in with the girl's demands for me to put an end to the dangerous man. I didn't need to ask who they meant.

I looked around the room to see if anyone else was seeing what we were, but they carried on, oblivious. This wasn't real, this was an illusion meant just for us.

'Listen, you sick fuck,' I said, leaning in as I spoke so no one else would hear me and wonder why I was threatening a pile of dead bodies, 'if you think this is going to scare me, you're wrong.'

David raised a hand: 'Job done over here though.'

'I promise, if you or anyone else tries to force my hand, or tries to take him out by yourself, I will fuck you up.'

I stood and turned away from the bodies, David following as I left the house and the bodies fell silent.

19

We needed to get back to the coven and find a way to track down Lorna before any more corpses piled up. Hopefully Eva would still be there and I could actually convince her to lend a hand.

'Just so we're clear, they meant me, right? That you should kill me?'

'Yes,' I replied.

'Blimey. Even the dead want me dead. I mean, I've not always been the most popular of people, but this is a new low, even for me.'

'That wasn't the dead speaking, that was some fool speaking through them.'

As we walked I felt eyes on us. I didn't turn to look, or to confront, I just kept us moving as quickly as possible. Once we were in the coven, we'd be safe.

'Um, Stella?'

'What?'

'I think we're being followed. No, I know we are, they aren't being at all subtle.'

A crowd was forming, ten or twelve Uncannies, more joining as we moved forward.

'Don't worry, we're almost at the coven, then they can try all they like, they won't be able to touch you.'

I sounded confident but I didn't feel it. Things were coming to a head; word of David had clearly spread far and wide since the altercation at The Beehive. The apocalypse man wasn't a rumour anymore. He wasn't someone you could wait for someone else to deal with. David was a threat and needed to be taken out before he turned everyone in London into ashes.

I wondered why they were hanging back, why they weren't attacking before we reached the safety of the coven.

I got my answer when we reached the blind alley.

Because there wasn't one.

Someone had blocked the entrance.

'Did you do that?' asked David, looking nervously from the solid brick wall in front of us, then over to the crowd of Uncanny stood calmly, waiting.

'No.'

I pressed my palms against the bricks and tried to find the way in, my fingers dancing over the stone, senses extending, desperately searching for a fault in the spell. I pulled magic into me, placed the words together in my head, and fed a spell into the wall, demanding the blind alley appear again and allow us entrance.

But nothing.

Whoever had done this was powerful, their magic stronger than I could counteract. They knew the coven was the one place David would be safe. The one place I could hide him away until my time to cure him ran out and he went boom. So they took the coven off the table and left us with no safe space.

No safe space and a crowd of scared, angry Uncannies ready to do what had to be done.

'We don't want to hurt you, Stella,' said one person in the group I recognised. A half-wizard on his mother's side who, fifteen years back, I'd rescued from a hex a pissed-off ex had placed on him that was turning his genitals to stone.

'Karl, you don't want to do this. None of you do.'

'What choice do we have? You know what he's going to do. You know of the portent. Why would you endanger us all like this?'

We had our backs to the wall – to the now missing blind alley entrance. My instinct was to run, but a quick glance to my left informed me that two groups had formed to block off both directions.

David stepped forwards. 'I'm not going to hurt anyone, I swear.'

I grabbed him back, placing myself in front of him as a shield.

'David, I need you to stay calm, okay?'

'What do you mean?'

'They're going to attack. We can escape, but they're going to attack, and if you switch like you did at The Beehive, I don't know what will happen. *You* don't know what will happen. So stay back, stay behind me, and stay calm. Please.'

David nodded, and I did my best to smile. 'Don't worry. I'll protect you.'

I pulled the magic into me, placing my feet into a boxer's stance and raising my fists.

'Who's brave enough to take the first hit?'

The two groups looked at each other, then to me, then swarmed us as one.

This fight wasn't like the one at The Beehive. Out there, in the street, there was nothing to dampen my attacks or theirs. But that was okay, I was strong, and I was used to fighting. That was my whole purpose for existing. Violence had been bred into me.

I didn't move far from my starting position. I held my ground, shielding David, as wave after wave of people surged forward, unleashing all sorts of magical attacks, not to mention fists and knives. One of them even swung an enchanted axe.

Despite it all, I stayed on my feet.

My body trembled as I opened it up to more and more of the magic in the air, starving my attackers of a strong connection by gorging myself on it. Willing it to be mine and mine alone as I blocked attack after attack and unleashed a fury of my own.

Bodies fell, blood splattered, bones cracked. The enchanted axe became enchanted kindling.

They had the numbers but I had the expertise. Thank Christ I was only dealing with your run-of-the-mill Uncannies. Nothing here was above my pay grade.

Soon enough there was a gap, a way out. I grabbed David's hand and pulled him after me as I swept my free hand back and forth in front of me, scattering anyone that got too close like skittles.

I placed the correct words together in my mind and shared a spell between myself and David: 'Run.'

And run we did, the spell letting us go a little faster, a little longer, than our bodies would normally allow. We took turns sharply, tearing through the street until the spell wore off and our bodies finally forced us to stop.

We staggered into an alley and collapsed on our backs, gasping for air, our lungs furious with pain, limbs shaking like we'd run a marathon.

'Holy... holy... shit....' wheezed David.

When I finally had strength enough, I pushed myself into a sitting position and flopped back against the wall.

David dragged himself over to sit beside me. 'Remind me... remind me never to piss you off,' he said.

We'd lost the pack, but more would come. More people, stronger people. Soon enough, either through sheer numbers or magical expertise, it would be more than I could handle.

'Someone has cut off the coven, so we need to try and stash you somewhere else. Somewhere safe enough until I can find a way to stop what's happening to you.'

'Do you think you can? What if there isn't a, you know,

"cure," or whatever? Maybe this is just the way it's going to be. Maybe nothing but death is going to stop this.'

I pushed myself up to my feet, my jellied knees threatening to keep me down. 'There's always a way. Always.'

David hung his head for a moment, then nodded. 'Okay. But what I said before still stands. I won't become a mass murderer. If it comes to it, you put me down.'

I went to argue, but the look in David's eyes stopped me. Part of me knew he was right. I would do everything I could to stop it, to stop him. To prevent him not only dying, but becoming a mass murderer in the process. But the very idea of... of *killing* him, it made me feel weaker than I'd ever felt in my sixty years of life. I had to find a way. No matter what my dead witches had said, no matter what L'Merrier demanded, I had to find a way to save him, and save everyone else, too.

'It won't come to that. I promise.'

He smiled.

'So what now? Where can we go that people won't be able to find?'

I had an idea about that. A favour that it was time to call in.

20

We found him at one of his usual haunts.

Razor, the head of his eaves clan.

'What the fuck do you two want?' he asked, hissing through his needle teeth.

Normally we'd have sat in The Beehive until Razor showed up, but The Beehive was currently in need of a drastic remodelling, so we had to do a tour of his other known drinking holes. It took us ducking into six different pubs until we found him, all the time trying to keep David out of view.

We took our place uninvited opposite Razor.

'We need your help,' I said.

Razor looked at me, then over to David, then back, his eyes blinking slowly, then he burst out laughing.

'I'm thinking that might be a no,' said David.

Razor spluttered to a stop, wiping the tears from his eyes. 'Too right it's a no. Are you mental? Why the fuck would I want to help either of you?'

I leaned forward and locked my eyes to his. 'Because you owe me.'

Razor's smiled dropped. 'How do you figure that one, Familiar?'

'Are you forgetting how I saved your clan's children? Not one, not two, but all of them. They'd have never woken up if I hadn't rescued them from the nightmare realm. I could have rescued the innocent and left your offspring to rot, but I didn't. Because I wouldn't. I saved your clan's future, and now you're going to grant me my favour, do you understand me?'

Razor glared at me fiercely, then broke eye contact, grabbing his drink, taking a swig and wiping the back of his filthy sleeve across his mouth. 'All the Uncanny of London want your friend here dead. How am I meant to help you with that, exactly?'

I smiled. 'You can build him a house.'

Eaves are low level Uncanny, but they do have one particular skill that I needed right now—that David needed—they could hide their homes. An eaves trades in secrets. In hearing things that shouldn't have been heard and passing the information on to anyone willing to pay the price; and that price was a taste of pure magic.

A person with that sort of a predilection will find themselves on a lot of shit lists, so they need a place they can lay their heads at night without keeping one eye open. The eaves have developed a way of using some of the magic they earn to create a strange network of spells, of misdirection, of shielding —layer after layer of it—that makes their homes almost impossible to find, no matter how many times you visit.

And that's what Razor and two members of his clan were now creating for me and David. A place for David to lay low. A place that only I knew how to get to and from whilst I figured out a way to save him.

I drip-fed Razor and his two grimy clan members magic while they worked, siphoning it from the air around us. It was a strange thing to watch. It looked like they nibbled at the air with their needle teeth, scraped and swatted at it with their filthy hands, their ragged, long nails clawing at the space in front of them as they walked steadily forward, almost like they were moles digging a tunnel into the earth.

They moved steadily through streets, down alleys, through doorways that should have led one place but now led somewhere else entirely. Across rooftops, through sewer tunnels, into tube train carriages, public toilets, libraries, until at last they stopped in front of a green door.

Razor turned to us, his two partners leaning against the wall either side of the door.

'There,' he said. 'Done.'

I turned in a little circle to see the surrounding area was a blur, impossible to make out. Like someone had smeared oil all over the view.

'I'll be able to find my way back,' I said, 'but no one else will be able to, right?'

Razor nodded. 'You were with us for the creation, you'll always be able to find this place.'

'Hey,' said David. 'Thanks, Razor. Really.'

Razor grunted. 'I may be scum, but I'm honourable scum.'

I raised an eyebrow at that.

'Well, maybe not honourable, but you did save our young. You deserve one good turn. But don't think you'll get another, this is us clean now. If you ever come back looking for another favour you'll be shit out of luck.'

'Got it,' I replied.

Razor snorted dismissively, then he and his two clan members turned and walked away, seeming to fade away into the indistinct blur as they did so.

David placed his hand against the green door. 'Will this work?'

It was our best shot at keeping him out of harm's way, but the only place I'd have been entirely happy with would have been my coven. Whoever had blocked our entrance to that was going to find themselves spitting teeth before this was all over.

'It'll work.'
I opened the door and we went inside.

21

I left the safe house as night fell and shivered, a sharp chill had invaded the air.

I wanted to stay with David, of course I did. Stay right by his side in the safe house to make sure nothing could get at him. But he was as safe as I knew how to keep him, no one should be able to unravel the maze Razor had set up, and I had another promise to keep.

To my coven.

To the bodies of a young family, tossed on top of each other like they were nothing but waste ready to send to landfill.

Lorna, the succubus, was still out there, and it was only a matter of time before she killed again.

I had to trust in Razor's work and carry on trying to put Lorna down, because that was my job. What I was created for. If I paused in my duty to take care of a personal matter, to solely concentrate on David's safety, then I was betraying my purpose.

So I left the safe house and I worried about David, worried that I wouldn't even be able to find my way back, no matter what Razor had assured me. After I found myself back somewhere I recognised, I stopped and attempted to find the path back to the green door, back to David, in my mind's eye; and there it was. As clear as fresh water.

'I won't be gone long,' is what I'd told David. I hoped it was true. I needed to take care of Lorna as quickly as possible so I could get back to him.

'I understand,' said David. 'I'm good here; I've got a TV, I've got food. You need to do your job, I don't want anyone dying because you're babysitting me, okay?'

I felt my stomach swirling with butterflies as I thought of him, but there was no time to indulge in any kind of stupid romantic feelings, if that's even what they were. I had a monster to hunt.

'Why are you calling me?' came Layland's voice into my ear.

'Has it struck again?'

'"It?" You need to pull your head out of your arse, Stella. We've got a murderer on the loose, that's all. Where's David? He's not answering his phone again.'

'I'm not his minder,' I replied, which actually, at the moment, wasn't true.

'Look, I've had about—'

I ended the call and pocketed my phone. That was good, no more attacks yet. At least none that had been discovered. Now I just had to find a way to locate Lorna before she struck again.

Before he left, I'd told Razor to let me know as soon as any of his clan spotted Lorna, but I had the feeling he wasn't going to be in too much of a rush to throw himself in with me after building David a safe house. He owed me that one, but right now I was hiding the most dangerous man in London. I couldn't exactly blame him for wanting to steer clear of me, to not let it be known that he was helping David.

So I headed for the coven.

I bought a cheap baseball cap and shades to try and stay incognito as I made my way home, making sure to check every few metres that I wasn't being followed, that I hadn't been spotted.

I made it to where the blind alley should open up, relatively sure that I'd made the journey unseen. The alley entrance was still blocked. It may well have been a waste of time, but my magic was at its most potent within the walls of my coven. If I could just find a way to get inside, to disrupt the blocking spell for even a moment, then maybe I could get past it. Get home and find a way of tracing Lorna.

Looking both ways before I began, I placed my palms flat against the wall and willed the magic around me to flow through me, to follow my command, to rush out of my hands and search the wall for a place of weakness. There was always a point of weakness in this sort of thing. Well, almost always.

'Yeah, not this time, love.'

I span around, heart jumping, to find Eva shambling towards me, one lit cigarette in her mouth, another in her hand.

'I was inside when someone pulled up the drawbridge,' she continued, gesturing with one hand at the wall blocking the blind alley entrance and scattering ash on the wind.

'You were in there? You were in there when this spell was cast?'

'I'm a heavy sleeper. Once I didn't wake up for almost a month. It's a gift.'

'Eva, focus, if you were in there, how did you get out?'

'It's only a one way block. They knew you were out, so they only had to stop you getting in, not getting back out again. They could make the spell stronger by only having it block one side of the alley, too.'

Okay, that made sense.

'I didn't even realise the thing was there until I stepped past it.'

'What did you do next?'

'Well...' she held up her cigarettes and pulled down her coat pocket to reveal a small bottle of vodka. 'I made breakfast.'

'How do we get back in?'

'We don't. That's way above what the lowly likes of us can dismantle. No, that thing'll last until the incantation naturally wears thin. And judging by the taste of it—' Eva ran a finger down the barrier, then licked it, '—that's not going to happen for a while.'

'Fuck!' I said, giving the wall a kick.

'Yeah, that'll help.' Eva unscrewed the cap from her vodka and took a swig.

'And that will?'

'It never hurts. Well, that's not true, it frequently hurts. But it hurts *good*.' She waggled her eyebrows and took another glug before sliding the bottle back into her pocket.

I'd had enough. Enough of the whole situation. Of the murders, of people telling me to kill my friend, of Eva's whole attitude; she was an insult to the name Familiar.

'You know, none of this started, the murders, until you showed up,' I said.

'Very true.'

'And you haven't exactly helped, in fact you seem very keen on not helping as much as possible.'

'That's my thing these days, being unhelpful. I've had hundreds of years of doing the right thing, it can get boring.'

'Maybe you're doing the opposite of helping.'

'Okay, I may be drunk, well, I am drunk, but you're going to have to get to the point.'

'Tell me why I shouldn't suspect you of being part of this.'

Eva raised her eyebrows, then spluttered and laughed, almost doubling over.

'Oh, that's a good one, that.'

I didn't really suspect her. Well, I didn't think so, but she was there and I was out of ideas.

'Eva, tell me why I shouldn't suspect you.'

'How bad is your nose, love? Do you really not smell that?'

I watched her, confused, as she leaned towards the wall now blocking entrance to the coven and gave it a sniff.

'I mean, the thing stinks.'

'Stinks of what?'

'Of very bad news. Of a very good reason why we should just walk away.'

'Stop being so fucking enigmatic and just tell—'

I stopped as I caught sight of something over Eva's shoulder.

Someone was stood on the other side of the street, watching us. They wore a long cloak, the hood up but enough of their face on show to reveal their identity.

It was Lorna. It was the rogue succubus.

22

Eva and I remained still, not looking directly at our observer. I didn't want to spook Lorna and make her bolt before I'd arrived at a plan of action.

'Didn't her mam, or boss, or sister or whatever tell you to stay out of that whole thing?'

I bobbed my head just slightly.

'Because, when a head of a succubus family gives you a not so friendly warning, it's best, in my experience, to run the other fucking way. And I believe I've already spoken about how much I despise the act of, you know, running.'

'I don't care. She's just murdered a whole family, including kids. Kids, Eva.'

'You're sure it wasn't me, 'cos it sounded like you thought I might be the big bad.'

'Shut up.'

'Oh, nice. I'll take that as an apology.'

Eva sighed, her brow creasing, as she swore around the ciggy that was still lodged between her lips.

'We can do this, Eva. Me and you, if we go at her, full force, we can stop all this.'

'Or just piss her off, and her whole family, and bring trouble crashing down on us.'

'This is what we do.'

'Not me. I gave it up for my health, love.'

I glared at her. I think she may have shrank a little. Was that something close to shame I saw momentarily twitch across her face?

'Eva...'

She looked away from me, didn't want to make eye contact.

'That whole mess just....' She looked at the wall that now stood at the entrance to the blind alley and inhaled through her nose, 'It smells like trouble. Trust me. It won't lead anywhere good.'

Lorna was on the move, heading away from us. I had to do this. Had to do it now.

'Eva, help me. She was six years old. One of the kids was just five and she sucked the life right out of her. Do what you were made for.'

Eva sagged, spat out the cigarette, then stomped it out under her boot. 'You know, I'm starting to not like you.'

I smiled. 'Let's get that bitch.'

We turned as one and ran towards Lorna, pulling in the magic around us as we moved, our fists starting to glow with energy that begged to be unleashed. To hurtle towards Lorna and blast her off her feet.

'Stop in the name of me,' said Eva, flinging a ball or orange energy in Lorna's direction. The succubus felt it coming and dropped onto all fours and started running, the magic sailing harmlessly overhead and detonating a post box.

'Shit it, she's a fast bugger,' yelled Eva.

We turned into a street more densely populated with foot traffic and people began to scream and scatter as Lorna barged her way through, still on all fours, the claws from her hands gouging holes in the pavement as she went.

You'd be surprised at the sort of sights the normal population finds a rational explanation for. This thing scampering through town wasn't some sort of beast from their worst nightmares, it couldn't be. No, more likely a strung out addict, high on a combination of who knows what, rampaging past. Better to get the hell out of the way than stop to look any closer.

I was relieved when Lorna ducked out of the high street and began to lead us down a warren of backstreets, before we emerged into an almost empty car park. I grunted as I flung a ball of green fire in Lorna's direction, catching her feet and sending her tumbling head over heels into a wall. Eva saw her chance and punched out a few rounds in a row, slamming into Lorna over and over, pinning her back against a wall as she screamed in fury and thrashed back and forth.

Both hands throbbing with power, I nodded to Eva, and we both unleashed a volley of hits, Lorna raising her arms to try and bat the assault away. I thought we had her on the ropes, when, with a screech, she pounced, taking me by surprise. I crashed down on my back, Lorna crouched over me, her face furious, mouth wide, ready to slurp the life out of me. I tried to wiggle myself free enough to punch her, but she was too strong, I was pinned like a butterfly.

A flash of yellow and Lorna was blasted aside by a burst of magic from Eva. I scrambled to my feet, ready to redouble the attack, only to find a traffic bollard hurtling in our direction.

'Shit—' was all Eva was able to get out before the heavy stone bollard smashed into us and knocked us to the ground.

I think I blacked out for a second. The world turned fuzzy and distant. I tried to claw my way back into full consciousness, aware that any moment Lorna could sit astride me and that could be that.

I felt someone grab my jacket and yank me into a sitting position, then slap me around the face.

'Hey!' I said, holding my stinging cheek.

'I think we need to take some ducking classes,' said Eva.

She helped me back to my feet, my head throbbing from

the impact with the ground. I looked around, but there was no sign of Lorna.

'Yeah, that cow legged it whilst we were taking a nap,' said Eva.

'Fuck. Fuck!' I punched a ball of energy out in frustration, wrecking a long out of use phone box and sending prostitutes' calling cards everywhere.

'Hey, that was a perfectly nice drunk person's toilet you just wrecked, there,' said Eva.

'That was it, that was our chance to stop her and we failed.'

'I'm sure she'll turn up again.'

'When? And how many more bodies will have piled up before we get another chance? How many more children won't get to grow up, Eva?'

Eva hesitated. 'Ah, fuck.' She pulled out her vodka, the bottle miraculously unbroken, unscrewed the cap and took a swig. 'Fuckity, fuck.' Another swig.

'What is it? What's wrong?'

'A lot of stuff.''

'Tell me.'

'I think… I think I might know where we can find her.'

I blinked in surprise then grabbed Eva by her coat, 'Tell me!'

'You're really not going to like this. I'm not, either. On a scale of one to ten, this isn't even a number. It's basically a big hole full of poo that we're in and it's just passed over our eyebrows.'

I yanked Eva closer to me, my teeth clenched, veins on my neck popping: 'Tell me where she is.'

23

I looked up at the sign and shuddered as a mix of fear, of fury, of disbelief danced up and down my body.

'Well,' said Eva, 'you happy now?'

I was a long way from happy. Maybe this was a mistake. Or maybe there'd be some sort of explanation that would make it all okay. Something gone wrong that could now be sorted.

Except I already knew that wouldn't be the case.

L'Merrier's Antiques.

The home of one of the most powerful wizards to ever walk the face of the Earth. A hero to my witches; to Eva's too.

'Come on,' I said.

I took a breath and opened the shop's door, the bell tinkling to announce our entrance. The shop was shrouded in gloom, the windows only allowing a few shafts of light to filter inside in long, stark fingers.

I pulled the magic into me, wondering even as I did why I was bothering. Would I really attack the mighty L'Merrier? What would be the point? It would be like a toddler throwing a tantrum in front of a grizzly bear.

'So, here you both are,' came L'Merrier's disembodied voice, sliding out of the shadows.

'Why'd you do it?' I asked, both fists crackling with strands of multi-coloured magic.

'You have come to accuse me of something? I, who make arch demons quake?'

'We get it, love,' said Eva, 'you've got a big head.'

A break in the shadows, and out slid L'Merrier, his hands clasped atop his stomach.

'When did you first suspect?' he asked.

Eva looked to me, wavering.

'Eva?' I asked.

'Oh, I'm not the only one who has been keeping secrets, am I, Eva Familiar? I can taste it on you.'

'The alley. The dead tramp in the alley way. I thought I got a whiff, but I couldn't be sure,' she said.

'Ah,' said L'Merrier, 'The Cumbrian Coven always did produce a finer stripe of familiar. 'Tis a pity what happened to them.'

'Why didn't you say anything?' I asked.

Eva looked at the floor.

'Because she is a wretched, broken thing, is that not correct?'

Eva scowled at him, 'You know what happened to me. To my coven.'

'Yes, and you have been pouting like a child about it for ten years, betraying your creators with the dawning of each day.'

'Eva?'

'When we first came here, to this dusty shop of old crap, I said I could smell his magic,' she said. 'That the place reeked of him. Well, I thought I got a hint of that stink on the corpse in the alley. But we'd been here directly before, I thought it was just because I still had the smell of this place in my nose.'

'More people have died, Eva! That's on you, that's on your conscience. You're a familiar, Eva, you should have told me!'

'There's nothing I *should* do, love. Not anymore.'

'Don't fight, you two, it is not Eva's fault that she has grown to be such a selfish coward, shirking her responsibilities. It's everyone else's. Is that not so, little one?'

For once, Eva didn't have anything to say. I felt betrayed, that was sure enough. Betrayed by L'Merrier, and now betrayed by Eva, another familiar, one of my own kind. Should I have been surprised that she'd kept the information to herself? That she hadn't wanted to get involved? I knew what Eva was. I knew how she lived her life. That, in the end, she got involved at all was the real surprise.

'So why'd you do it, L'Merrier?' I asked. 'Why turn a succubus feral and let her off the leash? Why'd you block the entrance to my coven?'

L'Merrier sighed. 'My goodness, but you are a slow one. I told you what needed to happen.'

David.

'You want David dead.'

L'Merrier spread his arms wide. 'Of course. Believe me, I take no pleasure in that fact, but I have the best interests of this city at heart. Something you should also have, Stella. I believe David detonating and wiping out the city would be a bad thing, don't you?'

'But why Lorna?'

'Simple. A distraction. Something to pull you away from him, to keep you busy. You're so dedicated to your purpose— unlike your misbegotten ally here—that I knew no matter what was happening with Detective Tyler, you would have to take care of a feral succubus. You would not just let it run riot whilst you stood by his side, his Uncanny bodyguard. If he is alone, if you do not have access to your seat of power... well, you can put together the rest, surely?'

L'Merrier wanted David dead, but he's not the kind of man to get his hands dirty. At least not for a century or more. He stays within the walls of his dusty little shop. That meant others needed to do the deed. Needed to murder David. If I was with him, L'Merrier knew I would fight tooth and nail to protect him. He needed David alone. So the rogue succubus, so the distraction to pull us apart.

I felt myself trembling with rage.

'People died, L'Merrier. Children died.'

He bowed his head, his brow creasing, 'Yes, and I will live with those deaths. I will remember their faces. Their names. And I will pay for each. But what I have done is for the good of all.'

'You know, love,' said Eva, 'You really are one special piece of shit.'

A movement in the shadows. It was Lorna, feral, eyes black, hands claws, stalking into view.

'Stay,' L'Merrier commanded, and the feral succubus stopped in her tracks, her face a mask of frustration. She wanted to lunge across the room at us, but L'Merrier's control kept her at bay. For now.

'As the truth is now out, it seems I must be more direct. Lorna here will now keep the two of you busy whilst I go and do what, unfortunately, must be done. For you. For me. For this city.'

'No!' I cried. He was going to leave and he was going to murder David. Murder my friend. Even as terror and fury coursed through my body, I wasn't consumed enough not to realise how big a deal that was. How big a deal all that L'Merrier had done to try and fix the David problem was. How big a deal it was that now he himself was going to walk out of his sanctuary and do the killing himself.

He didn't know David, not that it would have mattered if he had. London was in danger; at any moment David could rupture and the magical fallout would kill everyone in London. As far as L'Merrier was concerned, he was doing what was right. Doing what he saw I couldn't. Because he thought I was weak. Thought I was compromised.

And he was right.

But I didn't care.

He was still responsible for the deaths of innocents. I wouldn't overlook or excuse that. And I wouldn't just let him murder David.

'I won't let you kill him, L'Merrier.'

He looked at me, pity in his eyes, 'You have no choice. It must be so, and so it will be.'

'You don't even know where he is, big fella,' said Eva.

'Oh, I know.'

'Then you know I had the eaves build us a safe house,' I replied. 'You won't find him.'

'Familiar, that would work for most, but me? It is like a child hiding behind some curtains. I can see their feet poking out from underneath.'

With a sweep of his hand, Eva and I were thrown across the room, crashing into the wall and landing with a painful thump on the floor.

'Well, that's just bloody rude,' said Eva, standing up and pulling her fist back to punch out some magic.

'Eva!' I cried, but it was too late. She turned just in time to see Lorna springing through the air. The pair went down, rolling over and over into the shadows.

L'Merrier was at the door, about to open it, about to leave.

I summoned the magic into me, the sounds of Eva's struggle seemed distant as I focussed on stopping L'Merrier leaving. From stepping outside onto the streets for the first time in living memory to go and slaughter my friend.

'No!' I punched out a blast of energy, and another, L'Merrier turned smoothly, his robes floating, and deflected my attack back at me with the flick of a wrist, the impact throwing me across the room.

'For what it is worth,' said L'Merrier. 'I take no pleasure in this. None.'

I grimaced, 'Fuck you.'

He nodded and opened the door—

—to reveal Anya and the six remaining members of her family.

'We have come for our sister,' hissed Anya, eyes black.

'Oh yeah,' said Eva, staggering back into view, face bloody, after managing to wriggle free of Lorna's grasp, 'I might have passed on the news about you brainwashing their family member earlier. Whoops.'

24

If there was one force that could maybe—just maybe—cause L'Merrier a little trouble, it was the succubus family of London, working as one. And right now, that family was angry beyond belief.

They turned feral in a heartbeat and swarmed into the shop, surrounding L'Merrier, Jack and Jake joining them, as they launched an attack from all angles.

'Come on!' I said, waving Eva ahead.

'They seem like they've got things covered,' she replied.

But they didn't. They fought well, fought hard, but L'Merrier was a giant. Oh, they were certainly causing him to work harder than he'd like, but it was quickly becoming clear that this was only going to end one way.

I pulled in as much magic as I could and unleashed it in his direction, I think I even managed to make him wince a little.

'Enough,' he said, voice booming.

Anya, breathing heavily, raised a hand and the assault paused. 'You will die at our hands for what you have done to our sister, L'Merrier,' she said.

'I don't think I wish to be delayed any further, not while the future of this city depends on me, and so...'

He clapped his hands together, unleashing a shockwave that caused everyone around him to take a step back, ears ringing. The magic in the room rippled and turned dark. L'Merrier rubbed his hands together, coils of dark, purple energy rolling around his fingers, and then with a grunt he flung the power towards the shadows. We all held our breath, but all that could be heard was silence.

And then something happened.

Lorna stepped to one side, only she also stayed where she was. And then she did it again. And again. Each time she stepped aside she left behind a copy of herself, until there were twelve versions of Lorna, all influenced by L'Merrier, stood in a pack, growling hungrily at her own family.

'Good luck,' said L'Merrier, striding towards the exit, pushing a clear path for himself as he swatted his hand back and forth, knocking his foes aside.

'L'Merrier, stop!' I demanded as I tried to go after him, but one of the Lorna clones turned, her mouth a giant, silent scream.

She charged me. I heard the door's bell tinkle as L'Merrier left, but all I saw was the wild succubus attacking me, attacking everyone.

I felt panic overwhelm me. I was trapped here, and David was sat somewhere I'd told him was safe. Sat waiting for me to return and finally solve what was afflicting him, not realising for a moment that the mightiest wizard in the Uncanny Kingdom was en route to end his life.

I picked myself up from the floor after taking another hit from one of the Lorna copies, Eva lending me a hand.

'Now this,' she said, 'is a real knock-down, drag-out bar fight.'

'Eva, he's going to kill him! He's going to kill David and there's nothing I can do!'

'Yes there is,' said Anya, dropping in beside us. 'L'Merrier has made an enemy of my family with his actions, but that is for another time. Right now it is my priority to subdue and reclaim my sister, and I will. But this is not your business. Not your fight. You familiars leave here and go and take care of what is yours.'

'Anya, I... thanks. Thank you.'

She nodded and turned, charging down one of the Lorna's that was rushing towards us.

'Come on,' I said, grabbing Eva's coat sleeve and yanking her towards the exit.

'Leaving then,' said Jake.

'Looks like it,' replied Jack.

'This is a fun one, too.'

'You're missing out.'

A Lorna struck Jake across the face, leaving his cheek a bloody mess. Jake smiled, spitting blood, and fought on.

'You know, I think I bloody love that pair,' said Eva, as the bell tinkled and we got the hell out of there.

25

We paused a few streets from L'Merrier's to catch our breath.

'Okay,' said Eva, 'Time to get out of London town.'

I reached out and pulled her back, fury rising.

'Get out? We have to go and help David! L'Merrier is going to kill him!'

'I get the feels, love, I do, but that's Giles L'Merrier, if he wants someone dead, the worst place to be is at their side. It's time to get smart and see if we can get far enough away before your pal goes *boom*.'

She tried to pull me after her.

'No!

'Going after a succubus for a bit of a ruck is one thing, but this is suicide.'

I pulled my arm free of her grip and rounded on her, furious. 'Go! Run away then, that's what you're good at, isn't it? That's what you've twisted your life into, one long useless escape. I am Stella Familiar of the London Coven, brought to life by my witches to protect the people of this city, no matter what.'

'Even if it kills you?'

'Of course! I was born to protect this city until the last breath is knocked out of my lungs. And David... David is my friend. He's my friend and none of this is his fault. 'I'm going to spend every second he has left trying to stop him. Trying to save him. Because I have to.'

Eva looked at me. For the first time since I met her she seemed truly surprised. The mask of indifference, of inebriation, fell for a moment.

'Help me, Eva.'

She seemed to waver for a moment, then: 'Good luck.'

She turned and ran from view. If I'd stopped to think about how furious her running away made me, I'd have given chase. Have taken her down. Have punched some sense into her. Made her her join me. Help me. Help David.

But there was no time for that. I alone would have to be enough.

I turned and ran with the wind at my back.

Streets flew past, traffic, people, buildings, all a blur. I only saw one thing: David. Had it started? Had L'Merrier reached him? Was he already dead?

No, he was alive. He was still there inside of me, I could feel him. Feel his life still burning bright.

I realised with a burning certainty something I'd been dancing around. *I loved him.* Loved him fiercely and totally. The idea of him dying was beyond terrifying. It made me dizzy just to contemplate and threatened to turn my legs to rubber and drop me to the ground.

I loved Detective David Tyler.

Whatever that meant to me. Whatever it could mean for a familiar. Whether it was romantic, whether it was the kind of love I had for my witches, whether it was the love of true friendship, the first true friendship I'd ever had, I just didn't know. But it was true. It was real. And it *burned*.

There was no fast way to reach him. Every eaves' safe house

is the centre of the maze for those who know the right paths to take, the right turns to explore. It took time. There was no short cut. And so on I ran. Ran through doors that should open into shops but through which I found ourselves on a rooftop a mile away.

And on.

And on I went.

Down ladders that should have led me into the fairy-infested sewers, but instead delivered me onto grass in the middle of a park.

And on, and on.

A kaleidoscope of places. Of London. Flashes of places swirling past me in a seemingly random order with each new turn taken, each new door stepped through.

Had L'Merrier found it as easy to locate the safe house as he'd said he would? I could only hope he was bluffing and that it would have taken him longer than he'd like to unwind the tangle and find the true way there.

I knew I was lying to myself, but I had to hope.

Finally, I stopped, the safe house in front of me. The green door hung off a single hinge, some of the paintwork scorched back from the magic that had blasted it open.

I was too late.

L'Merrier had found him.

'David!'

I barged through the broken door and it crashed to the ground as the force of my entrance tore its remaining hinge from the frame. The air felt strange inside, like static crawling all over my skin.

I pushed on into the house. 'David, where are you?'

The house was silent, but the signs of L'Merrier's arrival were clear enough. Broken furniture, the smell of fire, scorch marks on the walls, on the carpets, broken glass and splintered wood crunching underfoot with each new step. A huge fight had taken place in the time it had taken us to get here.

Was it over already?

Would I step into the next room to find L'Merrier stood over David's broken corpse?

And then I found them.

L'Merrier was on his knees in one of the bedrooms, his eyes rolled back into his head, trembling.

David was stood in front of him, though his feet didn't quite touch the floor.

'David...'

He turned his head to me, his eye sockets leaking a burning, white light.

'An assassin,' he said, his voice echoing as he gestured to L'Merrier, who was now frothing at the mouth like a mad dog.

'David, it's me, it's Stella, your friend.'

He tilted his head to one side. 'I see you inside my head.'

David's body rippled, impossibly, bulging horrifically. The room shook, cracks appearing on the walls.

'David, please, you've got to try and calm down.'

The room shook again, the house complaining, coughing up dust that stung my eyes.

David turned back to L'Merrier. 'He came to murder. I do not like him.'

He waved a hand and wounds opened across L'Merrier's face.

'Maybe I will remove his skull. That will be a lesson learned.'

'David, stop! Just listen to me!'

The magic in the room was strange – tainted by the energy David had coursing through him. It stung to use, it was like breathing in sand, but I needed it. I pulled the power into myself, body shaking with the effort.

'David!'

He turned to me again, the fire in his eyes wreathing his head in a white hot tongue of flames. I needed to subdue him. Maybe if I could knock him unconscious, whatever switch had been flicked would turn off again. Would give me a new chance to find a way to stop this.

I circled him, throwing volley after volley of magic at him, hoping to knock him off balance, to take him down—even to make his face twitch would have been something—but it was like I was an ant attacking a mountain.

'Enough,' he said, and the floor beneath me opened like a hungry mouth and I fell, crying out in shock as my stomach lurched and I dropped hard on the floor downstairs.

I could see L'Merrier across the room, he'd fallen too, but remained silent.

The air began to crackle and down, gently, floated David. He emerged through the hole he'd created in the floor, descending with a small smile on his face. He was in no rush, and there seemed to be no anger in him. He was calm, comfortable, and ready to rip me to pieces.

'David, I know you're in there, I know you can—'

The words were cut off as I found myself flung through the air, head cracking against brick as I struck the wall. I didn't fall, he kept me there, pinned and helpless.

David did his curious head tilt again, then stepped slowly towards me. 'I am new. I am born. Why do you fight my creation?'

'David, listen to me, you have to hear me—'

'I can hear you.'

'No, please, I know you can fight this! I know you're in there, I can feel it!'

He was in front of me now and I strained with everything I had to move my hand, just an inch or two.

I touched his shoulder.

David stopped and the flames in his eyes sputtered, then disappeared. David sagged, face in his hands, as his grip on me disappeared and I fell to the floor.

David lifted his head, looking at me with his own eyes. He looked terrified.

'He came for me. The wizard came for me, would have killed me, and then... it just happened. It just swamped me, pushed me out of the way.'

'It's okay, David, I'm here.' I placed my hands on his arms, he was trembling.

'No, it's not, I can't—'

The room shook.

David wasn't back, he'd just bubbled up for a moment, dragged back by my pleas, by my voice, by my touch. But the monster was pushing its way back.

'David, you've got to fight it!'

He staggered back, fingers digging into his scalp as he screamed and thrashed from side to side. The house shook, walls cracking, windows breaking.

'David, don't go!'

He looked at me, eyes wide, and then he blinked and white flames erupted from his sockets. He was gone.

David came at me slowly, reaching out his hands, palms up, pure white energy dancing above them.

'David, please don't. Please.'

But there was no pity in his eyes. No understanding. Just fire.

A sonic boom, air rushing past, bright red flames erupting, knocking me sideways as David was lifted off his feet and smashed through the door into the next room. I looked up, head dizzy, to see the last thing I expected.

'Well, who wants to live forever, anyway?' said Eva Familiar.

26

Eva stumbled over the wreckage from the ceiling that littered the floor and came towards me.

'How are you here?'

'You think an eaves can hide its home from me, love? I'm Eva fucking Familiar of the Cumbrian Coven, bitch. I'm hundreds of years old, this nose can pin down a fart in a hurricane.'

'I thought you didn't do this anymore.'

'I don't. I didn't. But... Maybe I changed my mind a bit, okay? Because of you. Turns out I have a conscience; who knew?'

Relief coursed through me. Relief that I wasn't going to have to face this alone, relief that maybe, at last, Eva was truly acting as what she was. A familiar. A protector.

'Oi,' she said, pointing at the smile on face, 'Don't think I'm happy about it. I'm pretty sure I very much don't like you anymore.'

A hulking shape rose behind Eva: Giles L'Merrier. He looked shaken, but otherwise unhurt.

'Watch out,' I said, putting myself between Eva and the mighty wizard.

L'Merrier pulled a piece of chalk from his pocket and sketched a circle large enough to fit several people inside of.

'Now's not really the time to practice your doodles,' said Eva.

'Silence your foolish nattering.'

'You are a very rude gentleman.'

The house shook again and a white glow began to enter the room through the doorway. David was on his way back.

'Inside the circle,' L'Merrier commanded, and I found myself pulled towards it by invisible hands, Eva too.

'What are you—?'

A rush of magic detonated around us as David shot back into the room. It should have hurt, maybe even killed us, but instead it roared around us, repelled by an invisible bubble that L'Merrier had created.

'That's a neat trick,' said Eva.

L'Merrier grimaced and turned to me. 'The circle will not hold for long, he is too powerful and growing ever more so with each breath.'

'He's too much even for you,' I said, finding the idea strangely satisfying.

'Nevertheless, we must stop him. We will stop him. Either we do it or we die. Or everyone in London dies, Detective Tyler included.'

I looked at David, his eyes burning fiercely, his body twitching, distending, then snapping back into place as more and more of the Uncanny poured into him, filled him up, readied him to go critical and take us all with him.

'What can we possibly do?' I asked.

'Besides shit our pants,' added Eva.

'There is a war going on inside Detective Tyler. A fight for ownership of his mind that he is currently losing. I could sense it when I fought him, and I saw it when you, Stella, broke through to him for a moment. When his submerged self bubbled up to the surface. I believe you are the key.'

I pictured how his face had looked in that moments. The confused terror. It made my stomach hurt.

'You used the black arts to restore him to life, did you not?' L'Merrier asked.

'How could you...?'

'I am Giles L'Merrier, the man the devil calls, "*Sir*", I can taste black magic when I am in its presence. You are a foolish, small thing to play with such darkness.'

'He was dead! Mr. Trick had killed my witches and I couldn't let him murder David, too. I couldn't.'

I looked down in surprise as L'Merrier rested one of his meaty paws on my shoulder.

'I know,' was all he said.

'Well, this is all very heartwarming,' said Eva, 'but we still have a normal turned magic-godzilla-bomb knock-knocking on our door, and the way this bubble is looking, I don't think it's gonna stand up to much more punishment, do you?'

She was right. The field L'Merrier had created with the chalk circle was starting to become visible as it took more and more damage, David relentlessly throwing magic towards us as the safe house tore itself apart around his now grotesquely bulging body. He was no longer popping back into his normal shape, and glowing cracks were appearing across his skin, the magic burning to be released.

'What do we do?' I asked.

'As I said, I believe you to be the key. You are the one who was able to reach him. You will help Detective Tyler fight.'

Eva stumbled and grabbed on to me for support as another volley of magic pummelled against the barrier.

'How's that?' asked Eva.

'Stella, he knows you, trusts you. He is lost and afraid, cowering inside of his own mind as the thing he is becoming takes ownership. Of his body, his memories, his history. If I can project you into his consciousness, you can find him. He will trust and accept you, and you can help him fight back.'

'Couldn't you just pop inside and grab him yourself?' asked Eva.

'His mind neither knows me well, nor trusts me,' replied L'Merrier. 'The memories would not accept me, but they would accept Stella.'

He was talking about a form of astral projection, something beyond my powers, or Eva's, but not his. The ability to leave your own body behind and enter another state. To explore other realms, other universes, other people's inner worlds.

Another volley of magic hit and I felt heat lick my skin; the protection spell was almost dead.

'How will that help stop this happening again? Why won't the power overtake him again later?'

He clicked his fingers and a small box appeared in the palm of his hand.

'What's that for?' asked Eva, almost falling as the floor beneath us quaked.

'When you use the dark arts, there is always a price. A splinter of hell has embedded itself inside of Detective Tyler. I can see it within him now. After you locate his true self, you must find the splinter. Remove it. Place it within this box and bring it to me.'

I nodded and took the small box, sliding it into the inside pocket of my leather jacket.

'Okay, let's do this,' I said.

'One small problem,' he replied.

'Only one?'

'The circle will not allow you to pass through. When I release your astral form, I must break the circle.'

'Hey,' said Eva, 'wouldn't that, sort of, be bad news for those of us hoping to see tomorrow?'

'Time moves differently when in the astral form. For Stella, inside of David's mind, a second for us will be like minutes for her. She must move swiftly, or else he will turn us to ash, and London soon after. This is it familiar, the only chance we have left. This is all upon you now. The life of this city rests upon your shoulders.'

'I think what he's saying is: No pressure, love.' Eva winked, and I found I couldn't help but admire her attitude. She could have gone on her way, enjoying her traveller's life as best she knew how, rejecting the life she'd been born to. A life that had, apparently, treated her so badly. Instead she was trying to save someone she barely knew, but still facing it with a wink and a smile.

I grabbed her by the arm. 'Thanks. Thank you, Eva.'

'You can do it,' she replied. 'You're Stella Familiar of the mother-shitting London bloody Coven.'

I smiled. 'Yes I am.'

'The spell is almost dead, are you ready?' asked L'Merrier.

I looked at David, swollen to almost three times his normal size, his entire head engulfed in blinding white fire.

'Do it.'

I felt L'Merrier's hand grip the back of my head as he waved his free hand in front of us and the circle was broken.

David was screaming. Screaming in a voice I didn't recognise as his. Death shot towards us from his hands as L'Merrier leant close and whispered in my ear. 'Go....'

27

The first thing I heard were trees.

Branches, leaves, swayed back and forth by the breeze.

Then I felt the breeze myself, against my face, flowing through my hair.

I opened my eyes. I was in a field. No, I wasn't really in a field, I was in the memory of a field. David's memory. L'Merrier and Eva were back in the safe house, a heartbeat from death, and I was in the memory of a field, of trees, of sky, of grass, of wind.

'Who are you?'

I turned to see the back garden of a house, a small fence between it and the field. A young boy, maybe six years old, was looking at me, eyes wide, head tilted.

'Hello, David,' I said.

'How d'you know my name? Are you a friend of my mum's or something?'

Young David was small and skinny, a bowl-mop of hair that he kept pushing out of his eyes because it was past-due a cut, mud on his cheeks and on his hands from digging in the dirt.

'It's complicated,' I said.

'Oh, like maths you mean? 'Cos that's well hard and complicated, and I'm not even a stupid person.'

I'd never seen a picture of David as a child, but this was just how I'd imagined him. The house with the garden backing onto a field, he'd told me about this. It was in a small place called Hitchen, just outside of London, where he'd lived for a while growing up. This must be the field where one day some bad kids will torment him so badly he'll pee his pants. No wonder this memory burns strong, no wonder it's the first place I find myself after L'Merrier projected my consciousness into his.

'Is it okay if I climb over the fence to join you?' I asked.

David looked at me, then over his shoulder to his house, then back to me again. He nodded. 'Okay, if you're a friend of my mum's, I suppose that's okay.'

I gripped the fence and swung myself over as David dropped back onto his knees and picked up a trowel to continue his digging.

'What are you looking for?' I asked

'Buried treasure, of course.'

'Found any yet?'

'Nope, but I reckon there might be, like, a chest of gold, or a mummy down here, maybe. Something old and cool. It'll get me on the telly I'll bet, make me famous and rich and really popular. I won't have to go to school or nothing anymore.'

'Oh, of course.' I knelt down to join him, digging at the hole he was creating with my hands.

'I suppose, if we find anything together, you can have a share of the cut. Not as much as me though, 'cos I've already dug a pretty big amount of this hole before you even got here. That's just fair.'

I smiled. 'Oh, absolutely.'

We dug in silence for a few seconds.

'David?'

'Hm?'

'How do you feel?'

He shrugged, 'Okay, maybe.'

'Why just maybe?'

He stopped digging and sat back, thinking. 'Not sure.'

'Try to remember, David.'

He rubbed at his nose with his wrist. 'Hurts to try.'

'Hurts? In your head?'

'Yeah. Like, my head's too full of stuff. Sometimes it feels like it's getting fuller and fuller and it's just going to explode like a big balloon. Just go *Bang* and I won't be me no more.'

David's mind knew something wasn't right. His memories felt the change. The intrusion. He knew that he was under siege.

'You're not supposed to be here, are you?' he asked.

'I came to help you. Help you stop the balloon from bursting.'

He nodded, face grave beyond his years. 'Do you believe in monsters, Miss?'

'Yeah. I believe in monsters.'

He sat back, his legs crossed, digging for mummies forgotten. 'I'm not even talking about monsters under the bed, or in the wardrobe. I mean, I used to believe in that sort of thing, so I'd have my mum leave my bedroom door open a crack with the landing light on, just in case. But that's kid's stuff really, isn't it?'

'What sort of monster do you mean, David?'

He hugged his knees and closed his eyes tight.

'It's okay,' I said, 'you don't have to be afraid. I'll let you into a secret: My name's Stella, and I'm the person monsters run away from.'

He looked up at me, eyes wide with wonder. 'Really? You kill monsters?'

'I kill monsters. Well, bad monsters. Not all monsters are bad.'

Deadly Portent

'This one is. I know because I feel it here,' he said, placing a hand on his stomach.

'Then it's a good job I came here today, because getting rid of evil monsters is my thing. What does your monster look like, David?'

He hung his head again, then looked back up, eyes watery, and pointed to himself.

'It looks like you?'

He nodded. 'Like me, but I know it isn't. Though even my mum and dad thinks it is. They ask why I just did something and it wasn't even me. It was the other David, and they tell me off for making up lies and send me to my room to think about what I've done and why lying to my parents is a rotten thing. He's always up there waiting for me, then. The other me with the fire in his eyes that my mum and dad don't seem to notice. Why don't they see his fire eyes, Stella?'

'Because he doesn't want them to.'

David's eyes snapped wide and he began to push himself away from me in a panic.

'What's wrong, what is it?'

David pointed past me to the hole he'd dug, a beam of light was shining out from within.

I stood, pulling David up to his feet and placing him behind me, his hand gripping my leg so hard it hurt.

'It's the monster!' said David. 'It's other me with the fire eyes!'

An arm reached out of the hole we'd dug, shedding soil from its skin like scales. Then a second arm, the hands gripping the edge of the hole as a head rose into view, eyes burning bright and furious. Apart from the eyes, he looked just like young David. Same skinny arms, same unruly mop of hair.

'What do we do?' asked David, as the Other David pulled himself up out of the hole.

'Don't worry, everything is going to be okay.' As I said the words, I had to believe them. Had to believe that I was going to save him. I tried to pull the magic into me, to conjure something to punch out of my hand and burn Other David to dust, but there was no magic. No magic in the air, no magic inside of me. Just my astral form, inside of someone else's memories. I felt dizzy at the realisation as my body pulled again and again at nothing, not understanding the emptiness.

'It's okay, David, it's going to be okay.'

A shiver passed over me and I realised I couldn't feel David's hand gripping my leg anymore, couldn't sense him behind me.

There was a reason for that.

He wasn't there anymore.

'What did you do to him?' I yelled at Other David, now stood before me, calmly smiling. I knew what he'd done. He'd erased him. Pushed the real David out of this memory. Now the only David that existed here was Other David. Memory by memory it was taking over, replacing him, until this other version owned him completely. No, didn't own him, *was* him. There would be no David, just this thing with its fiercely blazing eyes. And when that happened—*if* it happened—David would tear open and London would die. Every person, normal or Uncanny, every family pet, every insect, every bird. All gone.

Other David stepped towards me and reached out a hand. I turned away, tried to run, but as I did the whole world seemed to be whipped away, like someone yanking a tablecloth from a restaurant table, the plates remaining still and unharmed upon it.

And then I was somewhere else.

It was getting dark, early evening, and I was stood in a park. In the distance I could see a set of swings. A girl was sat on one of the swings, a boy stood next to her. It was David, now a teenager.

He leaned in and kissed the girl.

What memory was this? His first real kiss? Or just some precious memory of an old girlfriend?

I began to move towards the set of swings, looking over my shoulders as I went, trying to find any sign of Other David appearing. I wondered what my plan would be this time. How would I stop David being pushed out of another memory?

I felt the small box L'Merrier had given me bouncing against my side as my jacket moved. A splinter, that's what he'd said. A splinter lodged in David's psyche, caused by the black magic giving him life. But where was it? Would I even know what it was if I saw it?

The girl had left, walking away from the direction I'd just come from. She turned and smiled and waved, young and happy and full of the fury of teenage love.

David waved back as he sat down in the swing, a big dopey smile on his face. He looked more like the David I knew now, though thinner, gawkier, with shaggy hair and a sprinkling of weak face fuzz.

'David,' I said.

He looked up, seeming to notice me for the first time.

'Oh, hey... do I know you?'

No, not yet, but one day.

'I don't have time to explain, he could turn up at any moment.'

He looked at me warily, obviously taking me for a nutcase.

'Right. Okay. I think I might just head off.'

As he turned I grabbed him by the arm and pulled him back. 'No, it's not safe, you need to stay with me.'

'Don't touch me you weirdo!' he cried.

'What do you remember?'

He blinked. Was that a twitch of recognition?

'I don't know what you mean.'

'I think you do. When you try to think back on your past, it's like there are holes, am I right?'

He shrugged, 'Everyone forgets stuff.'

'But not like this, not like you.'

Confusion crept across his face. 'We dug a hole.'

Digging a hole; he could remember that? But he'd been pushed out of that memory. Maybe something clung on, maybe you couldn't be made to forget everything.

'It's you. I remember you. I sort of remember you, I think. Only... we never met, but we did. A long time ago, but... I can't quite remember it. It hurts when I try, like it's a lie, or something.'

'David, you—'

A sudden light from behind me caused David to squint and turn his head away.

'No—'

I turned to see Other David moving fast towards us.

'Oh. It's the other me. But that's just a bad dream, isn't it? How can he be real?'

There was no time for explanations. I grabbed David's hand and pulled him after me as I ran.

We ran across the park, not looking back, just moving, just going, going, going. The world shot past, streaking like a painting that someone had just knocked a glass of water over. The image blurred, the colours ran, and when I finally looked back I wasn't holding David's hand anymore. Other David's eyes burned and I heard myself scream as I twisted, pulled my hand away, fell towards the grass and—

—I landed on a tiled floor, banging my head. The ceiling above me swayed drunkenly. I was failing. Another memory the real David had been pushed out of, more of him submerged under the new persona. I had to find the black splinter – had to search every memory until I had it. Did I have enough time? How much of the real David was left? How long did I have before L'Merrier and Eva were killed in the real world and this was all done with?

I sat up and looked around, rubbing at the back of my head.

I recognised the room, I was in David's kitchen. What memory was this, and where was David?

The hairs on the back of my neck stood up and I turned to find my answer. Other David was stood behind me. I pushed away, scrabbling back with my hands and feet, sliding across the kitchen floor, as there was a flash and a blast of air and then suddenly another me appeared in the room. I knew what memory this was. It was when I first met David. When, moments from death, Mr. Trick had yanked me out of the street and deposited me into his life.

And now David had been pushed out of this memory. I felt a surge of pure, wonderful fury ransack my body. How dare they rob him of the first time we ever met? Standing, I grabbed a chair and threw it towards Other David with a scream. I wanted to hurt this imposter. Wanted the chair to shatter his skull. Spill his brains. I wanted to hold him down and choke the life out of him.

Other David lifted a hand and stopped the chair in mid-air. He tilted his head, regarding me curiously, then with a flick of the wrist, launched the chair back in my direction.

I jumped out of the way, rolling and hopping back up onto my feet as the room blurred—

—I staggered, heart pounding. I wasn't in David's kitchen anymore. It was night time and I was in the street, close to the coven. So when was I now? What memory had I fallen into this time?

'David? David, where are you?'

I soon got my answer: he was nowhere.

I watched as a memory of me swayed and stumbled down the street towards home, clearly drunk as a skunk, as Other David accompanied me. The memory of me threw my arms around Other David.

It was the almost kiss. The drunken moment of stupidity on my part.

Other David leaned in and the fire in his eyes spread out,

enveloped the memory of me. Tendrils of pure white began to worm their way out of the fire and rubbed at the surrounding memory of the street like an eraser removing a mistake.

I ran from it and the world blurred once more as I—

—Another memory, and another. What good was I doing? Each memory went by faster and faster as every trace of the real David was removed. All I found were partial memories with Other David, his eyes burning furiously, at their centre. Time was running out and I could feel panic beginning to overwhelm me. To make me sweat and shake as I moved through each old recollection, desperately trying to find a true David, to find the splinter in his paw and remove it.

I was inside The Fenric. The members only Uncanny club in Mayfair. I walked up the stairs, calling out David's name, already fearing the worst. I'd walk all the way to the top, only to find Other David already here again. Another moment between me and David pulled out of him and stomped into the dirt.

There was noise up ahead, the crashing of furniture, the breaking of glass. I stepped into the bar, a figure was swaying back and forth in the centre of the room, like the building itself was rocking, buffeted by the waves at sea.

'Eva?'

David's memory of Eva turned to me, 'Don't mind me, I'm just giving this club a bloody good twatting.' An orb of fire appeared in her hand and she tossed it nonchalantly over her shoulder, the energy smashing into the bar and reducing it to splinters.

'Magic? How can you be using magic here?'

'Because I am actually here, a memory, not like you; an astral form projected into someone else's mind.'

I really hadn't expected her to say that.

'You know what's happening? How is that even possible? You're not you, you're just David's memory of you.'

Eva shrugged as she picked up a bottle of vodka and took a

swig. 'Beats me, love. Maybe his memory of me is just of one really top notch, one-of-a-kind magical bad-arse that would know they weren't real if such a, you know, situation occurred. Memory's a weird thing.'

I thought back to mine and David's actual encounter here with Eva, when we were called to take down some wild beast terrorising the club, only to find a drunk, indignant familiar trashing the place. I remembered what I'd told David about Eva. About how she was the oldest familiar in the country. Possibly the oldest ever. That she had power, knowledge and skill way beyond mine. It would seem that David had really taken that information to heart.

'So, what's the deal, then? I mean, I might be very, very, very, mildly tipsy, but I can sense things falling apart in here. This memory's not right for a start, is it? You and David should be stumbling in here to confront me, but oops, no memory of you or David, just me and an astral projection. Something's eating away at his subconscious.'

I took out the box L'Merrier had given me.

'Ah,' said Eva, 'black magic? You know it's really not smart to fuck around with that fuckery. Take it from someone who knows.'

'Did you use it?'

She bowed her head. 'No.'

It was strange to see her suddenly so sombre. Was she feeling something real, something true at last, even if she was only a memory of herself?

'What happened, Eva?'

'Do we have to? You've got someone to save and I've got alcohol to drink – we shouldn't waste any more time on memories.' She snorted. 'Well you should, clearly, but not me.'

'Eva, just tell me. Tell me why you're like this.'

Her shoulders sagged and she dropped onto the only chair she hadn't already shredded. 'My coven. One member of my coven. They... I couldn't stop them. None of us could. What do I do now, Stella? How much longer can I run from my purpose? It hurts.'

I opened my mouth to answer but the words caught in my throat as I felt a coldness prickle the back of my neck.

'Oh, who's this then?' asked Eva as I turned to see Other David step into the room.

'I'm too late, again,' I said. 'He's already gone, he's already erased the real David.'

'Oh,' said Eva, 'No, that's not true, I think he just ran into the Gents. He was white as a bastard.'

Other David turned to go, turned to hunt David down, to burn him away with the fire in his eyes.

'Eva, I need you to slow him down, can you do that?'

Eva opened her palm and energy crackled. 'Does the pope shit in the woods?'

'I don't think so.'

'Well, consider it done anyway.' Eva clapped her hands together, thick ropes of sizzling, brightly-coloured magic appeared between them as she began to pull her hands apart again and mould the spell. 'Oi, big lad, think fast!'

Other David turned in time to see a wave of energy explode from Eva and sweep him aside, sending him crashing through the window and plummeting to the street below.

Eva lifted one hand and blew on two fingers as though they were a smoking gun barrel.

'Less of the dilly-dallying, love, go find your boy.'

I ran from the room, from the memory of Eva, and sprinted down the corridor towards the Gents, barging the door open with my shoulder with such ferocity that I almost fell to the floor as I rushed inside.

David was curled up against the far wall head in his hands.

'David? David, is that you?' I approached softly, terrified that he'd look up and I'd see his eyes were on fire.

'David, it's me, it's Stella. I've come to save you.'

He looked up and I couldn't help but smile, my heart jumping. It was the real David. Memory after memory he'd been erased from, but I'd found him again at last. I ran to him and crouched, holding him, scared that if I didn't he would just blip out of existence.

'I found you. I found you, David.'

'Stella?

'Yeah?'

'I can't breathe.'

I released him from my bear hug, 'Sorry.'

'I knew you'd come. I wasn't worried for a second.'

'You're curled up on a toilet floor.'

'Just... having a breather.'

I pulled him up to his feet and tried to ignore how scared he looked. 'I've been searching all over for you.'

He smiled. 'Yeah. Sorry about that. That glowy-eyed bastard keeps turning up. Handsome guy though, am I right?'

I laughed. Even here, even now, he couldn't help himself, but when I looked at him again, I could see the worry in his eyes.

'I'm almost gone, Stella. There's hardly a thing left of me. I can feel myself getting colder as each bit of me is turned off. How are we going to stop... well, me? Other me.''

'I can save you, but I need your help.'

'I can already see the flaw in this plan, but I'll do my best.'

'Somewhere in your memories, somewhere in your mind, is a splinter. A slither of dark magic. You need to take us to it.'

'How am I supposed to know where it is?'

'Close your eyes, try to picture it. To picture the point where this is all emanating from. The paper cut that stings.'

David closed his eyes, his brow creasing. 'I'm not sure I can.'

'You have to try. So many people's lives depend on it; the whole of London depends on it.'

And *you*, David. That's what I wanted to say. *You* depend on it, and I can't lose you.

The Gents' door burst open and a great blast of air blew us back, pinning us to the wall.

Other David appeared in the doorway, eyes blazing.

'It's too late,' said David.

I grabbed his hand and looked into his eyes, our faces so close our lips almost touched.

'David, please, you can do this. I know you can. I believe in you.'

Other David began to walk into the Gents, the fire in his eyes engulfing his entire head. I tried to ignore how my heart was beating hard enough to burst out of my chest as I concentrated on the real David.

'I can't feel anything,' he said.

'You can, David. Just ignore what's happening in this room. This room doesn't matter. Just open yourself up and feel the intruder. Feel the sharp point that stuck into you when I brought you back to life. Take us to it.'

Other David lifted a hand and it erupted in white flame as he prepared to remove David from the memory.

'You can do it. David, you can do it, you can save everyone.'

His eyes snapped open and he inhaled sharply. 'I have it!'

Other David was yanked back suddenly, as though attached to a bungee cord. Eva poked her head into the room.

'Well go on then, bloody run!'

David grabbed my hand and pulled me after him as the room streaked and—

—A forest.

There were things out there. Hidden things, walking through the undergrowth. Monsters. I knew where we were. The only place that really made sense.

This was where we killed Mr. Trick.

Where David died and I brought him back to life using black magic.

Where this whole thing started.

'Come on,' I said, not letting go of David's hand.

'You know he'll follow us here,' replied David. 'He'll step into every memory I have until they're all his.'

'Then let's not waste any time.'

The splinter hung in mid-air in a clearing. It looked like a shard of black ice puncturing existence.

'This is what was left behind when you saved my life?'

'The dark magic, it rushed through your body, through your mind, and left a trace of itself behind. There's always a price to pay when you use the black arts, I knew that. But what choice did I have?'

I pulled out the small box L'Merrier had given to me.

'I need to pull out the splinter.'

I reached up tentatively, unsure what would happen when I touched the splinter. Would it burn me? Would it turn my hand to dust?

I breathed in once, then let it go. I gripped the splinter. It was cold. Cold enough to hurt. It was also stuck. I yanked at it, but it wouldn't budge.

'Stella,' said David, pointing past me. Other David, eyes aflame, was stood just beyond the treeline.

'Come on,' I said, grunting, trying again and again to pull the dark shard free, but it didn't budge an inch.

There were more Other Davids with every passing second. Other Davids from every stage of his life. They stepped out of the trees, one by one, a complete circle.

David began to pull the shard with me, both of us pulling at it desperately. Did it move? Was that a slight give?

The unseen monsters in the forest howled and the Other Davids grew in number with every breath taken. Tens, then hundreds, then thousands. Other Davids from every moment of David's life descending upon us.

'It's coming!' said David, clenching his jaw so hard his teeth threatened to shatter.

The Other Davids began to walk towards us.

'Come on, it's nearly out!' I cried.

Stella—

'What did you—?'

A wet hand on my leg.

I looked down to see something dark and withered and foul leering up at me with huge, yellow eyes.

I would have screamed if the realisation hadn't robbed me of breath.

It was Mr. Trick, or the memory of him at least. That's all it could be, surely? That was enough though. I let go of the dark shard in shock and fell to the dirt, bones jarring.

'Stella, what are you doing?' asked David, frantically pulling at the splinter as the Other Davids stepped closer and closer, ready to remove the last true David from his memories.

'It's him! Don't you see him?' But David didn't look down, he carried on pulling at the splinter.

Only you, Stella, I'm here for you.

Mr. Trick reached up and scratched at my neck with his ragged fingernails.

'Fuck you!' I yelled and kicked out. As my foot connected, his body crumpled and tore, like I'd just attacked a wet paper bag.

I felt more hands on me as David pulled me back up. 'Help me!'

I glanced down, but the memory of Mr. Trick was gone. I felt my neck throbbing, blood dripping.

No time for that. Not time for thinking or fear. I wrapped my hands around David's and we pulled. It was giving! It was moving, a tooth ready to turn and turn and finally—

—Out it came!

We both fell to the ground, the splinter gripped tight in my hand. I pulled out the box and placed the shard inside.

28

Everything was out of focus.

I was flat out on a hard floor, body aching.

'Oi, wake up, love,' came a familiar voice.

Blinking the world back to sharpness, I sat up. I was still in the safe house that Razor and his eaves family had produced for us, with Eva stood over me.

'I did it?'

L'Merrier stepped into view, holding the box out for me to see. 'Yes.' He rolled his wrist and the box disappeared.

'Christ, my head is killing me,' said David, rubbing at this skull as he sat up. I pushed myself over to him and held him tight.

'You're okay.'

'I knew you'd do it. Wasn't worried for a second.'

'Liar.'

'Okay. Maybe for a second, but no longer than that.'

I laughed as he wrapped his arms around me and we both did our best not to collapse from exhaustion.

. . .

I took David home and helped him up the stairs so he could collapse on his bed and get some sleep.

'I suppose you're going to need to do a little more flim-flam on Layland and the others, magic lady,' he said as he laid his head on the pillow and tried to keep his eyes open a little longer.

'I'll take care of it,' I told him. I wondered how sharp his memory was now. How many holes the experience might have left him with. But we could sort that out later. All that mattered for now was he was alive. Alive, safe, and no longer a threat to anyone. L'Merrier made sure that information got out fast, so no one would take it into their own hands to try and kill him again.

I inhaled sharply as I felt David's hand over mine.

'Thank you, Stella.'

The words caught in my throat for a second, tongue dry. 'It's my job, detective.'

He smiled, eyes drooping. I wondered if I'd ever have stopped him if I hadn't been able to prevent him going critical. If I'd have done the right thing and put the city first. Could I have done it? Would I have killed him? As I watched him drift off to sleep, his hand still upon mine, I thought I already knew the answer.

'Where is it?' I asked as I stepped into *L'Merrier's Antiques*, which now showed no signs of the huge fight that had taken place just hours earlier.

'The shard is destroyed,' he replied, sliding out of the gloom, his hands resting on top of his stomach as shafts of light danced upon his large, shaved head.

'People died because of you. Innocent people in my city.'

'Yes,' he replied.

'And you almost killed David, too. All because you thought

you knew best. Knew what was right. Knew what to do without ever even stepping outside of this fucking shop to find out for sure.'

I wondered what he would do. Would he attack me for speaking to him like that? Me, just a lowly familiar.

Instead, he bowed his head, for once unable to look me in the eye.

'I made... a mistake.'

'That's not all you made,' I said, stepping to him. 'You made a new enemy too.'

L'Merrier opened his mouth to speak, but I didn't wait to listen. I turned, disgusted, and walked out of his shop.

Eva was waiting for me back at the coven.

'You could stay,' I said.

'Could I?'

'London is a big place, and I don't have any witches. The two of us could keep the city safe together. We could be the new London Coven; two familiars protecting millions.'

She smiled as she pulled out a cigarette and lit it, taking a deep drag, then blasting the smoke out of her nostrils.

'Nice idea, love, but I don't belong here. If all this has shown me anything—if *you've* shown me anything—it's that I've been avoiding my responsibilities for too long. I need to go home. Which is a real pisser, believe me.'

Part of me was sad to see her go. Another friend, another familiar, it would make life... fuller. But how could I argue? The very idea of running away from London for ten years, like she had from Cumbria, made my heart skip out of rhythm. A familiar belonged where she was created.

'Thanks for eventually helping,' I said, smiling.

'Pleasure. Well, mostly. Apart from all the nearly dying bits.'

I walked with her to the door. As she stepped out into the

blind alley beyond, she turned back and winked. 'Thanks, love. Thanks for showing me the way home.'

'You're welcome.'

She wavered and squinted at me. 'By the way, that looks nasty, you should get it seen to,' she said, pointing to my neck. As the door closed I ran to the nearest mirror, pulling down the collar of my jacket.

Four red lines were scratched into my neck. They ran at an angle, one next to the other.

Only you, Stella, I'm here for you...

My legs began to wobble and I pressed a hand against the wall, lowering myself down until I was sat on the floor, other hand to the scratches that now throbbed.

It wasn't possible.

That had just been my astral form in an old memory.

'When Mr. Trick comes to town, all the uncanny shall fall and frown...'

I curled up on the floor, and closed my eyes.

The End.

LEAVE A REVIEW

Reviews are gold to indie authors, so if you've enjoyed this collection, please consider visiting the site you bought it to rate and review.

BECOME AN INSIDER

Sign up and receive **FREE UNCANNY KINGDOM BOOKS**. Also, be the **FIRST** to hear about **NEW RELEASES** and **SPECIAL OFFERS** in the **UNCANNY KINGDOM** universe. Just visit:

WWW.UNCANNYKINGDOM.COM

MORE STORIES SET IN THE UNCANNY KINGDOM

The Uncanny Ink Series
Bad Soul
Bad Blood
Bad Justice
Bad Intention
Bad Thoughts
Bad Memories

The Branded Series
Sanctified
Turned
Bloodline

The Hexed Detective Series
Hexed Detective
Fatal Moon
Night Terrors

The Spectral Detective Series
Spectral Detective
Corpse Reviver
Twice Damned

The Dark Lakes Series
Magic Eater
Blood Stones
Past Sins

Copyright © 2017 by Uncanny Kingdom.

All rights reserved.

No part of this book may be reproduced in any form or by any electronic or mechanical means, including information storage and retrieval systems, without written permission from the author, except for the use of brief quotations in a book review.

Printed in Great Britain
by Amazon